A DEADLY PAST MYSTERY

Marion Moore Hill

PEMBERLEY PRESS
CORONA DEL MAR

DEADLY
Design

ALSO BY MARION MOORE HILL:

The Deadly Past Mystery Series:
*Deadly Will*

The Scrappy Librarian Series:
*Bookmarked for Murder*
*Death Books a Return*

PEMBERLEY PRESS
P O Box 1027
Corona del Mar, CA 92625
www.pemberleypress.com
A member of The Authors Studio
www.theauthorsstudio.org



Cover design: Kat & Dog Studios
Cover illustration: Aletha St. Romain
Floor Plan of Poplar Forest: Courtesy of Thomas Jefferson's Poplar Forest and Mesick Cohen Wilson Baker Architects

Library of Congress Cataloging-in-Publication Data

Hill, Marion Moore, 1937-
Deadly design : a deadly past mystery / Marion Moore Hill.
p. cm.
ISBN 978-1-935421-00-9 (alk. paper)
I. Title.
PS3608.I4348D42 2009
813'.6--dc22

2009004854

The Deadly Past Mysteries are dedicated to all those who unearth and preserve the past, and who make it live again.

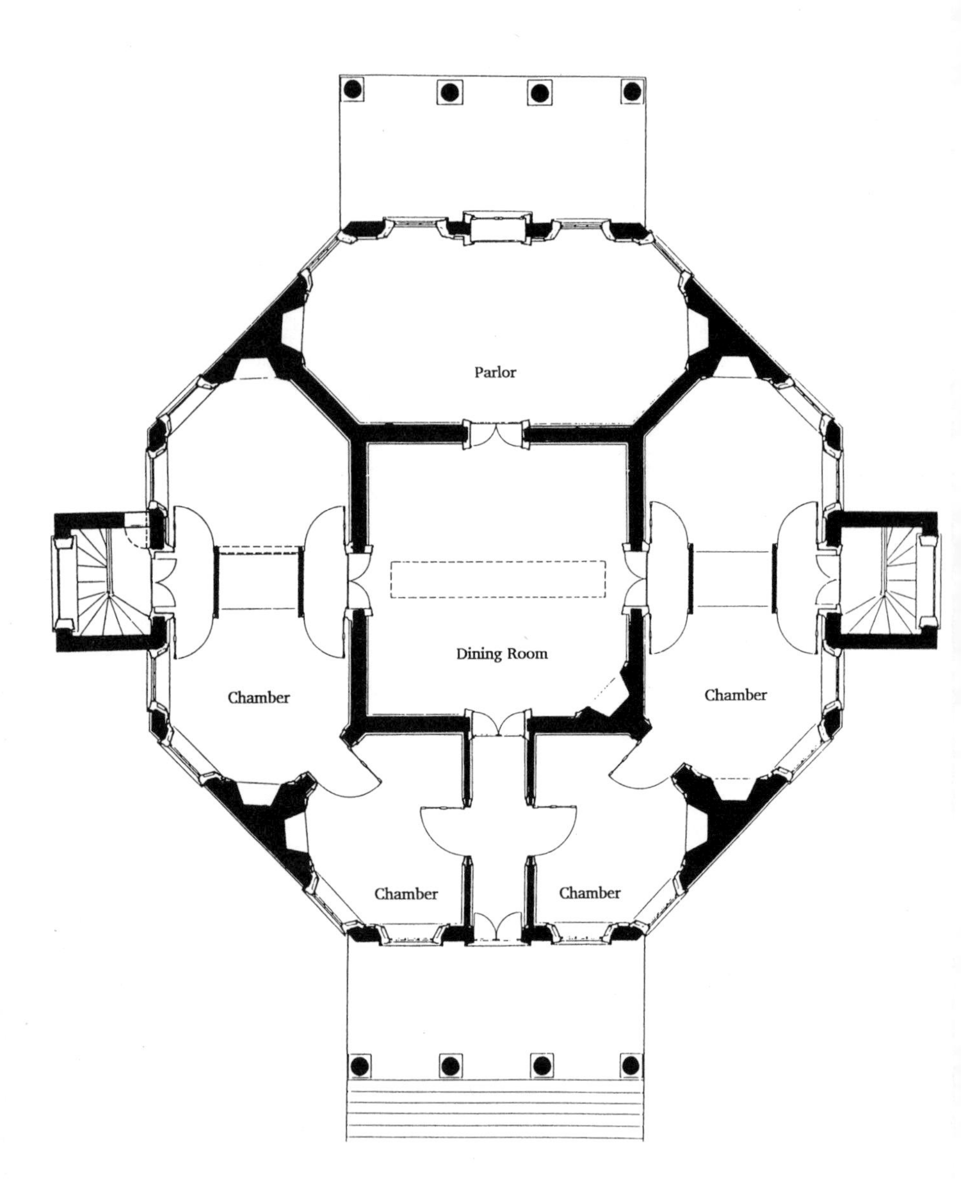


Floor Plan of Thomas Jefferson's

Secret Retreat

Poplar Forest

# Prologue

Monticello, September, 1806

"Why, Grandpapa?" five-year-old Virginia Randolph asked, her small hand patting a paper on the desk in front of Thomas Jefferson. "Why do you want a house with more sides?"

Her cousin, Francis Eppes, one month younger, left off peering at the drawing and climbed onto a chair.

"A very sensible question, Virginia," her grandfather said. "Who can tell her the answer?"

Jefferson glanced fondly around at his other grandchildren, ranging in age from almost-three to fifteen, all clustered about him in the book room at Monticello. They had just finished drawing straws for a book he'd received from a London bookseller, *The Visible World; Or, The Chief Things Therein; Drawn In Pictures.* Getting the longest straw had won just-shy-of-ten Ellen the right to read it first, and she cradled the prize to her bosom. Francis, who had drawn the shortest straw, would be allowed to keep the book once everyone had read it.

Teen-aged Jeff Randolph exchanged a knowing look with older sister Anne, the two in silent agreement to let the younger ones try to answer first.

It was seven-year-old Cornelia who replied to Virginia. "Because you get more light that way. Right, Grandpapa?"

"Very good, Cornelia. Light enters an eight-sided house from more directions than in a four-sided one."

A doting grandfather who often led his grandchildren in play, Jefferson also encouraged them to stretch their young minds with whatever knowledge they could absorb. He planned out courses of study for each, interested himself in their schoolwork, and, in a departure from the custom of the time, included them at table mealtimes so they could learn from adult conversation.

He now took a brick from the desk and held it up so all could see its pointed end. "You've heard me speak of the specially-molded bricks Mr. Chisolm is using to form the forty-five-degree angles needed to build my octagonal house. Do you remember what the type is called?"

"I know, I know!" not-quite-three Mary Jefferson Randolph cried, all but falling from her chair in her excitement. "It's a squint brick."

Jeff half-closed his eyes and peered obliquely at her, illustrating the name for the building block. Mary chortled, enjoying his big-brother teasing.

"Excellent," Jefferson said. "Now, who wants to run a foot race?"

A chorus of voices went up, and the children jostled each other in their hurry to get outside. As they left him, Jefferson's eyes fell again on the house plan in front of him. Poplar Forest would be a house like none other in the country.

Well, perhaps not quite. He had heard a Lynchburg merchant, someone he had only a nodding acquaintance with, hoped someday to build an octagonal house similar to his plan, and only a few miles from his Poplar Forest. Momentary annoyance gave way to a just acceptance. Jefferson hadn't originated the octagonal design, not totally. Octagonal plans for several kinds of buildings—churches, baptistries, garden temples, occasionally houses—had appeared in architectural books decades earlier. In fact, a German book on gardening that he'd purchased the previous year included a plan for a garden temple that looked much like his design for Poplar Forest.

He himself had already worked on a somewhat similar plan for a friend, but scaling down some of Poplar Forest's features. That friend lived in another part of Virginia, however.

Let the neighbor build his, Jefferson thought. It wouldn't be easy, based on his recent experience in Bedford County. His seasoned bricklayer Hugh Chisolm, who had laid out many building foundations over the years, had summoned Jefferson to do the Poplar Forest one himself, Chisolm having decided he was unequal to the task of laying out an octagonal foundation.

Jefferson had first-hand knowledge of the difficulties involved in such a design. But when had he shied away from a building project because it wasn't easy?

# ✯ Chapter One ~ 2002

Could her life get any better? Millie wondered as she tooled along U. S. Highway 221, eager to immerse herself and her son in the world of Thomas Jefferson, with time and money enough to enjoy it. The early-July morning felt fresh and cool after an overnight shower, and the rolling hills of the Virginia countryside seemed to draw her back to the early nineteenth century.

She and Danny had driven east from the Blue Ridge Parkway, he craning his nine-year-old neck for the first glimpse of what would be their temporary home, the small city of Lynchburg. Seeing a sign ahead indicating a turn-off to "Thomas Jefferson's Poplar Forest," Millie slowed her vehicle. She'd intended to go straight to the house in town that her friend Alice had rented, waiting until tomorrow to tour the third president's octagonal house. But knowing his retreat was so close tempted her.

As she hesitated, a motorcycle roared up behind her, its motor loud in the relative quiet of mid-morning. The helmeted rider slowed to let a car in the other lane go past, then zipped around Millie's car. She got a quick impression of burly strength in the way he sat his bike, the way his muscles filled out his blue T-shirt and jeans.

Then, suddenly, he braked hard and leaned into a right turn.

Millie's heart leapt into her throat. She hit her own brakes and jerked the steering wheel left. With tires screeching, she cringed, bracing herself for the strike of chrome on chrome, the impact of metal on flesh.

Miraculously, she missed him. As the biker completed his turn, she twisted the wheel back and fought for control of her car. The reflection in her side mirror showed the biker giving a thumbs-up sign, as he accelerated down the road towards Jefferson's retreat.

"Cool!" Danny cried, his small hands clutching the seat belt that had snapped taut.

Trembling from fright, Millie breathed deeply, trying to regain her composure. Her pleasant contemplation had been broken, her sense of well-being shattered by the incident. Before wrenching the wheel left, she'd thought the oncoming lane was clear. But what if that quick impression had been wrong? A head-on collision could have killed both her and Danny, plus people in the other car.

*That man's recklessness endangered several lives,* Millie imagined Sylva's indignant voice saying. The strong bond between Millie and her elderly Dallas friend often made her feel Sylva was traveling with her, commenting on events and people.

*Doesn't he remind you of someone?*

A memory flashed through Millie's mind, of her ex-husband riding his motorcycle in much the same fashion as this biker.

When she and Jack had gone together during high school, Millie had thought him dashing, adventurous. After they'd married, his devil-may-care attitude had increasingly worried her. When Danny was a tiny baby and Jack had threatened to take him for a ride on his motorcycle—to "introduce the kid to the open road and the wind in his hair"—Millie had come unglued.

Jack had stormed out that night. She hadn't seen him again for two years, and only then when he came to borrow money for a car payment. Foolishly she had given him twenty-two dollars she had saved towards a coat for Danny.

He hadn't paid it back, of course. A couple of months later, he'd surfaced again, wanting to borrow more. That time, she'd hedged, said she had none to lend, and the discussion had turned ugly. Jack had threatened to seek custody of Danny if she wouldn't give him money.

Anger and fright had gripped Millie, as if the walls of their drab living room had closed in, wedging her between. But somehow, from deep within, she had dredged up the courage to say a definite no.

Jack had made good his threat and filed for custody. He hadn't had much of a case, having been AWOL through most of his young son's life, but legal bills had worsened Millie's already difficult financial situation.

After that, fear had stalked her for months. When anyone knocked on the door, she'd felt sure it was someone with a subpoena demanding she appear in court. She'd dreaded collecting the mail, for fear there'd be an official-looking letter. But finally, the anxiety had dissipated. She now had only an occasional nightmare about losing her son.

Now the note of hero-worship she'd heard in Danny's voice troubled her.

"That was dangerous," she muttered to Danny. "We're very lucky we weren't meeting another car."

He twisted in his seat to gaze after the motorcycle.

Maybe she shouldn't go to Poplar Forest now and risk running into the biker again. But he probably wasn't headed to the historic dwelling, just taking the smaller road because he'd suddenly remembered a short cut to somewhere else.

As soon as she could do so safely, she reversed and drove back, this time taking the turn-off. They wound through a residential area, made a few turns, and soon were ascending a long hill. At its peak sat a classical-styled dwelling, red brick with white columns, topped with multiple chimneys.

Poplar Forest.

Millie caught her breath. Thomas Jefferson's own private getaway. And she'd be working here.

A few weeks ago, her friend Alice had phoned to invite her and Danny to join her in Lynchburg for the summer, to share a house and an experience in American history, a love they had in common. They had met last year when Millie had flown to Newark to pay condolences following the death of Alice's husband, Millie's fellow heir under an odd two hundred-year-old legacy. Earlier that year, Millie had unexpectedly received a letter from a lawyer, telling her that she was an heir of a relative she'd never heard of, Nathan Henry, who had died in the nineteenth century. Henry had based his unusual will, which involved accumulating interest on money for two centuries before legatees inherited, on the trusts Benjamin Franklin had created for Philadelphia and Boston. Nearly as excited over her ancestor's tie to a Founding Father as at the prospect of wealth, Millie had gone to meet her fellow heirs at the testator's Philadelphia mansion. But the experience had had a nightmarish side. Several of Henry's descendants, including Alice's husband, Hamilton Ross, had died because of someone's greed. Millie hadn't liked all her newfound relatives but had become fond of several during the few days in their company.

Hamilton Ross, for one. For another, Scott Wyrick.

In Philadelphia, Millie and Scott, a very distant relative from Colorado, had developed an easy camaraderie that had grown into something more. Millie liked his sense of humor, his strength in a crisis, his dedication to his teaching career, and his encouragement of her own academic efforts. Not to mention his intelligent dark eyes, broad shoulders, and shy grin.

When Millie had visited the widow Ross in New Jersey, the

women had bonded over common interests and their shared loss of Hamilton. So when Alice had found herself in Lynchburg for an indefinite period, volunteering at a historic site she knew Millie would love, she had made the call. Besides the prospect of a fun break from routine in Dallas, the invitation offered Millie an irresistible chance to involve Danny in her passion for history: a one-week camp in July in which he'd learn about Thomas Jefferson, life in another era, and archaeology. Millie had dropped the summer college classes she'd enrolled in, packed up the new Prius she'd bought with part of her inheritance, and set off with Danny on an extended "history trip" together—the first of many, she hoped.

Henry's legacy made such impromptu decisions possible, she thought now with gratitude. It had changed her life in other ways, too. She'd switched her education plan, from acquiring college hours slowly at night, working towards a computer major she didn't want at technology-oriented University of Texas at Dallas, to studying history and literature full-time at the Dallas campus of Texas Woman's University. She had also quit her day job as nurse's aide at the upscale nursing home where Sylva was a resident. And she'd bought things she and Danny needed, including the car and a small house with a yard. By the standards of many in the world, they were rich. But years of grinding poverty had made Millie cautious about spending.

Sylva had helped her gain some useful perspective on this. Millie had gone to visit her soon after Alice's phone call.

"I've just heard about a summer camp that sounds perfect for Danny," she'd told her. "You remember my telling you about visiting Alice Ross in Newark? Before I came home from Philadelphia last year?"

"Sure. The widow of your African-American relative."

"Well, she called last night." Millie told Sylva about Alice's volunteer work and the children's camp. "Doesn't that sound fun for a kid?"

"For a kid, nothing. I want to go! You're planning to do all those things with him, aren't you?"

"Hope so. I e-mailed from the Poplar Forest Web site to ask if I could be one of the adults helping with the camp."

The reply to Millie's message had said that the children's summer program already had enough volunteers, but it had encouraged her to volunteer in another capacity. Millie had opted to work at the archaeology lab with Alice. The dates and hours were fairly flexible, and she hoped she could make arrangements for a sitter for Danny, so she could work there longer than his one-week camp would allow.

"Great, Kirchner," Sylva said. "How long you plan to be gone?"

"Long enough for Danny and me to do a real Thomas Jefferson tour. We could see Monticello, Williamsburg, Richmond—lots of places associated with him."

"Excellent. I admire your restraint about spending your inherited wealth, dear—many your age would've blown it all immediately—but you also need to enjoy some of it."

"I worry that wealth which came suddenly could disappear just as fast."

"Understandable. You walked a difficult road before the legacy." A loving smile curved Sylva's pale lips. "While you're at Charlottesville to see Monticello, be sure to tour the University of Virginia. Did you know Jefferson designed his 'Academical Village' when he was already pushing eighty? He even planned its curriculum and hired the first faculty members. And they say old people aren't good for much!"

"I'd never say that. I know a woman who must be seventy-five if she's a day but acts like she's thirty."

"You're misinformed, my dear. The woman you're speaking of isn't a minute over sixty-two."

"If you're just sixty-two, then I'm Eleanor Roosevelt."

Sylva affected a curtsy as best she could in her wheelchair. "You've always been my favorite First Lady, Mrs. R, although I was very young during your tenure."

"No doubt. Franklin died more than sixty years ago, taking my First-Ladyship with him."

Sylva coughed several times, rolled to a bedside table for a lozenge, and popped it into her mouth. "The research you've been doing for that college course you're taking must've made you familiar with lots of Jeffersonian buildings."

"Yeah. It's an interesting assignment, to write about some lesser-known aspect of a prominent historical figure. I knew Jefferson had been an architect, but not how many buildings he planned, and how many others he influenced."

"He designed the state capitol in Richmond, didn't he?"

Millie nodded. "With help from another architect. Plus a number of houses. His own two, of course, and several for neighbors and friends. He even designed a few county courthouses."

"An accomplished man, Thomas Jefferson. Interested in, and knowledgeable about, so many subjects."

"True." Millie grimaced. "I just wish . . ."

"That he had managed to free all his slaves. Yes, we've had that conversation."

Millie heaved a sigh. "I know he inherited debt from his father-in-law, also that he personally absorbed expenses of being President that taxpayers would pay for today. But—the principal author of the Declaration of Independence, a slaveholder?"

"I'm not defending the practice of slavery, Kirchner. Lots of people before you have wrestled with the contradictions that were Thomas Jefferson. But when you get to be my age—there, I've said it, and I used to vow I never would—however, when you do, you'll realize that the same individual can be capable of both great good and great evil, sometimes at the same time."

Millie nodded slowly. "I know the Founding Fathers, and Mothers, weren't saints. But I revere them. And this—"

"Is hard to accept in anyone you admire. It should be. We mustn't ever accept evils like slavery. But we have to live with the knowledge that they've occurred, and try to prevent their happening again."

"'Try' is the operative word, isn't it?"

"People, and life, are works in progress. I'd be interested in knowing Alice Ross's 'take' on Jefferson. She must not despise him, or she wouldn't be volunteering at his home." Sylva coughed again. "And I'd like to read your paper about him when it's finished. Could I?"

"Sure. But I doubt you'll find it riveting."

"I could use a good soporific. Haven't been sleeping too well lately."

"A little arsenic in your tapioca could fix that."

"You amateur chefs. Always tampering with recipes."

Now, Millie felt Sylva was with her, as they followed a road that swept in front of the house, half-hidden behind a sea of boxwood bushes, and circled around it past a collection of frame buildings. They parked in a lot with several other cars and got out. Millie paused to drink in the sight of the structure from the rear, standing majestically a couple of hundred yards away.

She noticed something curious: The house had appeared from the front to be one-storied, but it was two stories at the back. The top level featured a gallery edged with white columns and a railing, the lower an arcade formed of brick archways. In the distance to the north and west, low peaks of the Blue Ridge Mountains offered a picturesque backdrop.

As she locked her car, she glanced around and saw, nestled between two cars a few yards away, a black motorcycle accented with chrome.

Uh-oh, Millie thought, the biker had been coming here.

Briefly she considered bundling her son back into the car and driving off. But they were here now, and what excuse could she give Danny for leaving?

She decided it would be silly to turn tail and run. So what if they all ended up on the same tour? Danny and the biker might not even recognize each other, away from their respective "rides."

Diverting her son's gaze towards the buildings, in the hope he wouldn't see the motorcycle, Millie eyed the house again. She hadn't visited Monticello yet but from viewing pictures knew it was considerably larger than Poplar Forest, yet Jefferson's two dwellings had an over-all similarity of style. Monticello was elegant, much-celebrated, a fitting residence for the man who had served as U.S. President, Secretary of State, Ambassador to France, and Governor of Virginia. But Poplar Forest, his private getaway, might show a side of him that even Monticello wouldn't. She wanted to see it. Today.

An idea came, a delaying tactic that might let the biker be out and away from the residence before she and Danny entered it. And it was something they should do anyway.

"We gonna go in the house, Mom?" Danny asked impatiently.

"Sure. But first, let's find the archaeology lab and say hello to Alice. She said she'd be working today."

They strolled past two small frame buildings and a clutch of vending machines and came to two boxy red structures with an open walkway between. A sign said the one on the right was the Maylia Green Rightmire Preservation Center, the restoration workshop. Shallow windows set into its outer wall displayed instruments of hand woodworking—awls, levels, planes—plus information on techniques used in building Jefferson's retreat.

"Look, Danny, these tools were the kind used a long time ago.

The people who've restored Poplar Forest used similar ones, to make it like the original."

Accustomed to odd enthusiasms from his mother, Danny glanced politely at the old implements. Then he moved to the frame structure on the left, the archaeology lab according to a sign, and peered into a large picture window.

"Hey, Mom," he called. "Look at the stuff people dug up here."

Millie joined him in viewing artifacts displayed on a shelf inside the window: part of a comb, bits of bone, seeds, and a cross-mended pottery bowl. An accompanying legend briefly explained the work of archaeologists.

"You gonna find bowls and stuff here too, Mom?"

"I don't know if I'll do any digging. From what Alice said, I'll mostly help in the lab, washing and labeling things other people have found."

"Oh." He wrinkled his nose in disdain. "Mom, how do they know where to find stuff? They dig up the whole place?"

"No, I'm sure they don't, but that's a good question. We'll ask someone here."

Past the window display could be seen a large room dominated by a huge conference table, holding a smattering of books and drawings. Enlarged photos of artifacts and excavation sites adorned walls. Alice had warned Millie that she'd be part of the exhibit seen by visitors when working in this main room.

"So you're saying I shouldn't scratch my butt just any time I feel like it?" Millie had joked.

"Your choice, if you don't mind Big Brother—or Small Sister—seeing you."

No one was in the big room now.

"Let's go in," she said to Danny. "But don't touch anything. We don't want to mess up important work."

From the small vestibule, doors led to the main room and a

smaller conference room. A set of steps ran upwards to where Alice had said the Poplar Forest library was located. Entering the main chamber, Millie saw two small offices on her left, no one currently in either, and a door at the back.

"Alice? You here? It's Millie and Danny," she called as they stepped through that portal.

"Come on through," Alice's raised voice replied. "I'm back in the kitchen."

They entered a small workroom centered with a table half-covered with brown paper sacks, their tops folded over and sides marked with black notations of letters and numbers. A large fortyish man, with twists of reddish-gold hair flopping over his eyes and clashing with his florid complexion, came out of an office on their right. He set a coffee mug on the table and extended a paw, which Millie took.

"Hi, Millie. Chas Locke, lab supervisor." He motioned to an open door on her left. "Alice is in there. So, you're going to be helping us out a while."

Millie smiled. "I hope I'll be a help, not get in the way."

"If you're anything like Alice, you'll be invaluable." He had a wide, placid face with a crooked nose that might have been broken at some time. He bent and offered a hand to Danny. "And you must be the young man who's in the children's program next week. Welcome, Danny." After a solemn handshake, Chas straightened. "Ever been around a dig, Millie?"

"No, but I am interested, and I'm a quick learner."

"No doubt. You'll find us a pretty casual bunch. Anything you don't understand, or want to know more about, ask any of us."

"Thanks. Actually, Danny was wondering—"

Alice came out of the kitchen, drying her hands on a cloth. "Millie, dear, so good to see you again."

They hugged. Millie introduced Danny, and he and Alice clasped hands.

"Hope you had a good trip?" Alice said.

"We did. Driving through the mountains has been lovely, the Smokies, then the Blue Ridge. Danny spotted a black bear in the Smokies. It's been fun, hasn't it, son?"

Danny nodded, shy with these new acquaintances.

"You started to say something," Chas reminded Millie, "about what Danny wondered?"

"Oh, yes. Danny was asking how archaeologists know where to dig, in order to find artifacts."

Chas nodded sagely. "A logical question, Danny. Sometimes letters and other old papers tell where buildings once stood. And by walking around over a likely piece of ground, archaeologists can often spot clues. For instance, a dip in the soil could suggest where a well, or fence post, or other feature once was."

"That makes sense," Millie said. "What do you tell Chas, Danny, for answering your question?"

"Thank you, sir."

Chas slapped the boy on his thin shoulder, waved goodbye to them and began examining labels on the sacks. Alice beckoned Millie and Danny into the galley kitchen, where she took a small mesh basket off the draining board and held it for him to see reddish-brown particles in it.

"These are pieces of brick, Danny. Most artifacts get labeled with a code telling exactly where they were found, but bits of brick just get collected and weighed. That helps the archaeologists figure out where a building stood and how big it was."

He nodded again, smiling slightly this time.

"Chas and I'll explain more to you on Monday, Millie," Alice went on. "Sorry our Director of Archaeology and Landscapes isn't here to greet you. One of her children was seriously hurt in an auto accident, and she's staying with her at the hospital in Richmond. The other archaeologist, Harold Drake, is out at the dig now, but you'll meet him next week. You two taken the tour yet?"

Millie shook her head. "I wanted to come say 'hi' first."

"Glad you did."

Danny asked to use the bathroom, and Alice directed him to a small room nearby.

When he'd left, Millie asked, "Have you heard anymore about that possible Jefferson house you told me about on the telephone—Highgrove, I think it was called? That really intrigued me."

A shadow crossed Alice's face. "Not about whether it's a Jefferson design. But something terrible happened a couple of days ago to one of the crew investigating it. A young woman named Paige Oberlin was murdered."

"How awful! While she was at Highgrove?"

"No, she was coming home from work, and had just stepped into the lobby of her apartment building, when she was attacked. Evidently someone had been waiting inside to rob whoever came in. He stabbed her several times and made off with her purse."

Millie shook her head. "That's horrible. You just never know these days, do you? Did she live there alone?"

"With a girlfriend, someone she'd known when she lived in Lynchburg as a teenager."

"Have they caught the person who did it?"

"No, the police have just started their investigation. They haven't released much information about it."

Hearing Danny return, Millie gave Alice a meaningful look and changed the subject. "We'll go take the tour now and let you get back to work." With this long a delay, she thought, the biker should have had time to see the house and leave.

"You buy tour tickets in the museum shop near the parking lot," Alice said. "One of our housemates works there, Jill Greene. Have fun. I should be home around three-thirty. You remember where I said the key to the house would be?"

Millie nodded.

On their way back to the main room, they told Chas goodbye. Busy examining contents of a paper sack, he waved absentmindedly

As they left the lab building, Millie noticed a nearby barn-like structure with big plastic-covered windows open to the breeze. A sign on the door read "Hands-On History."

"Oh, look, Danny," Millie said. "That must be where your camp will meet."

He chewed his bottom lip, apparently having second thoughts now that they were actually here. She felt a little apprehensive herself. What if he hated the summer program she'd enrolled him in? What if the other kids weren't friendly?

"We gonna go see it, Mom?"

"Not today, not unless they take us there on the tour. Today, we're just sightseers."

They entered the small museum shop and purchased tickets from a trim, athletic, rosy-cheeked blonde.

"Millie Kirchner," the blonde said with a smile, as she swiped the credit card. "And this must be Danny? Nice to meet you both. I'm Jill Greene." She handed back the card and offered her hand to each in turn. Then she leaned over the counter, blue-gray eyes sparkling mischievously. "Either of you like to play baseball?"

"I do," Danny promptly said.

"Thought you had the look of a ball player. I'm one, too. We'll have to have a game."

He grinned and nodded.

Jill completed the paperwork and told them their tour would begin outside in a few minutes. "See you later at the house, guys," she said, before turning to assist an elderly man.

Millie and Danny browsed briefly inside the shop. She found a few books of interest on Poplar Forest and Jefferson but decided to buy them later. Outside, they joined a half-dozen people clustered around a wiry-haired older woman who introduced herself as Clara, their guide. To Millie's relief, the motorcycle rider wasn't among the group. A girl about Danny's age exchanged diffident glances with him.

Clara led her charges across an expanse of yard towards the historic residence. A large rectangular sunken lawn stretched for a hundred yards or so behind it. A long wing extended off the house to the east, and two grassy mounds flanked the dwelling on either side. The tour paused near the western one, and Clara pointed out a small brick structure beside it, which she said was one of two privies, or "necessaries" as they had been called in Jefferson's day.

"How cute!" a woman in the group exclaimed. "Even the outhouses have eight sides."

"Jefferson did love that shape," Millie said. The women exchanged friendly smiles.

A balding man frowned. "Building an eight-sided house would've been lots more expensive and time-consuming than a four-sided one, wouldn't it?"

Their guide smiled. "Jefferson didn't necessarily go for what was easiest or cheapest. He loved light, and octagonal buildings let illumination enter from eight directions instead of four."

Millie glanced to her right again. This time her eye was drawn to movement beyond the sunken lawn. A stocky young man in jeans and a blue T-shirt strode out of a stand of trees in their direction.

That build, Millie thought. The blue T-shirt and jeans. The biker.

*Oh, no,* he seemed to be coming towards them. She debated what to do: make an excuse to leave, perhaps a sudden attack of tummy trouble; or continue the tour, praying the young man would keep his distance.

Danny had been sneaking glances at the little girl but chose that moment to look towards the trees. His glance flickered past them, then back. With a sinking heart, Millie saw his eyes rest on the biker.

Maybe he wouldn't recognize him, at least not if she could divert his attention. She slipped an arm around her son's shoulders and pointed up at the roof of the dwelling.

"Look, Danny, this house has four chimneys, so it must have four fireplaces. People had to use those for cooking and for heat before electricity, you know."

He frowned, informing her she was talking down to him, and glanced back at the trees. The biker had paused just outside the grove. He swiveled his head as if someone behind him had spoken. Millie saw his mouth move but couldn't catch any words. Then he retraced his steps and reentered the trees.

Clara spoke to Danny, and he turned towards her.

"Poplar Forest actually has nine fireplaces," she said, "two in each chimney plus a third in one. The house was largely destroyed by fire in 1845, and we think that extra flue may have caused it." She went on to explain that the pipe venting smoke from the third hearth had had a sharper bend than those for the others.

Danny appeared to ponder the fire story. Millie silently thanked Clara.

As they all followed their guide, she thought about where the biker had been. She wouldn't have expected someone on a tour to be over in those trees. Nor had she seen other sightseers with him.

He had been moving with casual ease, she recalled, like someone sure of where he was going. Maybe he wasn't a tourist but an employee here.

Millie frowned. She wouldn't necessarily have to see him regularly, or interact with him, even if he were. But her joy at the prospect of volunteering at Jefferson's retreat had now dimmed.

# ★ Chapter Two

Millie had no leisure to worry about the biker. Clara led her group around the house and up the front steps onto the columned porch, where she paused just outside the door.

"This was Jefferson's concept of an American villa," she said. "He was a great admirer of the Italian architect Andrea Palladio and took many architectural ideas from him. He also copied elements of houses he saw while in Europe. Jefferson very much enjoyed the process of building and remodeling—'putting up and pulling down,' as he expressed it—and kept working on Poplar Forest over a seventeen-year period, from 1806 to 1823."

She pointed out the original carriage turnaround in front of the house and said that in Jefferson's day a road had encircled a five-acre area around the house, within the sixty-one-acre tract he had called the "curtilage," which also contained outbuildings.

Millie glanced at Danny. He was wearing the lethargic expression that said he was bored but willing to indulge his mother awhile longer. She had taught him to be polite when adults were speaking, but politeness didn't necessarily translate to rapt attention.

The guide told how Jefferson had acquired the property, along with numerous slaves and heavy indebtedness, as the inheritance of his wife, Martha, on the death of her father, John Wayles. Poplar Forest was principally a tobacco-growing plantation then, she said, and tobacco continued to be an important cash crop for Jefferson, though he also grew wheat and other crops of more use and less damaging to the soil.

"He first came here in 1773 and didn't return until 1781, during the Revolutionary War. He was then Governor of Virginia, and fled here with his family after the British nearly captured him twice—first at Richmond, then at Monticello. During that 1781 visit, the Jeffersons stayed in the overseer's house, which wasn't terribly comfortable, especially since his wife was in frail health. But Jefferson had time during the stay to write much of his only published book, *Notes on the State of Virginia.*"

Millie listened, interested, but a small part of her brain still mulled questions about the biker. Maybe he wasn't an employee but a tourist looking around the grounds after his tour finished?

Clara led them inside and through a narrow entry hall, which divided an elongated octagon into two small bedrooms. Emerging from the spare hallway, they stepped into a large two-story central room flooded with light from a skylight. Startled at the contrast, tour members paused.

"Wow," one man said. "Isn't this something! Especially after that dark hall."

Danny's eyes had widened on stepping into the impressive space, and he looked at Clara with renewed interest.

The guide smiled. "Exactly the reaction Jefferson wanted. He meant this room to surprise and awe. It's a perfect cube, 20 by 20 by 20 feet, and the skylight illuminates it beautifully. After he began building here in 1806, he would visit periodically, sometimes as often as four times a year. In 1809, he began using the residence as his retreat from the many visitors and the activity that sometimes overwhelmed him at Monticello. In 1823, he stopped coming due to failing health, and gave the place to his grandson, Francis Eppes. Jefferson died three years later, at the age of eighty-three.

"This house was important to him as a place where he could read, think, and find solitude. But family members did come with him, and he entertained a few close friends and neighbors here."

Tour members strolled around the graceful dining room, then into an octagonal room on the west side, which Clara said had been Jefferson's bedroom. Millie stood looking out a long window, thinking that the President himself must often have stood in this very same spot. Danny, she noticed, had started to fidget. She laid a hand on his shoulder and whispered in his ear.

"Not too much longer, now."

He gave his one-shoulder shrug, as if to say he wasn't so sure about that.

While other tourists enjoyed the view, Millie took advantage of the lull to ask Clara if she knew of other Jefferson-designed buildings in the area.

Clara confidently shook her head. "Poplar Forest is the only one here, although several around Charlottesville and other parts of Virginia were either designed or influenced by him. Some in Washington, D.C., also. He didn't design the White House but did contribute ideas. There's even a building in Louisville, Kentucky, that may be his design."

Millie nodded, recognizing information she'd read while researching her history paper about Jefferson as an architect. "I understand some of his long-time builders constructed houses in his style for years after he died."

Clara smiled. "Correct. The style is now called Jeffersonian Classicism. James Dinsmore and John Neilson were particularly gifted among his builders. Some say Neilson even surpassed Jefferson as a designer."

Millie hesitated, unsure whether to mention Highgrove by name since it hadn't been authenticated. But she decided it might be of interest to Clara. "Actually, I've heard about an old house near here that's being investigated as a possible Jefferson design. Highgrove?"

"Really!" a stout woman near Millie asked. "Wouldn't that be exciting, to discover a new Jefferson building after all these years?"

Clara smiled indulgently. "That's interesting, but I'm afraid it's most unlikely it'll turn out to be his design."

Millie said no more, and Clara again took up her narrative.

"The restoration of this house is now complete, except for a few entablatures and facings that were intentionally left unfinished, so visitors can see elements of Poplar Forest's construction."

Millie noticed that Danny and the little girl he'd exchanged glances with had finally broken the ice and were talking in low tones. She'd have liked to hear their conversation but thought her son should have some privacy, even from his mom. She only hoped that in his boredom he would not grow too rambunctious and disturb the group.

*Being a parent's largely a matter of balance,* Sylva often said. *Protect and help when you need to, but otherwise, let the kid be a kid.*

"This house, as Jefferson designed it, wasn't to everyone's taste," Clara said, as she led them through the dining room into the bedroom on the east, noting that it looked out over the recently reconstructed office wing. "As I mentioned, Jefferson gave Poplar Forest to his grandson a few years before his death, but the grandson and his wife found it too odd in design and too remote in location. After owning it five years—and after Jefferson's death—they sold it to a neighbor. It remained in private hands until purchased for restoration by the non-profit Corporation for Jefferson's Poplar Forest."

The house had been remodeled by one of the non-Jefferson owners, she added, making it a more typical farmhouse, better suited to the needs of a family. In this room, for instance, the ceiling had been lowered eight feet, an attic installed to provide more storage and accommodation for guests, the dining room moved downstairs, and a staircase added on one wall of the former dining room.

"Removing the skylight made this room much darker, of course, and all the changes took away the special character of Jefferson's design."

Poplar Forest's floor plan was unusual, no doubt about it, Millie thought. But if she had owned it, she wouldn't have dared alter a design by Thomas Jefferson. Staring unseeingly at an ornamental frieze near the ceiling, she let herself escape into a fantasy of being a privileged dinner guest in Jefferson's time, conversing at table with the knowledgeable owner and his family, eating fruits, vegetables, and other foods grown on the plantation.

She would have been served by slaves, of course, one aspect of Jefferson's life that always made her uncomfortable. If she had lived then, would she have accepted her fellow humans' involuntary servitude as easily as most people seemed to have done? She'd never know, of course. However much she studied life two centuries ago, she could never get fully into the mindset.

As if reading Millie's mind, a thin female tourist raised the subject of Jefferson's slaveholding past, calling him a hypocrite for espousing independence for the colonies but not granting it to individuals he owned. Clearly used to such comments, the guide patiently listed occasions when Jefferson had spoken out against the institution of slavery, calling it "a great evil."

She went on to say that the system had been well entrenched, particularly in the South. Plantations could not have existed otherwise, she noted. "And many in the North preferred to look the other way, to finance the slave trade, and to go on enjoying goods produced by the plantation system.

"We should also remember that Jefferson was one of the biggest landowners in the state. As such, he was responsible for the livelihood and sustenance of many people besides his own family."

"But some of the Founding Fathers did free their slaves," the woman insisted. "George Washington. And Ben Franklin."

"True. But Franklin never owned many slaves to begin with. Washington, like Jefferson, owned hundreds but freed them only at his death. Also, Washington left an estate large enough to support his freed slaves the rest of their lives, whereas Jefferson was heavily in debt when he died. His belongings, including Monticello and most of his slaves, had to be sold to pay his creditors.

"Admittedly, he wasn't the best of money managers. But much of his financial difficulty was caused by having to take on other people's debts."

The thin woman frowned, looking thoughtful.

"Jefferson did free a few slaves during his lifetime," Clara added, "sometimes by allowing them to escape without pursuit. And at the end of his life, he asked that his creditors allow him to free five slaves, which they did."

Given the times and Jefferson's personal situation, Millie admitted to herself, perhaps he had done the best he could. If she'd lived then, would she have done better? Even as well?

Millie saw that Danny and the girl had broken off their conversation, and he was now standing at a window, looking out over the office wing, lifting and relaxing his shoulders in mute expression of ennui. All at once, she saw him tense, alert to something he saw outside.

"Mom!" he said, his high voice carrying, although he'd partly modulated it for his surroundings. "There's that man again!"

With a sense of foreboding, Millie hurried to the window. Sure enough, the biker was striding across the lawn near the wing, this time carrying his helmet.

"Yes," she whispered, her heart pounding with renewed anxiety, unable to deny the biker's identity but equally unsure what else to say. She could hardly deliver a lecture on the evils of reckless driving, not here. She decided not to make a big deal about it now, hoping to find the right words later to voice her concern. "Maybe the man works here. We'd better move on now." Putting an arm around her son, Millie nudged him away from the window.

"You said Jefferson freed several slaves," a woman on the tour said, as the group walked back through the dining room. "Was Sally Hemings one of them?"

"No, the Hemings family was a large one, and all those freed were related to her in some way, but not Sally herself. Her brother James, who was Jefferson's body servant and chef, was freed as the result of a deal between master and servant. James taught his Paris-trained cooking skills to his brother Peter in return for manumission. But Jefferson later regretted freeing James, who drifted from one job to another, became an alcoholic, and finally committed suicide. Jefferson thought James hadn't been sufficiently prepared to be on his own."

"What about Sally, then? Did she remain a slave all her life?"

"No, she was freed by Jefferson's daughter after his death. Sally finished her life in Charlottesville, living with her sons Madison and Eston, who were among the five freed in response to Jefferson's deathbed request."

Danny didn't seem to have paid attention to the exchange, Millie noticed. Just as well, she thought. They would need to talk about slavery one day, undoubtedly, but one serious talk, about the biker, would be plenty for now.

The tour reached the fourth and rear octagon, which had been the parlor or living room, another light-filled room where Jefferson had often read and written. They walked around the elegant space and looked out through large, full-length windows onto the back gallery and sunken lawn. Clara mentioned the oddity that Millie had noticed earlier, that the house was two stories at the back though it appeared to be only one from the front.

"Jefferson enjoyed tricking the eye," the guide explained. "He incorporated surprises into both houses and landscapes that he designed."

She led them back through the house to the entrance and told them about other interesting features of the property to view on their own. After thanking her for the tour, Millie and Danny went to the basement, where they watched a film about archaeological work at Poplar Forest and looked at exhibits about the construction and restoration of the house. A few hundred yards from the house, they saw a stick frame of a building that marked the site where a slave cabin had once stood. Millie was struck by how small it was to have housed an entire family, maybe even more than one.

In the office wing, which jutted off the residence to the east, they saw several service rooms, each entered by its individual door from a covered walkway. These included the kitchen, where a counter held a row of cooking eyes of various sizes that had allowed the preparation of French sauces and other delights for the diner-in-chief's taste. They climbed to a vantage point and looked at underpinnings of the flat roof covering the wing. A placard explained that Jefferson had designed the intricate system of gutters and joists, with its triangular peaks, to channel water off the terras roof, on which the famous owner and his companions had strolled of an evening, enjoying an unparalleled view of the countryside.

As they climbed back down, a man from the tour spoke to Millie. "Quite a roof, isn't it? Just imagine, four thousand hand-carved shingles. No wonder Jefferson's houses took so long to build."

Millie nodded. "It didn't help that he was away so much during construction. But at least he trusted his experienced builders to make some decisions themselves, not always to be waiting for instructions by mail."

As she and Danny left the office wing, ready to head to the car, she saw from the corner of an eye two men coming towards them from a grove of trees beyond the wing. One was the biker, still carrying his helmet, the other an older man, short, pear-shaped, and bald, wearing jeans and a tan sport shirt. Oh, Lord, she thought, what now?

The two were deep in conversation, walking rapidly enough that they'd probably catch up with Millie and Danny on their way to the parking lot. She pointed to the graceful arcade on the lower floor of the house.

"Look, Danny, aren't those arches neat? This is a really unusual house, isn't it?" Pretty lame, she thought.

He looked at the rear of the house more closely, nodding slightly.

"I bet it would've been fun to be one of Jefferson's grandchildren, playing all around such a neat place."

". . .frustrating as hell," she heard the biker mutter as the two men came even with her.

"But you've just started to look outside . . . ," the other replied, his voice trailing off as they went on past.

Danny turned to look after them and pulled on Millie's arm.

"There he is again, Mom, the guy on the motorcycle."

She nodded, her insides in turmoil. Of all the dumb things to do today, she berated herself. If we had gone on into Lynchburg like I'd planned, we wouldn't have seen this guy again today.

Millie wondered if the men were both employees here, sightseers who'd struck up a conversation, or one of each. Maybe the biker had toured Poplar Forest, then strolled about the grounds and begun talking with one of the employees.

She hadn't really expected he'd be coming here. That might be her bias showing, however; some bikers probably were interested in history. When she thought of motorcycles, though, she couldn't help thinking of Jack. He would not have been interested in coming here.

As Millie and Danny walked behind the biker and his companion—with deliberate slowness on her part, so the men would have a chance to get well away before mother and son reached the parking lot—the two men parted with casual waves to each other. The biker continued towards the parking lot; the other veered towards the archaeology and restoration buildings. Reaching the two similar structures, he disappeared between them.

Millie slowed even more. Soon she heard the noise of the cycle starting up. The clatter rose, then abated, as the biker evidently rode away.

As they reached their car and crawled in, an idea occurred to her. Alice had sent a map before they'd left Dallas, on which she'd marked locations of several sites she knew would interest Millie, including areas of historic homes and a cemetery that contained graves of a few Revolutionary War veterans.

"What say we pick up some burgers and have ourselves a picnic?" she said to Danny.

He perked up at that. "Sure. Where we gonna eat it?"

"You'll see," she said. "It's a place Alice told me about. She says it has lots of nice flowers and trees. Bet you'll like it. Anyway, Alice won't be home for a while, and we're not on a schedule today."

As they drove out of the parking lot, Millie saw the empty space where the motorcycle had been. Yes, she and Danny would need to have that talk.

They bought sandwiches and drinks at a fast-food place, then by using Alice's map soon found their way to Old City Cemetery. Just inside the iron gates, Millie took a graveyard map and brochures from a holder, followed a trail a few hundred yards, and parked under a shade tree, and they sat in the car, munching their lunch. As Millie finishing eating, she screwed up her courage and began.

"Danny, you know that man we saw on the motorcycle? And again at Poplar Forest? I know you thought he was 'cool,' zooming around on that bike like he was having lots of fun. But you do know he could've caused a bad wreck, don't you?"

Her son looked at her, not saying anything.

"I had to turn the steering wheel really hard and really fast to avoid hitting him. If we'd been meeting another car at the time, you and I both could've been killed. And we could've killed people in the other car. That would not have been cool, would it?"

He looked down at his lap and slowly shook his head.

"We were really lucky. And the guy on the motorcycle was lucky, too. He might've been killed or badly hurt, himself. Plus, if we, or other people, had been hurt, he could've been in lots of trouble for causing the accident. This was serious, understand?"

He nodded, still looking down. "I guess."

Her heart turned over, seeing him look so forlorn. Enough for now, she decided. She was under no illusions that the problem was solved, for good, but at least they had made a beginning.

Hitting Danny's shoulder lightly with a fist, she said, "Ornery as you are, as much trouble as you are, I love you, and don't want to lose you. Now, shall we go look around?"

He hopped from the car, relieved the lecture was over. They prowled among the tombstones, enjoying the tranquil setting and attractive plantings of apple trees, shrubs, herbs, and many varieties of antique roses. One of the brochures mentioned five small museums on the cemetery grounds that sounded interesting, especially the Hearse House and Caretakers' Museum, which housed a turn-of-the-century hearse; the Station House Museum, a reproduction of a World-War-I-era railway station; and the Pest (Pestilence) House, where smallpox victims had been quarantined during the Civil War. But the museums could be toured only by appointment, so they would have to return another time.

Danny didn't seem to mind, and Millie realized he was getting tired. Much as she enjoyed history-related sightseeing, she shouldn't demand too much of him, maybe turn him off history entirely. But she couldn't leave without seeing the graves of the Revolutionary War veterans.

They found the oldest part of the graveyard, but Millie was disappointed to see that much of the lettering on these tombstones was no longer legible. One old grave, however, had apparently been better protected from the elements by its positioning beneath the branches of an ancient-looking tree. The name and death date on the stone were readable as Ephraim Hayes, 1807. That was the year after the cemetery had been established, according to one of the pamphlets, so this was clearly one of the first interments here.

In what apparently had been a phrase below the date on Hayes's marker, most of a word could be read: "Discov--y."

"Discovery," Millie said aloud. "What do you suppose Ephraim Hayes discovered, that was important enough to put on his tombstone?"

Danny gave his "who cares?" shrug, as if someone's centuries-old "Eureka!" moment couldn't possibly matter now. Millie laid a hand lightly on his shoulder, and they walked together to the car.

# ✯ Chapter Three

Following the map of Lynchburg that Alice had sent, a red dot marking the location of the house she'd rented, Millie found the historic Rivermont section. Here, estate-sized, tree-shaded yards surrounded stately houses, many of them restored Victorians with multiple porches, turrets, gingerbread trim, and stained-glass panels. Millie had once considered such structures monstrosities, relics of an era far removed from her beloved American Revolutionary period. Undoubtedly Jefferson, with his preference for classic, clean lines, would have found the style garish and overdone. But Millie now realized she appreciated Victorians for their lushness, attention to detail, and evocation of a bygone age.

*If a thing's worth doing, it's worth over-doing,* Millie could almost hear Sylva say.

"There it is, Mom!" Danny cried. "That one's yellow, and it's the right house number."

They had passed the dwelling he indicated, so Millie stopped the car, reversed, and pulled into the drive. She sat for a moment admiring the double-galleried structure, pale yellow with dark gold and rust accents. The photo Alice had e-mailed hadn't fully prepared Millie for those imposing columns, arched windows, and dual mansard roofs that topped the main structure and an adjoining square tower at one end.

They got out, and Millie found the key where Alice had said it would be, in a saucer hidden in a pot of yellow snapdragons beside the sidewalk that led from driveway to front porch. Dashing up the front steps, Danny jumped onto the porch swing and pushed off with a tennis-shoed foot. She fumbled with the door lock, then swung wide the entry to a long reception hall with a staircase along one side, doors to other rooms and the entrance to a smaller hallway on the other. They took a quick tour through a long parlor across the front, then a formal dining room and bedroom behind it. Behind those were a breakfast room, kitchen, laundry room, and bath. The bedroom had to be Alice's, Millie decided. She'd said she was converting a den/playroom into quarters for herself, because she loved to cook and wanted to be handy to the kitchen. A door between the laundry room and bath opened onto a back porch, and another off the breakfast room exited to a flagstone terrace which wrapped around the dwelling from front to back.

Danny was hungry again, so they left unexplored the smaller hall that went from the hallway to whatever environs lay beyond. In the kitchen, a lengthy typed note on the refrigerator gave basic information about the house and neighborhood and offered a plate of cookies on the counter and a pitcher of lemonade in the fridge. They sat at the counter munching shortbread and sipping lemonade, while Millie looked around the kitchen. She admired the way it blended new and old, with modern appliances, handcrafted pecan cabinets, granite countertops, a wide window over the sink, and a many-paned door opening to the breakfast room.

After putting their dishes in the sink, they took an old-fashioned cage elevator to the second floor and found the rooms Alice had chosen for them, across the hall from each other at the back of the house. They would share a bathroom, and Jill and the other renter would share another. Danny's room had bunk beds and lots of built-in drawers, Millie's a bay window complete with window seat.

"Such luxury," she murmured to him, anticipating happy hours of reading in her room.

"Yeah!" Danny said, flinging himself onto the window seat. She joined him, lolling against the wall of the bay, and they grinned at each other.

After they carried in their luggage and other belongings, Millie moved the car to a lot behind the house and across the alley, where Alice had arranged for them to park for a fee. Millie helped Danny organize his drawers and then set up her new laptop computer in her room. She had rationalized the expense as needed for e-mailing friends at home and elsewhere. Deciding to leave the arranging of her closet and bureau drawers until later, she made two phone calls to say she had arrived safely.

The first was to Scott in Boulder, Colorado. They usually spoke at a later hour, after he'd stopped studying for the day, but he'd said to call earlier today if she could.

"Sounds like a one-of-a-kind house," he said when she'd finished describing Poplar Forest. "Wish I could take the summer off and join you in Virginia."

"How're the studies progressing?"

"Okay. But there's a reason they're called comprehensive exams. There's so much they could ask me. But I've been thinking—maybe I should take a day or two off and meet you in Charlottesville. My best friend from grad school took a job there and has been after me to visit."

"Charlottesville. Sounds good. I do want to take Danny there while we're in Virginia."

"Excellent. Let's plan on it. Can't wait to see you again, sweets." He paused, then added hesitantly, "Think Danny'll ever get used to me being part of your life?"

"I do hope so. But it may take a while." Millie lowered her voice, though she hadn't heard Danny coming from his room. "It's been just the two of us all his life—except for brief appearances by Jack the Rat, when he wanted something."

"I still can't believe you were married to someone stupid enough to let you get away."

"He was the one who left. Couldn't handle being a father."

"As I said, stupid. Danny's a neat kid."

"He is. But I think he's afraid to get attached to you. Several of his friends have dealt with multiple dads going in and out of their lives." Millie cleared her throat. "And—I guess I'm okay with that. I don't want my kid getting hurt."

"Millie—"

"I know. I'm sure you and I made the right decision, to keep things simple while our lives are in different places. But the impermanence of our relationship presents problems for Danny. He and I've talked about it—he doesn't understand what you *are* to him. He can't call you his new dad, and 'Mom's friend' sounds iffy."

"I see that. But I need to finish my graduate program here, and I don't feel I could move Aunt Charla to Dallas. They say with Alzheimer's patients, the fewer changes in their environment, the better.

"But," he went on in a more cheerful tone, "one really good change has happened at her nursing home. There's a new nurse's aide who's kinda adopted Aunt Charla. Jolene does lots of nice things for her—brushes her hair gently, reads to her sometimes on her break, even brings her son Larry to visit on her day off. I'm trying to return the favor by tutoring Larry in reading."

"You have important ties to Boulder, I know."

"But I'm not going away, Millie. We're part of each other's lives now."

"We are. And I care for you, too, Scott. But in my experience, just when you're most hopeful, that's when life smacks you one in the eye."

"Losing your mom suddenly, the way you did, had to make you leery about the future."

"It did. But I'm far from unique—other pre-teens lose parents to suicide. Anyway, I didn't mean to drag this conversation into the pits. Think you can stay in Charlottesville a couple of days, so we can tour both Monticello and UVA together?"

"Probably. My grad-school buddy, Brian, is teaching this summer, so he won't expect me to spend all my time with him. Plus, he's already seen both Jefferson locales several times with visiting family and friends."

"I'm really looking forward to touring them."

"Me, too. I've always liked history, but finding out our goofy ancestor actually knew Ben Franklin piqued my interest more. Great talking with you, babe, but I'd better hit the books. Love you."

When their call ended, Millie phoned Sylva at Waverly Manor in Dallas. She had called her elderly friend twice from the road and as always felt her spirits lift on hearing the dear voice. Millie told her impressions of Lynchburg and mentioned the near-collision with the motorcycle, which she hadn't thought to tell Scott about.

"What an awful introduction to Poplar Forest!" Sylva said. "Sure you and Danny are both okay?"

"We're fine. I've probably made it sound like a closer call than it was."

"I doubt that. If anything, you underplay danger to yourself." She asked if Millie had found Alice well.

They chatted a while, Millie relieved to find that Sylva was no longer hoarse as she had been before they'd left. Just as Scott could not abandon his Aunt Charla, Millie would find it difficult to leave Sylva, who had been like family to her. She wasn't sure how, or if, they would ever resolve their distance problem.

Soon, Alice arrived home, brewed a pot of coffee, and told them about interesting sights and activities in the area. The women sat on the back porch, sipping coffee and watching Danny investigate the large backyard.

"Sorry I was out of touch on the trip," Millie said. "It felt good to not even check e-mail every night at motels. I figured you could call my cell phone if you needed me."

Alice nodded. "I try not to let technology run my life, too. I've leased a computer and printer and set up an office on the second floor, down the hall from you, but I refuse to let the internet take all my time."

"You were hoping to get more renters to share the costs. Had any luck?"

"I thought I had a third-floor bedroom rented to two women, but they backed out. So it's just the two of you, Jill, Cynthia, and me. Fortunately, we're getting a good deal on the rent. The owner's traveling overseas and mainly wants responsible tenants who'll look after the place. She's a friend of my sister's, so I gave Belinda as a reference."

"I met Jill today, and she seems friendly. What's Cynthia like?"

"More reserved than Jill but nice. She's an elementary teacher from New Mexico, here working with the children's summer program. She shares our love of the American Revolutionary Era."

Alice gave a little laugh. "Unlike the rest of us, Jill isn't a history buff. She followed her boyfriend to Lynchburg. Of course, she took the classes for volunteers, which anyone who represents the site to the public—docents and museum-shop people—has to take."

"I'm glad the archaeologists agreed to waive those classes for me. I couldn't have managed to come while school was on. You said Jill followed her boyfriend. What's he do?"

"He's the archaeologist investigating Highgrove."

"Really! So does she give you regular reports about how that work's going?"

"No, not much. Jill's only interest in archaeology is loving one particular archaeologist."

"Did she know the young woman who was killed?"

Alice nodded. "Jill goes out to Highgrove sometimes to hang around Luke, so she knew Paige. How well, I can't say."

"Still, that must have been horrible for her. You mentioned a crew investigating Highgrove. Besides Luke and Paige, how many?"

"Jill says the firm that employs Luke sent a team of four, including two other men. And she's mentioned a male volunteer who spends lots of time there."

Millie heard a car pull into the drive and stop. Alice stood, saying that must be Jill and Cynthia, who carpooled on days when their schedules meshed. Millie went with Alice to greet the arrivals. Danny followed them inside.

Cynthia Cisneros proved to be a petite Latina with lustrous long hair, a winsome smile, and a manner that at first seemed standoffish. But when they had all put together a simple soup-salad meal and sat eating at the dinette table in the breakfast room, her initial shyness melted, especially once she and Danny discovered a shared interest in plants. He told her about growing geraniums and petunias in window boxes at their old apartment, and spring onions and potatoes in their present backyard. She told him about the many varieties of cacti and succulents around her small town near Santa Fe, and described the yucca plant that produced New Mexico's dramatic state flower.

Jill and Danny also found a common interest, knock-knock jokes. Her raucous laugh rang out easily and often.

Millie gave an internal sigh of relief. The women populating her son's new world were making him feel included, and he seemed to like them. A few times that day, she had worried that she might have made a mistake in coming. First there'd been that run-in with the motorcyclist, then the news about the murder. When she had envisioned a few weeks at Poplar Forest, she had never imagined she could be bringing Danny to a place with any danger. Now, after meeting her housemates, she felt reassured. They might easily never see that biker again, and since Paige's murder had occurred in her apartment building, it probably had nothing to do with either Highgrove or Jill. Now if the summer program proved to be as much fun as it sounded . . .

In a lull between jokes, she asked Cynthia how things were shaping up for the camp.

"Will you be my teacher?" Danny asked.

"No, the Education Assistant at Poplar Forest is the teacher. She's really good. But she'll have several volunteers helping. I'm a helper."

He nodded slowly, as if trying to envision this new learning environment.

"I'll bet the Hands-on History building is fun," Millie said.

Cynthia smiled. "It is. I'd love to take it home to show my own students."

"S'pose I can see it while we're here?"

"Sure. It'll be open to the public on weekends once the camp's over."

"Good. Did you know a lot about Poplar Forest before coming here to volunteer?"

"I'd seen the house twice, then attended a one-week archaeology field school for teachers last summer. But I still had to take the training for volunteers. Fortunately, our spring break came at the right time, so I could do it."

"What are you doing this week to get ready for camp?"

"Going over the agenda, getting our assignments, preparing workbooks for the kids. And we really have to know our stuff. Kids ask off-the-wall questions sometimes."

"You may want to spend time in the Poplar Forest library while you're here, Millie," Alice suggested. "The librarian's very helpful and will steer you to sources for anything you want to read more about. From the first, Poplar Forest was intended as a teaching resource, so there's a strong focus on how the house was built initially and how it's been restored. Lots of classes come on field trips, and the instruction given follows Virginia's Standards of Learning guidelines."

"I can't wait to get started." Millie turned to Jill. "Are you enjoying your work in the shop?"

"It's okay. We've been busy this week, lots of people in."

"Mom, can I be excused?" Danny had eaten most of his food while the adults talked and was now squirming in his chair.

"Okay, I'll be up soon." When Danny had gone, Millie broached the subject that had been on her mind. "Alice told me about that young woman's getting killed—Paige Oberlin. Have you heard anymore about who might've done it?"

Jill's rosy checks paled. "No. I try not to think about it; it was just so terrible. But everywhere I go in Lynchburg, people are talking about it."

Millie nodded sympathetically. "Alice said Paige worked with your boyfriend. What was she like?"

"Reserved. But she had a real dry sense of humor. I didn't always know when she was kidding. I invited her to go shopping with me one time—trying to get to know her better, you know, since she was Luke's crew member—but she said she wasn't into shopping. She invited me instead to go see some old church with her. She was really into poking into old things. I didn't go, of course. That's just not my thing."

"Paige and I would've gotten along, I bet," Millie said with a slight smile.

"Whatever. Just imagine—getting attacked when you're almost safely home." Jill shook her fair head. "What a waste."

"Was Paige very young?"

"Twenty-six. She was an intern assisting the architectural historian that's working with Luke. Highgrove was Paige's first job for the company, and she was glad it brought her back to Lynchburg."

"Do her folks still live here?"

"They're both gone, and she was an only child. But she seemed pretty close to the friend she shared the apartment with, Monica something."

"Do the police have any leads?"

Jill gave a clueless look and shook her head. "The paper said the stabbing appeared random— someone looking to steal money from whoever happened into the building. But I guess the police don't tell the media everything. Luke's been questioned twice—all the crew, in fact—so the police must not be satisfied yet."

"Suppose they think someone she knew did it and made it look like a mugging? That'd be even worse, in a way, than being a random victim."

"Yeah." Jill chewed a thumbnail, looking thoughtful. "Yeah, it would."

# ✯ Chapter Four

"So Luke gets assigned to various archaeological jobs by his company?" Millie asked.

Jill nodded. "Yep. He's a contract archaeologist." With a superior look, she explained. "He does what's called 'public archaeology' or 'rescue archaeology.' Ever hear of the Historical Preservation Act?"

"Sure. It was mentioned in one of my sources about Jefferson the architect. Anyone wanting to develop land containing an Indian grave or other historical feature that could be disturbed by construction has to consult appropriate specialists before going ahead."

"Yeah. And Luke's one of the experts they'd call in. He researches the history of a property, digs test pits to determine the age of structures, that kinda stuff."

"Does he think Highgrove is a Jefferson building?"

"He says it's too early to say." Jill's finger traced the edge of her plate. "Highgrove's in kinda bad shape. It was tied up several years in a legal battle over unclear wording in somebody's will, and nobody lived there during that time. It was originally several miles from town, but it's in the city limits now. Luke says the owner's getting lots of calls from developers about the big tract of land it sits on." She turned as Danny came back into the room. "Hey, kiddo, get lonely upstairs?"

Danny gave a one-shoulder shrug, laid down a young-adult novel he'd brought with him, and sat beside Millie. Realizing he probably didn't yet feel comfortable in the huge, unfamiliar house, she laid an arm over the back of his chair. She'd have liked to tousle his hair or give him a hug, but he'd likely interpret either gesture as "babying."

"So Highgrove's in danger of being sold to developers?" Millie asked.

"Yeah. The owner could get lotsa money if she sold."

"What about the house, then? Would it be moved somewhere else and restored?"

"Who knows? My mom worked with a group in Maryland that rescued a historic house, and she says it's not easy. Somebody's got to raise funds, work with the right experts, and jump through legal hoops. Doesn't happen by magic."

"I'm sure you're right. Still . . . any chance I could get a look at Highgrove? It sounds worth seeing, Jefferson design or not."

"I'll call Luke and ask." Jill started to build a fence of toothpicks for Danny's amusement. "I work in the shop tomorrow, but if Luke agrees, you and I could go over there Friday."

"That'd be great! I'd love to see it before I start working on Monday. Want to see another old house, Danno?"

He looked up from his book. "Do I hafta, Mom? It sounds boring."

He'd been a good kid today, Millie thought, not whining when she'd wanted to see Old City Cemetery in addition to the earlier sightseeing. "I guess not. I can probably see Highgrove later."

"Speaking of houses," Cynthia put in, "don't you love the one Alice found for us?"

"I do."

"It's a huge place," Alice said, "so we may have to keep in touch by phone when we're in different parts. We all have cells, though, and the land lines have several extensions."

"Good," Millie said. "You mentioned a third floor. What's up there?"

"Mostly rooms filled with the owner's furniture and boxes. The mansion has an interesting history, according to the realtor who manages it. She says the man who built it was an eccentric, quite wealthy but distrustful of banks. A story persists that he squirreled away cash in a bunch of secret hidey-holes he had installed when the house was built."

Danny's eyes grew large. "Maybe there's still money inside the walls!"

Jill's hand slipped, scattering her toothpick fence. Cynthia and Danny helped her retrieve the bits of wood from the floor.

"I very much doubt it," Alice said with a grin. "More likely, someone's imagination ran wild because they thought this big, ornate place looked like a house that should hold secrets. Or maybe the realtor manufactured the tale to make it appealing to renters."

Millie chuckled. "And I'm told I'm a cynic."

"Makes a good story," Alice said, raising her brows. "And who knows? Maybe Danny'll find a secret trapdoor in the floor of his room." She gave him a mock-severe look. "Don't be pulling up any floor-boards, young man, not without consulting your mom or me first."

His half-smile suggested he wasn't sure she was teasing. A wink from her assured him she was.

"We'll need to work out how to manage the cleaning and cooking chores," Cynthia said. "Alice has been doing most of both, but we mustn't be unfair."

They decided each would clean her own room and they'd divide the cost of having someone do the common areas. On weekends, they'd plan the next week's meals. All liked to cook, so each would prepare at least one dinner a week, and the cook for a given day would be excused from clean-up. Each would post her weekly work schedule on the refrigerator, with any other plans that affected mealtimes, and let the appropriate chef know when her dinner plans changed.

Alice and Millie planned to carpool on days they'd both be working, and Alice offered to look after Danny on her day off.

"Speaking of that, I'm off tomorrow. If you and Jill could go to Highgrove then, instead of Friday, he could stay with me."

"That'd be great, Alice," Millie said. "Thanks. Would that be a possibility, Jill?"

"I'd have to switch days with a friend who works in the shop, but she owes me a favor. I'll check with Luke first."

"I could baby-sit sometimes, Millie, when you work and I'm off," Cynthia offered.

"Me, too," Jill said.

Danny laid down his novel. "Can't I stay by myself while you're gone, Mom? I'm too big for a sitter."

"You're growing up fast, Danno, but I don't want you staying alone. Lots of things could happen that a nine-year-old wouldn't know how to handle."

"Billy French stays by himself after school, and he's in my grade."

"I said no, Daniel John."

Recognizing the full-name signal that meant his mother's patience was wearing thin, Danny heaved a sigh, grabbed his book, and stalked from the room. The four women exchanged glances.

"That went well," Cynthia said with a teasing glance at Millie.

"Didn't it?"

Alice chuckled. "Kids want independence—at least they think they're supposed to—but I bet he's relieved you said no."

"It's great that you're all willing to help look after him. We'll work out a fair hourly rate, and I'll try not to abuse your kindness."

"You won't pay me," Alice said with a smile. "I don't have grandkids, and this'll be fun. But I won't speak for Cynthia or Jill."

The others agreed to accept a fee. "You really don't mind paying us, Millie?" Cynthia asked.

"You kidding? I can't believe I'll have good sitters in-house."

"Danny's a great kid," Jill said. "You've done an amazing job with him."

"Thanks."

Cynthia nodded. "It can't have been easy, without his father there to help."

"Jack wouldn't have been much help, even if he'd been around," Millie said with a wry grin. "He's not exactly mature himself. In and out of trouble ever since I've known him, never made a wise choice about money in his life. Danny's better off without that great role model."

The housemates compared notes on current men friends. Cynthia said she had recently broken up with a long-time steady, who hadn't taken it well.

"Ted keeps calling and begging to get back together." She wadded her napkin into a tight ball.

"Some men are hard to discourage," Jill said knowingly. "You have to be firm."

"I'm not good at that. I hate to hurt guys' feelings." Cynthia said she'd gone out with another volunteer a couple of times since arriving in Lynchburg but merely as friends. "I tend to lose myself in whoever I'm dating. Then when the break-up comes—and it always does—I have to go searching for what's left of me."

"Luke doesn't absorb a woman like that," Jill said. "Not that I'd let him. We're pretty serious, but I have two more years to go on my degree before we can get married. I wouldn't mind being officially engaged, though—" She fingered a sparkly ear bob.

Taking the cue, Millie said, "Pretty earrings. Are they real diamonds?"

"Yeah," Jill said, looking smug, "and valuable. My rich aunt willed them to me because I'd admired them so much. I wear them all the time—can't stand their languishing in a vault somewhere. All my family know how I love real gems—looking at them, wearing them, reading about them—especially unique stones that've been stolen, lost, cursed, or have a salacious past." As she spoke, Jill's blue-gray eyes gleamed like jewels themselves.

"Everyone's heard of the Hope Diamond," she continued, apparently launched on a favorite topic, "but there're other fabulous stones with interesting histories. Take the Star of India, which is a huge star sapphire that was the object of an infamous burglary. And the Scarlet Star's even more interesting, I think. It's a blood-red star ruby, set in a gold ring that was owned by several crowned heads of Europe before being lost during the French Revolution. It resurfaced in the possession of a titled Englishwoman traveling in Europe, and she brought it to this country. It disappeared again, this time in Missouri—in a stagecoach accident, of all things. I was reading an article about it just last night. The English lady often didn't wear the ring but carried it about her person in a pouch with a fleur-de-lis pattern on it—all part of the mystique about that incredible stone. But she worried about stagecoach robberies and gave the ring to her maid to hide in her bustle, assuming the maid would attract less notice from thieves than her expensively dressed mistress. Both women were thrown from the coach when it overturned on a rocky patch of ground, and the pouch apparently popped out then. The Star was never found."

Jill gave them a skeptical look. "A stagecoach has an 'accident,' and a valuable gem goes missing at the same time? Puh-lease. Bet the maid was working with a conspirator to steal the ring. Boy, would I love to get my hands on that beauty!" She clasped her hands together as if cradling the stone.

"Rubies are one of the oldest precious stones," she said in a lecturing tone. "Most people don't know that the finest deep red ones are worth more than diamonds of comparable weight. I do adore diamonds, and they're what people mostly want for engagement rings, but rubies are so gorgeous."

She smiled with a self-importance that had begun to annoy Millie. But now the self-centered bragging seemed to mask insecurity. Anyway, Millie decided, she could forgive much because Jill was friendly to Danny.

"I plan to be a broker of precious stones some day," the monologue went on. "Or maybe I'll go to work for Sotheby's."

"Very specific goals," Millie observed.

"I know what I like, and I know what I want." Jill touched her earring again. "Luke gave me a necklace once with a pendant that looks like a sapphire, but it's not genuine—I can tell. I've dragged him into a few jewelry stores, trying to teach him about real precious stones, but he doesn't seem to care. Men! How about you, Millie? You serious with anyone?"

Millie told them about Scott and their mostly long-distance relationship. "We're taking things slowly. It's a big adjustment for Danny, seeing me with any man. For years, I was too busy to date."

"He doesn't like having to share his mom," Cynthia offered.

"I guess. And to tell the truth, I'm enjoying just being able to attend school full-time and afford occasional treats for Danny and me, like this trip. I do care for Scott, enjoy being with him, but—well, we'll see how it all works out. Or doesn't."

*Millie Kirchner, cockeyed optimist,* Sylva observed in Millie's mind.

They all pitched in to clean up the kitchen, and then Alice showed Millie the washer and dryer. As they left the laundry room,

Alice asked how she and Danny liked their rooms.

"Love them. I'm so glad you found the house and invited us to join you."

"My pleasure. Bet the library's your favorite room, right?"

"Library? I don't recall seeing that."

"Ah, you haven't been to the tower yet."

"No, I'm pretty sure I'd remember a tower and a library."

Alice beckoned her along the long hall towards the front of the house, turning left into the smaller passage that Millie and Danny hadn't investigated earlier. It ran behind the parlor and ended at large double doors, which Alice said separated the main structure from the tower. She opened them to reveal the library of Millie's dreams.

A huge fireplace, its grate empty for summer, dominated one end of the big room. Nearby, sat a cozy arrangement of deep leather chairs, lamps, and a rosewood table. Carved wood paneling lined the walls, save where full bookshelves soared two stories high. A rolling ladder gave access to an upper-level catwalk, as did a spiral staircase in one corner of the library. On the wall beside the stairs, Alice opened French doors to reveal another flagstone terrace, smaller than that on the other end of the house. Millie could hardly wait to begin enjoying the booklovers' retreat.

But she excused herself to go check on Danny, fearing he'd be lonely or scared in this roomy new place. Climbing the stairs to the catwalk, she strode around it to a door into the main house, glancing at book titles as she went. One section featured travelogues, another tomes about famous military battles, yet another books on Thomas Jefferson and related topics, including the Louisiana Purchase. It looked like a great library for browsing, Millie thought, especially the Jefferson section.

Reentering the main structure on the second floor, she followed a corridor past the office Alice had fitted out, passed Cynthia's and Jill's rooms, and reached her own. Seeing that Danny's door across the hall stood open, suggesting he'd recovered from his pique, Millie tapped on the facing and went in. She found him lying across the lower bunk bed reading an adventure novel they'd bought during a stop at a bookstore in Knoxville.

The bulletin board she had helped Danny hang earlier now held snapshots of his Dallas friends. His collection of action figures marched across the built-in desk, and the puzzle books he had used for entertainment in the car were stacked neatly beside them.

"Like your room okay?" Millie asked, brushing an errant hair from his eye.

"Yeah, it's good." He continued reading.

"This is a big house, isn't it?"

He nodded.

"Too big, maybe?"

He shrugged.

"I'm right across the hall, in case you get scared during the night, or need to ask me anything."

"I won't get scared."

"Okay. But I'm handy if you need me."

When she started to leave, he looked up. "What we gonna do tomorrow, Mom?"

"I may go to Highgrove with Jill. If I do, you can stay with Alice. Okay?"

"Okay."

"Whichever day we don't go to Highgrove—Thursday or Friday—you and I can look around town some more. Alice told me about several other sections of historic houses—"

He scrunched up his face. "Bor-ing."

"—but I can see those another time. She also told me about some nice parks and an interactive museum for kids. It's called Amazement Square and has exhibits you can touch, plus lots of ladders to climb and tunnels to crawl through. Sound fun?"

He turned up his face and grinned. "Yeah, okay."

She supervised his preparations for bed, then went back to the library's second floor and looked at the Jefferson collection. A cache of books on Lewis and Clark reminded her she knew little about this important part of Jefferson's presidency.

Might be time to remedy that, she thought. Selecting two volumes, she carried them to her room.

Millie had just curled up in the window seat and begun to read when Jill tapped on her door, which she had left open in order to hear if Danny called.

"I talked to Luke," Jill said. "We can see Highgrove tomorrow. He said that'd be better than Friday, because he needs to go to Roanoke then. I called my friend, and she's agreed to trade with me. Luke's glad you're interested." Jill rolled her eyes. "He likes to show off when he's on an interesting job."

"Great!" Millie said. "Thanks for arranging it."

"'No problem. 'Night, now."

Millie took up her book again, an illustrated history with maps, photos, and paintings that brought alive the journey to explore the vast uncharted lands Jefferson had acquired in his bold deal with Napoleon. As she read, she began to see as individuals the forty-plus explorers who had given up home, family, and safety for more than two years to undertake the mission.

John Colter, for example, a man of great strength and excellent hunting skill, had left the expedition a few weeks before it returned to St. Louis to become a fur trapper in the West. Initially, his story about having seen steam rising from the ground and mud boiling in sulfur pits had been ridiculed as a tall tale. But the area Colter had described later became Yellowstone National Park.

A reproduction of a Charles M. Russell painting, titled "Big Medicine," showed expedition members around a campfire with their Indian hosts. Near the fire, a Hidatsa chief rubbed the chest of York, William Clark's slave who'd accompanied him on the journey, trying to see if the blackness of York's skin would come off. A caption explained that, though most Indians along the Missouri River had seen whites before, blacks were a novelty to them. The Indians consequently wondered if York was a painted white man or, if not, whether his blackness was a sign of extraordinary powers.

Millie stretched, yawned, and decided to take a break. Sliding the book into a drawer, she got out a sketchpad and pencils and caricatured each of her housemates: Alice as a mother hen, gathering all her chicks (with faces like those of the four younger residents) into a nest around her. Cynthia looked fetching in overalls and a straw hat, surrounded by cacti and yucca. Jill was an overly made-up child in showgirl costume, flashing precious jewels from head to toe.

Millie considered the drawings. As initial impressions, they weren't bad. But she wondered how a few weeks in the company of these women might change how she saw each.

She put her drawing supplies away, prepared for bed, wrote a few e-mails to friends back home, then searched online for information on Lynchburg restaurants. She found menus for several and went to the office, intending to use the printer and computer there to print them off. Stepping into the room, she heard someone sniff.

Cynthia sat bent over the desk, her face buried in one hand. At Millie's step behind her, the snuffling paused and Cynthia looked up. "Oh . . . hi, Millie."

"I'm sorry," Millie said, easing backwards. "I didn't realize anyone was in here. I can come back later."

"No, don't leave. I will." Cynthia wiped a tear. "I can feel sorry for myself somewhere else."

"Anything I can help with?"

Cynthia took a long breath and released it. "Depends. You know how to get someone out of your life who's determined to be in it?"

"Your former boyfriend?"

"Ted prefers 'current boyfriend.'"

"Oh."

"Exactly. I got another e-mail insisting I get back together with him. How can I make him understand it's over?"

Millie considered. "You may have to be really blunt. Sometimes that's the only way to get through to someone."

"I hate this." Cynthia stood and turned to leave. "But thanks for listening, Millie."

# ✯ Chapter Five

The next morning, Millie and Jill walked to the parking lot behind the mansion. As Jill unlocked an old white Chevy Cavalier, Millie did a double take. The car beside it looked exactly the same, down to model and year.

"Amazing. How do you know which is yours?"

Jill bent beside the mate to her auto and pointed at a spot on the rear fender. "Cynthia's car has this little dent down here. See? You kinda have to know it's there. Besides, hers is usually cleaner than mine. Spending time and money to keep an old heap sparkling clean seems a waste to me."

They headed for the northwest part of Lynchburg, north and east of where Poplar Forest lay in Bedford County. The day was dreary, dark clouds threatening rain. Passing through commercial and residential areas, they arrived at a long stretch of undeveloped land, where Jill swung her car into a driveway. They bumped along the broken drive, weeds tufting its center, for a quarter mile or so, until the forest thinned to reveal a house perched on a rise in its own grove of trees. It had an over-all similarity to Poplar Forest, but its front wasn't partly obscured by boxwood bushes as was that at Jefferson's retreat. They pulled up by the dwelling, parking to its left beside a black Pathfinder, a blue double-cab pickup, and a tan sedan.

As she got out, Millie studied the classic lines of the structure. It looked very much like Poplar Forest, except that Highgrove's portico was narrower, its fanlight-centered pediment shallower, and it had two columns instead of four. Too, the roof here was higher, with what appeared to be an added-on attic room between the four chimneys. And, unlike the restored Poplar Forest, Highgrove showed its age. Once-white trim and the upper parts of the columns were fire-blackened. Near one end of the house, a wooden housing hid part of the brick wall and roof, apparently concealing damage and protecting the interior from weather. Yet in spite of obvious problems and general seediness, the house retained a grandeur.

Millie felt her heart skip. This old dwelling might have been designed by Thomas Jefferson! And she was seeing it before its debut to the world.

It probably wasn't his design, her internal pessimist warned. The odds against discovering a "new" Jefferson building after two centuries must be astronomically high. Still, she could hope.

To the left of the house, in front of the vehicles, someone had placed several lawn chairs in a half-circle, shaded by a tall oak. Beside them stood a shed. Beyond that, Millie saw what had to be an active archaeological dig, with thin uprights linked by string, a pile of dirt, a wheelbarrow between two tall sawhorses, shovels and other implements, and a table holding supplies.

Two men in T-shirts and jeans, faces and arms tanned, came around the left side of the house.

"Welcome, ladies! Glad you made it." The speaker was in his late thirties, tall, lean, and blond, with a moustache like a pale yellow caterpillar. He planted a quick kiss on Jill's cheek and offered Millie a slender hand. "Luke Brooks."

"Millie Kirchner." She shook hands, and, given his thinness, was surprised by the strength of his grip.

"This is Ron Tuttle," Luke said, indicating the man with him. "He's the architectural historian who's working with me on a site plan for Highgrove."

Ron was a few inches shorter than Luke, stocky, round-faced, and forty-something, with thinning brown hair. His grin and handshake were lackadaisical, but his dark eyes were quick and sharp.

"I hear you're an admirer of Jefferson," he drawled. "So'm I. Good to meet another fan."

"Jefferson would've been a fascinating man to know, wouldn't he?"

"And a complicated one. I've probably read every book ever written about him but don't feel I fully understand him."

Another man came striding towards them from a side door of the house. Luke introduced him as Nolan Unruh, a volunteer helping the investigative crew. A faint hint of tobacco smoke clung to him.

"Nolan's into Jefferson too," Ron said. "Even plays him sometimes in reenactments."

"No kidding." As Millie shook hands with the muscular man about her own age, she decided that if such a dark-haired, sturdy young man could transform himself into a believable Thomas Jefferson, he must be a talented actor. Not only had Jefferson had reddish-blond hair and been a head taller, his bearing had been erect and dignified, whereas Nolan tended to slouch. As for facial features, Nolan's rounded, almost pug, nose hardly suggested Jefferson's patrician one. Nor had the Founding Father boasted a deep cleft in his chin.

Makeup and costuming would help, of course. And many people wouldn't be aware of Jefferson's height or stance, knowing his likeness merely from head-only portraits on money and in textbooks.

If any of this trio had been born to play the nation's third president, Millie thought, it would be Luke. But he'd need to shave off that silly moustache.

Millie took a deep breath, and said hesitantly, "I understand a colleague of yours was killed recently. I'm sorry. That must be difficult for all of you."

Ron blinked rapidly three times, then focused his gaze on a tree behind Millie. Luke and Nolan glanced worriedly at him, then at each other.

"It is," Luke agreed, staring down at the ground. "We all liked Paige, and she was a great help here, especially to Ron. She was his intern, you know."

Ron nodded, eyes still averted. Too emotional to speak, Millie thought. But he would naturally feel Paige's loss keenly, having worked closely with her.

"Will you be getting a replacement for your crew?"

Ron looked at Luke.

"We hope to, eventually," Luke said, with a hunch of one shoulder. "Right now, the company has no more interns to send."

No one spoke for a moment. Then Ron broke the awkward silence to say to Millie, "Nolan's family has owned Highgrove since it was built in the 1800s."

"Really?" She couldn't blame him for changing what was clearly an uncomfortable subject.

"Yep, my great-great-however-many-greats-it-was-granddaddy, Hiram Wixon, was the original owner." Nolan looked appreciatively from Jill to Millie. "You ladies certainly brighten the job site."

Millie smiled in acknowledgment of the compliment but returned to the intriguing matter of the house. "If your ancestor built Highgrove," she said to Nolan, "wouldn't some of your relatives know who designed it? Especially if it was Jefferson. Surely that would've been passed down in the family?"

"You'd think so, wouldn't you? But I don't recall any such family lore."

"And wouldn't there be old letters that mentioned Highgrove's origins, or financial records from when it was built?"

"Wish it were that simple. Not everyone was as obsessive about record-keeping as Jefferson. And old letters? I come from a long line of neat-freaks, thrower-outers—the opposite of pack rats. Only thing we have on Highgrove's origins is an old sketch of a floor plan that Granddad gave my aunt and that she's lent to Luke. It's dated 18—, with the last two numbers smudged, so the date could work for a Jefferson plan. But there's no architect's name on it, and it's too amateurish to've been drawn by the third prez himself.

"I've looked through lots of Jefferson's papers—reams of them are available to the public now—but found nothing to show he ever designed anything for my ancestor. That suggests he didn't, but it's not definite."

Luke nodded. "It's not always easy to tell whether Jefferson designed a structure or not. He sometimes drew plans for friends, or consulted casually on designs by others. And records for many buildings got lost over time."

Millie gazed at the façade of the dwelling. "This must've been quite a house once. Did you live here when you were growing up, Nolan?"

He chuckled, as at a good joke. "Nah, my folks lived in a different house Granddad owned, in one of the 'less desirable' parts of Lynchburg. Mom inherited it when Granddad died. But we used to visit here often, and a cousin and I played all over the place as kids. My grandparents were the last to actually live here. Wanta take a look at the dig, Millie? I'd never helped at an archaeological site before, and this one's pretty interesting."

"Sure. I'd like to see—"

"Actually—" Luke began, speaking at the same time as Millie.

Both broke off as the whine of a motorcycle came fast up the drive. Everyone turned to look. The bike was large and new-looking, black with chrome accents. The rider's helmet partly obscured his face, but something about his burly physique, the way his hands gripped the handlebars, seemed familiar to Millie.

Uh-oh, she thought. This was the same biker she and Danny had seen near Poplar Forest, the one who had nearly caused a wreck.

The rider flashed past them, swung his bike in a tight turn, and headed straight towards Millie. She leapt back just as he turned aside. He circled the group, skidded to a showy halt near Jill's auto, briefly idled the bike, and shut it down. Climbing off, he removed his helmet, revealing a shock of light brown hair. With a slight swagger, he came over to them and handed Ron a small paper bag.

"This Hell's Angels wannabe," Luke said with wry amusement, "is my assistant, Whit Young. Millie's Jill's housemate, Whit. She has a thing for old Tom Jeff and came to see what may be one of his designs."

"Cool." Whit offered his hand. "Sorry if I scared you, Millie. But I did have the hog under control."

Millie shook hands and said a chilly hello. His smile and manner seemed amiable enough, but his presence here came as a shock. Even worse was discovering that he was Luke's assistant, and thus had a connection to her housemate Jill.

It would be impossible to ignore him with these kinds of links between them, but for the moment she would keep her distance.

Turning to Nolan, she indicated the blackened pediment, and said, "Looks like there was a fire here at some time."

"Lightning struck a few years ago," he said. "Fortunately, nobody was living here then."

"And what happened at that end? Is that wooden cover hiding damage of some kind?"

Nolan nodded. "A tree fell across the house just a coupla months ago. Damaged the attic and two of the walls. The court had awarded the place to my Aunt Julia by then. She had a company come out and remove the tree, and had the hole covered to keep out rain, but real repairs await the results of these guys' investigation."

"Then Highgrove will be restored to what it was originally?"

His smile faded. "I've no say about that; the court decreed otherwise. Lord knows what Aunt Julia'll decide. She may turn Highgrove into a theme park."

"You're kidding, right?" Millie shuddered at the idea of a house like Jefferson's elegant Poplar Forest being run with profit in mind: a fast-food buffet in the majestic dining room, balloons flying from the chimneys, signs endorsing products wrapped around the stately columns.

He shrugged. "Who knows? I've heard her say history fanatics'll shell out to see anything that's even remotely connected to a Founding Father. Yeah, she'll make it pay, somehow."

"I'm one of those history fanatics," Millie said with a smile. "And even if Jefferson didn't design Highgrove, I'm all for preserving interesting old houses. Preferably by dignified means."

"Woman after my own heart," Ron said with his slow smile.

Something about him, his bright eyes perhaps, made Millie suspect that real energy lay behind that indolent manner.

"Mine, too," Nolan said. "But I'm not the one who'll decide Highgrove's fate."

"You must care about what happens to it, though. You're here now."

"Yep, the place exerts a nostalgic tug on me. So Luke, Ron, and Whit let me hang around and help out a little."

"I appreciate getting to see Highgrove before any . . . changes get made."

"Don't let Nolan give you that 'help out a little' crap." A corner of Luke's mouth lifted in the merest of grins. "He's actually keeping an eye on us for Aunt Julia, to make sure we don't rip something off."

"Are you taking time from a job to volunteer here, Nolan?" Millie asked. "Or are you independently wealthy?"

"I wish. No, I design Web sites for businesses and individuals. I mostly do that evenings and weekends."

"Flexible hours. Nice."

"Come on, Millie." Luke claimed her attention now. "I'll take you through the house." He waved the other men off to their work. "Catch you later, guys."

"Why don't you show her the dig first, Luke?" Nolan said. "This is a good time to see it, Millie. I helped Whit uncover it earlier, but then Ron needed batteries for his flashlight and Whit went to get them. So nobody's started working the dig yet."

"I . . ." Glancing from Nolan to Luke, Millie saw the archaeologist frown. He resented having his role as boss challenged, she realized, and said no more.

"I'll show her the house first," Luke said firmly. "Don't worry, Nolan—we'll get to the dig. Later."

With a shrug, the volunteer followed Ron and Whit around the side of the house. Luke, Jill, and Millie went up the front steps and entered.

"We think this front part's pretty much as originally built," Luke said, "except for that attic add-on. But if TJ did design this house, he'd turn over in his grave to see what somebody did at the back."

Unlike the plan at Poplar Forest, where a middle passage dividing the octagon led directly to the dining room, Highgrove's entry was a small foyer that opened into an octagonal parlor with fireplaces at both ends. A lone chair holding a camera sat by a mantel with a chunk of brickwork missing, and the pail shelf on a stepladder held a large flashlight and a few small implements. Much of the front wall was sooty and grimy. But even in the sparse light of a gloomy day, the room had an air of majesty, the damage to ceiling and one wall as shocking as a gouge through an old master.

"I see where the tree struck," Millie commented, gazing up at the broken ceiling. "Was that also when the bricks got knocked out of that fireplace?"

"No, that happened when the tree-service people were taking the tree out, before Ron and I got involved." Luke waved a hand at the broken mantel and the chair beside it. "Ron's about to start photographing and examining that hearth."

Millie glanced into the hole in the brickwork. "The wall must be really thick here. Even in this dim light, I can tell there's a cavity that goes quite a way back."

Jill bent to look into the aperture, started to rise, then turned to peer into it again. "Yeah. Really deep."

"You're seeing this room on an ugly day," Luke said, "so it doesn't show to best advantage." He flipped on the lights in a graceful chandelier suspended from the high ceiling. "That wall's thick, as you said, Millie. When two octagons angle together as they do here, the space between the ends forms a deep triangle. Jefferson used that space at Poplar Forest to hold fireplaces. The fireboxes in adjoining rooms sit at right angles to each other within the triangular wall, sharing a chimney. The unknown architect of Highgrove used the same arrangement here."

"You're very familiar with Poplar Forest, aren't you?" Millie commented. "But I suppose you have to know Jefferson's buildings inside and out, to figure out whether Highgrove fits."

"That helps. The other guys and I go over to Poplar Forest occasionally and walk around comparing it to Highgrove. One of the archaeologists there, Harold Drake, works for the same company we do. Whit and Harold share a mobile home in the south part of Lynchburg, between here and Poplar Forest."

Ah, Millie thought, that would explain why she'd seen Whit at Jefferson's retreat yesterday. He'd been neither a tourist nor an employee but a friend of an employee. The man with him must have been Harold.

"The floor plan of Highgrove is really similar to Poplar Forest's," Luke went on. "Both houses even underwent the same types of remodeling. The dining rooms, for instance—"

He showed them a central square smaller and darker than the one at Poplar Forest, its ceiling dropped to allow addition of the attic. The lower ceiling and absence of a skylight made Highgrove's dining room distinctly not awe-inspiring.

In a side chamber off the dining room, another elongated octagon, they saw more damaged brickwork from the fallen tree, higher on this fireplace wall than on that in the parlor. An alcove bed divided the room into two.

"Charming," Millie murmured. "I want an alcove bed."

"Don't we all?" Jill said, yawning and turning away. "Think I'll go wait in the parlor."

Her lack of interest surprised Millie, until she realized that Jill must've seen Highgrove numerous times before.

Across the dining room from that octagon was another, also with an alcove bed. At the rear of the house, instead of the fourth long octagon Millie expected, they entered a square room that Luke said Nolan's grandparents had used as a family room. A few chairs were scattered around, indicating the crew probably took breaks here. Opposing doors opened into a bathroom and a walk-in closet, both shaped like the ends of octagons. Any fireplaces that had been in the octagon had evidently been bricked up. This was the travesty he'd been speaking of, Luke said—chopping an originally eight-sided room into three unprepossessing parts.

Behind the erstwhile family room came a sizeable rectangular kitchen furnished with decades-old avocado appliances. On a gray Formica dinette table stood an array of artifact bags like those at Poplar Forest. A stack of mesh trays and a rag or two lay beside the double sink. In one corner at the back of the room, Millie saw a railing and the top of a set of steps going down.

"This is the original kitchen, remodeled to add plumbing and electrical appliances," Luke said. "Those stairs could've been added after it was built, especially if Jefferson was the designer. He hated staircases because they take up so much space in a house, and sometimes included them only as an afterthought. Poplar Forest was actually under construction before he added stairwells to his design."

He explained that this kitchen hadn't originally been the very back of the house, according to the old floor plan Miss Unruh had lent him. On it, a long service wing had jutted out the rear, containing kitchen, cook's quarters, storage, and two unnamed rooms he thought might have been used for house slaves. The service wing, except for the kitchen, had been demolished at some point, and other rooms built off both sides of the kitchen, one of these used by the Unruhs as a pantry, the other as a "junk room." Luke and Ron had set up their project office in the latter.

As Luke talked, enthusiasm for the special puzzle that was Highgrove showed in his animated face. Was this what Jill termed "showing off"? But surely he was entitled, Millie thought.

"Like Poplar Forest," he went on, "Highgrove would've functioned better as a personal retreat than as a family home. Neither one has much space for entertaining, and both have awkward traffic patterns for servants."

"Can Highgrove be put back as it was originally?" Millie asked.

He shrugged. "If Miss Unruh's willing to part with enough money. It won't be cheap."

"Jill says you're doing some excavating in the basement?"

"Yep, trying to date the original structure. I'll show you."

They went down the steps at the back of the kitchen into a huge paneled room, dank and musty-smelling.

"Jill's not crazy about the basement," Luke said, wrinkling his nose. "Can't say I blame her. Nolan's uncle started finishing the space years ago, but he gave up after doing this rec room—most likely on account of the dampness and odor."

From somewhere above, Millie heard a low rhythmic tapping, like someone chipping ice. The day was warming up, and a cold drink sounded good. Maybe she'd get one on her way back through the kitchen.

Luke opened a door into an unfinished area with bare brick walls and dirt floor. "It does make our job easier that this part was never completed. I'm working near that wall now, trying to locate a builder's trench."

"Why do you need to find that?"

"When a builder's trench is filled in, any trash that's around gets tossed in. So if a trench contains objects that can be dated—a bent or broken coin, a sherd of pottery produced only in certain years—we can determine the earliest date a structure could've been built."

Millie looked around. A hole about two feet square had been dug near an outside wall.

"I'll also dig units near the other foundation walls." Luke led the way back upstairs, talking as they went about the process of dating a structure.

They went through the kitchen to the project office, which was currently empty of other crew members. A counter on one wall held a collection of books, a microscope, and several marked paper sacks. A table and chairs stood nearby. On the opposite wall, a large picture frame displayed a montage of snapshots showing Highgrove crew members in a variety of poses. Millie looked over the photos as Luke told about them.

One showed him, Ron, and Whit striking a pose on Highgrove's porch, all three grinning, the ends of Luke's moustache lifted by a breeze, Whit's face glowing with sunburn, sunlight glinting off Ron's wedding band. Luke was holding up a pottery sherd, which he now told her had been their first real "find" at Highgrove. It had been sent off for expert analysis, but it appeared to be a type of pottery produced in the late eighteenth century.

"Then I understand why you all look smug," Millie said.

In another shot, Nolan and Whit were placing a grid marker to begin the outside dig, Nolan mugging for the camera, Whit frowning in concentration as he tightened a strand of twine on a pole. In another, Nolan poured dirt from a bucket into a rectangular box that Luke called a shaker screen, strands of dark hair flopping into one eye. In yet another, Ron and a young woman, whom Luke identified as Paige, stood over a microscope talking and smiling, as if discussing some discovery they'd made.

"She was lovely," Millie murmured, studying the pictured woman's delicate features, generous smile, expressive hazel eyes, and auburn hair tied back in an attractively artless way. Paige had somehow managed to look both brainy and ingenue-like. Ron's grin at her seemed that of a friend, not a boss.

"Sad," Millie said, "a promising young life ending that awful way. What was she like?"

Luke mused. "Easy to work with. Pulled her weight and then some. Liked a good joke. Not flamboyant, but no prude either. Loved poking into old buildings—houses, churches, whatever. Even Miss Unruh, Nolan's aunt, took a shine to Paige, and that lady's no easy sell."

"So you all miss her. For herself, I mean, not just as a hard-working colleague."

Luke swallowed hard. "Yeah, she was a friend. It doesn't seem real that she's gone."

"Do the police give any indication whether they're getting close to finding her killer?"

Luke paused in the act of rubbing his chin. A second later, he replied.

"If so, they haven't shared the fact with us."

"It must be nerve-wracking not to know. Jill said you guys have been interviewed more than once."

"She did, eh?"

"I'm sorry. Was I not supposed to know that?"

"No, no, it doesn't matter. At least not to me."

He glanced towards the parlor, from which more small sounds issued—a clink, then a tiny grating or rubbing, like a tool brushing plaster. Ron must be at work in there now, Millie guessed.

Luke looked at her, lips parted as if to say more, then shook his head and shrugged. Turning to the pictures again, he pointed to one taken looking down into a square-edged hole.

"See those darker spots?" he asked. "They show that dirt has been disturbed at some time to build a feature."

Luke continued explaining photos. Millie wondered what he had been about to say to her—something about Paige? Clearly, he was disturbed by the continued questionings by the police. They would suggest that the police suspected a connection between Paige's death and the place where she had worked. Did they also suspect one of her co-workers of having something to do with the murder?

On the surface, the scene at Highgrove seemed exactly what it was supposed to be, an archaeological dig with researchers and volunteers working in harmony side by side, but what if there were something darker going on here?

Millie thought of Whit and how unexpected it had been to find a biker, a reckless one, on the archaeology crew. But the other men seemed nice and normal, and apparently liked him. Could she be letting her memories of Jack prejudice her? But Paige Oberlin had worked with all these men, and someone had killed her. Conceivably even one of them? At any rate, Millie sensed some secret here, beyond the mystery of Highgrove's origin.

Minutes later, Ron came in from outside, entering though the side door next to the project office. "How d'you like our house, Millie?"

"Love it. Don't you hope it turns out to be a Jefferson design?"

"Hope doesn't come into it," he said with mock severity. "We're scientists."

"I didn't mean to suggest you'd skew your findings." She noticed his mood had improved since they'd talked about Paige. She probably should avoid that subject with him.

Ron chuckled. "Just kidding. It would be fun to find a 'new' Jefferson property, though of course we can't let our wishes influence us. You going to take Millie out to the dig, Luke?"

"Yep. She can get her hands dirty if she wants."

He led Millie out the door that Ron had entered and across the side yard. The sun had come out, the clouds now mere wisps of smoky gray. Luke paused beside the dig, a plot of earth about ten feet square criss-crossed with taut lengths of twine fastened to uprights.

"Jill said you'll be working in the lab at Poplar Forest," he said, and explained how the area to be excavated was divided into a grid, with unit coordinates designated by letter-and-number codes, which were then marked on artifact bags and cards that remained with their samples through the washing-labeling process.

"Occasionally, items from a later period intrude into a site—if, say, the area got dug up at some point for a garden, fence posts, or whatever—so artifacts from more than one period might sometimes be found together. Archaeologists have to try to piece together what happened at a site from all the clues."

Millie smiled. "Detective work."

"Exactly. And this is a job you have to get right the first time. You can't excavate a site twice."

Near the dig, Whit poured dirt from a bucket into a shaker screen, which was balanced on two tall sawhorses. He rubbed the soil around in the box, most of it falling through into a wheelbarrow between the sawhorses.

"Whit mostly works here," Luke went on. "Nolan helps sometimes, though he mostly hangs around Ron. He's especially interested in Highgrove's interior structure."

Whit picked two bits of material from the box and showed them to Millie. "Here's what I'm finding now. This is schist—rock with layers of mineral in it—and this other is a chunk of brick."

Millie recognized the brick particle from similar ones at Poplar Forest, but to her untrained eye, the two pieces looked nearly the same.

He pitched the brick into an open paper sack beside the wheelbarrow and the schist onto a nearby pile of screened and discarded dirt from the dig.

"Wanta join the fun, Millie?" Whit asked.

She wouldn't have chosen to work with him, given their brief history, but he didn't seem to have recognized her. And he was friendly. If she wanted to learn more about archaeology and Highgrove—and she did—she would have to make up her mind about him. She decided to give him the benefit of the doubt, for now, and try to learn more about him.

"Guess so," she said. "Jill will surely let me know when she's ready to leave."

Luke handed Millie a pair of gloves. "This work's murder on manicures."

She donned the gloves and followed Whit's lead in pushing dirt around in the wooden-sided box.

"I'll get another bucketful," Luke said to Whit. "You and Millie continue screening." He grabbed a pail, a trowel, and gloves and headed for the dig.

Whit and Millie worked in silence at first. He mostly seemed intent on his work but would occasionally gaze intently at some part of the terrain, as if seeing new details in the familiar surroundings. To break the silence, she asked if he read a lot about Jefferson, as Ron did.

"Yeah, quite a bit, though not as much as Ron. But Nolan's the real TJ expert. He's won contests with his Jefferson knowledge."

"Really? National contests?"

"Regional. A Thomas Jefferson fan club holds this big celebration every year on the prez's birthday, including a Jefferson-knowledge contest. Nolan's won it several times."

"Impressive. So Nolan wins consistently?"

"There's one other guy he goes head to head with each year. Nolan lost to him the last time."

Presently, Nolan came from the kitchen with two cans of cola, handed one to Whit, and offered the other to Millie.

"Hey, Millie. Cold drink? This is thirsty work."

"You go ahead," Millie said, realizing he'd intended the second can for himself, unaware she was out here now. She wished she'd remembered to get that iced drink when she'd come through the kitchen. "Did you see Jill in the house? She impatient to leave?"

Nolan popped the top of his drink. "She was in there but didn't say anything about leaving."

"Going to work out here a while, Nolan?" Whit asked.

"Yeah, might as well. Change of pace and all."

"I understand you're quite an authority on Jefferson," Millie said to Nolan. "Congratulations on winning those contests."

He shrugged off the compliment, but a little smile betrayed his pleasure in it.

They all chatted about the weather and their own lives. Millie learned Whit was from Missouri, near St. Louis. When she mentioned her plan to use Lynchburg as a base for traveling to Jefferson-related locales around the state, he chuckled.

"That'll keep you busy a while. You can't go far in Virginia without tripping over something connected to American history, much of it to Jefferson."

"He was a plenty smart guy, you have to agree," Nolan put in, setting down his soft drink and joining the others at their work. "Also gutsy, like with the Louisiana Purchase. Especially considering its legality was questionable."

"I don't know a lot about that," Millie admitted. "But I'm reading about Lewis and Clark now, so I'm sure I'll get to it."

Nolan and Whit sipped their drinks. Whit wiped his forehead with the back of a gloved hand.

"It's neat to visit Highgrove while you're investigating it," Millie said. "Before it gets restored."

"*If* it gets restored." Nolan frowned.

Luke brought a bucket of dirt from the dig and substituted it for the empty pail, grabbed a new paper sack off a table, marked a code on it, then switched it with the filled one. Folding the top of the latter, he carried it to the house.

"Couldn't your aunt set up a foundation or something?" Millie asked Nolan. "Get grants to help her finance the restoration?"

"Maybe," Nolan said. "I don't keep up with that stuff."

"You said you lost a court case over Highgrove. What would you've done with it if you'd won?"

He gave a wishful grimace. "Fixed it up and lived here. I love the old place. Takes me back to my childhood." Nolan took a long drink from his soda can and swallowed.

Whit's eyes wandered over an area behind Nolan. Millie followed his gaze but saw only an old tree stump a hundred yards away. He stared at it a minute or so, then returned his focus to Millie.

"Glad you're getting into Lewis and Clark," he said. "All us guys read about them. Paige knew a lot about Jefferson but wasn't into 'derring-do,' as she called the expedition."

At mention of Paige, a respectful silence fell over the group. Millie stole a glance at Whit, then at Nolan. They looked at each other, then at her, expressions equally morose. Beneath the sadness, she sensed tension, as if something had gone unsaid, but Millie could pick up no sense of guilt or accusation between them. Whatever the secret was, the two men seemed to share in it equally.

Whit returned to the topic of Lewis and Clark, recommending to Millie a few books he especially liked. She recognized one title as being a book she'd picked out to read at the mansion. She straightened to ease a kink in her back. Nolan lifted the bucketful of dirt Luke had brought and held it over the shaker screen.

"'Us guys focus on different aspects of the expedition," Whit said. "I'm most interested in the captains, Meriwether Lewis and William Clark. Clark didn't officially hold that rank, you know, but Lewis insisted on calling him 'Captain' so the other men would see both as qualified to lead. Luke studies maps and other items the explorers brought back, Ron the Indian tribes they met. You're most interested in what happened to expedition members after the trip ended, aren't you, Nolan? I saw a book on that in your car that time you gave me a ride. When my bike was on the fritz?"

Nolan paused in the act of tipping the pail, his expression thoughtful.

"Yeah," he said at last. "Yeah, I do recall that."

"Seems like the expedition included some colorful characters," Millie said. "You recall the title of that book, Nolan?"

He shook his head. "No, sorry. Anyway, it turned out not to be as interesting as I'd expected."

Millie lifted a particle of material from the screen. "Hmm, what's this?" She removed a glove and grasped the object more firmly. It crumbled in her hand, a lump of dirt. "Shoot, I thought I'd found something."

Whit grinned. "Wish I had a nickel for every time I've said that."

"You must've heard a lot about Lewis and Clark where you grew up, Whit," Millie said. "Since they started from near St. Louis."

"Yeah. My grandparents live at St. Charles, the actual organization point. Gramps was a big L&C buff, so he and I used to talk a lot about the expedition, even retraced parts of their route one time."

"It must be neat to share such an interest with your granddad," Millie said wistfully. She had never known any relatives besides her mother.

*I love my grandkids, and I'm sorry you didn't get a chance to bond with your grandparents,* Sylva spoke in Millie's mind. *But relatives can be a mixed blessing. Don't feel too sorry for yourself.*

Still, Whit's revelations of his love of history and his closeness with his grandfather made her think better of him. Those were hardly the kinds of disclosures a "hardened biker" would make.

As Whit told about a collection of Lewis and Clark memorabilia his grandfather had amassed, Millie glanced past him and saw Jill stroll from the house to her vehicle, moving with an air of studied casualness. She held one arm close to her body.

What now? Millie wondered.

"Granddad's getting on in years," Whit said. "Before he goes, I'd love to be able to solve one of the mysteries about the expedition."

The word "mysteries" caught Millie's attention. She wasn't yet knowledgeable enough about the famous journey to have spotted any unsolved puzzles.

"Like what?"

Whit narrowed his eyes and swallowed hard, as if he'd wandered into a conversational area he hadn't intended. "Like . . . oh, I don't know . . ." He cleared his throat, then went on with more assurance. ". . . like whether Meriwether Lewis's death after the expedition returned was actually suicide. But there are several unanswered riddles, and Grampa'd be so proud if I could solve one."

"But wouldn't that be impossible after so long? Generations of scholars must've picked through all the sources in agonizing detail."

"Damned straight," Nolan said with an air of amused tolerance.

He had been quiet so long while she and Whit talked, Millie had forgotten he was there.

Over his shoulder, she saw Jill standing beside the open passenger door of her car, bent over, as if taking something from the glove compartment, or putting something in.

"Maybe not," Whit replied. He noticed her looking past him and followed her gaze. Evidently satisfied she was wondering whether to continue work or not, he turned again to the screen. "New evidence could still turn up. Like maybe a letter or something would surface from a witness not heard from before. Obviously, it's a super-long shot, but I can dream."

Her mind half on Jill, half on Whit, Millie didn't at first notice the small object in the shaker screen. Spying it, she picked it out.

"What's this?"

Whit took off a glove and examined the object, handling it with care. "Smooth. Piece of bone, maybe. Oh, look, there's a tiny hole. See, at the side here. Could be a fragment of a necklace." He handed it back.

Millie removed her gloves and examined the piece, imitating his caution. "You're right, it might be from a piece of jewelry. Or maybe a button. Notice how flat it is?"

He leaned closer and eyed Millie's find again. "Could be that. We'll ask Luke."

"Ask me what?" The archaeologist returned from the house carrying a small ice chest, which he set down nearby. "Coke, anyone?"

"Thanks, I am thirsty," Millie said. She showed him the piece. "Could this have been part of a button? Or a necklace? See the small hole here?"

He opened a soft drink, handed it to her, and took the artifact. Turning it over, he held it up to the light. "Good eye, Millie. It'll get its own little sack, and I'll check it under the 'scope later. May have to put you on the payroll." He carried the object to the table that held markers and bags, both plastic and paper.

Whit raised his hand to Millie in a "thumbs up" sign.

Nolan lifted one brow. "Coulda fooled me."

"Ready to go, Miss Budding Archaeologist?" Jill's voice came from behind her.

Her sudden appearance made Millie jump. "Oh! Sure, let me wash my hands first."

Nolan gave Jill a long, steady look. She flushed, turned her back on him, and joined Luke. Millie removed her gloves, went to the kitchen and washed her hands, then returned to the dig.

"Jill's waiting in the Cavalier," Luke said. "When she's ready to go, she's ready." He grinned. "Come back out any time, Millie. We'll put you to work."

She smiled. "I'd like that. In fact—" In spite of her initial feelings about Whit, Millie was now fairly sure that her bias against him had been unreasonable. And now, the tiny discovery she had made had given her the archaeology bug. She made a quick decision. "Could I volunteer here a few hours a week, in addition to my work at Poplar Forest?'

"You want to? Sure! We're short-handed with Paige . . . gone. You couldn't exactly replace her—she'd had course work and experience, after all—but I can tell you learn fast."

She agreed to talk over her Poplar Forest schedule with Chas and Alice, then give Luke an idea when she could come to Highgrove.

"Great!" he said. "It doesn't have to be the same day of the week every time. And partial days are fine, too. We can use you for however much time you can spare. Nolan's here every minute the rest of us are—he'd probably sleep here if his aunt'd allow it—but then he has ties to the place. We won't require the same dedication from you."

"Good. But I am interested in your project, so I'll definitely make time."

When Millie reached Jill's vehicle and climbed in, she glanced back at the dig. All three men waved as the Cavalier drove away.

Whit hadn't turned out to be such a bad guy—so far. But he did have a reckless streak. For Danny's sake, she wouldn't entirely let down her guard around him.

As for the crew as a whole—those looks passing among the four whenever Paige was mentioned had appeared distinctly nervous. There was something they knew about her that was troubling them. Millie wondered if they had shared that something with the police.

# ★ Chapter Six

Jill didn't speak for several minutes, not until they'd exited the Highgrove property and headed south. She seemed nervous, looked into the rear-view mirror often, and didn't respond to Millie's attempts at conversation. Millie wondered what had caused the change from her earlier jovial manner. Perhaps Jill was miffed over Luke's attention to her? But they hadn't flirted; he had simply responded to her interest in his project.

On the way to Highgrove, Jill had said she'd take a different route home, to show Millie parts of the town she hadn't seen. Without comment, she now turned onto a different street from the one they'd traveled before.

Millie wondered about that odd bit of behavior when Jill had walked to her vehicle almost furtively. If she'd lost something there on an earlier visit, then found it today, why hadn't she simply mentioned the fact? Millie considered the articles women commonly carried in purses that might be embarrassing, like a condom or a diaphragm. But few young women today seemed discomfited about such things, and Jill wasn't easily abashed, from what Millie had seen.

Yet she had blushed and turned away when Nolan had stared at her. Was something going on between Jill and Nolan behind her boyfriend's back? But Jill seemed committed to Luke.

Millie told herself to forget it, that whatever there might be between the two of them was none of her business. Nor was it her affair if Jill had lost something at Highgrove, found it again, and hidden it in her vehicle's glove compartment.

But her mind wouldn't leave the questions alone. Sniffing loudly, she reached a hand towards the button on the glovebox.

"Okay if I look in here for a Kleenex?"

Jill thrust a hand out to forestall her. "No! I mean, I don't keep any in there. May have one in my purse, though." She opened a blue clutch bag beside her, fumbled in it, and produced a tissue.

"Thanks." Her ploy foiled, Millie pretended to use it to blow her nose.

"Isn't Luke just the cutest thing?" Jill suddenly gushed. "And so smart! Being given such an important assignment, young as he is!"

The change in her attitude jolted Millie. She eyed her companion, who was now grinning a little too broadly. Millie wondered if Jill had introduced the subject of Luke as a distraction. Whatever was in that glove compartment must be really embarrassing.

Millie agreed that Luke must be well thought of by his employer.

"He's a great guy," Jill went on. She chewed her lower lip. "I just wish he didn't play his cards so close to his chest."

Millie didn't reply, not knowing what to say.

"I've found this perfect engagement ring online." Jill fingered one of her diamond earrings as she warmed to her favorite subject. "We've been to several jewelry stores, but they mostly stock the same old thing. I want something different. This ring online is an emerald, not huge, but the cut and setting are gorgeous. I showed it to Luke, and he said he likes it, too. He didn't exactly promise to buy it for me, though."

"Maybe he's planning to surprise you with it."

"I hope he . . ." Jill's voice trailed away.

"If he's visited jewelry stores with you, he must be intending to get engaged. Looking at rings is a pretty obvious prelude to marriage."

"You'd think so, wouldn't you? But—well, actually, it's always been my idea to go into the stores." She negotiated a turn and sped up on the straightaway. "But I've never said it was to look at engagement rings. Luke knows my career plan. He knows I love looking at jewelry."

Jill's unaccountable nervousness had disappeared. But Millie felt increasingly uncomfortable with the personal turn the conversation had taken. She concentrated on a section of nice houses they were traveling through.

"Trouble is," Jill went on, "he never says much to give his feelings away—whether he prefers a particular ring, or if he's looking forward to seeing me wearing his ring. He just never refers to our future together."

As she listened to the monologue, Millie wondered if the relationship was more serious to Jill than to Luke. And maybe she was a little too focused on the ring, not so much on the marriage?

"Perhaps—" Millie hesitated. "You think Luke feels pressured? By the trips to jewelry stores?"

Jill's head whipped towards her. "Pressured! We've been seeing each other over a year now! Pressured, my eye!"

"I just thought—"

"If anything, I've given him way too much time. I was engaged twice before, you know, and both proposals came less than three months into the relationship."

"But you didn't marry either of those guys?"

"Nope. The first one wanted us to be engaged secretly for six months or so—no announcement, no ring, no picture in the paper—while he tried to convince his parents I was the right one. They didn't like me, for some reason."

A plaintive note in Jill's voice suggested that the little girl in her still hurt over not being universally liked. But her next words dispelled Millie's sympathy.

"If we'd gotten married, I'd've made sure his parents didn't come around much." She heaved a sigh. "But I decided, if he was ashamed to let the world know we were engaged, he wasn't the guy for me."

"I see."

"My second fiancé bought me the teeniest, tiniest solitaire I've ever seen. Couldn't have been more than an eighth of a carat. Obviously he didn't love me much." Again, that hint of pain behind the caustic words.

"Maybe that's all he could afford," Millie said gently.

"They were losers, Millie. I'm much better off with Luke. Only . . ."

As Jill rambled on, they passed near Lynchburg's downtown, and Millie realized she was developing a fondness for the place. She liked the way present and past co-existed against the timeless backdrop of the Blue Ridge, the city's downtown nestled against a hillside above the James River. Reading about the area online before leaving on the trip, Millie had learned that the James was one of the longest rivers in the country whose entire length was within a single state. It rose in the Alleghenies, bisected Virginia west to east, and had been a factor in American history since the first English settlement, Jamestown, was founded near where the river flowed into Chesapeake Bay.

*Don't romanticize the place too much, Kirchner,* Sylva's voice warned. *Human beings live here, bringing all the problems that come with that.*

And Scott tells me *I'm* too pessimistic, Millie thought.

Jill was frowning, apparently having realized she'd lost her audience. Millie felt a twinge of guilt for letting her mind wander so long when her companion had been talking. She tried a gambit to revive the conversation.

"I saw a picture of Paige today in the project office at Highgrove. She was very attractive."

"Yeah," Jill said shortly, then more amiably, "and not stuck-up about it."

"Did she have a boyfriend?"

Jill frowned. "I—can't say for sure. When I'd ask Paige, she'd give me some non-answer, like 'My heart belongs to Thomas Jefferson.' I asked her once what that meant—was she seeing someone or not? But she just gave me a mysterious smile and clammed up.

"I asked the guys on the crew, and they'd only say Paige didn't talk about her love life. Well, duh, they could know something, whether she told them or not. I mean, there are signs. Luke's maybe the worst, Mr. Buttoned-Up, especially about discussing people he works with."

*Not such a bad way to be.*

Jill cut her eyes at Millie. "I think Paige was having a thing with one of the crew, and that's why no one would talk. But I don't know which one." She drew a shuddering sigh. "I hoped it wasn't Luke. Just in case, I used to drop in unannounced at Highgrove. Never did catch them at anything, though."

"Luke doesn't seem the two-timing type," Millie said soothingly, then finished more lamely, "if there is a type, I mean."

So Jill had suspected her boyfriend of seeing Paige on the sly. A motive for murder, if there ever was one, Millie thought. Then she felt shame for thinking such a thing of her new housemate.

"Did you know Paige well?"

"Not real well, I guess. I'd see her at Highgrove, of course. Sometimes I'd eat lunch with all the crew. And Luke and I went to a party once that Paige and her roommate gave. God, just think, we waited for the elevator in that same lobby where she got killed." Jill shivered.

"What's the roommate like?"

"Smart like Paige, but more outgoing. Monica never meets a stranger. Most of the people at that party were her friends rather than Paige's, I'm sure. She's shorter, a little chunkier than Paige, but cute. And she laughs more. Paige—well, I've mentioned her dry sense of humor. But she was dead serious about her work. Luke and all his crew are."

Millie nodded. "Paige's death must've hit Monica hard, especially since it happened in their building."

"I'm sure. I heard her parents tried to get her to move back home afterwards, but Monica likes her independence. She did agree to look for a different apartment, though." Jill turned into their street.

"Do you enjoy going to Highgrove? Apart from getting to see Luke?"

Jill made a face. "It's okay. Sometimes he and I go walking when he takes a break, and that's nice. Otherwise, it's fairly boring watching them dig, or poke at walls, or update records. Everything moves at a snail's pace."

"Have you considered volunteering there yourself? That might make it more interesting."

Jill pulled into the parking lot and stopped before replying. "I don't mind getting dirty when I play sports, but digging for what somebody dropped a couple centuries ago? No, thanks."

Realizing Jill hadn't heard her making arrangements with Luke for volunteering, Millie said she would be going out to Highgrove some to help.

"Really?" Jill said, narrowing her eyes. "Why? You have the hots for one of the guys? Not Luke, I hope."

Millie replied that she wanted to help find out if Jefferson had indeed designed Highgrove.

"Yeah, you like that history stuff, don't you?" Jill rolled her eyes, but her grin was friendly.

They went into the house and found Alice and Danny busy in the kitchen, the former manning a deep fryer, the latter sprinkling sugar on freshly cooked crullers that were draining on paper towels. Alice had helped him cut the doughnuts from dough, he said proudly.

"Those look terrific!" Millie exclaimed. "And it happens I'm starved."

"Yeah," Jill said as she filched a sugary ring.

Alice said Cynthia was upstairs, lying down with a headache. Millie wondered if she'd heard from Ted again. Selfishly, she hoped Cynthia's boyfriend troubles weren't going to cast a pall over the household.

"We've got pork chops, Mom," Danny went on. "Alice let me peel the potatoes, and I'm gonna mash 'em. I helped make the salad, too."

"This young man has the makings of an excellent chef," Alice said.

"He is a real help, isn't he?" Millie said, glowing with pride.

"Alice is good at games, too, Mom."

"So you didn't miss us at all, huh?" Jill teased. "Want to hit some balls after supper, Chef Danny?"

"Sure!"

Millie heaved a deep grateful sigh. How had she gotten so lucky? To have this great chance to learn Jeffersonian history and live with companionable women who seemed to like both her and her son?

Something will turn up to ruin this golden summer, a negative thought came.

*Crap, Kirchner! Let yourself enjoy good things,* Sylva's voice countered. *Worrying about the future just gets in the way of appreciating today.*

So, am I too optimistic—romanticizing Lynchburg—or too pessimistic? Which? Millie mentally asked.

*Find the balance, dear. Balance is the key to living triumphantly and with joy.*

After dinner and cleanup with a silent, worried-looking Cynthia, Millie went into the library, where she found Jill leafing through a tall, faded blue-backed book. She was breathing fast, as if she'd been running.

"Find something exciting to read?" Millie asked, glancing at the title on Jill's book, *Horticulture in the Shadow of the Blue Ridge*. "Hmm, I thought Cynthia was the resident plant enthusiast."

"Oh, you know—" Jill's voice was breathy, nervous. "Never hurts to know—something—" she glanced at the book cover—"about the local vegetation." Her eyes shifted to a column of shelves a foot away.

"That book looks too old to have up-to-date information. Well, guess I'll see what I can find to read."

In the mood for a good novel, Millie browsed in the section Jill had glanced at and found a collection of Victorian fiction. The very thing to read in this lovely old mansion, she thought. Thumbing through a copy of Charlotte Brontë's *Jane Eyre,* she watched her housemate's movements out the corner of one eye. Jill continued to page through the old volume on gardening for another minute, then quietly slipped it onto a shelf beside her.

"Guess I'll head up to my room." Jill gave an overly dramatic yawn.

Millie nodded, watching her leave. Unable to shake the feeling that Jill had been up to something, she laid down the Victorian novel, found the volume on horticulture, and leafed through it. Nothing about it appeared likely to appeal to someone of Jill's tastes. The book seemed almost a random choice.

Was that what it had been? Jill had sounded and looked out of breath. Had she been reading something else, something she hadn't wanted to be seen with? Had that something anything to do with whatever she'd stowed in her glove box? And on hearing someone coming in just now, had she quickly hidden the embarrassing volume and grabbed the first one handy?

Millie looked over the shelves near where Jill had stood. None of the books looked hastily or incompletely returned to a slot. The shelves in this section and part of the next housed old atlases, dictionaries, and references on birds, wild life, trees, and minerals. The clutch of novels where Millie had found the Brontë tome began on the lower part of the shelf unit to the right of the horticulture book and continued into the next column, all well-thumbed works by writers from Jane Austen to Anthony Trollope.

Books on minerals, Millie thought. Including precious stones, Jill's passion?

She looked through tables of contents in a few reference works on minerals, then flipped pages of the texts. Most were technical discussions of the composition of various kinds of rock, but in one she found a chapter on precious and semi-precious stones used for jewelry. Millie paged through the section carefully but found nothing about Jill's current interest, spectacular gems that had been lost, stolen, or supposedly cursed.

Anyway, why hide a book on jewelry when Jill had made no secret of her love for it? She was often seen around the mansion reading such material.

Giving up on the question for now, Millie browsed more along the library shelves, marveling at the range of reading interests mansion residents must have had through the years.

Later, Danny was abed and Millie was reading the Brontë novel in her room when a tap sounded at her open door. Cynthia entered, wearing pajamas and hair curlers, her eyes red as if from weeping. She took a chair near Millie's and emitted a long sigh.

"Ted still being difficult?" Millie asked sympathetically.

"He's coming here Saturday, Millie. To win me back, he says."

"Do you want to see him?"

Cynthia shook her head.

"Did you tell him not to come?"

"I tried, but . . . I don't know if he even heard me."

Millie considered. "A face-to-face talk might be good. If you tell him, very firmly, when he arrives that you can't see him anymore, maybe . . ."

"Oh, Millie, he'll just lay a huge guilt trip on me, go on and on about how much he loves me and how he's devastated not to be with me every second . . ."

"He sounds needy."

"Yeah. But I keep remembering how good we were together at first. He was fun and romantic—would shower me with unexpected gifts. But then I decided I was losing myself in the relationship. I didn't tell him so, which I should've done, I know. I just started making excuses for not going out, that kinda thing. But the more I pulled away, the tighter Ted clung. He begged me not to leave, said he'd kill himself if I stopped loving him."

"That's emotional blackmail."

"I know. But what can I do, Millie? What if he really did commit suicide? I couldn't stand having that on my conscience."

"Can you talk him into getting counseling? Sounds like he could use some."

Cynthia sighed. "I guess I'll have to see him tomorrow, go out to dinner with him one last time and explain again how I feel. Tell me the right words to say, Millie, to make him understand without hurting him."

"I'm not sure such words exist, Cynthia. From your description, Ted sounds like a person who's not impressed by words, only by actions."

Cynthia sat looking at the wall, her eyes filled with unshed tears.

"I'm no expert on relationships, Cynthia," Millie finally said. "Far from it. But I don't see how spending time with Ted, trying to be kind to him, can help you break it off."

A tear dropped from one of the dark eyes. Cynthia wiped it away. "I know. But when he leaves a long message on my voice mail about how much he misses and needs me, I can't seem to ignore it. I am cold and distant when I call back, though."

"Your replying at all probably gives the impression there's still a chance."

Cynthia studied the front of her house slipper. "I've decided to change my cell phone, and I won't give Ted the new number. But he knows the phone numbers here, and I don't want us to have to change those. Please, Millie, tell me what to do. You're so sensible. Alice is, too, but she's lots older and I doubt she could relate. I—don't think Jill would understand at all."

Millie took a deep breath. "I'll tell you what I think I'd do. I can't promise it would be right for you, though."

"Understood. What?"

"I would either call or e-mail Ted, whichever I felt more comfortable doing, and tell him firmly that the relationship is over and he mustn't come this weekend. I wouldn't explain or leave any wiggle room, just say I'd moved on and hoped he would too."

"Moved on? Should I pretend I'm seeing somebody else?"

"I wouldn't. Besides the dishonesty, a lie could cause more trouble. If he should come here and learn you're not really with anybody—well, you know. By 'moved on,' I just mean you no longer see him as part of your life."

"You're probably right. I know you are. But e-mail seems so cold, and a phone call—Millie, I'd never get off the phone with him. Once he started begging me to come back, he'd go on and on. And I couldn't just hang up."

"You may have to. That might be the only way to end such a conversation."

Cynthia clutched her head with both hands and moaned. "Oh, Millie, I hate this. When I finally told Ted I didn't think we should see each other anymore, he seemed too stunned to argue. But now every time we talk, whether it's one of his 'reasonable' days or otherwise—he gives me a list of reasons we should get back together. I can't come up with a good enough rebuttal."

"You don't have to, Cynthia. This isn't a matter for argument."

"But—"

"You asked what I would do." Millie tried to be patient, but her patience was wearing thin. "I wouldn't try to argue with Ted. That would imply you agree this can be decided by logic. Matters of the heart aren't mathematical theorems, to be proved or disproved. They're about liking or disliking. If you told me you didn't like chocolate ice cream, there'd be no point in my listing the merits of chocolate ice cream. You either like it or you don't.

"If you don't want to go with Ted anymore, don't go with him. Period."

"You make it sound so simple."

Millie hugged her housemate. "I know you're concerned about Ted's feelings, Cynthia. But sometimes two people want different things and one ends up getting hurt. I'd tell Ted firmly that it's over, no argument, no discussion. If he should try to contact you after that, I wouldn't respond. It sounds harsh, but it'd be kinder in the long run than giving him false hope."

Cynthia heaved a long sigh. "I'm sure you're right, Millie, but I don't know if I can do that. Anyway, thanks for listening and for your good advice."

"Anytime. Good luck."

"I'll probably need it."

Millie suspected she would, too. She had given Cynthia

good advice, but it would be up to her to decide whether to take it. Cynthia's revelations about Ted's use of emotional blackmail disturbed her, though. Often, that kind of desperate possessiveness went hand in glove with spousal abuse. What had seemed a minor threat to Millie's enjoyment of these living arrangements, now appeared to have the potential to grow into something worse. She hoped she hadn't exposed herself and Danny to a situation that could turn violent.

She went upstairs, saw Danny settled, prepared for bed herself, got out her drawing supplies and caricatured the crew at Highgrove. Luke Brooks she depicted as a clown in baggy pants with a lightbulb nose and a pale straggly moustache that extended well past his ears. Whit Young was a daredevil unicyclist balanced precariously on a high wire. Nolan Unruh was also a performer, gotten up as Thomas Jefferson playing his violin in the Revolutionary-themed musical "1776." Ron sat in the audience, a spectator with a wry grin that suggested he could tell secrets if he chose.

After a moment's thought, she did one more sketch, Jill as a secretive mole, her tiny head peeking out of a hole, her nearly invisible eyes and ears barely discernible above the ground.

Millie studied the drawings, wondering why she'd depicted the people as she had. Luke wasn't a clownish figure, except for that incongruous moustache. And why had her view of Jill changed so radically from the jewel-bedecked woman of that first day?

Maybe her muddled portrait choices reflected her own uncertainty about the motives and agendas of her new acquaintances.

# ☆ Chapter Seven

Three days remained before Danny's camp and Millie's volunteer job could start. On Friday, they went to Amazement Square and saw exhibits about electricity, gravity, the James River, and a Monacan Indian village. Danny climbed and crawled his way through four floors of ladders, tunnels, and slides. They ate a sack lunch afterwards in a park, the day bright and not too hot, with a gentle breeze blowing. After swinging on swings and watching ducks swimming on a small pond, Millie sat on a park bench, reading her novel, while Danny practiced headstands on the grass a few yards away.

"Lovely day, isn't it?" a plump matron called as she walked past with a Welsh corgi on a leash.

Millie glanced up and smiled. "Yes, the weather's great."

Danny, spying the short-legged dog from his upside-down position, dropped to the ground and bounded upright almost in a single motion. He ran up and reached an eager hand towards the dog. Then he drew it back, apparently recalling his mother's cautions about touching strange animals.

"Is it okay if I pet your dog, ma'am?" he asked, dancing a bit in his excitement.

The friendly owner gave her consent. Danny patted the foxy

head while the corgi wagged its long tail, eyes bright and interested in this new acquaintance. With a pang, Millie remembered her promise to get a dog for Danny once they got a house with a yard. He'd asked for one numerous times while they'd lived in the apartment, but the landlord hadn't allowed pets. After she'd bought the house and they'd moved in, she'd stalled, saying she was too busy with class work to help him train an animal, which was true. Guiltily, she vowed her first priority when they returned home must be to visit animal shelters with her son.

Millie chatted with the dog's owner a few minutes, while Danny fondled the canine's head, gingerly at first, then with a confident grin as it licked his face. Soon, owner and dog walked on. Danny's wistful expression tore at Millie's heart.

He played awhile longer. Then they went by the public library to sign up for cards and to browse the holdings. Danny had brought some of his favorite books from home, and they'd bought a stack at the Knoxville bookshop, but he'd now read all his new acquisitions. They checked out novels for him and volumes on Lewis and Clark for her, to supplement the mansion library's collection of the latter. In all those shelves at the mansion, there were no books for children.

On the way home, Millie noticed a couple looking into a store window, holding hands. The man looked familiar. As she watched, he turned his head, and she saw his face.

Whit Young.

Millie glanced at the young woman again. Shorter than he, with a curvy figure and dark, curly hair, she had a laughing, pretty face.

So, Millie thought, Whit has a girlfriend. She shouldn't be surprised—he was good-looking and had an amiable manner—but somehow she hadn't pictured him as part of a couple.

Millie and Danny returned home tired and hungry to find Jill in the kitchen heating a skillet for individual omelets, small bowls of grated cheese and chopped veggies beside her on the counter. Luke had gone to play baseball with guy friends, she explained in an irritated tone, so she'd opted for a quiet Friday evening at home. Millie and Danny chose ingredients for their omelets, washed up, and joined Alice and Cynthia at the dinette table. Jill cooked and served each portion, then sat beside Danny with her own.

"This is great!" he said around a mouthful of soft egg and cheese, clearly revived by the food.

"It's really good, Jill," Millie agreed.

They told about their day, Jill and Alice offering occasional comments. Cynthia said little, her gentle face shadowed.

After supper and supervising Danny's preparations for bed, Millie spent a happy couple of hours reading in her room. One book she'd chosen was the journal William Clark had kept while on the historic journey, telling of hardships endured, victories won, and the variety of humans and creatures encountered. Although she enjoyed his first-hand account, she found herself going back and forth between it and other volumes that discussed the trek from a broader historical standpoint.

She was glad she'd decided to read about the expedition, one aspect of Thomas Jefferson's presidency she hadn't much considered before. It was awesome to contemplate how great his influence had been on the country, and what a length of time it spanned, from the Colonial Era to the nineteenth-century expansion of the West. According to her reading, Jefferson had long thought about the need for such an expedition, which he'd launched before Poplar Forest was built. It was hard to reconcile the dates of the adventure, which had started out from St. Louis, with the red brick and white trim of Poplar Forest, so quintessentially eighteenth century, but the two were almost contemporary. Obviously, the subject of Thomas Jefferson offered meat for many an interesting history paper to come. She would have to see what resources on Lewis and Clark were in the Poplar Forest library.

Millie was so eager to start her volunteer job that the weekend seemed too long a time to wait.

A knock sounded at Millie's door. It was Cynthia again, her pretty face drawn and anxious. With a pat on the bed, Millie invited her to sit down beside her. Her gentle housemate looked so hopeless, Millie slid a comforting arm around her.

"I called Ted today," Cynthia reported. "I told him, very firmly, that what we'd had was over and I wasn't going to submit to anymore emotional blackmail."

"Good for you."

"He started crying and pleading with me to change my mind. He sounded so pitiful that I almost gave in and said I'd go back with him. Finally, I hung up."

"I know that was tough—" cheered by this progress, Millie gave her an encouraging hug—"but I'm sure you did the right thing. He will get over you, much as he doesn't think so now."

Cynthia sighed. "Unfortunately, things didn't end there. He called back a few minutes later, really mad. Told me I couldn't ditch him so easily, and said he'd see me tomorrow. Oh, Millie, he's coming anyway. What'll I do?"

Millie's heart sank. "Do you think he could get violent?"

"He never has before."

"But you think it's possible?"

"I guess he might. He has an awful temper. Millie, what should I do?"

"If you're genuinely afraid, you could go to the police and see about getting a restraining order. I don't know what the law is in Virginia—whether he'd have to have actually hit you first, or made a specific threat, or what—but you could certainly find out."

"Oh—I wouldn't want to do that. It would be humiliating to have to say I was afraid my boyfriend might hurt me."

"Better than letting him actually do it." Millie studied Cynthia's woebegone face. She swallowed the impatient words she was tempted to say. She would never forget how helpless and alone she had felt when she had feared that Jack would come to take Danny. "Well, what about this, then? You could go somewhere before he arrives. Is he flying in from New Mexico tomorrow?"

"Late morning."

"Why don't you clue Alice in, and then she and I can present a united front when he comes. We'll tell him you've left and don't want to see him, ever again. Maybe that'll discourage him."

"But what'll Alice think of me?"

"Probably that you're being very sensible. I suspect she understands way more about people than you and I together do."

"Okay, I'll go talk to her now. Thanks, Millie. You're a real friend. By the way, I did change my cell phone—here's the new number." Handing Millie a slip of paper, she left.

In spite of her brave words to Cynthia, Millie dreaded the encounter with Ted. She had had enough trouble with Jack to last a lifetime, and the last place she wanted to be was in the middle of someone else's relationship dispute. It certainly wasn't how she had envisioned spending her summer. At least she and Alice would have each other for support. She considered calling the police herself to alert them of a potentially explosive situation at this address tomorrow. But she doubted they could do anything without Cynthia's participation.

It occurred to Millie that her pretty housemate might be overreacting. But she thought Cynthia too levelheaded to fret unnecessarily.

Millie's cell phone rang. When she heard Scott's voice at the other end, she almost wept with joy. They had e-mailed each other at least once a day since she'd arrived in Virginia, plus talking occasionally by phone, but she hesitated to call too often for fear of interrupting his concentration.

"How'd you know I needed to talk to you right now?" she said after their greetings.

"Psychic, of course. What's going on? Danny been hurt?"

"No, nothing like that. One of my housemates has a boyfriend problem, and it seems I've gotten involved." She explained Cynthia's situation and mentioned her apprehension about the morrow.

"Sweetness, be careful." Concern was heavy in his voice. "Maybe I'd better catch a flight there myself, first thing in the morning. No, shoot! I promised to take Larry to sign up for a library card. Well . . . he and I'll have other chances to do that."

"Scott, you can't come here! Not that I wouldn't love to see you, but you're busy. And you shouldn't disappoint Larry. Besides, you can't ride to my rescue every time there's a hint of unpleasantness."

"This sounds like more than just a 'hint of unpleasantness.' The guy could lash out at anybody who gets in the way of his seeing your housemate. Maybe Cynthia should stay there and face him herself. Or you should leave with her."

"I couldn't let Alice deal with him alone, especially since I feel partly responsible."

"How are you responsible? Sounds like this is Cynthia's mess, not yours." Anger joined worry in his voice.

"When she confided in me, and I gave her advice, I became involved. Maybe I shouldn't have, but I did."

"So alert the police. Or—you met any big bruisers you could get to hang around, just in case?"

Millie thought about the men she had met since arriving in Lynchburg. Chas was big, and might conceivably be called a "bruiser," although he didn't strike her as that type. Luke was thin, but Whit, and Nolan, and Ron were all husky.

Cynthia was a private person, however, and Millie doubted she'd want her boyfriend problems told to anyone locally.

"I think Alice and I can handle this, Scott. She's pretty savvy, and I'll keep my cell phone handy in case I need to call for help.

Besides, Ted may accept Cynthia's decision, if it's given through third parties, and go home without causing trouble. Please don't worry."

"I can't help it. Millie, I can come there. Just have to check flights and pack a toothbrush."

"No, Scott, but I appreciate the offer. I can't tell you how much."

"Phone me tomorrow, sweets, soon as you know anything. I'll be waiting. I won't be able to concentrate on studying till I know you're safe."

"I will. Love you."

"Please be careful, love."

More than ever now, Millie wished the weekend were behind her and she could start labeling treasures at Poplar Forest.

Saturday at breakfast, for Jill's benefit Cynthia mentioned that she'd be going to Roanoke for the day to see a friend. After Jill left on a tennis date, Cynthia confided to Millie and Alice that she actually knew no one there but would mostly be seeing movies. She asked Millie to call her after they heard from Ted and said she might decide to spend the night in Roanoke, depending on how things went.

"If he asks when I'll be back, just tell him you don't know—which is true, of course. I might not make it back today."

"Leave it to us," Alice said. "And try not to worry."

Cynthia beamed, the first real smile Millie had seen her wear for days. "Thanks, both of you, so much."

As it turned out, Cynthia didn't miss running into Ted by much. Just a few minutes after she drove away, Millie and Danny were hanging sheets on a clothesline behind the Victorian, which she liked to do on sunny days to save on energy use, when she heard from in front of the house a screeching of brakes, then the slamming of a car door.

"Go ahead and hang the pillow cases, son," Millie said, securing the end of a sheet with a clothespin. "I'll help you with the other sheets when I get back."

"Bet I can hang one all by myself, Mom."

"Okay, if you want to try. I might be a little while." Better she should have to re-wash bed linens that had fallen on the ground, Millie thought with a quickening pulse, than have Danny come in with her and maybe witness a tense scene.

Striding through the house and up the hall to the front entry, Millie made sure the cell phone in her slacks pocket was on. She found Alice talking through the screen door to a sturdy young man with brown hair worn in a burr cut. His expression and stance appeared low-key, almost deferential, not what Millie had expected of Ted.

Still, she was glad to see Alice had latched the screen door.

"I see we have a visitor," Millie said, with a smile that included both the man and her housemate. "Hello."

Raising one eyebrow quizzically, he nodded to her.

Alice looked relieved to see Millie. "I was just explaining to Mr. Loftis that Cynthia's gone and I don't know when she'll be back."

He frowned. "There must be some mistake. Cynthia wouldn't leave when she knew I was coming."

"Alice is right," Millie said. "Cynthia left, and we don't know when she'll return."

Ted grinned boyishly, a smile Millie guessed many women found irresistible. She could see why Cynthia had found him attractive.

"I may as well own up," he said, like a small lad caught in mischief. "Cynthia and I had a little tiff on the phone yesterday, and she told me not to come. She didn't mean it, of course—that's just her way. We've had plenty of little arguments before, and we always make up. I decided to catch an earlier flight than I'd planned, so we'd have more time to spend together this weekend.

"And—" with a flourish, Ted produced a tiny box from his shirt pocket—"I'm bringing her this." He eased open the diminutive container to reveal an exquisite diamond ring.

Alice exclaimed at its beauty. For a moment, Millie wondered if Cynthia might have misunderstood this young man, who seemed so engaging, so genuinely in love, so—

*Get a grip, Kirchner. Doesn't he remind you of someone you know all too well?*

Sylva was right, Millie realized. Jack Kirchner, Danny's father, could be tremendously appealing when he wanted to be. For that matter, she'd read that abusers and serial killers were often charmers, lulling their victims into a false sense of security.

"Cynthia doesn't want to see you," Millie said, managing to keep her voice calm. "Please leave."

The young man again smiled seductively. "I'm sure she said so, before. But she'll definitely want to see me now—she'll want this ring. And she'll be mad at you if you keep us apart. Come on, lovely ladies," he wheedled, "where can I find my darling Cynthia?"

"It's no use asking us," Millie said. "We've no idea where she is."

He grinned and wagged a playful finger at her. "I don't *believe* you." Turning to Alice, he said, "You'll tell me, won't you, ma'am?"

"I can't tell what I don't know," Alice said firmly.

"You do remember what young love was like, don't you, Alice?"

For answer, she folded her arms and eyed him unsmilingly.

"At least let me come in and wait for Cynthia. She'd want you to make her boyfriend welcome. After all, we're practically engaged."

"You need to leave, Mr. Loftis," Alice said. "Now."

He tensed, and his smile faded.

"I will, if you'll give me Cynthia's cell phone number. I seem to've misplaced it. I can just call and explain things to her—including my nice surprise—and I'm sure she'll come right back from wherever she's gotten to."

"Cynthia does not want to see you or talk to you—ever—again." Alice emphasized each individual word.

He chewed a lip, as if debating his next move. Muscles flexed in his powerful shoulders. Millie's heart skipped. She wondered if he might wrench open the screen door and attack them. Slipping a hand into her pocket, she took out her phone, ready to dial for help.

If Ted had contemplated violence, he thought better of it. "Just tell Cynthia I was here," he said evenly. "And be sure to mention I brought her a special surprise. I'll be in town a while. She can call me on my cell."

He strode down the steps, arms held away from his body in the manner of a much heftier man, perhaps a weight-lifter. Millie wondered if he'd been larger at some time, or if the posture was an affectation, a way to appear tough.

As he drove away, the women looked at each other.

"That is a man who's capable of meanness," Alice said with a sigh. "I hope Cynthia stays away from him."

Millie nodded emphatically. "And he from her. From all of us. But somehow, I'm afraid we haven't seen the last of Ted Loftis."

# Chapter Eight

Millie called Cynthia's new cell phone number and told her Ted had been there but had left. "He did say he'll be in town awhile and for you to call him on his cell."

"You told him I don't want to see him, didn't you?"

"Yes. Alice and I both did."

"Thanks. I—" Cynthia hesitated. "I don't think I'll come home until tomorrow. Maybe he'll decide overnight to give up and go home."

"I hope so. Take care, Cynthia."

Millie then dialed Scott's cell phone to reassure him that Cynthia's ex had left without violence.

His relief matched her own.

In early afternoon, Alice completed a grocery list and prepared to drive to the market.

"I won't be here for dinner—I'm eating with Belinda and Dave—but we need several things for the next few days. I hate to leave you and Danny alone, though, in case that Ted should come back. Want to go to the store with me, then to Belinda's? She wouldn't mind setting a couple of extra plates."

Jill, also, planned to be out. Millie was a little nervous about being the only adult in the house, but she said, "No, thanks. If anyone comes to the door, I won't answer unless I'm sure it's not Ted."

She waved Alice off. That evening, she and Danny played games inside and kept the doors locked. To her great relief the rest of the day proved uneventful.

Cynthia stayed away until Sunday morning, arriving home with small gifts for her housemates: a DVD for Danny, cologne for each of the women.

"How'd you know Shadowfire is my favorite fragrance?" Jill asked with a pleased smile.

"I peeked at the bottles on your dressers. Did I get the right scent for you, Alice? Millie?"

They both thanked her, saying she had chosen correctly for them. Millie felt touched that Cynthia had noticed all the women's preferences.

"You must've been having a good time in Roanoke, to stay overnight," Jill said, her voice full of curiosity. "Say you have friends over there?"

"Friend, singular. She and I were in school together. She married right out of college, and she and her husband moved to Roanoke. They divorced a couple of years ago, but she liked Roanoke and stayed on."

"You hadn't mentioned having a friend living so close. You guys do anything fun while you were there?"

"Mostly just visited. We did go shopping a while yesterday, though. That's when I got your gifts. Oh, I saw a gorgeous ring in a jewelry store window that would look great on your hand."

"Yeah? What was it like?"

Millie inwardly chuckled at the adroit way Cynthia had changed the subject. Mentioning jewelry was a sure-fire way to shift Jill's attention. But . . . had Cynthia lied a bit too easily?

Later, Jill went out with Luke, and the other women prepared chef salads for lunch while Danny played in the back yard.

"Tell me everything he said." Cynthia's voice held resignation. "And what you both said."

Alice and Millie related their dialogue with Ted.

"So he really scared you two?" she asked plaintively, when they'd finished. "I've remembered some things about him this weekend that I hadn't thought much about—maybe hadn't let myself think about—incidents that bother me now."

"What sort of things?" Millie asked.

"Once at a family gathering, he teased a young cousin until she cried. And when we were at a nice restaurant one night, he chewed out a waitress because the food was slow coming out. I rationalized both incidents then as being small and unimportant, but I recall feeling uncomfortable.

"Ted's good to animals, though, at least to the hunting dogs his dad owns, and I'd told myself that made up for his lapses with people. Now I'm not so sure."

"Good to animals, horrible to people," Alice said. "Nice fellow."

"He said he'll be in town for a while," Millie reminded Cynthia. "You aren't home free yet."

Cynthia sat a moment without speaking. "So he thinks he can buy me with a diamond?" she finally said. "I'm not Jill."

"What should we say if he tries to phone you?" Alice asked.

"That I don't want to speak to him. You mean he hasn't already tried, since he left yesterday? That surprises me. You had any suspicious hang-ups?"

Millie and Alice both said no. Then another possibility occurred to Millie.

"Was anyone on the street, watching the house, when you drove in today? In a parked car, maybe."

"Not that I noticed. Oh—I see what you mean—that the reason Ted didn't call was, he knew I wasn't back because he was watching for me. That's scary."

"Cynthia, I have a bad feeling about that young man," Alice said. "Why don't you talk to the police or an attorney, find out what you can do to protect yourself against him?"

"But he's never hit me or anything, never even threatened to. Just worrying that he might isn't evidence. I couldn't prove he has evil intent—I'm not even positive he has." Cynthia laughed nervously. "Maybe I should start dating a cop."

"Not a bad idea," Alice said. "Know any?"

"Unfortunately, no." Cynthia tapped a finger on her cheek. "There's a local fellow, Toby Bannister, who volunteers with me, and we've gone out a couple of times. But he's not a big guy and claims to be a devout coward. Probably an exaggeration, but I doubt I should look for help there."

"I think it'd be a good idea for you and Jill, or someone, to carpool to work every day," Alice went on. I suggest you tell her what's going on. If there's even a possibility Ted's dangerous, she has a right to know."

Millie sighed. "Please don't take this the wrong way, Cynthia, but I'd rather Danny not go to and from camp with you next week."

Cynthia's eyes widened. She seemed about to protest, but then her shoulders drooped. "Guess I can't blame you. And Jill will have to know—I see that—so she won't ever leave the house unlocked. I can imagine Ted sneaking in and hiding, to 'surprise' me."

"Danny'll have to know, too, I suppose," Millie said sadly. "I had hoped to spare him that, but we can't risk his inadvertently letting Ted use him somehow. Okay, you tell Jill, and I'll tell Danny." Reluctant to destroy another bit of her son's innocence, she fixed Cynthia with a steady look. "We're not overreacting, are we? Is it possible Ted isn't the menace we're treating him as?"

Cynthia spread her hands. "It's possible, sure. I'm sorry, but I'm not clear about much of anything these days. Not when it comes to him."

They had lunch, and then Cynthia began preparing soup for the evening meal, saying that cooking relaxed her.

Later, Jill and Luke returned from Natural Bridge, several miles west of Lynchburg, bringing superb digital photos of the huge limestone arch that Jefferson had once owned and had called "the most sublime of Nature's works." A picture Luke had taken of Jill leaning against one of the stone pillars, which rose a couple of hundred feet above her head before curving to meet its opposite column, revealed the feature's massive scope.

"Can we go see this bridge, Mom?" Danny asked. "It's awesome!"

"Sure, later on. Before we head home."

"Like to stay for supper, Luke?" Cynthia shyly offered. "There's plenty."

Jill threw a sidelong look at their housemate, and Millie realized that Cynthia's invitation might not bode well for household harmony.

"A home-cooked meal?" Luke said. "You bet! Thanks."

For dinner, Cynthia served a green chile pork soup, which she said was her grandmother's recipe.

"Your grandmother must be a terrific cook," Millie said.

"She is. I come from a line of good cooks. I've always been more of a gardener, myself, but *mi abuelita* and *mi mamá* insisted I learn some basic recipes." She turned to Danny. "*Abuelita* means granny, and of course, *mamá* means mom."

"I know. We study Spanish at my school. And one of my friends is from Mexico."

*"Hombre, ¡qué listo eres!* How smart you are!"

*"Gracias, señorita,"* Danny said with a grin.

"Outstanding food," Luke said. "Ron'll be green with envy.

Mexican food's his favorite."

"I'll be cooking again in a few days," Cynthia said with her shy smile. "Probably enchiladas, maybe *calabacitas*—that's a squash and corn dish. You should bring him over."

"Name the date and get outa our way."

Jill stiffened, looking from Cynthia to Luke and back again. It wasn't hard to guess her thoughts, and they weren't friendly to Cynthia.

"I guess you get tired of restaurant food when you're on assignment, Luke?" Millie asked, hoping to ease the awkwardness.

He nodded. "For sure. Ron and I occasionally microwave food at the motel, but that gets old too. Whit and Harold—Whit's roomie—sometimes eat out with us."

"I'll be cooking roast beef next Wednesday, and it's a huge chunk of meat," Alice said. "Would you and Ron like to join us?"

"Absolutely! Thanks, Mrs. Ross."

"You and Ron spend a lot of time together, don't you? At work, sharing a room, cooking and eating together. It's good that you get along."

Luke grinned. "We sound like an old married couple, don't we? But we do have individual interests. He likes to look at old buildings—logical for an architectural historian—Paige was the same way—so he's in his element in Lynchburg. I like to hike solo on one of the good trails around here, or play baseball with a pick-up team at one of the parks. When I'm not seeing Jill, that is—my favorite pastime." He winked at her.

Millie noticed he'd said Paige's name without the mournful expression he'd worn when she had asked about her a few days before. His memory of her must be fading, she thought, or maybe he could now recall happier memories.

After dinner, Luke and Jill sat in the swing on the front porch, while Cynthia and Danny played Scrabble on the terrace near the kitchen. Millie and Alice did dishes, then joined them. The day's heat had waned, and a cool breeze dried Millie's damp temples.

She skimmed passages in a book on Lewis and Clark she'd brought out with her, more and more appreciative of the courage and quick-wittedness required for such a journey into the unknown—or at least the little known—since few accounts of life in what had become the western United States would have been available to them. The book's author gave much credit for the mission's success to Thomas Jefferson himself, for his "masterful planning."

After a while, Millie told Danny to go up and get ready for bed. Still reading his novel, he rose and stumbled towards the back door.

A little later, in his room, she sat with an arm around him and told him about Ted in a matter-of-fact tone, emphasizing that no one knew for sure that he would try to harm anyone. They were just being cautious.

Danny didn't speak for a minute, watching his mother's face with wide, frightened eyes. The expression broke Millie's heart. She would have endured much to be able to erase it, forever. But she couldn't protect him from all dangers, all worries and fears.

"He's not mad at you, Danno—probably not at anybody except Cynthia. And we don't even know he'd try to hurt her. But just in case he might, we all have to be smart and careful, and help her stay safe."

He thought a moment. "I could loan her my slingshot, Mom."

"Thanks, sweetheart, but you'd better keep it. You're the only one who knows how to use it, anyway." Actually, Cynthia probably knew, too, Millie realized, since she had grown up with five brothers.

"If that man comes here, Mom, I can shoot him."

"Let's not plan on your doing that, sweetie. Don't try to hurt him, or do anything that would cause him to hurt you. The best thing you can do is stay away from him. Okay?"

He slowly nodded.

"Try not to worry about this, Danno. I just thought I'd better tell you, so you can help us always keep the doors locked." She showed him a wallet photo of Ted that Cynthia had lent her, reserving another copy to show Jill. "This is the man we're trying to keep away from Cynthia.

"If he should ever come up to you, Danny, here or anywhere—maybe ask you to help him in some way—don't do it. Just come and tell me. Or Alice, or Cynthia, or Jill."

"Okay, Mom. If none of you're around, should I find a policeman?"

"Yes, that's a good idea. But I hope you'll never even see Ted Loftis."

When she returned to her room, she started reading a library book. A few minutes later, Alice appeared at her door. She put her finger to her mouth in a shushing action and beckoned to Millie to follow. Millie gave her a quizzical look, since her friend wasn't the intrigue type, but followed her downstairs to her room.

When they were closeted in Alice's bedroom, the older woman took a large carton from her closet and placed it on the desk. Opening it, she removed handfuls of tissue paper, then unwrapped and unfolded a woman's long dress—scarlet, with an Empire waist.

"Alice, how lovely!" Millie cried.

With an enigmatic smile, Alice removed and displayed more women's garments—long dresses and skirts, short jackets, bonnets—and laid them across the bed. Even with Millie's scant experience of expensive clothing, she could tell they were of costly fabric and fine workmanship.

"Alice, these are beautiful," Millie said, fingering a red woolen cape. "Did you find these at a vintage clothing shop?"

Her friend chuckled. "Would you believe a thrift store? My sister Belinda manages one downtown, and when anything special comes in—anything that might have value as an antique—she asks me to look it over. She knows I'm interested in old things."

She held various garments up to Millie and concluded that they'd been made for someone with a tinier waist, fuller bust, and shorter stature. Pressing a dress of white muslin trimmed with red ribbon against herself and twirling slowly, Millie imagined she was the gown's original wearer, arraying herself for an evening of gaiety.

"These must be really old," she said. "But aren't they in great shape?"

Alice stroked the high waist and low neckline of the dress Millie held. "I'd guess a couple of centuries old. The Empire waist was big then. As for the fabric, white muslin was worn by wealthy women as a sign of status. It soiled so easily that servants were needed to maintain it."

Millie nodded and looked over the other garments. "Lots of bright fabrics and trimmings. I'll bet red was her favorite color."

Alice sniffed. "Mothballs and cedar. I don't think mothballs were even invented when these things would've been new. They probably got stored in a cedar chest at first, then were re-packed with moth balls later."

"Maybe packed and re-packed several times over the years. Wonder what they'd bring for the thrift shop."

"A tidy sum. But I'm not expert enough to price them. I'll suggest Sis get appraisals from a couple of reputable dealers." Alice turned again to the open box and removed a half dozen faded crimson-backed books. "Look at these, Millie. They're evidently someone's diary. Wonder if they belonged to the same young lady—at least I visualize her as young—who wore the clothes?"

"May I see one?" Millie took the volume Alice handed her and paged through, stopping occasionally to scan a passage. She flipped other pages, then gave it back with a sigh. "Trying to read that will be an exercise in frustration. The entries aren't dated by year, just 'Wednesday evening' or 'Sept. 26.' And they're so sketchy you can't get any sense of who the writer was. It's like she jotted bits of information as reminders, then left space after each entry so she could flesh them out later. Only she apparently never did."

Alice nodded. "Maybe she felt obliged to keep a journal—because doing so was the fashion among other ladies she knew, or perhaps a favorite aunt suggested it—but her heart wasn't in it. I don't know that fuller entries would be more interesting, anyway. Her thoughts seem to've been full of new frocks and handsome young men, nothing substantial. But I guess I'll skim all the volumes. Maybe there'll be something more interesting later on."

"Hope so, for your sake. I'm afraid reading six volumes about boys and clothes would render me senseless."

"I know they'll probably be deadly dull. But I feel I need to read them all before getting rid of them, just in case they really do contain something of merit."

The women re-folded the garments, padding them with tissue to prevent creases, and returned them to the carton. Alice said she'd take it back to Belinda and recommend getting the garments appraised. The journals, her sister had said, were Alice's to dispose of as she saw fit.

Bidding her friend good night, Millie went upstairs and curled up with a Lewis and Clark book.

# ☆ Chapter Nine

The next morning, Cynthia and Jill carpooled to Poplar Forest, Jill having agreed that her housemate probably shouldn't travel alone while Ted might still be around. Alice brought Millie and Danny in later. He was nervous but excited about his first session of the Archaeology, History and Restoration summer field camp for children. Alice took a route that brought them in at the back of Poplar Forest and parked in an unpaved lot with a dozen or so other vehicles behind the boxy red buildings containing the archaeology lab and restoration workshop.

"I usually park back here," Alice explained. "Seems more convenient than the main lot. But either's fine, Millie, when it's your turn to drive. Chas uses the main lot, because he likes to approach the house the more scenic way, from the front."

As planned, Cynthia met them behind the archaeology building and took Danny to the nearby Hands-On History Center. Alice led Millie up a set of back steps and through a storage room containing equipment such as cameras and metal detectors, plus shelves holding white lidded boxes that she said contained site materials that had been washed, labeled, and examined. Chas greeted them and said the director was still out. He told Millie to get her day-to-day instructions from Alice but gave a few basic cautions about handling excavated materials.

"Never try to work with more than one artifact bag at a time. If you're unsure about how to do something, ask Alice or me or one of the archaeologists. We'd rather answer the same question a dozen times than have you guess and maybe mishandle material." He opened several glass-topped drawers in a cabinet in the main room to show her artifacts of special interest found at Poplar Forest. Then saying Alice would explain the rest of the procedures, he went to his office off the small workroom—the labeling room, he called it.

Moving between kitchen and labeling room as needed, Alice demonstrated for Millie how to properly clean and label artifacts, recording each step in a log book so anyone looking for a particular sample could tell where it was in the handling process. Following her example, Millie practiced the washing, labeling, and recording procedures. Alice said she'd later show Millie how to enter artifacts in a computer database, using special software. Items of particular interest would also get photographed, she noted, especially those sent out for expert analysis.

"Most of the analysis work happens in winter, after the archaeologists close the dig," she went on, "though I'm helping Chas do preliminary analysis now. The archaeologists will decide, based on what they've found, how a site was probably used, how each artifact fits into their theory, and so on."

In the kitchen, Alice picked a bent bit of metal from a mesh tray that held Millie's washed material. "This is part of a nail, made right here on the plantation. Jefferson tried to run totally self-sufficient operations, here and at Monticello. He didn't quite succeed but came close. As with the bricks, we don't label all the nails."

Millie heard the back door open and close, then the rumble of a male voice, not Chas's.

"That's Harold," Alice said. "I'll introduce you."

The women dried their hands and went into the labeling room, where Millie again saw the short, bald man she'd seen with Whit on Friday. Alice introduced him as Harold Drake, a contract archaeologist assisting with archaeological work at Poplar Forest. He finished jotting something on a clipboard and shook Millie's hand. A genial smile briefly creased his doughy face, then disappeared.

"Heard good things about you from Alice and Chas," he said. "Like Lynchburg so far?"

"I do. And you?"

"It's fine. Yeah, I like it." Harold wore jeans and a short-sleeved brown shirt, both a little too snug on his pear-shaped body.

"Where's home for you?" she asked.

He chuckled. "I don't actually have one, or not a settled home. Since college, I've mostly been moving from dig to dig. In my rare 'off' periods I stay either with friends or at my sister's house in Maine. A nomad lifestyle's easier to maintain when you're not married, of course. I understand you'll be helping at Highgrove, too?"

"That's right. How—? Oh, of course. You live with Whit."

He nodded, placed the clipboard in an office beside Chas's, grabbed a billed cap off the desk, and came out again.

"So you work for the same firm that employs Luke, Whit, and Ron?" Millie said.

"Yeah, we furnish experts for digs all over the world. I've worked in Turkey, England, and Alabama, to name just a few. I understand you have a young son with you?"

Millie told about Danny and her hope he'd learn to share her passion for history.

"He'll be hooked after a week in the Hands-On History Center." The smile darted out again. "Wish I'd been able to see that when I was a kid."

As Harold talked, Millie recalled the first time she'd seen him, walking with Whit near the office wing. Whit had been expressing frustration over not finding something, and Harold had reminded him that he'd just started looking outside.

Hmm, Millie thought, so Whit was looking for something outside. At Highgrove, perhaps?

Of course. She recalled Chas's explanation to Danny about how archaeologists knew where to dig. They simply looked over a likely area, searching for clues such as depressions in soil.

Whit must be scouting out other likely dig sites at Highgrove.

Chas came out of his office and filled a coffee mug from a carafe.

"Gorgeous medallion, Chas," Alice commented. "You make it?"

He lifted the highly polished black pendant from his chest, a pleased flush further reddening his florid face. "Yeah, this is one of my pieces. Glad you like it."

"What's the stone?" Alice said, touching the disk's smooth surface. "It reminds me of jade, but I've never seen jade that dark."

"You've a good eye. This is Absolute Black 'jade.' It's denser than a true jade and takes a higher polish."

"You're becoming a real professional, Chas. This is wonderful workmanship."

"Thanks. I'm pretty happy with the way it turned out."

Alice explained to Millie that Chas was studying to be a lapidary and worked part-time at a local jewelry store in addition to his part-time work as lab supervisor at Poplar Forest.

"Interesting combination," Millie remarked. "You studying to be an archaeologist as well?"

He laughed. "No. I'm here mainly because I'm a Jefferson fan. Poplar Forest wasn't open to the public when I was a child, but I'd ride my bike past it, pretending I lived here as Jefferson's son. I used to pester my parents and schoolmates with interesting tidbits about him—I must've been an insufferable kid." He grinned and pushed a reddish curl from one eye. "If you're wondering what I'll do when I grow up, I hope to own my own jewelry store. But history and Poplar Forest are major interests of mine, too."

Adding his compliment about the medallion, Harold said he needed to get out to the dig and left. Chas returned to his office. Alice told Millie she'd be in one of the offices off the main room if she had questions.

"I'm checking e-Bay," she went on, "in case a piece of really old pottery should turn up that matches a sherd found here. Could help us date the artifact." She smiled. "Not everything you find on e-Bay is genuine, but stranger things've happened."

Millie spent the first part of the morning washing sackful after sackful of excavated material. She and Alice stopped mid-morning for a break, sitting over coffee at the table in the labeling room.

"Washing and labeling aren't exciting, but they're vital in archaeology," Alice said. "An artifact that has lost its context, or provenance, is useless."

"Jefferson would approve of all the care you take with samples," Millie observed, "having been such a meticulous record-keeper, himself."

Alice smiled. "Researchers studying him and his houses are luckier than most scholars who write about that period. He recorded what crops he planted and when, even the amounts he paid for household items. The restorers of Poplar Forest not only had his own plans of the house but also his notes about construction, like the lengths and numbers of boards needed to build it."

"It's almost as if he knew people in the future would study his every move, so he helped them out."

"I think the Founding Fathers all had a sense they'd be important in history, Jefferson more than most. But observing and recording what he saw also seem to've been part of his nature. He was a real scientist, the father of archaeology in America—among other things."

"A true Renaissance man."

After working a while longer, the women prepared to go home for lunch. Before they left, Millie asked Chas about her work schedule. He told her to plan it with Alice, since as a volunteer she'd have flexibility. She explained her interest in Highgrove and said that, if it was okay to take the rest of the day off from the lab, she'd begin helping there this afternoon. With a smile, he waved her away.

"Wish I was going with you," he said. "I saw the place just after the crew started work—Harold arranged it with Whit—and it's a fascinating place. I can believe Jefferson did design it."

Cynthia rode home with Alice, Millie, and Danny, since Jill would be working through the afternoon. On the way, Danny regaled the women with details of his first day at camp. He had learned the names of several other kids at camp and especially liked one boy, Kevin Reynolds, whose family lived in Lynchburg. The students had been divided into groups of four, a volunteer docent assigned to each bunch. The children had toured the house and grounds, including the slave quarter site, familiar territory to Danny from seeing Poplar Forest a few days before. Another first-day activity had been a scavenger hunt, requiring the children to find answers to a list of questions about various exhibits and features at Poplar Forest.

"I already knew some of the answers, Mom," he crowed. "Like how many sides are in the privy and what cross-mending means. Remember, the sign in the picture window where you work says that's when you fit together pieces of a dish that were found in different layers of dirt."

"I remember."

The teacher had also taught a time-crime lesson, showing slides of people digging illegally in places where the property owner hadn't agreed they could, or where they'd failed to get the required permission from the State of Virginia.

"Did you know you're not supposed to hunt for artifacts in a public park or forest, Mom?"

"I did."

"And you shouldn't dig up a grave or take flowers off a grave in a cemetery."

"Useful to know."

"Miss Hazel said it's good to collect old stuff, but we shouldn't mess up anything to get it, or take anything that doesn't belong to us."

Millie nodded, glad her son had made a friend and learned respect for the past, all in his first day. She noticed Cynthia was unusually quiet, though, smiling at Danny's enthusiasm while saying little.

"You're learning a lot, Danno," Millie said. "Good for you."

"It's fun."

*Learning is fun—too bad some kids, and adults, never realize that.*

They had lunch and Alice returned to the lab. Cynthia said she'd lock the doors of the mansion and she and Danny would stay inside, reading or playing games.

Millie changed into an old shirt, cut-offs, and moccasins, suitable garb for a hot, dirty job like sifting soil, and took along a floppy hat, sunglasses, and sunscreen. She drove north and west to the driveway Jill had taken a few days earlier, thinking with high anticipation about the work to come.

*And you would be partly responsible for solving the mystery.* What if Highgrove really should turn out to be a Jefferson design?

Humming to herself at the prospect, Millie saw on the hill ahead of her the remarkable old dwelling. Though not as majestic as Poplar Forest, Highgrove was clearly no ordinary house, its chimneys proud and straight like a triumphant fist clenched in the air. She reached the house and parked beside it, next to Luke's pickup. Nolan's sedan, Ron's Pathfinder, and Whit's motorcycle sat nearby.

Hearing a voice, she turned and saw Ron, cell phone to ear, stretched out on one of the lawn chairs. Crew members often took breaks here rather than inside, Luke had told her, because the house was stuffy on warm days. Although Nolan's ancestors had added plumbing, electricity, and heating, his grandfather had vetoed air-conditioning, which he hated. Presumably, the grandmother either had felt the same or had adapted. Millie doubted the temperature in Highgrove would ever reach the level of her cramped Dallas apartment one summer, however, when the air-conditioner had been out for two days.

Near the arrangement of lawn chairs sat a storage shed with a wide door to accommodate bulky equipment. Luke had told her that first day that the archaeologists stored wheelbarrows and other equipment there when not in use and locked it at night. Glancing towards the small building, Millie thought she saw movement behind a window.

A trick of sunlight on the pane, she decided.

"... can't find it, I tell you ...." Ron's voice was muted, but insistent, not angry but determined to be understood, to be believed. "I know ... it's a special ring ... yes, very special ... but I just don't know where ... " He sighed. "Sure, I'll keep looking."

Hearing him speak with frustration about being unable to find something, Millie felt a sense of *déjà vu,* remembering Whit's similar words to Harold. Only it was clear that Ron was looking for a ring of some kind.

Uncomfortable about overhearing his private conversation, Millie hastened up the walk and climbed the front steps. Luke had told her to come on in when she arrived, since crew members might all be occupied and unable to answer a knock. She twisted the doorknob and entered. The parlor looked much the same as it had last week, except the chair and camera were in a different spot beside the fireplace wall. No one was here.

"Hi," she called softly, "it's Millie."

No response. She walked through to the dining room, then the kitchen, seeing no one in either room or in the open-doored project office. At that moment, the outside door opened and Whit stepped inside, removing a set of headphones from his ears.

"Hey, Millie. Didn't hear you drive up. I was listening to my iPod." He unclipped the small device from his belt.

"I saw Ron outside but had about decided the rest of you were gone somewhere," she said.

"Nah, I was just leaning against the house back there, fiddling with the volume." He laid the headphones and iPod in the office. "Luke's probably in the basement. He usually is.

"And Nolan—"

He broke off as a dark head of hair, followed by burly shoulders, appeared at the top of the stairs from the basement. Nolan finished his climb, registering surprise on seeing Millie.

"Thought I heard voices up here. Welcome, Millie."

"Thanks." She turned to Whit. "How's everything going at the dig?"

"Good, good. Ready to go to work?"

She said she was. He took a cola from the fridge and offered her one. "But there's coffee made if you'd prefer. Luke likes it sometimes even in warm weather."

Millie opted for a cola, donned her hat and sunglasses, and followed Whit outside, Nolan bringing up the rear.

The three of them stood at the sawhorses, rubbing dirt through the shaker screen. Millie saw that Ron was standing beside his vehicle, taking something from the glove compartment. Another *déjà vu* moment, she thought, recalling Jill's puzzling actions on Thursday. Her curiosity changed to amusement, though, as Ron emerged from the Pathfinder, biting open a packet of snacks.

He walked on to the house. Shortly afterwards, Luke came out. Spying Millie, he asked how she liked working at Poplar Forest, and they chatted a few moments.

Nolan left the shaker screen, took a lidded ashtray from his car, walked a distance of fifty yards or more from the dig, and lit a cigarette. Millie recalled smelling tobacco on him and realized he probably was forbidden to smoke in the house or near the dig. After a few minutes, he put out his smoke in the ashtray, closed the lid, returned the container to his car, and resumed his place at the shaker screen.

An automobile motor throbbed in the distance, then came closer. The crew turned to look. As a maroon Lexus burst from a line of trees along the road, Nolan grinned ruefully at Millie.

"Herself approacheth. Prepare to bow."

Millie watched the car zoom into the clearing, jerk to a halt beside her own car, and disgorge a pencil-thin elderly woman wearing jeans, a sleeveless blue vest over a white T-shirt, and low boots. Probably older than Sylva, she exuded energy, purpose, and dignity. Her iron-gray hair was worn in a mannish style, almost a burr cut, with no attempt to hide the hearing aids in both ears. The cane she carried seemed more pointer than walking aid. She gestured with it towards the dig.

"Anything new out here?"

Luke strode out to meet her. "Welcome, welcome, Miss Julia. Nothing much at Whit's site, but I've found something in the basement that'll interest you." In courtly fashion, he offered an arm and she laid her hand on it, apparently their ritual. "Come meet our new volunteer, Millie Kirchner from Dallas. Miss Julia Unruh, owner of Highgrove." He added that Millie was volunteering at Poplar Forest for the summer but was also giving Highgrove a few hours each week.

The sharp black eyes behind owlish glasses evaluated Millie. Apparently satisfied, Miss Julia said a curt, "Hello, good to meet you."

Millie replied in kind. Then Miss Julia's gaze moved on to Whit. She nodded without smiling.

"Hello, Aunt Julia," Nolan said with a wide grin.

"Nolan." The corners of the severe mouth lifted slightly.

Luke claimed her attention again, and she accompanied him to the house. As their voices diminished, Millie heard him mention finding in a builder's trench part of what he thought was a leather apron, before they disappeared inside.

Millie smiled at Nolan. "Your aunt appears to be a formidable woman, one who knows what she wants and usually gets it."

"You got that right. She's a tough old broad."

"But she did speak to you—even smiled a little. No lingering hard feelings from the court case?"

He and Whit exchanged glances.

"You might say my aunt and I have reached an uneasy truce," Nolan finally said.

"Has she children and grandchildren? Cousins of yours?"

"My aunt never married. We're each other's only relative now."

"Is she retired from some profession?"

"She's a professional pain-in-the-ass, and not likely to retire from that."

Millie frowned at the flippant non-answer. He had the grace to look sheepish.

"My aunt was a legal secretary for many years," he said. "Invested her money wisely and now owns lots of rental property. I think she considers Highgrove just another valuable piece of real estate, but it's more than that to me."

He looked again at Whit, but his fellow crewman's eyes were on a boulder-strewn hillock a couple of hundred yards away.

"If you're each other's only family," Millie persisted, "won't she likely leave Highgrove to you in her will?"

Nolan laughed, a bitter sound.

"Millie, innocent Millie," he said. "Aunt Julia has a will all right, leaving me the magnificent sum of one dollar. She took great pleasure in showing me the document, which she made right after winning in court. Most of her money and investments go to her alma mater, Vassar, except for ten thousand dollars she's leaving to the City of Lynchburg for a museum."

"I see. Sorry."

Nolan's eyes swept the house from chimneys to foundation. "Well, it's just a house, I guess."

Millie studied him, saw the longing in his eyes. "It isn't just a house to you, is it? Such a shame your aunt won't even let you have Highgrove after she's gone. You're the one who cares for it and would look after it."

He shrugged, gave her a sad grin. "Yeah, well, life's like that sometimes."

Needing to use the restroom, Millie removed her gloves and went into the house. She had finished and was getting a glass of water in the kitchen when she heard Luke and Miss Julia coming up the stairs from the basement.

" . . . Whit can't . . ." Miss Julia's words mostly couldn't be understood, but a few stuck out in emphasis.

The pair had evidently paused on the stairs, Miss Julia facing the stairwell. Luke's low-pitched reply was unintelligible, as if he faced the basement.

Miss Julia was speaking again. "No! I'm sorry . . . don't agree . . . either him or Ron . . . security . . . do not give him . . . . under no circumstances . . . don't trust him . . ."

Realizing she'd already heard too much of a conversation not meant for her ears, Millie set her empty glass by the sink and hurried out the door.

Miss Julia's words lingered in her mind, however. The dowager Unruh was clearly suspicious of someone. Maybe several someones. Whit, for one.

While Nolan was in the house on a restroom break, Millie decided to talk to Whit privately about the thing that had been on her mind.

"I need to tell you something, Whit," she began. "Do you remember a few days ago when you were riding on Forest Road, at the turn-off to Poplar Forest? When you braked suddenly in front of a car?"

His frown deepened. Then his brows shot up, and he grinned. "That was you? Oh, yeah, the turn came up on me suddenly. I almost missed it."

"I noticed."

"Sorry, Millie, I'm usually more careful. Did I scare you?"

"You did. Unfortunately, my son thought you were 'cool.'"

"Ah." He waited to hear more. When she didn't go on, he said, "This a major problem between you and me?"

"Major, maybe not."

"But you do see it as an issue?"

She averted her eyes, then looked at him again. "I'm thinking ahead, figuring that there may come a time when you and Danny will meet."

"And that would be a problem, how?"

"Would you please not brag to him about your motorcycle? Or insist on taking him for a ride?"

"You asking me to lie to your boy? If he should tell me he likes motorcycles or says he's seen a neat bike, am I expected to act like I've never ridden one myself? Or must I tell him what dangerous evils they are? Exactly what do you want from me, Millie?"

She took a deep breath and let it out slowly. This hadn't been a good idea. She had thought she might avert trouble later by tackling the problem head-on, but he clearly wasn't going to cooperate.

"Whit, no. I don't expect you to lie. But I'd appreciate it if you don't bring up the subject of motorcycles with Danny. And—I'd rather he not ride with you."

"Because you think I'm reckless." He spoke so quietly she barely heard him.

She met his eyes. "Yes. From what I've seen."

Whit held her gaze with his own. Then surprisingly, he said, "Okay, you've got it." He ran a hand through his shock of hair. "I am sorry I scared you, Millie."

"Thanks, Whit. I appreciate this very much."

"No lying, though."

"No lying. We agree on that."

Nolan came from the house, and the three began screening again. Then Miss Julia and Luke came out and walked towards the Lexus.

"So you can't give me an estimate of when you'll know?" she said to him. "I'm not getting any younger, Mr. Brooks."

"Sorry, I can't, Miss Unruh. This will take as long as it takes."

"Any chance you'll get a new intern soon? Help speed up the process? Not that anyone's likely to be as good as Miss Oberlin."

"Not so far as I've heard. But we are lucky to have a couple of volunteers now."

Miss Unruh glanced at the little group by the shaker screen, and Millie thought she saw the old woman's lip curl.

# ★ Chapter Ten

When Millie arrived home, she prepared dinner with Danny's help, layering lasagna and making salad dressing while he tore lettuce and spread slices of Alice's homemade Italian bread with butter and garlic. His chatter was still of camp and his new friends. Cynthia picked at her food, saying little. After dinner, Alice suggested Cynthia go lie down while she and Jill did dishes.

Jill nodded. "Sure, go ahead."

The gray-blue eyes held sympathy, reminding Millie again that Jill's usual self-serving manner could not be the whole woman. She wondered if her blonde housemate carried a secret sorrow, making her hide her softer side for fear of being hurt again.

Cynthia thanked them and left. Millie and Danny settled into easy chairs in the mansion library, each with a book from the public library.

Hers contained details of York's bittersweet story that she hadn't read before. He had grown up playing with Clark, who was about his age, had acted as Clark's body-servant, had accompanied him on the trail to the Northwest. The slave's strength, hunting prowess, and usefulness as a curiosity to the Indians they encountered soon made him invaluable to the expedition. The Indians' fascination with York's rich coloration, distinctive appearance, and dancing ability gained the explorers help at more than one crucial point.

Slaves were typically denied the use of weapons, but Clark's body-servant had carried one on the journey. And when the expedition party voted on a site for its winter quarters, York's opinion had counted equally with the opinions of white explorers.

Unfortunately, his taste of equality came to an abrupt end when the expedition returned. He again became nothing more than Clark's slave, denied even such basics as the right to live with his wife, who was a slave belonging to a neighbor of Clark's. Nor did York's name appear on the "official" list of expedition members. And when a grateful President Jefferson awarded land and money to the triumphant returnees, York—arguably a vital part of their success—received nothing.

Likewise Sacajawea, the Indian woman whose knowledge of the wilderness and the Shoshone language had been critical to Lewis's and Clark's triumph. She also had been a slave, the book said, sold to her trapper husband, Toussaint Charbonneau, by the rival Hidatsa tribe that had kidnapped her as a young girl. She, like York, received no reward from the U.S. Government.

So much for personal freedom and equality in the newly independent United States, Millie thought sadly. But she reminded herself that slavery had been embedded in the culture in those days, a fact that even heroism on a high-profile presidential mission couldn't erase.

*It was a different time, Kirchner. No amount of wishing, no attempt at revisionism, can change that.*

Millie and Danny read a while longer. Then he went to bed, and she went down to Alice's room.

"I'm about to turn in," she said, pausing at the door. "How're you getting along with those old diaries?"

"Come in a minute, and I'll show you some passages. It's getting more interesting."

She took a red-backed book, slips of paper marking pages, from her nightstand drawer. They sat on the bed, and she turned to one of the marked pages. Millie read the entry, noting that it was fuller and thus clearer than those she'd seen earlier. But the date, April 29, was still maddeningly incomplete. April 29 of what year? What century? She read two other entries as Alice turned to them.

"Our diarist is getting serious about one young man in particular," Millie observed. "Someone she calls 'Dear Effy,' whom she met when she visited her cousins in Kentucky."

"'Very tall and slender,'" Alice intoned, a faraway look in her eyes, "with rugged features and a 'precious raven cowlick.'"

Millie chuckled. "You're a romantic, Alice, reading Effy's description so often you've memorized it."

"Now this one." Alice turned to an entry many pages later.

"So," Millie said after reading it, "Effy went off on a long trip, a 'perilous journey.' The diarist doesn't know if she'll ever see him again. I wonder if she ever did."

"I don't know, yet." Alice flipped to a later passage. "But she did hear from him again."

Millie read the entry and looked up with a smile. "She says he returned safely, as far as Missouri. That's good. But I wonder why Missouri."

"And then," Alice said, turning to another page, "the lovers ran into another stumbling block. Her father opposed their marriage." She waited for Millie to read the paragraph. "Effy had to 'prove himself' before he'd be allowed to seriously court this young woman."

"You ever learn her name, by the way?"

"Not really. She mentions one place that Effy calls her his 'dearest Prissy,' but probably that was a pet name, like Effy."

"He must've been an enterprising young man. She said Effy was working hard in Missouri, trying to earn a stake that would impress her dad. Don't they sound like star-crossed lovers, *à la* Romeo and Juliet?"

"Something like that. Except their families weren't fighting, maybe only because they hadn't met yet."

Millie grinned. "Can one be a cynical romantic? If so, you are. Keep me posted on what you learn about them. You've got me interested now."

"I wish Prissy's handwriting weren't so hard to read. Plus, she tends to abbreviate long words."

"At least she's using complete sentences now. Be grateful for small favors."

Millie returned to her room, mulling over the clues in the diary. Prissy could be a nickname for Priscilla. But "Effy?" She tried out different names—Everett? Ephraim? Now why did that latter name ring a bell?

Then she remembered where she had seen the name Ephraim before. On the tombstone in Old City Cemetery. Someone named Ephraim had died in Lynchburg in 1807. The date had struck her because it was the year just after the founding date of the cemetery.

She wondered if the man buried in the cemetery could be Prissy's "Effy." The date would certainly go with the Empire-style clothes that had been donated along with the diaries. Wouldn't it be fun if the two were the same? Perhaps Alice would find out "Effy's" last name as she read on, and they could check it against the tombstone.

Millie turned to her library book and was deep in reading, when a tap sounded on the door. She looked up to see Jill standing there.

"Okay if I come in?"

"Sure. Sit down." Jill plopped into a chair near the window seat.

"Lewis and Clark, eh?" she said on noticing Millie's book.

"Yes, I was reading about York, William Clark's slave who went with him on the expedition, and got to wondering if Clark ever set him free. That would've been an appropriate reward for all he'd contributed, worth a lot more to him than money."

"Yeah, I'm sure. The books don't tell whether he ever became a free man?"

"Some may. If so, I haven't found them yet. If he did get his freedom, there should be a manumission document somewhere."

"Manumission? What's that?"

"It was a paper that former slaves carried to prove they weren't runaways, that they'd been granted their freedom. Otherwise, a freedman might've been captured and enslaved again."

Jill frowned thoughtfully. "Important document, then. Ever seen one?"

"No, but you could probably find an example in a museum, or online."

"Nah, it was just a passing thought. What I really came in for was to ask if you'd like to go to Williamsburg next week. Someone in the shop wants to trade days, but I wanted to make sure of my plans before I commit. You mentioned wanting to see Williamsburg, and I've never been."

"Sure. What day were you thinking of going?"

"I'm scheduled to be off Thursday, but if I switch days I'd be off Friday. Which day would work better for you?"

"Either day's fine."

"I'll switch then, and you and I can see Williamsburg next Friday."

""Terrific. Okay if Danny goes too?"

"Why not? He's a good kid."

"Then it's a date."

Tuesday, Millie woke an hour before her alarm was set to

sound and shut it off, intending to get up and have a leisurely breakfast. She woke again an hour and a half later, chagrined to see she'd now have to hurry. She jumped up, woke Danny and helped him choose attire for the day, then rushed downstairs. Unfortunately, Alice was straggling into the kitchen too, having also overslept.

"I was wondering about you guys." Cynthia stood at the sink rinsing a bowl. "I didn't hear anybody else up, so I woke Jill, then got ready and ate some cereal. I'll check my e-mail while she's getting dressed, and then we need to leave."

At least Cynthia seemed somewhat more chipper than last night, Millie noticed.

Alice made coffee and toast while Millie quickly packed lunches. Danny came in, yawning, submitted to a check of hair and clothing, and sat down with a glass of milk and toast. Cynthia returned, her lovely face stricken.

Bad news in the inbox this morning, Millie guessed. She reminded herself Ted was Cynthia's problem, not hers, though she felt involved anyway.

Leaving Jill nibbling on a piece of toast, Alice and Millie gulped breakfast themselves, rushed to get ready, and with Danny piled into the Prius.

"I almost never oversleep," Alice lamented, "but I had a hard time dropping off last night. I guess when the alarm went off, I didn't hear it. May have to get a louder alarm."

"I just need to get up before I shut mine off," Millie said ruefully. She drove the speed limit all the way, and they arrived at Poplar Forest only a few minutes later than usual. Danny went to the Hands-On History Center, while Millie set to work washing and Alice labeled. Mid-morning, the women took their break in the main room. Chas brought in a cup of coffee and asked if he could join them.

"Sure," they both said.

"You worked here long, Chas?" Millie asked as he sat across from her.

"Couple of years."

"You married? Have a family?"

"Not married yet. As for family, I helped Mom look after Dad for several years. He died last fall. It hit Mom hard, even though he'd been ill a long time and was a tyrant to be around."

"Does she live with you?"

He hesitated. "No, but it's probably just a matter of time. I can see her failing."

"Sorry."

He shrugged. "Nothing anyone can do about aging. Danny liking his program?"

She gave him a brief summary of her son's first day.

The front door opened, and tentative steps entered. It was Jill, looking especially pretty in a Wedgwood-blue pants outfit that matched her eyes. Chas jumped awkwardly to his feet, nearly upsetting his coffee cup.

Jill's gaze swept the trio at the table, and she grinned. "Anybody here forget something?" She held two lunch bags aloft.

"Our lunches," Millie said, taking the sacks. "I remembered to make them, just not to get them here. Thanks, Jill."

Alice seconded her. "Jill, have you met Chas Locke, our lab supervisor? Chas, this is our friend and housemate, Jill Greene."

Jill eyed him without enthusiasm. "We actually have met, when my boyfriend Luke and I were in the jewelry store last week. You showed us some rings, remember?"

"Yeah, I do. You work in the museum shop, don't you? I've seen you a few times, getting out of a Cavalier parked in the main lot and going in the shop."

"Yeah, I do. Well, better get going. Take it easy, everyone."

"Wait!" Chas said. When Jill turned, wearing a puzzled frown, he flushed. "I could tell you really like nice jewelry. Would you like to see some semi-precious stones I've cut?"

*Is this the modern version of "Come up and see my etchings"?* Millie could imagine Sylva saying.

She stifled a chuckle.

"*You* cut?" Jill said skeptically. "You're a lapidary?"

"I've taken some courses. See this medallion? It's a piece I just finished."

She touched the pendant on his chest, eyeing it critically. "Hmm, not bad. So, are you an archaeologist or a lapidary?"

"Neither, now. The reason I'm working here is that I'm interested in Thomas Jefferson and Poplar Forest."

He went on to say he'd helped found a Jefferson fan club.

"I heard about that," Millie said. "Whit told me Nolan Unruh has won a Jefferson-knowledge contest the club sponsored. Several times, I believe."

"Yeah. But not the last one." His face darkened. "*I won* it."

"Oh, so you're his competition."

Jill yawned, apparently uninterested in his Jefferson expertise. Reading the signs, he returned to what clearly interested her most, his jewelry-making. He said he planned to own his own jewelry store some day, and her look of polite sufferance changed to real interest.

"No kidding." She drew her brows together, considering. "You know, I would like to see the pieces you've made. I'd like that a lot."

"Great! You busy Friday evening? We could go from here to get a sandwich, then head over to my place."

She hesitated, then smiled. "Yeah, I'll be here on Friday. Sounds like a plan."

"Great! What time do you finish work?"

They firmed up arrangements, and Jill left. Seeing the admiring way Chas watched her swing out the door, Millie hoped he had also noticed the possessive way she'd spoken of Luke as her boyfriend.

When it was time for Danny's camp to be over, Millie collected him and they rode home with Alice, her son chattering the whole drive about what he'd done that day. The children had learned about colonial brick making, mixed mud with their feet, molded bricks, and built a miniature kiln.

She listened to him prattle, happy to hear him so thrilled about learning. After lunch, Alice returned to work, while Millie and Danny played a game. A few hours later, Alice was home again, and she and Danny started work on supper. Alice noticed they were low on milk, and Millie went to get some.

When she returned home, she found Cynthia in the porch swing, wearing a tank top and cut-off jeans, one bare toe listlessly moving the suspended seat back and forth. Millie asked if she'd heard from Ted since Saturday.

"Not *from* him, but—Millie, I think I saw Ted today. When we were outside with the kids, and they were making bricks, I saw someone dart behind a tree several yards away. I'm not absolutely sure it was him, but whoever it was held his arms the same way Ted does, away from his body, you know, like some muscle-bound weight-lifter."

Millie recalled Ted's strut as he had left the mansion Saturday. He did indeed walk that way.

"Maybe he'll be content to just watch you from afar." The words of comfort sounded lame even to Millie's own ears.

Cynthia only grimaced. Millie carried the milk inside, then helped finish the simple supper. When the macaroni and cheese had baked, she summoned Jill from upstairs and was opening the front door to call Cynthia when she heard voices outside.

Swinging back the door, Millie saw a young man talking to her housemate. He had curly black hair, an athletic physique, and an open, sensitive face. Cynthia, smiling now, introduced him as Toby Bannister, a fellow volunteer in the Poplar Forest children's camp.

"I was driving by when I saw Cynthia on the porch," he explained, "and I remembered her saying she lived in a great old Victorian house. I stopped, hoping for a better look." He glanced at his watch. "Crap. I bet this is a bad time. You ladies are probably about to sit down to dinner."

"We are, actually." Cynthia looked hopefully at Millie. "Think there'd be enough food for—"

The cheeriness in her voice suggested she hoped the answer was yes.

"For Toby to stay? Sure, we made lots. Probably way too much for the five of us, but you know how hard pasta is to judge. Supper's nothing fancy, Toby, but you're welcome to join us."

"You serious?" He looked from Millie to Cynthia. "Great! I didn't intentionally drop by at mealtime, but I won't say no."

"Will that be okay with your mom?" Cynthia asked. "Is she expecting you for dinner?"

"Nah, this is her bridge night. Dad and I batch it on Tuesdays. I'll give him a call, and he'll eat his frozen dinner in front of the TV. He likes to do that, anyway."

Toby and Danny, recognizing each other from camp, touched fists and grinned a hello. Toby asked to use a restroom before dinner, and Danny showed him to the one by the laundry. While they were gone, Cynthia told the others Toby was a local man who installed cabinets for a kitchen remodeling firm, also a great admirer of Jefferson and Poplar Forest. Since he liked kids too, he was spending part of his vacation volunteering. She and Toby were just friends, she said. Millie wondered, after seeing her perk up at his visit.

When Toby and Danny returned, everyone sat at the dinette in the breakfast room. Toby had an easy, joking manner, treating Millie and Jill as friends, Alice as a respected aunt, and Danny as a buddy. Millie could see why Cynthia liked him. They learned he had no siblings, only his parents as family.

"Except for Danny and me," Toby said, "it's all women here—to state the obvious—so how's about some gift ideas for an older lady? My mom has a birthday coming up."

"What's she like?" Cynthia asked. "It'll be easier to make suggestions if we know something about her."

"She's female. You probably guessed that. And she'll be—forty-seven, I guess."

Alice winked at Millie. "Older lady, huh?"

"And . . . ?" Cynthia's hand revolved in a "come on, give" motion.

"And she's my mom. A good one. A really good mom."

"Zheesh." Cynthia placed both hands over her face.

"Does your mother have any hobbies, other than bridge?" Alice asked. "Does she cross-stitch, paint, garden?"

He gave her a blank look.

"Does she like to read?" Millie suggested. "Have a favorite author?"

Toby shrugged. "She reads the paper, and recipe books."

"Okay. You know of any cookbooks she'd like to have?"

"Nah. She has about a million. If I bought her one, I'd be sure to get one she already has."

"She into sports?" Jill asked in a bored, being-polite tone. "Golf, tennis, hiking, swimming?"

*"My* mom?"

"Then buy her a nice brooch. You can never go wrong with jewelry."

"And Jill would know about that," Alice teased her.

"Oh, yeah, you're the one who's nuts about jewels, aren't you?" Toby said to Jill.

She frowned at Cynthia. "Do you tell everything you know about us to all your friends?"

Cynthia started to reply, but Toby forestalled her, spreading his hands helplessly and saying with a self-deprecating grin that he knew nothing about shopping for women.

"No kidding," Cynthia said with good-natured scorn. "You'd better learn before you get married. Being able to buy a great gift for a woman is a survival skill."

"Teach me, please, Cynthia?" he begged, palms together at his chin. "Mom'll never give me hints, I don't have a sister or aunt to ask, and my male friends are as clueless as I am."

Cynthia lifted her eyes ceiling-ward. "What gifts have you given your mom in the past?"

"I shouldn't tell. A matched set of potholders wouldn't impress you, would it?"

"Please tell me you didn't give her that."

"Not so far, but I may get desperate enough."

"Okay, Rule Number One: Don't give a woman anything utilitarian—cookware, bed linens, whatever—unless you know it's something she really wants. Even then, you should probably add something personal as well. When's your mom's birthday?"

"Not for a couple of weeks. I usually sweat about it a while, then go to a department store and grab the first thing I see."

Cynthia shook her head slowly back and forth.

"Okay," she said, fixing him with a business-like stare, "this week's too busy, but after camp's over, you and I'll hit a mall. I'll show you some 'don't' gifts and some 'do' gifts."

"Great!"

Since he was a local man and an admirer of Thomas Jefferson, Millie asked if he knew about the fan club she'd heard mentioned.

"Sure, I was a member of the Jefferson Geniuses, as we modestly called ourselves."

"Was it a large group?" Millie asked.

He hesitated. "We were up to about twenty-five towards the end."

"May I ask why the group disbanded?"

He sighed. "It doesn't reflect well on any of us. When I first joined, it was lotsa fun. We'd get together once a month, drink a little beer, talk about Jefferson. Then guys began writing ditties and limericks about our group—the raunchier the better—and made up and performed skits about all things Jeffersonian. Still cool. Then somebody got the idea to host a Jefferson Day on his birthday, April 13.

"The first couple of years, even that went great. We drew crowds. There'd be a parade of people wearing period costumes; musical performances featuring the violin, his instrument; cooking and eating contests using foods from the Jefferson cookbook; and kids' games like he played with his grandkids.

"The centerpiece of the day, what everything else built up to, was the Jefferson-knowledge contest. We had college history profs contribute questions about his life, and contestants went through elimination rounds until the two best competitors were left to duke it out. Probably sounds tame to anyone who wasn't there, but the suspense was terrific. We had a no-wagering rule, but plenty of money changed hands under the table."

"So what happened to end it?"

"People started taking the J-knowledge contest way too seriously. Rivalries developed, spectators got hostile, and it became less and less fun. Then last year, Chas Locke and Nolan Unruh were the last two standing. Nolan had won twice in a row, and Chas was president of the Geniuses at the time. The judges declared Chas the winner, but Nolan claimed Chas had learned the questions beforehand and had an unfair advantage. When Chas left the building that night, a couple of drunk guys who'd bet on Nolan jumped him. All three landed in the emergency room, Chas with a broken nose, the others with various injuries.

"We tried to carry on with the group, but hard feelings between the two factions . . . well, attendance at meetings dropped off and we finally disbanded."

"Over some dumb history questions?" Jill scoffed. "So-o-o-o-o not important."

Toby shrugged. "Depends what you think's important. I bet you'd fight for a gorgeous ring or bracelet you wanted."

Jill looked down at her plate. Millie wondered about the reaction, since she usually seemed impervious to teasing about her jewelry obsession. To bridge the awkwardness, Millie said she'd just heard about the rivalry between Chas Locke and Nolan Unruh.

"Really? Who told you?"

Millie explained how she was acquainted with each man.

"Those two always had to out-do each other in anything related to the club," Toby said. "Cooking and eating contests, Jefferson lookalike competition, everything."

"Jefferson lookalikes? Those two?" Millie had thought Nolan an unlikely choice to play Thomas Jefferson in a reenactment. But Chas, with his wide face and languid gait, seemed just as improbable. She had to admit, though, that his red-blonde hair was a closer match to Jefferson's than Nolan's dark brown locks.

Toby grinned. "I know, I know, makeup can do only so much. But they were both good in the role."

Jill was silent the rest of the meal, then volunteered to clean the kitchen alone. More out-of-character behavior, Millie thought.

Toby requested a tour of the mansion, and Cynthia obliged. Then they joined Millie, Alice, and Danny in watching a sitcom on the television in the parlor. During a commercial break, Toby wandered about the room, eyeing the Victorian ornaments and furnishings. A beer-stein collection in a glass-enclosed corner cabinet caught his eye, and Alice told him the steins had been a fancy of the original owner of the house. When he asked if he could open the door for a closer look, she hesitated.

"I suppose so, if you'll be very careful. I'm sure those aren't terribly valuable, or the owner wouldn't have left them here. But as renters, we'd be liable for any breakage."

"I wouldn't want to break one of these beauties, myself," he replied, reverently lifting a hand-painted ceramic mug with a scene of cupids frolicking about two lovers. "I have a few steins, but nothing as neat as these."

He fingered mug after mug, from the tall and elegant to the squat and substantial. Some were in animal shapes, others painted or engraved to commemorate events or organizations. With a sigh, Toby closed the cabinet and reclaimed his seat.

When the sitcom ended, Alice, Millie, and Danny rose, excused themselves, and told Toby they'd enjoyed meeting him.

"Likewise," he said with a grin. "Thanks for letting me horn in on that delicious meal."

Danny went upstairs, Alice to her room. Millie got a glass of water in the kitchen. Jill had completed her chores and left. A thought occurred to Millie, a possible reason Toby's off-handed comment about jewelry had struck such a nerve with Jill at dinner. Maybe she'd dropped one too many hints to Luke about an engagement ring and they'd had a row.

*Not your problem, Kirchner.*

Right as usual, Sylva, Millie thought.

# ✯ Chapter Eleven

Later, in her room, Millie started another library book about the expedition. Its first few pages mostly reiterated material she'd already read, so she rapidly skimmed the rest. Near the back, an appendix listing members of the expedition caught her attention. She had already read some about their individual contributions, and had seen references to a return party of men chosen to leave the expedition early, to bring President Jefferson the maps and samples of flora and fauna collected to that point. But here was information new to her: a grouping of twenty-five men under the heading "Temporary Members of the Party."

One name on the list seemed to jump out at her, that of Ephraim Hayes.

Ephraim Hayes. That was it. That was the name she had read on the gravestone in Old City Cemetery.

Millie looked up Hayes in the book's index and read the few references about him in the text. He had been friends with William Clark in Louisville, Kentucky, where Hayes had been apprenticed to his master-bricklayer father. He had served in the army, held the rank of private, and been recruited by his friend Clark for this special military assignment. Good at hunting and swimming, skills important during the trek through the wilderness, Hayes had apparently acquitted himself well on the expedition, except for being accused once of stealing shot from another man's pouch.

The explorers had wintered that first year in what later became North Dakota, a season so brutally cold that the Missouri River froze. Fortunately for the men and their mission, Mandan Indians helped them make it through alive. The next spring, the main party continued westward, but the smaller "temporary party," led by Corporal Richard Warfington, returned to St. Louis.

So Hayes hadn't gone all the way to the West Coast, Millie thought. Had he been glad to return, or had he felt cheated of the rest of the adventure?

Surely, it couldn't be the same man. Why would this Ephraim Hayes have come to Lynchburg after his journey to the north ended, rather than returning home to Kentucky?

Wait, though. Another word on that gravestone, mostly readable, had been "Discov--y." And the more formal name for the Lewis and Clark Expedition was the Corps of Discovery.

The death date would fit, too. The return party had started back south in early 1805 and must have reached St. Louis some time that same year. Hayes could conceivably have come on to Lynchburg then and died here more than a year later. But if so, what had brought him here?

Could it have been Prissy?

All at once, Millie felt light-headed. Could it be true, that the Ephraim Hayes in Old City Cemetery had been part of the famous band of explorers? Unlikely, maybe, but not out of the question. And if he had come to see his sweetheart here, that would explain why he had traveled to Lynchburg. The diary had referred to a "perilous journey." Could it really have been the Lewis and Clark Expedition?

She booted her computer and navigated to a Web site for Old City Cemetery. It featured a searchable database of records about persons interred there. Elated, she quickly typed in Ephraim's name. But there, her luck ended. The record for him contained no more information than had his tombstone.

Millie sat back and stared at the screen. It had grown late and she was tired, but she had to share this mystery with someone who would appreciate it. Alice would be asleep, and it was far too late to phone Sylva's nursing home. Cynthia might be abed, also. Anyway, Millie hesitated to bother her amid the Ted difficulties. Even if Jill were awake, she probably wouldn't see, or care about, the significance of what Millie had learned.

But Scott would be awake, still studying. She dialed his number, and he answered. After some affectionate words, she told him about the Hayes mystery.

"Wow!" he said, as enthusiastic as she could have wished. "No kidding. You're going to follow up on this, aren't you?"

"I'll try. I guess I can start by calling the cemetery office, to see if they know anymore about Hayes than is on their Web site."

"Yeah, that sounds good. And you might find a death certificate in court records, or a death notice in an old newspaper."

"Oh, Scott, wouldn't it be fun if I could prove what happened to Hayes after he apparently dropped from sight?"

"Not only fun. You should be able to get special credit from your college's history department, probably get an academic paper or two out of it, maybe even a master's thesis. No, you're a long way from working on a master's. You couldn't sit on such information that long."

"I haven't really been thinking in terms of those possibilities."

"You need to start thinking like an academic, sweets, so you can claw your way to those hefty salaries university profs draw."

"Ah, I see what's keeping your nose to the grindstone, that financial bonanza you're expecting."

"Absolutely. The Nathan Henry windfall's a pittance beside

that."

"Mm-hmm."

"Friendly warning, sweets. Better keep the information about Hayes under wraps until after you've researched and verified it and are ready to present it to the world. There are history profs and doctoral candidates out there who'd kill for the information you've stumbled onto."

"Sounds ominous."

"Cut-throat opportunism isn't confined to Wall Street, m'dear."

On Wednesday, Millie worked in the morning at Poplar Forest, taking time out to phone the Old City Cemetery office and ask if anymore was known about Ephraim Hayes than appeared on his tombstone. She was told she'd need to speak to the Archivist and Curator, who wasn't in at present. Disappointed, she returned to labeling. When Danny's camp ended for the day, Millie drove him and Cynthia home. As before, his talk was all about what he'd done that day, pounding mortar, plastering walls, and laying brick with mortar.

"Miss Hazel said I'm a real good bricklayer, Mom."

"That's great."

After lunch with the two of them, Millie went to her room, determined to learn something more about Ephraim Hayes if possible. She tried Old City Cemetery again and was relieved to get to speak to the curator. He said he'd been told of Millie's inquiry and had double-checked the archives for a file on Ephraim Hayes.

"Sometimes the descendants of an individual who's buried here, or another researcher, will submit information about the person. But regrettably, we've nothing on Mr. Hayes except what's on the tombstone and in our online database."

He added that the graveyard's official burial records went back only to 1914. As for other records, no full household censuses for that part of Virginia existed until 1850, no official state birth or death records until 1853. Virginia hadn't used death certificates until 1912.

"So I'm afraid information on people buried in the cemetery before 1850 is sketchy at best."

Millie's spirits sank. "Can you suggest any other approach, then? I searched online for obituaries in old newspapers but found nothing for Lynchburg that early."

"A few papers did exist then, though none published for the 'masses.' These were essentially gentlemen's political and business journals, printed once a week or twice a month, heavy on state and national news. As for obituaries, only people of prominence in town would have merited those. Mr. Hayes, I gather, wasn't such a man."

"Probably not, no."

"The only other thing I can suggest is to check with Jones Memorial Library. Jones specializes in local history and genealogy and has quite a few old papers on microfilm. I know they have some issues from before 1800, though they're spotty until about 1820." He gave an e-mail address for the library.

Millie thanked him for his help. She was about to ring off when she heard his voice again.

"Um, miss, may I inquire if you're researching Mr. Hayes for a book or an academic paper?"

"I'm—not sure at this point."

"Then I feel I should tell you that you're not the only one interested in him. Two different individuals have asked about him in recent months. I checked the archives just in case one of them had brought us information to add to our file on Mr. Hayes. Neither has. But if you're planning an academic work, you may want to hurry its publication."

"Really. Two other researchers? May I ask who they are?"

"I'm sorry, but I don't think I should give out that information. Just as I won't reveal your name to another researcher."

Millie thanked him again, said goodbye, then sat staring into space. On the one hand, she felt vindicated that other researchers considered Ephraim Hayes a worthy subject. On the other, she'd be disappointed if someone told the world about him before she could. And if others had been working on their projects for some time, they might well beat her to publication.

Even so, she now felt more of a sense of urgency about solving the puzzle of Ephraim.

Armed with information about the Jones Library, Millie went to its Web site and found a listing of early Lynchburg newspapers among the library's holdings. She learned that issues of two papers, the *Lynchburg & Farmer's Gazette* and *Lynchburg Weekly Museum,* were available from the years 1795 and 1797 respectively. Later years were listed for other newspapers, but the years 1805–1807 weren't included for any.

She telephoned the Jones library just to be sure, explaining what she had learned of Ephraim Hayes from the cemetery curator and the library's Web site and asked if the library had other materials that might help her. The staff person she spoke with expressed regret but said the cemetery curator had been correct about the available sources.

That evening, Luke, Ron, Whit, and Nolan appeared at the big Victorian. Luke had called Alice the previous night, asking if the latter two could be included in the dinner invitation. She had agreed, but mindful of Millie's concern about Whit, asked that he ride with Luke rather than bringing his bike. Unfortunately, Alice forgot to inform the other women of the changed guest list until shortly before the men's arrival. Millie and Cynthia were fine with the change. Jill wasn't.

"This is getting outa hand, isn't it?" she said crossly. "First, it was Luke staying for dinner, then Luke and Ron being invited over, then Toby wheedling his way in, and now it's Whit and Nolan coming, too? Why don't we just open the doors to anyone who happens to pass on the street?"

"What's the big deal?" Cynthia asked. "It would've been awkward for Alice to say no when Luke asked, since she'd already invited him and Ron."

"The big deal is, we're all supposed to decide anything that affects us."

"I'm sorry, Jill," Alice said. "It didn't occur to me any of you would have a problem with adding two more, since we've plenty of food. I'll be more careful if there's a next time."

Jill considered, finally saying, "Oh, I suppose it's okay, this once." She rubbed at her left earlobe, adorned only with a tiny stud. Jill's ears and neck sported a reddish rash.

"Is that sore?" Millie asked, touching her own ear in sympathy. "You allergic to something?'

"I guess so," Jill said, "though I don't know what it is. Doesn't hurt, just itches. It flares up now and then. I use topical cream and antihistamine, and it goes away after a while. So far."

"You may want to see a dermatologist," Alice suggested. "Find out what's causing it."

"Yeah, maybe. Worst thing is, I can't wear my favorite earrings."

All the men came in Luke's four-seater pickup. He made introductions, and Alice led the way to the formal dining room. Millie noticed Jill sneaking glances at Ron, Whit, and Nolan, her expression sometimes petulant, sometimes wary. They sat three on one side: Jill, Luke, and Ron, and four on the other: Whit, Cynthia, Nolan, and Danny, with Alice and Millie at the ends. Over a tasty meal of tender beef, Alice asked how the work at Highgrove was coming.

"Pretty well," Luke said, wiping breadcrumbs from his blond

mustache. "I've found a couple of things in a builder's trench, including a hunk of bottle glass, that may help us date Highgrove."

"So if those items were early enough," Alice said, "that'll tell you Highgrove was probably designed by Jefferson?"

"*Possibly* designed by him. The floor plans of Highgrove and Poplar Forest are very similar, but we need stronger proof than that. Theoretically, someone who'd visited Poplar Forest could have then drawn a plan that copied Jefferson's ideas. Unlikely as that seems."

"From what I've read," Millie said, "people have claimed lots of houses were designed by him, but mostly their claims couldn't be proven."

Ron smiled lazily. "Yeah. It's been said that if he'd designed half the buildings attributed to him, he'd never have had time to be President." He patted his stomach. "This meal's terrific, Mrs. Ross. Good as Michelle's—my wife's—cooking, and that's saying something. Thanks for letting me share it."

"I appreciate the invite, too," Nolan said, grinning at each of the women in turn. "I couldn't face another meal that I'd cooked."

Cynthia was smiling a lot tonight, Millie noticed, especially at Luke. She seemed to hang on his every word, a fact not lost on Jill, who grew quieter as the meal progressed. Danny eyed his new male acquaintances warily. Millie realized how seldom he spent any time with men. He had no male role model in his life. She longed to reassure him everything would be okay. But she, too, felt a certain tension in the room. Was it only due to Jill's jealousy?

"I have a proposition to make to you ladies," Luke said halfway through dinner. "What about letting Ron and me eat here a couple of times a week? We'd pay well for the privilege."

"Yep," Ron seconded.

Cynthia's eyes lit up. "Sounds like a good idea to me."

"Me, too?" Nolan said, scratching his pug nose. "Great food, great-looking women, and a great old house—what's not to like here?"

"I won't ask to make it four," Whit said, "though it sounds like a good deal. I'm the main cook at home—days we don't eat out—and Harold wouldn't appreciate me bailing on him twice a week."

Millie glanced at Jill. She was staring at her plate, jaw clenched.

"Ple-e-ease allow us to eat with you, ladies," Luke begged. "You'd make three poor, sad men very happy."

"I won't lower myself to whine," Ron said with mock haughtiness. "But—" He crumpled, as in defeat. "Oh, heck, I will if it'll make a difference." He said the last words in an annoying whimper.

Millie laughed. "Abject surrender, that's all we're looking for."

Luke mentioned a sum each man could pay per week, considerably more than she had expected.

"That sounds generous, gentlemen," Alice conceded. "But we need to talk it over and get back to you."

"Guess that'll have to do." Luke grinned beseechingly at Jill. "Put in a good word for us, will you, sweetheart?"

She didn't look at him, her eyes fixed on the tablecloth near Ron's plate. She stared for a minute, then raised her eyes in challenge to his. A pink flush crept up Ron's neck. Nolan smiled at his own plate, as if secretly amused.

"It sounds great to me," Cynthia said again to Luke. "Of course I . . . can't speak for everyone." Her tone changed when she noticed Jill's frown.

"How about you, Danny?" Luke seemed to see him for the first time and to realize his opinion might count. "Like to have us guys here a coupla times a week, so you won't be so outnumbered?"

Danny gave a noncommittal shrug.

"Like baseball, Danny?" Whit said. "How about a game after supper?"

Danny smiled weakly. "Yeah. Okay."

"But first," Nolan said, "how about a tour of this fine example of Victorian architecture? I love old houses."

"Me, too," Ron seconded.

After they'd all finished eating, Alice showed Ron, Nolan, and Whit around. Luke, having seen the house before, joined the other women and Danny in clearing the table.

*Check out Luke Brooks, kitchen helper,* Sylva spoke in Millie's mind. *He must really want those meals.*

The tour and clean-up over, Whit and Luke pronounced themselves ready to play baseball. "How's about we choose up sides and everybody play?" Luke said. "Alice, you in?"

"No, thanks. My baseball-playing days are over."

"I'll pass, too," Ron said. "My knee's been giving me trouble lately."

"You just want to make time with Alice," Nolan said with a knowing grin.

"Couldn't hurt. She's a great cook."

Alice smiled indulgently, as she might've looked at her own son.

Luke polled the others. Jill reluctantly agreed to play, Cynthia with more enthusiasm. Millie declined.

"I'd make the sides uneven," she said. "Besides, you'll need people to cheer."

"Chicken." Nolan made clucking sounds and flapped his arms.

"I admit it," Millie said. "You've found me out."

"Okay if I take another look at your library?" Ron asked. "It's what I want in a house one day."

"Sure," Alice said. "We'll be out back."

On the large lawn behind the Victorian, illuminated by a pole light, Whit, with Danny's willing assistance, chose for bases a corner of the house, a bush, a tree root, and a flat rock. Then they drew straws for team assignments. Millie and Alice watched from chairs on the back porch as Jill, Danny, and Whit competed against Luke, Nolan, and Cynthia. After a while, Ron dropped into a chair beside Millie.

"Great library," he said, clasping his hands above his head. "Michelle's about ready for me to settle somewhere, so we can build our dream house and have a more normal life."

"Where's your wife living now?"

"Richmond. I go over there most weekends."

"You have kids?"

"Nope. Maybe later." He gazed into the distance. "Michelle's pretty focused on her career right now. She teaches psychology at a community college and is researching her doctoral dissertation."

Millie said she hoped to be doing a dissertation in history some day. "You plan to get a more settled job soon, so you can have that library?"

He shrugged. "Probably not soon enough for Michelle. If the company keeps giving me good projects like Highgrove—well, we'll see."

Jill had a strong pitching arm and seemed to play harder with each smile that passed between Luke and his pretty teammate. If he wasn't deliberately trying to make Jill jealous, Millie thought, he must be clueless about her feelings.

The older players—Whit, particularly—treated Danny as a valued competitor, and he was loosening up around them. All the men played ably, Nolan and Whit moving awkwardly but with surprising dexterity considering their burly physiques. Slenderer Luke played with grace and speed. But Cynthia was the one who surprised Millie most. Her petite body packed real power at the bat, and she threw with confidence and accuracy. When the game ended after the agreed-upon five innings, her team up by one, she garnered compliments from everyone but Jill, who wore a pasted-on smile.

"I grew up with five brothers," Cynthia said with a laugh, "so I learned to hold my own at sports. But everybody played well tonight. Danny, *jugaste muy bien.* You did great."

*"Muchas gracias, señorita."*

"Most valuable player on our team," Whit said. "Oh, but you were really good too, Jill."

"Thanks," she said evenly, wiping perspiration from her forehead.

They piled into chairs on the back porch, and Millie and Danny went to get soft drinks for everyone. Returning with a tray, Millie noticed Jill wore an angry frown. Had someone said something offensive to her? Or was she still miffed over the unexpected additions to dinner? Or was Luke's obvious interest in Cynthia the explanation? With Jill, Millie thought, it could be any one of those or a combination of all three.

Soon, Millie told Danny to go up and get ready for bed. After brief resistance, he did. The adults sipped their sodas and chatted about the game. When Nolan excused himself to go to the bathroom, Millie leaned across his empty chair to ask Whit if they could talk privately. With a shrug, he followed her to a corner of the porch.

"I wanted to say I appreciate your not bringing your bike," she said, when they were alone. "Danny knows you have one, but I'm glad you didn't force the issue tonight."

"No problem. I like your kid. And I may even feel the same way myself if I ever have one."

Millie returned to her seat, grateful he was being so cooperative, yet also wondering why. He didn't need to ingratiate himself to get in on a possible meal deal. Maybe he really had thought about what she'd said and put himself in her position.

The men soon left, and Millie helped Cynthia carry glasses to the kitchen, her mind on the events of the evening. Tension had sparked around Jill, her jealousy of Luke and Cynthia, her unfriendly looks at the other men, her long gaze at Ron's plate.

And why had that stare seemed to unnerve him? Ron impressed Millie as a man who took life in stride, kept his own counsel, didn't let much bother him. Paige's death had affected him, no doubt. But then, who wouldn't be troubled by a colleague's sudden, brutal death?

She couldn't help noticing, though, that she had just spent a whole evening in the company of the entire surviving crew at Highgrove and no one had mentioned Paige. Not once.

# Chapter Twelve

After seeing Danny to bed, Millie sat in the breakfast room with the other women, debating Luke's meals proposition. Alice and Millie said they'd go along with whatever the others wanted. Cynthia wanted to take the proposed deal, pleading financial need.

"This summer is turning out to be way more expensive than I'd planned," she said, her lustrous dark eyes pleading. "What the guys would pay us would help so much."

But Jill remained opposed. "We've barely started eating together as a group ourselves. Adding people would mean more tastes and schedules to consider. I just don't think it's a good idea."

"We'd need consensus on something like this," Alice said. "If even one of us is opposed, I don't think we should do it."

"Please, Jill," Cynthia said. "I'm having a hard time financially."

Jill's expression softened momentarily, then it hardened again. "Okay, here it is. I don't like the way you come on to Luke."

"Come on to him? I was trying to be nice to your friends. I thought you'd appreciate that."

"You didn't seem to try all that hard to be nice to the other guys."

Cynthia's mouth worked, as if she wanted to say something but was trying not to.

"What can I say, or do, to make you change your mind?" she finally said.

Jill looked at her a long moment. "I don't think you can. Luke's an attractive guy. I can understand your interest in him. But he's mine."

"If he really is, you shouldn't have to worry, should you?"

Jill said nothing more, but her expression said she was thinking plenty.

Millie thought about the interchange between the two housemates. On the one hand, she could understand Jill's jealousy. But she didn't seem angry at Luke, only Cynthia. And surely he was at least as much to blame?

The conference over, she retired to the tower library, curled up in an easy chair, and sat reading one of several books that the Poplar Forest librarian, on learning of her interest in Lewis and Clark, had checked out to her. This one was a compilation of entries from journals men on the trip, other than the two captains, had kept.

When she left the library later, she stopped by Alice's room and told her of her suspicions that Prissy's "Effy" was one Ephraim Hayes, a member of the Lewis and Clark Expedition, who was buried in Old City Cemetery.

"No way!" Alice said. "How did you find that out?"

Millie told her about coming across Ephraim Hayes's tombstone on her first day in Lynchburg and how she had seen his name again in one of the books on Lewis and Clark.

"I never would have put the two together," she said, "if you hadn't found those references to Effy in the diary." She asked Alice to keep the discovery to herself since she couldn't be positive her hunch was right. She told her she was hoping to be the first to write a paper on Ephraim Hayes, and asked Alice to let her know if anymore references to him turned up in the diaries.

"You know I will," Alice promised.

"I'm trying to discover what he did between arriving back in St. Louis and coming to this area, but so far, no luck."

They promised to keep each other informed, and Millie went cheerfully to bed.

On Thursday, Danny's enthusiasm for field camp continued unabated. The children had screened dirt actually taken from the dig and bagged any artifacts found. In his portion of soil, Danny had discovered a nail and a piece of brick.

Millie went to Highgrove in the afternoon, assured that Cynthia and Danny would both stay inside until Alice, then Millie, came home. Arriving at the old house, she again entered without knocking, her moccasins noiselessly crossing the foyer.

"Oh-h-h-h-h," Ron's wavery voice came from the parlor. Then Millie heard what sounded like a tray of glasses breaking. Something heavy thudded to the floor.

She dashed in and found Ron, hanging by both arms from the chandelier, his expression anxious, his legs swinging free. On the chandelier, crystal danced against crystal, creating ripples of music, reflecting light in all directions. The stepladder lay on the floor beneath and to one side of Ron.

"Millie!" he cried, when he spotted her. "Just in time!"

She righted the ladder under his foot, and he found a step. Carefully, he released the arm of the light fixture and slowly climbed down, his hand trembling as it gripped a ladder leg. Then he let go and jumped the last couple of feet.

"What happened, Ron?"

"I don't know." He dusted off his hands. "I was standing up there, examining that chandelier, when all at once the ladder went backwards out from under me."

"You must've leaned a little too far forward."

He frowned, obviously perturbed. "Maybe. But I get up on ladders all the time. Never fallen before."

Millie looked up at the light fixture, still swaying slightly.

"At least the hardware held you. Is this the original fixture, converted from candle-power to electricity?"

"It doesn't go that far back," he said more calmly, "but it's fairly old. Guess I wasn't in real danger if you hadn't come in—this ceiling's high, but I coulda dropped straight down from the chandelier. If I'd fallen off the ladder, though, in no telling what awkward position, I'd probably'a busted something, maybe been out of commission a while."

He scratched his head. "It's odd, though. I didn't feel over-balanced right before it happened, yet suddenly I had nothing holding me up. If I hadn't caught the chandelier arm, I'd have splayed out all over the floor."

She convinced him to sit down and relax while she brought him a drink. He agreed and went to the office. She was standing at the sink, running water into a glass of ice, when she remembered an oddity about the accident.

As she'd rushed to Ron's aid, nearing the center of the room, from the corner of one eye she had seen a movement near the baseboard. She replayed the scene in her head, recalling details.

Something had raced along the baseboard, away from her and Ron, towards the door into the dining room. A mouse? Had a rodent caused Ron's accident?

She took him his drink, relieved to see him sitting with his feet on the desk, reading a professional journal. She went back to the parlor, still recreating the accident in her mind. The movement she'd seen hadn't been that of a mouse scampering, she decided, more like a snake. A long snake. A long, straight snake.

But something was wrong about that. The thing hadn't moved with the coiling action of snakes.

Still puzzled, Millie headed out to the dig. Whit and Nolan

were standing by the sawhorses, and she briefly told them what had happened.

"Ron okay?" they asked in unison.

"Seems to be. Just shaken up a little. He said he hadn't felt he was losing his balance until suddenly the ladder fell out from under him."

"Strange," Nolan mused.

"Yeah," Whit agreed. "But you know what? My grandma falls sometimes for no reason. She says she has no warning, no dizziness or anything, just all of a sudden she's on the floor."

Millie looked at him doubtfully. "She's probably a lot older than Ron, though."

"Sure. But we don't know that her falls are age-related, since the doctors can't figure out what's causing them. I'm just saying maybe it's a similar thing."

They screened a while in silence. Then Millie commented on the fact she'd found Nolan working at the dig today, although Luke had said he mostly helped Ron inside.

Nolan and Whit looked at each other. The former muttered that he liked being outside in nice weather. Millie nodded. It wasn't important, anyway.

With another glance at Nolan, Whit offered a different explanation. "Ron's been kinda short-tempered today. I suggested Nolan stay outa his way by helping me, till Ron's more his old self."

"Something wrong? He not feeling well?"

Whit shrugged. "Delayed reaction to Paige's death, I think. The police interviewed all of us twice, soon afterwards, and everybody was in shock then. By the time you and Jill came out last week, her death—awful as it was—was starting to fade a little. But then the police interviewed each of us again today, and I guess Ron's having a hard time putting it behind him. He worked closer with her than the rest of us."

"It devastated everyone when we heard she'd been killed," Nolan said. "But Ron's reaction at first was . . . oh, never mind."

"What?" Whit said. "You trying to suggest something, Nolan?"

"No. No. Forget I said anything."

"You must've been getting at something."

Nolan grimaced. "It's dumb. I was just thinking that Ron seemed more cheerful right after her death than I'd have expected, given his closeness to her and all. 'Course, people don't all grieve the same."

Whit was silent a moment. "You're right, now I think of it. Almost as if he was relieved she was gone. No, can't be. We must be remembering wrong."

"You're right. Ron's a good guy."

They worked awhile longer, and then Whit said it was time for a break. They all trooped to the kitchen, where Nolan doled out soft drinks. He and Whit took theirs outside. Carrying hers, Millie wandered into the dining room, noticing details she'd paid little attention to on her other visits. She could imagine herself at table in the dining room, a skylight where the attic was now, or lounging in the current family room back when it had been an octagon. In many ways, Highgrove must have been an almost-twin of Poplar Forest before the alterations began.

Millie moved on to the parlor, silently in her soft footwear. Ron was standing by the damaged section of fireplace wall, shining his torch into the cavity. That seemed a little odd, Millie thought. She'd heard more than one crew member say he'd moved on from that section of wall.

"Find something interesting in there, Ron?"

He jumped as if pricked with a knife. "Oh, Millie!" His voice shook slightly. "I heard the guys leave and thought you'd gone with them." He glanced into the aperture. "No, of course not. Why would you think there'd be something in the wall?"

"Figure of speech. Okay, did you find anything interesting about it?"

Ron let out a breath. "What I mostly notice," he said in a steadier tone, "is its similarity to the triangular walls at Poplar Forest. You enjoying your work here as much as you do there?"

She smiled. "Both are interesting, in different ways. Highgrove's more intriguing, I guess, since less is known about it."

He grinned, at ease now. "That's the way I feel. Excuse me, I need to go write something down before I forget it." He clicked off the flashlight, set it on the chair a few feet away, and headed towards the office.

Curious about what had interested him, Millie switched on the torch and aimed it into the hole. By its strong light, she saw that the cavity went far back, into the deepest part of the triangle. At the rear, a scooped-out area marred an otherwise smooth strip of mortar between two rows of bricks. The concrete was thicker around the depression, Millie noted, than in other mortar strips in the wall.

Was that difference what interested Ron? What could account for the hollow? Had Ron perhaps scraped out a portion of mortar to be used in some test, part of his work as an architectural historian? She knew little about how such experts worked.

But if so, why hadn't he said as much? The crew all seemed willing, even glad, to explain what their work entailed. And why had Ron seemed so jumpy when she'd surprised him?

That evening after dinner, Millie was in her window seat reading when Jill stopped by, carrying a soft drink can and glowering. Millie laid down her book and asked her in. Jill sat in the desk chair, placing her soda on the desk.

"Something wrong, Jill? You look worried."

"Yeah . . . I couldn't decide whether to mention this or not—" she shook her head—"but I think I should tell somebody about it. Someone's been going through my bureau drawers."

"Really? How can you tell? I mean, my drawers get pretty disarranged. Unless things were obviously flung around, I'm not sure I'd know."

Jill sipped from the can. "I'm not a neat freak—not about everything—but I am picky about my socks and undies drawers." She gave Millie a speculative look. "Does Danny ever get into your things without permission?"

Millie sat up straighter. "No. You saying you suspect him?"

"Not really, I guess. But it's kind of worrisome, you know?"

"I've taught Danny to respect other people's property," Millie said, trying not to sound angry, "and he's really good about that."

Jill sighed and rubbed at the back of her neck. Millie saw that the rash on her throat and ears looked slightly less red than before.

"I didn't mean it as an accusation, Millie. I like your kid, you know that. But I thought he might've been looking for something to play with, and—well, forget it."

"Danny isn't a perfect child, but he's not a sneak. When do you think this intrusion happened?"

"I'm not sure. I'd noticed something was different this morning—my bras weren't arranged the way I usually keep them, dark colors together, light ones together. Today, a black one was mixed in with the whites and beiges. I don't know how long it might've been that way—I've dressed in a hurry several times lately—and just figured I'd absentmindedly put them in a different order than usual.

"But just now I was laying out clothes for tomorrow, so I wouldn't have to rush in the morning, and I saw my sports socks were stacked funny. I don't wear those much, mostly for tennis, but just thought I would tomorrow. That's when I got to thinking. It's worrying me."

"Anything else in your room bothered? What about your closet?"

"Some of my shoes might be in different positions on my closet floor than I left them. But I'm less sure about those." Jill drank more soda.

"But why would anyone want to go through your things? You don't have the British crown jewels stuffed into an old boot, do you?"

Jill choked on her drink, set down the can, and coughed several times.

"Besides," Millie went on, "I can't imagine that anyone in this house would do such a thing."

"Actually, I'm not so sure about Cynthia."

"Cynthia! Why her, for goodness' sake?"

"Can't you see how jealous she is of Luke and me? I wouldn't put it past her to go looking for keepsakes he gave me, to steal or destroy them."

"Oh, Jill, surely not."

"You have noticed she's attracted to Luke?"

Reluctantly, Millie nodded. "But liking him is a long way from prowling through your belongings in a mad hunt for gifts he gave you. Cynthia's an object of obsession, but I really doubt she's obsessed herself."

"Well, who else could've done it? Not you or Alice. If not Danny, or Cynthia, then who?"

Millie considered. "The guys ate here last night, remember. I'm not suggesting any of them would do such a thing either," she hurriedly added, "only that others besides the four of us might've had opportunity."

"That's true. But none of them— Oh, that sneaky little friend of Cynthia's—Toby? He was over here Tuesday. After dinner that night, I sat on the porch awhile, then came back in to get a magazine and go upstairs. Cynthia was sitting in the parlor alone. I found a magazine and, as I was about to leave the room, Toby came walking in from the direction of the kitchen. He must've gone to the john back there. But what if he also nipped upstairs?"

"Why in the world would Toby go through your things?"

"Probably a pervert who likes women's clothes."

"Come on, Jill. You must be mistaken."

"About him, possibly. But not about somebody being into my stuff."

"You didn't seem sure of that a few minutes ago."

"Well, now I am. Talking about the possibilities made me more certain."

"Whatever you say."

After Jill left, Millie sat in the window seat staring out at the darkened lawn below and wondering if her housemate had overreacted. If not—if someone really had searched her room—had it been one of the men who'd come to dinner? Thanking back on the evenings with Toby and the Highgrove crew, she realized that any one of them could have gone up to Jill's room, Ron when he'd supposedly been looking over the library, the others when they'd been to the restroom. But why would they, any of them? With the possible exception of Luke, they probably wouldn't know which room was Jill's.

Then she recalled the tours they'd all been given.

But why Jill's room, in particular? Or was she right, that the guilty party had gotten a thrill out of pawing through a woman's intimate apparel? Thinking about each of the men, she couldn't believe that of any.

If Jill was correct about the intrusion, and if none of the men had done it, then the intruder had to be one of the housemates. Not Danny. Not Alice. Millie would take an oath it wasn't either.

That left Cynthia. Unless Jill had concocted the story, to try to make Cynthia look bad.

# ★ Chapter Thirteen

On Friday, the last day of Danny's camp, the children got to identify and date artifacts, draw sketches of a few, even cross-mend a broken saucer.

"Wow!" Millie said when he told her and Alice. "You've gone way beyond what I've done so far."

His proud grin made her day.

Jill wasn't home for supper, having gone as planned to eat with Chas, then to see his stonecutting handiwork. Millie had heard her on the phone Thursday, telling Luke why she couldn't go to a movie with him tonight. From Jill's end of the conversation, it sounded as if she'd presented her plans as payback for his spending the previous Friday evening with male friends rather than her, also that she'd embellished her interest in Chas, trying to make Luke jealous. Her sullen expression afterwards suggested he hadn't responded as hoped.

Millie increasingly suspected Luke was much less invested in the relationship than Jill was.

*Not your problem, Kirchner.*

The remaining housemates celebrated the end of Danny's program by ordering pizza and watching a DVD of a new G-rated film. Unfortunately, it proved disappointing, thin of plot and full of improbable dialogue and familiar chase scenes. Danny, Alice, and Millie groaned at clichés and hurled derogatory comments at the screen. Cynthia mostly remained quiet, distracted.

After the movie, Alice played a board game with Danny while Millie and Cynthia did clean-up. As they worked, Millie commented that Cynthia seemed troubled and asked if anything new had happened about Ted. Her friend sighed.

"Not exactly." At Millie's quizzical look, she went on. "That is, I've had a few odd messages in my inbox that are probably from him. They're signed 'The Once and Future.' The sender's I.D. comes in as TOAF, which I don't recognize."

"Probably stands for 'The Once and Future.' What kind of messages?"

"Mostly stupid questions, like, 'Do you still eat honey on ice cream?"

"I take it you do like honey and ice cream together?"

"Sometimes, yeah."

"Would a lot of people know that about you?"

Cynthia considered. "People I've grown up with or known a long time, but probably no one in Lynchburg. I don't think I've eaten ice cream that way a single time since I've been here."

"Hmm. I see what you mean. That's not a detail someone could just guess about you. TOAF must be someone you know."

"Yeah. Ted."

When Jill got home, Danny, Alice, and Cynthia were all in their rooms. Millie chose to read in the parlor for a change and was seated there in an easy chair when Jill bounced through the front door and into the parlor. Jill flung her purse on a table and herself onto a couch, grinning at her housemate.

"How was your evening with Chas?" Millie asked. "Have fun?"

Jill's strident laugh rang out. "He's such a klutz—can hardly walk for stumbling over his own feet. It's kind of surprising, since you have to be pretty steady to cut precious stones."

"Hmm. Chas has a shuffling gait, but I hadn't noticed him being clumsy. Maybe he's nervous around you."

"He's smitten, all right." Jill self-consciously rubbed the rash on her ear. "But wow, he does make gorgeous jewelry."

"So he really is good. You going to see him again?"

Jill hesitated. "He's no competition for Luke, but he's so great at what he does— He showed me a rough piece of garnet and offered to make me a pendant. I know I shouldn't have, but I flirted outrageously with him. And of course I said I'd love to have a garnet pendant."

"Oh, Jill."

"I know. It was mean, since he has no chance with me. But Millie, you should see his work. He showed me a piece he's re-shaping for his mom, a diamond dinner ring she inherited from a cousin. He's really talented."

"Who knew Chas was such an artist? But please, Jill, don't string him along and then break his heart. He's a nice guy."

"I'll be as gentle as possible when I give him the push. That'll be after he finishes the pendant, naturally."

Millie frowned.

"I know, I know," Jill said. "You don't approve. Good thing this isn't your decision, then, isn't it?" She grinned again.

But this time, the smile was sheepish.

Saturday Millie did some errands, than drove around through historic sections of town Danny wouldn't want to see. In one such area, she passed a brick Methodist church, obviously quite old. She was tempted to stop and look around but decided she needed to get home. Maybe another time.

As she drove, she thought about Ephraim Hayes. He had left North Dakota—the area that was to become North Dakota—

during the spring of 1805 with Corporal Warfington's party and must have reached St. Louis some time the same year. Ephraim had died at Lynchburg in 1807, so there might be a period of several months, perhaps a year, unaccounted for. Had he stayed in St. Louis awhile, returned to Kentucky, or come on to Lynchburg right away? Or had he gone somewhere else entirely before fetching up here?

She seemed to have reached a roadblock in her Lynchburg research. Maybe she should try tracing Hayes in St. Louis . . .

Her cell phone rang. She pulled into a cross street, parked, and answered. It was Scott, saying he was taking a break from studying and hoped this was a convenient time for her to talk

"This is fine," she said, apprehensive that something might be amiss, since his usual time to call was evening, not afternoon. "Is something wrong?"

"No, just wanted to hear your voice. You seemed discouraged about your research when we talked last night. You thought of any other possible sources on Ephraim?"

She told him her plan to try the St. Louis angle. "If I could physically go there, that would be ideal," she said wistfully. "But with my volunteer work and the sightseeing I've promised Danny, I don't see how I can get there for a while."

"I wonder if either of the other researchers has found out anymore. Too bad the curator couldn't give you names."

"On the one hand, it seems there's no real hurry, since whatever's available about Hayes hasn't come out in all this time. But if *I* could find out what I already have—"

"So might others. Let me think about it. Maybe I can pull my head out of seventeenth-century England long enough to come up with an idea."

"Don't worry about it. Something will turn up, as Dickens's Mr. Micawber always said."

"Wish that something could be me," Scott replied, his voice

suddenly husky, "arriving on your doorstep about now. I miss you, Millie."

"I know. Me, too. But it's not long now until we see each other in Charlottesville."

"And I have a mountain of material to get through before then. Till Charlottesville, then."

Millie drove on home, saw that Danny was involved in a Monopoly game with Alice, and went to her room to start her St. Louis search. She found few court records for upper Louisiana, as the area had been called then, from the early 1800s. But she did learn a newspaper had been published there then, the *Missouri Gazette.* Unfortunately, no really early editions were available online.

Jill had gone out with Luke and friends, but the other women sat in the parlor after dinner watching a history special about John and Abigail Adams. The telephone rang. Alice glanced at a Caller ID on the table beside it.

"Anonymous," she told Cynthia. "Should I answer or let the machine catch it? Oh, shoot, I forgot to reset the darned thing."

"It could be Ted," Cynthia said. "Let it ring."

The phone rang fifteen times. Finally, Cynthia jumped up and snatched the receiver. Alice muted the television.

"Hullo." Cynthia's chilly tone turned to barely controlled fury. "Give it up, Ted! What we had is over! I don't want to see you again—ever!"

Millie heard a crackle at the other end. Cynthia's free hand balled into a fist.

"I don't care if you brought a hundred priceless diamonds with you," she said, her voice quaking. "Go back home, Ted. Please. You and I are finished. I don't hate you, and I hope you don't hate me, but we don't belong together. I'm sorry."

The noises from the phone this time sounded louder, more

insistent.

"You *will* forget me and move on, Ted. You'll find someone else. I'm not the one for you."

Cynthia listened to the voice at the other end several minutes, alternately shaking her head and grabbing her hair.

"Ted!" she finally said, desperation in her voice. "Ted, I'm hanging up now. Go back to New Mexico and have a good life. Don't call me anymore. I won't pick up if you do, no matter how many times the phone rings." With trembling fingers, she laid the receiver in its cradle, then dissolved into tears, hands over face.

Alice went to her and wrapped her in a motherly hug. Cynthia sobbed on the older woman's shoulder a few minutes. At last her snuffling slowed, then stopped. She stood, said a choked "Good night," and went upstairs.

The other women looked at each other, Millie with the uncomfortable feeling of having witnessed a too-intimate exchange.

"I suppose we should've left the room during that call," Alice said doubtfully. "To give Cynthia privacy."

"Probably. Then again, she might've been glad of our moral support."

"True."

They sat quietly a few moments. Then Alice turned up the TV sound. Millie stayed to watch the rest of the program but couldn't have passed a quiz about how it ended.

Sunday, Cynthia and Toby went to a mall, returning a few hours later with gifts for his mother. They had first bought a box of attractive stationery in buff and navy, colors he remembered she liked. Then while browsing through a bookstore he'd recalled hearing his mom mention a novel she'd heard about on a TV talk show and wanted to read. He proudly displayed the finds to Cynthia's housemates.

But Cynthia wasn't as lively as Millie would have expected,

given the shopping triumph. When Toby left, Millie drew her housemate aside and asked what was wrong.

"I saw Ted again, Millie," Cynthia replied woefully. "When we were coming out of the mall. He darted behind a pillar, but I'm almost positive it was him."

Millie hugged her. "Did Toby see him, too? If so, that could help if you decide to go to the police. Another witness, besides you, who saw him following you."

"No, he didn't. And I've been too ashamed to tell him about Ted."

"Cynthia, you haven't done anything to be ashamed of. Let your friends help you."

Cynthia shrugged, one fingernail tapping the chair arm.

Monday morning, Millie and Cynthia strolled together to the parking lot behind the Victorian. Cynthia planned to ride to Poplar Forest with Millie, to do further research in the library there on an area of knowledge about the house she felt needed strengthening, revealed by children's questions during camp.

"Glad to see you're looking more cheerful this morning," Millie remarked.

Cynthia smiled. "I think I overreacted yesterday. I'm probably seeing Ted everywhere these days, just because I'm watching for him. Anyone who looks the least bit like Ted . . . "

She gasped.

They had reached Millie's auto and were climbing into the front seat. At Cynthia's quick intake of breath, Millie followed her gaze to the old white Cavalier nearby. Its left front tire was flat.

"Oh, shoot," Cynthia said, crawling back out. "I did not need that today."

Millie got out, too, and watched her friend squat beside the automobile to examine the tire. "This one's practically new, too. I can't believe my awful luck."

"You must've picked up a nail."

"Yeah." Cynthia stood and dusted off her hands. "You'd better go ahead, Millie. I don't want to make you late. Since Alice is off today, I'll ask her to take me somewhere to get this fixed."

"Okay, then. Hope you don't have to buy a new tire."

"I may go ahead and get one anyway—this proves the folly of going without a spare."

"How long you been without?"

"Nearly a month. I had a flat while driving here, and that tire was in bad enough shape that I ditched it. But the others weren't bald, and my spare—the one that's flat now—was new, so I figured I'd get by a while. I won't start back home without buying a spare, though."

Cynthia frowned. "I wonder— No, I'm probably being paranoid."

"You're thinking someone did it on purpose? Ted, maybe? That'd be a juvenile thing to do. And it wouldn't earn him any brownie points with you."

"Ted can be petty when he's ticked off. Maybe he'd do this to show me I can't get away from him, so I may as well take him back. Ew-w, if he caused my flat, he was really close to our house last night. Or early this morning."

Millie squeezed Cynthia's arm in sympathy.

Over dinner that evening, Cynthia reported that she hadn't had to replace her tire after all. "It did have a nail in it, but they were able to repair the puncture."

Millie wondered why, in view of the good news, her housemate looked and sounded even more worried than she had earlier. At Jill's quizzical look, Cynthia told about her morning's discovery.

"So it was just a bit of bad luck?" Millie said.

Cynthia sighed. "I'm not so sure of that. Someone's been in

my car." She explained she had opened her glove box to enter the tire repair in a small notebook record of auto expenditures but had noticed the compartment's contents weren't as she'd left them. "I always stack things in a certain way in there, so I can quickly find what I need: notebook on top, then proof of insurance, then the car manual, then whatever maps I'm carrying. Things were all out of kilter."

"Are you sure Ted was the one who did it?" Millie asked.

"No, but who else would it have been?"

"Maybe somebody thought you had something valuable in there. You ever carry spare cash in there, for instance?"

"No, only the things I've mentioned." Cynthia made a fist and leaned her chin on it. "Ted could've messed up my glove compartment on purpose, so I'd know he'd been in there. Same thing with putting the nail in my tire, just showing me he's still around and still has power over me."

"You need to file a complaint, get that guy off the streets," Jill said.

Brusque as her words sounded, Jill's glance at Cynthia looked kind. Millie wondered about the two personas of Jill Greene, one part warm-hearted, the other cold, as if she feared to appear vulnerable. She seemed sometimes to be at war with herself.

Later that evening, Millie was in her room reading when Cynthia came by. When they were seated in chairs close to each other, Cynthia said with a catch in her voice that she hadn't told everything at dinner. Millie waited in apprehension.

"I didn't mention this earlier," Cynthia said. "but I saw Ted today. I know it was him this time. When I was getting out of Alice's car, after we'd been to get the tire fixed, I glanced up the street, and he was sitting in a maroon SUV, just watching me. The SUV must've been a rental—I didn't recognize it—but it was him, I'm sure."

"I'd say that definitely makes him a stalker. Did Alice see him too?"

"I—didn't think to point him out to her. Seeing him like that startled me so, I didn't know what to do, what to think."

Millie laid an arm across Cynthia's shoulders. "I think it's time you check into getting a protective order."

Cynthia put a tissue to her face and sobbed into it, long and hard.

"I hate the whole idea, Millie," she said at last, lowering the sodden ball of paper. "I might have to go to court, to testify, and it would all become public. Everybody'd know."

Millie clasped her tighter. "You may have to choose between privacy and protecting yourself, Cynthia. But people wouldn't think badly of you anyway, only of him."

Feeling Cynthia's shoulder quiver under her hand, Millie decided to suggest another possibility. "I guess you could hire your own bodyguard. Of course, that would be expensive."

Cynthia shook her head. "No way I could afford that. Staying in Roanoke, having to buy a tire, are wreaking havoc with my budget as it is."

Millie hesitated. Friends and relatives were known to be notoriously bad about repaying loans, but it was a risk she'd have to take. Cynthia's situation seemed desperate.

"I could lend you money to pay a bodyguard. For a while, at least." The words sounded odd coming from her own lips. Until a few months ago, she hadn't imagined she'd ever have "extra" money to lend anyone.

"I won't take a loan from you, Millie, even for a day," Cynthia said, with a grateful smile. "But I love you for offering." She sighed. "Okay, I guess I'll go tomorrow and see about getting a restraining order against Ted."

"Good. He might never try anything violent, but you never know. Hang in there, Cynthia. You're smart and strong, and you will get through this."

"Thanks, Millie. You're a great friend." Cynthia hugged her tight.

# ★ Chapter Fourteen

Tuesday, Millie drove Danny to his friend Kevin's house for a play date, while the other housemates rode to work in Alice's car. Kay Reynolds had phoned Millie yesterday with the invitation, saying her son missed Danny since camp had ended. The Reynoldses lived in a rambling brown bungalow with a shady front yard and toys on the porch. Millie went to the door with Danny and met his friend Kevin, a thin, talkative child, and Mrs. Reynolds, a willowy, energetic brunette a few years older than herself, whom Millie liked immediately. The boys greeted each other with fist bumps and headed for the backyard and Kevin's swing set.

Millie worked for a while at Poplar Forest, then drove out to Highgrove. This time she found Luke at the dig with Whit and Nolan. He said he'd finished his work in the basement.

"Do you archaeologists ever work weekends or evenings?" Millie asked.

"Been known to," he said with a grin. "You offering?"

She smiled. "No, my time's pretty full. Just wondering."

"We don't punch a clock, and I'll work late to finish something I'm in the middle of. But I like my off time to be really 'off.' Whit likes to come out here early mornings, before any of the rest of us get here."

Whit brought a bucket of soil over in time to hear the comment. "Yeah. Guess I'm just a morning guy. It's great to be out here then, before anybody else is around."

"So anyone can come onto the property any time, without getting permission?"

Luke smiled. "What are you suggesting, Millie? That someone is sneaking and screening? I doubt many people know this place is here, as off-the-beaten-track as it is."

"But there's no real security, right?"

"A police car patrols the area. As for the house itself, I guess somebody could get in by breaking a window, though no one ever has. Ron and I're the only ones with keys—besides Miss Unruh, of course—and she insists we guard them with our lives. She's picky, is Miss Julia."

So, Millie thought with satisfaction, that answered one of her questions. Miss Julia really had denied Whit a key. What was it that made her not trust him? Did she know something in his background that made her suspicious? But if that were the case, wouldn't she refuse to have him here at all?

Midway of the afternoon, they all took a break, refreshing themselves in the house. Then Whit went back out, saying he liked walking around the property in his free time. Luke and Ron sat in the project office, comparing thoughts on some aspect of their work, Nolan kibitzing nearby. Millie wandered to the parlor, which she had decided was her favorite room.

Ron's accident still troubled her—the fact he hadn't felt off balance before it happened, the fact he claimed to be careful, and the mysterious movement she'd seen just after he yelled. She'd turned it all over in her mind since that day and kept coming back to one question: Had someone caused his fall?

She didn't think that long, straight thing dashing along the baseboard had been a snake. She'd never seen or heard about any snakes in the house. Maybe it had been some sort of rod, pushed out from the dining room by someone, then withdrawn?

She replayed the incident from this perspective and decided it would fit the details she'd noticed.

But if she was correct, what had the perpetrator done with the rod? It would have had to be fairly long, not something one could conceal on one's person.

Millie walked through the house, looking for anything that might have been used but saw nothing suspicious in any of the rooms. Nothing improper or exceptional anywhere.

She went outside and walked around the dwelling, looking carefully for anything that might have been used to shove or grab a ladder leg. Nothing.

Millie was rounding the last corner of the house when she noticed the storage shed's door stood open. She strolled over and went inside, walking around the small space to peer closely at its orderly contents. A tier of shelves held trowels, dust pans, shaker screens, balls of twine, and other articles used in archaeological work. In corners of the room and against walls stood straight-edged shovels, ladders, and a three-legged apparatus like the total stations she'd seen surveyors use. She was standing beside the tier of shelves, ready to give up, when she noticed something wedged behind a tall ladder, a long rod with a hook at one end.

She nearly dropped her soft drink. This must be it! The thing that had been used to cause Ron's "accident," what she'd initially thought was a mouse or snake racing along the baseboard. This rod could have shot out from the dining room, grabbed the ladder leg, jerked it to throw Ron off, and darted back. She had witnessed its return trip from the corner of an eye.

And then the rod had been hidden in here, perhaps waiting for an opportune time to move it elsewhere.

But who had wielded it? Someone who had it in for Ron personally? Someone who wanted to delay work at Highgrove? Such a fall wouldn't likely have killed the architectural historian, but he might have broken a limb, which could have slowed the investigation. Part of it, at least.

The architectural-historian portion. And Paige had worked in that area too. Maybe her killer had expected her death to hamper the work more than it had. So Ron had been targeted next.

But who would want to impede the work, enough to kill one of the workers and try to injure another? Nolan might want to delay things, to annoy his aunt, but surely he wouldn't have killed for such a reason. Anyway, from what Millie had seen, he seemed to be genuinely contributing to the investigation, not trying to slow it.

The perpetrator must be someone regularly seen at Highgrove, however: Luke, Whit, or Nolan.

Or Julia Unruh herself. She apparently dropped in often, and even a frail elderly woman could wield a rod. But Millie couldn't see the straightforward, outspoken woman doing something so sneaky. She could almost as easily imagine Sylva doing such a thing.

Anyway, Miss Julia's approach to the job site hadn't been at all subtle the day Millie had met her. It was hard to believe she could arrive unnoticed. And why would she want to delay work she'd commissioned and was paying for?

Others did come here occasionally, of course, including Jill and Harold. But neither had been here the day of Ron's "accident."

Not that she had seen, that is.

Jill had shown no interest in coming back to Highgrove since the day she'd brought Millie out. Of course, Paige was no longer here, an object of Jill's jealousy.

Puzzling over the many unexplained questions, Millie stepped from the storage shed and gazed around her. The hilly, woodsy setting chosen for Highgrove enhanced the unusual house beautifully. As Millie eyed a rocky hillock a hundred yards or so from the excavation, a movement on it caught her eye.

Whit stood on a ledge partway up the outcropping, poking a hand into a crevice. What the—? Millie watched as he ran his hand along the cleft, apparently unaware anyone was watching.

He drew his hand from the opening, looked at his watch, and clambered down the rocky projection. Millie turned away and walked around the collection of vehicles, then headed back towards the dig as if she'd been to her car for something and was returning to work.

"Been for a walk?" she asked Whit when their paths converged.

His eyes flicked from her to a tree behind her and back. "Oh? Oh, yeah. Like I said earlier, I like to walk around when I'm on a break. Relieves my muscles after standing at the shaker screen. And you never know, I just might spot traces of an interesting feature from years ago, like a shed or a privy."

"Up on those rocks?"

His eyes widened. Then he looked down at his hands, clearly nonplused.

"Oh, not there, of course," he said, recovering. "I climbed up there to see the area better—sometimes you can spot things from above that aren't apparent on the ground—and then I noticed something down in that crevice. Thought it was a piece of metal, maybe even an old coin somebody'd dropped when the house was being built. Wishful thinking, of course. Turned out to be minerals in the rock glinting in the sun."

As they talked, Nolan stepped from behind the vehicles, holding his lidded ashtray, obviously having walked away from the dig to smoke. He opened his car and put the ashtray inside.

"Others enjoying this fine afternoon, I see," he said with a smile.

The men eyed each other speculatively, then returned to the dig and began to work.

Millie waited by the lawn chairs a minute, thinking and

wondering.

Had Whit been looking for something in particular in that crevice, not necessarily an old coin? And did Miss Julia suspect him of having a hidden agenda, the reason she didn't trust him with a key?

But for that matter, was Whit the only crew member who might be up to something at Highgrove? Millie had heard Ron say he was looking for a ring of some kind. Here, or elsewhere? And Nolan? Maybe he, too, suspected Whit of some nefarious activity to do with his beloved Highgrove? Had he really been walking around smoking, or had he been watching Whit from some vantage point? He hadn't been behind the autos the whole time, because she'd walked around them herself.

Millie had reached no conclusions by the time she took her leave.

She picked up Danny on the way home from Highgrove, finding him tired but happy. He and Kevin had played catch in the backyard, also Scrabble and a video game, had eaten peanut-butter-and-jelly sandwiches for lunch, and had helped Mrs. Reynolds weed a flower bed.

"Busy day," Millie commented.

"Yeah. Mom, can I have Kevin come over?"

Millie considered. With Ted around, bringing another child into the house might not be a good idea. "That'd be great, Danno, but I'll need to think about it. I do like Kevin, though, and his mom.

He whined for a few minutes, but soon he turned his attention to a Yorkie being walked along the sidewalk.

That evening over dinner, Cynthia reported the outcome of her visit to the police station that day. Alice had dropped her off as she went to the thrift shop to join Belinda for lunch, then picked her up.

"In Virginia," she said in a voice not quite steady, "a protective order can only be issued in domestic situations. My relationship with Ted wouldn't qualify. Apparently I could go before a magistrate and get a warrant because of the harassing phone calls, but that's only a class three misdemeanor and carries a maximum punishment of a $500 fine." Cynthia sighed. "Ted's family has scads of money, and his dad never says no to him. I can't imagine a fine like that would faze Ted."

"What about his watching you from the parked car?" Millie asked.

"The police said I did right to let them know about that, but for a stalking charge to stick, I'd have to be in fear for my 'life or well-being,' and it would require more than one act of stalking. And in Virginia an arrest has to actually be made before a stalking protective order can be issued.

"As for the flat and my glove compartment's being messed up, I have no proof he was involved. His fingerprints might be found on the glovebox, but that'd prove nothing. They could still be there from when we were seeing each other.

"The police told me to keep good records as to dates, times, and locations of occasions when Ted seems to be stalking me. If I later go before a magistrate and go under oath, that's when the record of stalking incidents would be important. But for now at least, no restraining order."

"Sorry, Cynthia," Millie said.

"I'm actually kind of relieved, I guess. I was feeling sad and a little guilty."

"Guilty? Why guilty?" Jill asked.

"Ted and I meant something to each other once. It doesn't seem right to involve the police."

"I bet every abused wife who's ever had to get a protective order against her husband has felt the same way," Alice said. "Loving somebody, but being afraid of him, would be awful."

"I can't say I love Ted now. His possessiveness has pretty much wiped that out. But I did once have high hopes for the relationship."

"So you're mourning its death. Understandable."

The next morning, Danny wasn't up yet when the four women sat down to breakfast together, for once without anyone's needing to rush off immediately. Alice dropped a bombshell.

"I think someone tried to get into the house last night."

Her face was shadowed with worry. Three pairs of anxious eyes fastened on her.

"Alice!" Cynthia gasped. "What happened?"

"It was quite a while after I'd gone to bed. I couldn't get to sleep. As I lay there awake, I heard a scratching noise from the direction of the dining room. I pulled on my robe and slippers and crept over there. Then I realized the sounds were coming from outside, by the dining-room windows."

"What did you do?" Millie asked.

"I didn't even think of calling the police, not then. I assumed it was an animal under that bush beside the windows, causing a branch to scrape against the house. I flipped on the dining-room light, and the sounds stopped. I didn't hear anything more the rest of the night, but I didn't sleep well, either. As I was finally drifting off, it occurred to me the noise had sounded too methodical for an animal, that maybe someone had been trying to pry a window open."

"You should tell the police today," Jill urged. "Sounds like Ted's getting more desperate."

"I'll bet it was Ted," Cynthia said. "Please tell the police, Alice. If I should ever have to apply for a restraining order, it could really help to have a prowler report on file about this address."

"You're right, of course," Alice said. "Middle-of-the-night thinking isn't apt to be my best. I'll go by the police station this afternoon."

At work that morning, Millie asked if it would be all right if she helped Harold at the dig. Chas and Alice both agreed, so Millie put on sunscreen and went on out. Harold welcomed the help, and they worked at a shaker screen in silence at first. Then he asked how things were going at Highgrove, obviously trying to make conversation. Although she assumed he'd have heard from Whit, she mentioned Ron's near-fall, watching his face carefully as she did so.

"Yeah, Whit told me about that," he said. "Funny, I had Ron pegged for a more careful guy."

"You think he was just careless, then?"

"Ladders can be tricky. You think everything's just fine, and then the thing moves on you."

If he had knowledge about any other cause, Millie noticed, he hid it well.

"Have you worked with Ron on any digs?"

"No, we've talked when I've gone over there, of course, and when he occasionally comes over here. You go to Highgrove often?"

"Not very. I seem to have more things to do than time to do them."

"I'd like to go again myself, but with the archaeology director out, I'm needed here."

"You probably get daily reports on Highgrove from Whit, don't you?"

He smiled slightly. "Those usually amount to 'same old, same old.' Anyway, it's interesting to get another perspective. What do you think of Highgrove?"

"It's a neat old place. I hope it gets restored." Millie noticed the glint of something small in the shaker screen and picked it out.

"I do, too. Whatcha got?" Harold took the shard of flat, clear glass from her and inspected it.

Since Alice had said to bag some materials separately, Millie asked the procedure for glass.

"This is window glass. We don't label each individual piece of it, just a small amount for recognition purposes. Put it in a separate bag, though. And never mix more than one type of glass together. Mirror glass, lamp glass, pieces of a drinking vessel—bag each separately."

Harold told Millie that the site being excavated had been identified as an old drain but that the archaeologists weren't certain yet what it had drained and from where. They had found a number of items apparently tossed in it as trash.

He took two bottles of water from an ice chest and offered Millie one. She gratefully accepted.

"You meet Miss Unruh yet?" Harold asked.

"I have. She visited one day when I was there. You know her?"

He hesitated. "Not exactly. She was there the day Whit first showed me around. She seems to be a lady of very definite opinions—about the way things should be done, about people, about everything."

"That was my impression, too. I hear she's picky about who can have a key to Highgrove."

He didn't speak at first, and Millie feared her blunt words had angered him. But she hadn't been able to think of a more diplomatic way to ask if Harold knew the redoubtable Miss Julia was suspicious of his friend Whit.

"You noticed that, did you?" he finally said evenly. "Yeah, I guess 'picky' is the word for Miss Unruh. But she's the boss."

Neither spoke for a minute. For something to say, Millie asked if Harold had known Whit long.

"Several years. I stayed with friends near St. Louis once when I was between jobs, and his grandparents lived next door. Whit came to see his grandparents one day, and he and I got to talking over the backyard fence. He was starting college at the time, trying to figure out what to do with his life, and I told him about archaeology as a career. He decided that was for him. When he finished his program and was ready to get his first job in the field, I helped him get on with my company. When the job came up at Highgrove, I recommended he be assigned there."

"So you're a kind of mentor for him." Millie stretched to ease her back. "Whit mentioned he and his granddad are huge Lewis and Clark buffs. Are you interested in them too?"

Harold twisted his compact body as if to ease a cramp. "Yeah, I am. Whit's grampa's neat. He has this great collection of L&C memorabilia that he picked up at flea markets and such."

"Sounds interesting. Like what?"

"He's especially proud of a couple of letters by members of the expedition, written after it was all over. They— Hmm . . ." He stopped, considered, then went on, seeming to choose his words more carefully. "They don't mention the trip itself, unfortunately, just day-to-day stuff like you write to friends and family. But he's had them authenticated as really being by the L&C explorers."

"I bet those are valuable letters."

"Probably. But they'd be worth a lot more if they contained new information about the expedition. Why didn't people in the past think of these things?"

Millie smiled. So Harold did have a sense of humor, after all.

She read late that evening. In one of her Lewis and Clark books, she came across a whole chapter on York, giving several possible endings to the slave's story. One had it that Clark gave York his freedom on their return in 1806, in gratitude for his help on the trip. However, letters and journals written by Clark and others refuted the story, speaking of York as being Clark's slave years afterwards.

Too bad, Millie thought. That story had the ending she'd have chosen, the appropriate one as she'd told Jill.

In another version, York had either escaped or been given his freedom sometime after 1806 and had traveled back to the Northwest. A trapper had reported seeing him living with Crow Indians, as a chief of that tribe, in what later became Wyoming. But the book's author noted that other evidence indicated the trapper had been mistaken, that the black Crow chief he'd seen was more likely one of two other African-American men known to have lived with the Crows about that time.

In yet another account, the one the author considered likeliest, Clark and York had had a falling out sometime after their return from the expedition. Exactly what had happened between master and slave was open to conjecture, but letters and journals suggested that York had grown insolent, resentful at being treated as a slave after enjoying so much freedom on the trail.

Why shouldn't he have felt that way? Millie thought.

Comments by Clark in letters he'd written indicated he'd tried to bring York to heel with various punishments over ensuing years, one day giving him a "Severe trouncing," another time hiring him out to a harsh master in the hope that cruel treatment would quench the fires of rebellion. No less a figure than Washington Irving, after visiting Clark in 1832, reported that Clark said he had set York free, giving him a wagon and team of horses with which to start a drayage business in Tennessee. York had contracted cholera and died in that state, Clark told Irving.

An ignoble end for a valiant man, Millie thought.

She should show this to Alice. The two women had discussed York once or twice as Millie read about the epic journey, and Alice would be interested in the three versions of his end. Although doubtful her friend would still be awake, Millie put on a robe and slippers and carried the history downstairs.

Sure enough, she saw no light around the edges of Alice's

bedroom door. Disappointed though not surprised, Millie went to the kitchen, made a cup of herbal tea, and carried it to the back porch. She sat there in the dark, looking out over the gloomy backyard. The night was very still, no wind, no traffic noise. An anemic moon cast shadows across the lawn from the garage and a large bush.

Something stirred beside the shrubbery. A limb? No, not that—no breeze was blowing. Millie blinked twice, strained to focus her eyes. Whatever it was moved again. Something a shade darker than the shrub. Too high off the ground for a cat, or even a big dog.

A human? Oh, God, Millie thought. Is this Alice's prowler, returning for another try? Is Ted planning to break in, to get to Cynthia?

She blinked again, then riveted her eyes on the bush. She thought she detected movement there, but in the dimness, she couldn't tell what had caused it.

Should she phone the police?

But she wasn't even sure any live creature was there, much less a human bent on meanness. If she called, and the police found no trace of a would-be intruder, they'd conclude she was a hysterical female with a vivid imagination.

So what? Better a little embarrassment than harm to her housemates, herself, or, worst of all, her son.

But if she called in a false alarm, and then a real intruder broke in later, she wouldn't be a credible witness against him.

Debating with herself, Millie continued to stare at the shrubbery and surrounding murkiness until her eyes smarted from the effort. If anyone had been there before, she couldn't tell it now. If someone had, perhaps he had seen her on the porch and fled? A few feet to her left, a high window in the kitchen overlooked the porch, and she had left the overhead fixture on after making tea. A shade covered the window, but light spilled around the edges.

Enough to reveal her presence to an observer?

Maybe she had let her imagination run away with her, Millie told herself. She squeezed her eyes shut, then opened them wide, trying again to penetrate the darkness. Murky and mysterious it was, but serene.

She finally stood and entered the house, locked the back door, checked that all other doors and windows were secure, turned out the kitchen light, and went upstairs to bed.

She tossed and turned awhile, her dreams troubled by a vague, unnamed fear.

At breakfast, while Danny was still abed, Millie told the other women about the possible return of Alice's prowler last night. Cynthia urged her to tell the police, but the others agreed with Millie that she had no real evidence anyone had been there, much less anyone bent on harm.

That evening after dinner, Millie and Jill sat in the parlor watching a television program. When the phone rang, Jill jumped up to answer. Signaling to Millie not to bother turning down the TV volume, she carried the phone to the other end of the room. At first Millie barely heard her low-pitched voice, but it became gradually louder. When she hung up, she see-sawed her hands above her head in glee.

"That was Chas," she said.

Seeing she was eager to talk about the call, Millie lowered the sound.

"He's been working on my pendant," Jill said with a grin. "He was describing the cut to me. It's going to be so gorgeous."

Millie smiled. "He finished it yet?"

"He's almost through shaping the stone. Then he has to set it and add a chain."

"So you'll be getting it before long?"

"Not as soon as I'd like. His mom's birthday's coming up, and he wants to finish her ring first. Oh, Millie, I can't wait!"

She frowned. "Too bad I can't combine Chas's qualities with Luke's, to get an ideal man."

*The problem with searching for a perfect mate is, would a perfect person want any one of us?*

# ★ Chapter Fifteen

Late Friday morning, Millie maneuvered her car into a parking space near the Visitors Center in Williamsburg. Danny had chosen to go to a roller-skating party he'd been invited to at a local rink. Learning from Kevin's mother that she and other parents would supervise, Millie had agreed he could go.

"We could see Williamsburg later, just us two," she had told Danny as he was trying to decide between the outings. "That might actually work better. Jill and I could do sightseeing this time that would bore you, and I could also scope out things you'd like, for when you and I go back."

Thus assured, he had cheerfully agreed.

Millie smiled at Jill now as they climbed out of the car. "The Historic Area's a bit of a hike, but a walk sounds good to me. Unless you'd prefer catching the shuttle at the Visitors Center?"

Jill stretched her arms wide, her shiny pink purse dangling from one hand, and yawned. "Unless it's miles away, walking's fine. But let's not wait too long for lunch."

They looked the part of tourists, Millie thought, in their wide-brimmed hats, sunglasses, and running shoes. Each carried bottled water, Millie in her commodious beige shoulder bag, Jill in a pink water-bottle caddy hooked to her belt. They followed signs to the

Visitors Center, a modern concrete-and-glass structure with a concrete plaza and benches in front. There, they collected maps and literature and watched a film about the restoration of Williamsburg, sponsored by John D. Rockefeller, Jr. Called Middle Plantation at one time, Williamsburg was now effectively two towns: the 301-acre Historic Area of restored or reconstructed Colonial buildings, and the modern small city that had grown up around it.

They walked across a pedestrian bridge to the Historic Area and opted to eat sandwiches outside in the fenced yard of Chowning's Tavern. Choosing a table near a grape arbor, they looked through literature while eating. Millie thirstily downed half her glass of iced tea. Jill expressed no preferences about places to see first, so Millie chose the Governor's Palace, Bruton Parish Church, and the George Wythe House.

Glancing up, she saw a burly young man with a wide nose and unusually large ears, wearing a flat green cap, sitting at a nearby table watching them. As her gaze reached him, he dropped his eyes. She didn't recognize him, but something seemed familiar about his stocky frame and relaxed way of sitting.

Your vivid imagination, Millie, she told herself.

The women finished eating, then sauntered along Duke of Gloucester Street, the principal thoroughfare of Colonial Williamsburg, while Millie read aloud about the 1699 creation of the town and street by Virginia's General Assembly: Both had been named after the same man, who was at one time the Duke of Gloucester, then became William III, King of England.

"'The august avenue known as Duke of Gloucester Street,'" Millie read, "'began as a narrow Indian trace that rose to the dignity of a horse path in the seventeenth century....'

"'Often referred to as the "main street" or the "great street" in the eighteenth-century, Duke of Gloucester Street was to be ninety-nine feet wide and run nearly a mile straight from the

College of William and Mary on the west to the Capitol on the east.' And get this, Jill: It wasn't supposed to ever be changed, 'either in ye Course or Dimensions thereof.'"

"Imagine putting a restriction like that on a street today," Jill said, eyebrow raised. "No changes in length or width, ever? Modern city fathers'd stroke out."

"And listen to this." Millie read a passage about potholes in the early days of Williamsburg: "'Carriages and horses making their way downtown—the Capitol end of the city—sank from view on Duke of Gloucester Street and rose again as they climbed in and out of gullies and ravines.'" She chuckled. "That's what I call a pothole!"

Jill grinned. "So they're not a twentieth-century invention, after all."

Millie gazed around at the restored and reproduction Colonial-era buildings lining the street, which President Franklin D. Roosevelt had called "the most historic avenue in all America." The town had been lovingly restored, building by building, beginning with Bruton Parish Church in 1905 and continuing in the 1920s as Rockefeller realized a dream of reclaiming the deteriorating historic town for future generations.

At street's end, a large emerald lawn called the Palace Green led visitors' eyes to a magnificent three-story brick Georgian structure, the Governor's Palace. Millie and Jill strode through the gate, guarded by a stone unicorn and a stone lion. A cheery young matron, wearing mobcap, apron, and full-skirted eighteenth-century dress, led them and others through the three-story building, telling facts about life here in the palace's heyday. For instance, laundry had been done once a month, she said, the clothing boiled in lye soap. The original house dated from 1722 and had been occupied by seven Royal Governors and a few Virginia governors, including Patrick Henry and Thomas Jefferson.

"It was Jefferson who moved the state capitol from Williamsburg to Richmond," the guide said. "The Revolutionary War was going on, and he thought a more inland location would be safer from British attacks."

Downstairs, the group saw a banqueting hall, some of the earliest Venetian blinds in the country, and an entrance hallway where muskets and the English sovereign's coat of arms were displayed. Their guide told them the hall had been one of several receiving areas.

"The butler would screen and rank visitors to determine where they should wait and whom they should see," she explained. "Those of lower status didn't make it upstairs, sometimes not even inside the building, while higher-status visitors were shown to the governor's upper middle room."

"Guess I'd have been out in the alley somewhere," Millie muttered to Jill.

"Me, too," she giggled.

Upstairs, the guide pointed out walls of black walnut, the wood of choice for paneling in the early eighteenth century because it was plentiful in Virginia. The house had been built over a period of sixteen years, contained about ten thousand square feet of space, including a cellar with eleven wine bins, and had been staffed by twenty-five slaves and other servants. Royal governors had often entertained townspeople with dinners and galas, she said, but their hospitality was sometimes declined because of events. After Royal Governor Francis Fauquier dissolved the House of Burgesses during the Stamp Act crisis in 1765, fewer than a dozen townspeople attended the king's birthday celebration here.

As the two women exited the building, Millie looked down the sweep of Palace Green, which teemed with tourists crossing from one historic building to another. A few lounged on the grass, including—

The same man she had seen in Chowning's yard, the one with

the green cap. He glanced her way, then looked back at the map he'd been studying.

The women meandered along the green to the handsome two-story brick Wythe House. Inside, they saw a dwelling that, although comfortable by late-eighteenth and early-nineteenth-century standards, looked especially modest just after seeing the elegant palace. Wythe, a guide explained, had been an unpretentious man in spite of being a prominent lawyer, scholar, and legislator, the first law professor in America, a member of the Continental Congress, and a signer of the Declaration of Independence. He had also been Thomas Jefferson's teacher, law partner, and friend.

Millie wondered why Wythe wasn't better known outside his home state of Virginia. She hadn't heard of him before studying Jefferson for her history paper. Perhaps Wythe's modesty had put him at a disadvantage among the many larger-than-life figures populating that period of history?

Wythe had been a "quiet abolitionist," the guide went on, freeing his own slaves and providing for their support until they could earn their own living.

Too bad Wythe's protégé Jefferson hadn't managed to emulate him there, Millie thought.

But to be fair, their situations had been different. Both had been sons of planters, but Wythe had never become a part of the Virginia planting aristocracy as had Jefferson. The senior Wythe had died soon after George's birth, so the junior one had never known his father, much less felt duty-bound to imitate him. But Thomas had known and admired Peter Jefferson, who had died when Thomas was fourteen, an impressionable age. Little wonder the boy had followed his father into managing the plantations he'd inherited from him.

Fourteen years old, only five years older than Danny is now, Millie thought.

And two years older than she had been when her mother had committed suicide. Although her own situation differed from Jefferson's in many ways, both had seen their young worlds abruptly ripped apart by the death of a beloved parent. The realization made her feel kinship to the nation's third President.

"Hey, space cadet," Jill said in an undertone, touching Millie's shoulder. "Going to continue the tour with us or drop out?"

Glancing past Jill, Millie saw that the guide and other visitors were leaving the room. "Sorry, I was wool-gathering," she muttered as they hurried to catch up.

Upstairs, the guide pointed out an optical illusion: The second-story windows, though shorter and narrower than the first-floor ones, contained the same number of window panes, giving the impression of a larger structure. Not unlike the surprises Jefferson had enjoyed putting in houses, Millie thought..

When the formal tour ended, the women viewed fine gardens and outbuildings on the Wythe grounds, then walked next door to Bruton Parish Church, which Millie's literature said had been the first cruciform-shaped church in Virginia. A small bell-tower entry led to a serene-looking sanctuary, where several other tourists strolled about. In the sanctuary, neat box pews on both sides faced a raised pulpit. Opposite the chancel, a canopied chair sat throne-like inside a railing. A guide in the sanctuary told them the church had been attended by many famous Revolutionary leaders, including Thomas Jefferson, George Washington, Patrick Henry, George Wythe, Richard Henry Lee, and another man Millie didn't recall hearing about in history classes, George Mason.

Another important figure of the Revolution she hadn't known about, Millie thought. Would she spend a lifetime trying to learn about the heroes of her own country?

In one of the enclosed pews, all by himself, sat the young man with the large nose and ears. He had respectfully removed his green cap. Though he paid Millie and Jill no notice this time, seeing him in so many places at the same time as themselves struck Millie as unusual, to say the least.

Over the years, the guide was explaining, Jefferson would have sat in various places in the church, depending on his station in life. While at the College of William and Mary, he'd have been in the balcony at the back, the place designated for students. Later, when studying law with Wythe, he would have sat on the left side—the men's side—probably near the rear. The church stopped having men's and women's sides about the time of the Revolution, the guide noted. When a member of the House of Burgesses, Jefferson would have sat in a pew near the front of the church. As Virginia's governor, he had occupied the place of honor, the canopied Governor's Chair. Most parishioners had sat in the walled pews, which gave both privacy and protection from drafts.

Besides having Revolutionary leaders among its congregants, the guide said, the church had played another role in American history. As passions flamed prior to the war, special services had been held in reaction to the passage of the Stamp Act and to the closing of the port of Boston by the British. Millie briefly imagined herself attending one of those meetings, hearing impassioned words that, however much she and most other colonists dreaded war, helped make it inevitable.

"I'm about done in," Jill complained as they exited the church. "Where can we get a cold drink and sit down?"

Millie consulted the map's listing of dining establishments. "Merchants Square isn't far, and there are several restaurants there. Oh, there's a café at the college bookstore, too. How's that sound? You can rest while I hunt books for Danny."

"Sold. Can't wait to get off my feet."

They entered the College of William and Mary Bookstore, a long, deep, welcoming space in what, according to Millie's online research preceding this Williamsburg trip, had once been a department store. Millie briefly envied William and Mary students their opportunity to study in such a historic setting, at the second oldest college in the nation next to Harvard. But she couldn't pull up stakes and move to Virginia, not with her ties to Texas.

The bookstore held the usual sweatshirts, textbooks, and other collegiate paraphernalia, but shelves and alcoves also displayed lots of popular fiction, juvenile books, and, to Millie's delight, many works on American history and its personages. Glancing up, she spotted the café, a second-floor gallery open to viewing from downstairs. Diners sat at small tables, chatting and looking down on shoppers. Millie and Jill climbed steps near the front of the store, bought ice cream and soft drinks at the café counter, and collapsed at a table. Jill set her purse on a chair, stretched her arms over her head, and sighed with relief.

Quickly downing her food, Millie left Jill resting her feet and went downstairs to browse. She found books for Danny on the Virginia Colony and on York's adventure to the Northwest. For herself, she chose books on Williamsburg and Jefferson.

She was carrying her finds to the checkout counter when Jill came hurrying towards her, eyes wide and anxious.

"Millie! You seen my purse? I thought I had it with me in the café, but when I started to leave I couldn't find it."

Reflexively, Millie glanced at her own shoulder bag. "No. But you did have it up there. You paid for your food before we sat down, remember?"

"Yeah. And I laid the purse on a chair by our table while I was eating. But it's not there now. Oh, Millie, what'll I do?"

"Did you search all around the restaurant?"

"Sure. But come help me look again before I alert the cops. I don't think I could possibly have missed that bag—shiny pink plastic?—but just in case—"

Millie paid with a credit card, then followed Jill back up the stairs. They methodically checked around the table where they had sat. A middle-aged woman seated near the balcony railing called to Millie.

"Did you lose something, dear?"

Millie explained Jill's predicament. The woman asked what the purse looked like, and Jill described it. Their friendly inquisitor nodded sagely.

"I thought you must be the owner. When I was getting my food just now, I saw your bag over there by that cooler. 'Someone's laid that down while they looked at sandwiches,' I said to myself, 'but they'll be back.' I didn't like to leave it there, where anybody could get it, so I turned it in to the counter girl."

Jill clasped the woman's hand. "Oh, thank you! Thank you so much! Can I give you a reward?"

"Of course not, dear. I couldn't take anything for that small service. I hope someone would do as much for me if I needed it."

Jill reclaimed her purse and sat at a table looking through it.

"Nothing's missing, thank God! But how strange, that somebody would pick up my bag and move it like that."

"Probably another shopper thought it was hers, then realized it wasn't," Millie soothed. But she didn't believe her own words. Jill's glossy pink bag was distinctive, unlikely to be mistaken for anyone else's. Still, nothing had been taken. "I wonder how the person managed to pick it up, though, without your noticing."

Jill considered. "I did close my eyes for a few minutes, relaxing. It must've happened then."

Millie glanced around at the others in the café. The helpful woman had left. At one table, three teenagers huddled in low-voiced conversation. At another, two adults and two youngsters chattered noisily. A young man in a green cap stood looking at merchandise on a rack near the back wall. No one seemed to be paying any attention to her and Jill.

Green cap.

*The same man you saw three times before, at Chowning's, at the Governor's Palace, and in Bruton's Church.*

So another tourist is going all the same places we are, Millie thought. Nothing so odd about that. Plenty of visitors must make similar choices.

But coupled with the purse mystery, the multiple appearances began to seem more than coincidence.

Jill sat thoughtfully a few minutes, then seemed to reach a decision. Leaning closer, she said in an undertone, "Millie, would you keep something for me for a while—just in case." With her right hand, she fished in the pocket of her bottle caddy and brought out something small, hiding it under her left hand. Right fist closed, she held it above Millie's hand as it lay palm up on the table. "I trust you, Millie, and I think this'll be safer with you."

What in the world? Millie wondered as Jill opened her fist barely enough to release whatever she held, then folded Millie's fingers around it. Millie felt something flexible and smooth, like a plastic sleeve. And something small and hard inside it.

"Why all the cloak-and-dagger?" she whispered. "What'd you give me?"

Jill glanced furtively around. Apparently satisfied no one was listening, she murmured, "My diamond earrings. I can't seem to get this darned rash cleared up, so I haven't been wearing 'em lately. Whoever was in my room didn't find them, but just in case, I've been keeping them with me. Now, with losing my purse, would you keep them, Millie? Just till I can wear them all the time again. Any would-be thief won't be expecting you to have them."

Millie looked around, then whispered, "But I don't see anyone we know anywhere around here. Who'd know you're carrying valuable earrings with you?"

Jill sighed. "Maybe I'm being paranoid, but—will you keep them for me, Millie? Please?"

"Jill, are you sure? What if I should lose them?"

"You won't. You're too careful and level-headed. And you're the only one I can trust to do this. Luke doesn't even get how important jewelry is to me." Her voice dropped even more, and Millie had to strain to hear. "Just in case something should happen to me, I want my younger sister Rachel to have my earrings."

"What're you talking about?" Millie's voice rose in consternation. At a gesture from Jill, she lowered it again. "Why should anything happen to you?"

"Nothing will. But just in case . . .

"Millie, I'll give you Rachel's contact information tonight when we get home. But it's important you know I'd want her to have anything I have of any value."

"What's going on, Jill? You're scaring me."

"I can't explain everything now. Just remember all my possessions must go to Rachel, if . . . you know."

"No, Jill, I don't know. You make it sound as if the mob's after you. What's up?"

"Maybe I'll decide I can tell you more later, Millie. But I need to think some things through first." Jill raised up and looked carefully around, then bent towards Millie again. "I guess I'd better tell you this much, though. I have one other thing that's especially valuable, much more even than my earrings."

"More valuable? Jill . . ."

"It's safer where it is, for now, so I won't give it to you to keep. But I will let you know its location—later—so you can get it and give it to Rachel, just in case . . ."

"Would you stop saying 'just in case' and tell me what this is about?"

"Please, just help Rachel find it, if anything should happen to me."

"Why don't you tell *her* its location? So she could get it herself? And why don't you put your earrings in the same safe place?"

Jill smiled wryly. "It's complicated. That place isn't always easy to get into. Besides, Rachel's scatter-brained. She'd mess up somehow. But you're so smart and sensible, Millie—" She took a deep breath. "Don't tell Luke about any of this. He wouldn't understand. Will you do this for me?"

"I—don't know, Jill. Would I be doing anything illegal?"

"No! Of course not!" Jill's eyes didn't quite meet Millie's. "Please. There's no 'mob' after me, as you put it. What I have hidden is just something I want to preserve and hand over to my sister."

"O . . . kay, I guess. But if I find out there's anything illegal about this—"

"You won't. Thanks, Millie. I hope I'll be able to get my earrings back soon and wear them again."

Millie opened her big shoulder bag, slipped her closed hand inside, and dropped its contents into a side pocket. Jill smiled, then frowned.

"You won't lose *your* purse, I hope."

Millie hugged the bag close to her body and whispered, "I'll take good care of your earrings, but I hope I won't be keeping them long."

As they rose and left the café and the bookstore, Millie said with forced heartiness, "Have we done enough sightseeing for today?"

"I have."

They sauntered towards the parking lot, chatting about what they'd seen in Williamsburg, although half Millie's mind was replaying what had just happened, and wondering what Jill's mysterious hidden item was.

"When you drive over here with Danny," Jill said, in an obvious effort at light conversation, "you should rent him a costume. He'd enjoy dressing up."

"True. Maybe I'll even get one for myself. Since Williamsburg's a 'pretend town'—a reproduction of the original, however authentically restored it is—it seems fitting that Danny and I pretend we're original residents. He'll want to take a wagon ride, I'm guessing, and see some of the reenactors: Jefferson, Washington, Patrick Henry. Oh, and we'll have to learn about Colonial gardens and Williamsburg's pirate connections.

"But I'm glad to've had an 'adult' look at the town first. Glad we did this, Jill."

"I've enjoyed it. Maybe I'll get Luke to bring me back, if I can tear him away from Highgrove."

They reached the parking lot. As she opened the door of the Prius, Millie glanced behind and saw the same young man she'd noticed several times before. He walked past their row without glancing her way, but something in his demeanor suggested he wasn't unaware of her. The thought spooked her. She didn't know him—surely she'd have remembered those prominent ears and nose—but something about him seemed familiar.

And why did he keep turning up in exactly the same places she and Jill did? Colonial Williamsburg wasn't huge but certainly big enough that they shouldn't keep stumbling over each other.

Unless someone had planned it that way?

# ✯ Chapter Sixteen

That evening, the five housemates sat on the side terrace, enjoying the cool of the evening, after a simple supper. Danny was tired after his roller-skating party but had clearly enjoyed it. Jill was tight-lipped over Luke's having decided to go solo hiking. The doorbell sounded, and Alice walked around the house to see who was there. Millie heard voices on the porch, then the front door opening and closing.

A few minutes later, Alice came out the kitchen door, carrying saucers, forks, napkins, and a large knife. Toby followed, looking sheepish and holding a long foil-covered pan. Danny laid down his book and rejoined the others.

"Toby's mom sent us something nice," Alice explained. She placed the dishes and utensils on the table, took the pan from Toby, and removed the foil. "Mm, doesn't this look good."

"It's a fresh apple cake she makes a lot," Toby said apologetically. "It is really good, though, especially when it's just made, like now."

He winked at Danny as he spoke, but Millie saw her son had eyes only for the loaf pan.

"It's very thoughtful of your mom to bake us a cake," Cynthia said with a wide smile.

"Least she could do, after you fed me a meal, all impromptu."

"No problem," Millie said. "We enjoyed having you."

Some of us did, she mentally amended. Jill hadn't been thrilled. And now she was scowling at their visitor.

"Thanks." Toby folded his arms, looking awkward.

"Have a seat, Toby, and join us in some cake," Cynthia said. She served Danny a piece, saying with affection, *"Toma, m'ijo.* Have some, sweetie."

*"Muchísimas gracias, señorita,"* he responded, attacking his cake.

Toby perched on a chair near Cynthia's. "I'll sit for a minute, but no cake, thanks."

As Alice cut and dished out servings, Millie and Cynthia handed them out.

"This particular recipe," Toby went on as if feeling further explanation was needed, "is made from a starter—like sourdough, Mom says—and you're supposed to make it regularly, two cakes each time, and give one away. She calls it a friendship cake. You give one to a friend, along with the recipe and some of the starter. Alice already put that in your fridge. Not the recipe, just the starter. So then the friend gets saddled with—I mean, gets to make—this delicious cake. Regularly. So regularly."

"It's a nice idea," Cynthia said, resuming her seat.

"Yeah. But frankly, I'm sick of apple cake. It's good, but we have it way too often. And now Mom's running out of people to give the second cake to." He watched Cynthia as she took a bite and closed her eyes, savoring it. "It really is good. I know I'm not selling it well . . ."

"It's wonderful, Toby," Cynthia said. "Please thank your mom for us."

Others echoed her.

"Sure you won't have some with us, Toby?" Alice asked.

"No, thanks. There's some waiting for me at home. But I'll pass your compliments on to Mom. Of course I don't report negative comments to her, so feel free to say what you really think."

Millie glanced at Jill, half expecting her to make a smart-aleck remark. But she apparently liked the cake, judging from the way she was scraping her saucer.

When all had finished eating, Toby insisted the women keep their seats while he did dishes.

"Oh, I'll take care of that," Cynthia offered, getting to her feet. "I'll wash your mom's pan and put the other things in the dishwasher."

"You will not," Toby said indignantly, gently pushing her back down. "My mom brought me up right. Let me do this, please. Just relax, every single one of you."

"At least let me show you where the detergent is," Alice said, starting to rise.

Toby raised a hand, palm outward, signifying "halt!"

"Keep your seat! The Great Tobolski can divine even that mysterious location." Toby closed his eyes and put a hand to his forehead. "I have it—your detergent is . . . under the kitchen sink." He made a sweeping bow. "Seriously, Danny can help me carry things to the kitchen, but then even he has to come back and sit down."

"Guess you win," Cynthia said with a pleased grin. "Thanks, Toby."

He and Danny carried dishes and utensils into the house; then Danny returned and took up his book. Millie and Jill told more about their day of sightseeing, and Cynthia talked of her work that day helping prepare the Hands-On History Center to open to the public. She would be working there tomorrow.

Eyes glued to his book, Danny rose and sauntered into the house. His toe caught the edge of the door facing, and he glanced up to check his route ahead. He left the kitchen door ajar, and soon Millie heard the toilet by the laundry room flush. Then her bookaholic son stumbled out, chuckling at something he read.

A few minutes later, Toby came out carrying the clean cake pan.

"I'll be going now. Thanks, everyone, for your compliments on my mom's baking. They'll make her happy."

"We thank you, Toby," Alice said, "for the cake and the clean-up. Please tell your mother we very much appreciate her thoughtfulness."

Others chorused similar sentiments, and Toby left.

Millie read for a time in the library, then went upstairs to tell Danny it was his bedtime. He nodded, but his eyes didn't leave his book.

"Get ready for bed, Danno. Then you can read half an hour more. Then lights out."

"Aw-w, Mom, I'm nearly finished." He showed her that only two pages remained of the novel. "Just a little longer, please."

"Finish those two pages, then." While he read, she straightened the underwear and socks in his bureau drawers. When he clapped the novel shut, she said, "That must've been a terrific read."

"Yeah, it was good, Mom."

"You were so engrossed when you started into the kitchen, I was afraid you'd fall," she teased, recalling similar incidents in her own long reading career.

"I could see where I was going," he protested. "On both sides of my book."

"So you didn't bump into the kitchen table, or into Toby?"

"No, Mom. Anyway, he wasn't in there."

"Not in the kitchen, when you were going to and from the bathroom?"

"Nope—Mom, can we go back to the library tomorrow? I've finished all but one of my books."

He was devouring all the age-appropriate books in the local

library's young-adult section at a rapid pace, Millie thought. Good for him.

"Probably."

Danny had begged to invite Kevin over, and Millie had decided he could come on Saturday, when she'd be home. Ted hadn't been sighted for a few days, so she hoped he had left town. Kay Reynolds brought her son over.

"Thanks for having Kev here today, Millie," she said as the women stood on the front porch. "I've been wanting time to myself, to use a spa afternoon my husband gave me for my birthday." She stretched her thin arms gracefully above her head. "Mm, just think, for the next few hours I'll be pampered outrageously. You ever done that?"

"No," Millie said with a smile. "Maybe some day."

"Every mother should, at least once."

She left, and the boys set up one of Danny's board games on the back porch. Millie cleaned their bedrooms and bath, then gave the boys soup and sandwiches for lunch. They started on another game, and she tidied the kitchen, then went upstairs to check e-mail. When she returned and opened the back door to offer the boys cold sodas, she saw they were no longer on the porch. She hadn't seen or heard them inside when she'd come through the downstairs, so she hurried out and looked around the yard.

Lord, she thought, what are they into now?

At first, she didn't see them. Then she noticed both boys reaching through the back fence, petting a large dog that stood in the alley, its leash held by someone partly hidden by a bush in their yard. Millie guessed the animal was a golden retriever-collie mix.

Guilt gripped her at the reminder of her unfulfilled promise to Danny.

*A kid needs a dog, Kirchner. Danny would learn things about responsibility and friendship and loyalty that he mightn't learn another way.*

Sylva was right as usual.

The dog's owner might be a neighbor, she thought, and she hadn't yet met them all. Millie strode across the yard towards the little group at the fence, a hand out in greeting.

"Hello, I'm Millie Kirchner. I see you've met my son Danny and his fr—" Millie broke off as she saw the dog-walker at closer range. Something about that posture, that face, that burr cut—

Ted Loftis.

"Go back inside the house, boys!" she said, gripping a shoulder of each and turning them to face the Victorian. "Now!"

Danny gave the dog a last regretful pat, shrugged at Kevin, and led the way. His friend looked from Millie to Ted to Danny, eyes wide and curious, then followed.

"What are you doing here?" she said to Ted, her voice shaking with fright and anger. "Cynthia's made it clear she doesn't want to see you anymore."

He smiled. "No law says I can't walk my dog in this neighborhood, is there?"

"There are laws against stalking."

"Stalking?" He grinned unpleasantly. "If I wanted to stalk Cynthia, I could do way better than this. Any judge'd laugh her out of court."

He shook the lead attached to the animal's collar. "Whatta ya think, Killer? Think she'd have a case?"

*Killer.*

The unfortunately named dog, long-haired, golden-tan with sable and white markings, looked with soft dark eyes from one human to the other. Millie thought she detected fear when they reached Loftis. She wanted to pet the animal herself but feared that Ted might see her doing so as weakness.

"Killer" wagged his tail as he looked longingly after the

boys.

"Don't worry," Ted said. "Killer doesn't live up to his name. Too bad, really. But when I saw him at the shelter, I had to have him. You oughta get your kid a dog. He wants one, bad."

"You need to leave, Mr. Loftis."

"You gonna make me, cutie? You'll notice I'm not on your property. So you've no right to give me orders. None at all."

"If you don't leave immediately, I'll call the police." Unfortunately, she didn't have her cell phone with her, she realized. But he couldn't know that.

He grinned. "Oooh, I'm scared. The police'd tell *you* to quit harassing *me.* But just to keep you from embarrassing yourself that way, I am going to leave. For now, that is. C'mon, Killer." He yanked on the leash, and the dog followed him down the alley.

A cold trembling seized Millie. She clasped her arms about herself in an attempt to control the fit of shaking. Fortunately, Cynthia was working in the Hands-On History Center, which had opened to the public today, so she hadn't been in danger. Nor had Ted threatened Millie, or her son, not in so many words. Yet his presence had seemed to exude danger.

Undoubtedly Loftis had brought that precious dog in order to ingratiate himself with Danny, to get into the house or learn information that would help him get to Cynthia. Millie would have to have a serious talk with both boys, try not to scare them unduly, but make it clear that Danny—and Kevin when he was here—must have no contact with Ted Loftis. Even if he offered candy or other inducement, even if he had a hundred sweet-tempered animals with him. She would also have to fill Kay Reynolds in about the situation.

And that could mean Danny wouldn't get to play with Kevin again, at least not here.

Resentment drove out fright. How dare Loftis presume to exert this kind of control over all their lives?

And that poor dog. Would he be beaten, Loftis taking out on a creature that couldn't escape, his frustration over failing at whatever plan he'd hatched?

Then she recalled Cynthia had said Ted was good to his father's hunting dogs. So maybe he wouldn't hurt "Killer."

Unless he was good to the hunting dogs just to stay on his father's good side.

Sunday afternoon, Millie and Danny went to the Reynolds home. When Kay had come to pick up Kevin on Saturday, before Millie called the boys from the back porch, she'd told Kay about Ted's ploy. Predictably Kay had feared possible harm to Kevin if another encounter occurred. But as the women discussed the problem, it became clear that neither wanted to separate her son from his new friend. They decided the boys would have to play together at places other than Millie's house. So Kay had extended the invitation for Sunday.

Immediately on the Kirchners' arrival, Danny and Kevin headed for the backyard. The mothers watched them from the bow window in the Reynolds' breakfast room while sitting over cups of tea. The low sound of a tennis match came from a television in the nearby den; Mr. Reynolds was a sports addict, his wife said resignedly, "all sports." Kevin's younger sister was asleep in the nursery.

"Kev really liked that dog yesterday," she commented. "Too bad its owner's such a jerk."

"Danny's crazy about dogs. Visiting shelters is number one on our "to do" list when we get home."

"Ashley—Kev's little sis—is allergic, unfortunately. So far we've managed to placate Kev with goldfish and turtles, but I doubt that'll work forever."

"Some breeds are apparently better than others. Maybe Ashley could tolerate a poodle or a chihuahua."

"I suppose—"

The doorbell rang, and Kay went to answer it. Soon, she reappeared in the kitchen, followed by a short, pretty girl with curly dark hair, a curvy figure, and a friendly manner. The girl looked familiar, Millie thought. Kay introduced her as Monica Dusin.

"Monica and I have known each other since I was in high school," she explained to Millie. "I baby-sat her, and now she sits for us. Have a seat, Mon. Tea?"

"Yeah, thanks."

"How's work at the apartment coming?"

"I'll be moving in tomorrow," Monica said with a pleased chortle. "Can't come too soon. Living with the folks again is getting to me."

Kay served Monica tea and sat down. "Your folks restrict your coming and going? I wouldn't have expected that of your mom."

"No, not that. She just wants to do everything for me."

"I could get used to that, myself," Kay said wistfully. "For a while, anyway. Millie, Monica's moving into this darling apartment a few blocks from here. At least it's darling now, after she's added new curtains, lively artwork, and lots of imagination."

"Don't forget elbow grease." Monica scratched a bit of white paint from her left forearm and laughed again. "I had to really scrub that kitchen stove, and, as you can see, I've slapped lots of paint around. Some even got on the ceilings and walls."

"I bought my first house a few months ago and fixed it up like you're doing," Millie said with a grimace. "It was worth all the effort, though, to get out of that dreary apartment."

As they compared notes on dwellings, Monica said with a sigh that she'd hated to leave her previous apartment.

"Landlord problems?" Millie asked sympathetically.

Monica and Kay exchanged a look.

"No," Monica said. "It was a landlady, actually, but she was fine. I just needed to change."

"Did you have to move far?"

"No. No, not far." Monica glanced at Kay again, then sipped her tea. "I suppose I might as well tell you, Millie. If you haven't heard about it yet, you will. My roommate was murdered in that apartment building, and my parents insisted I find another place."

"Oh, you're—"

"Paige Oberlin's roommate. Yeah, I was."

Millie explained she was volunteering at Highgrove and the other crew members had told her how much they missed Paige. "They all say what a terrific person she was. I'm sorry I didn't get to meet her."

"She and I were so different, but we got along really well."

"I understand she lived here a few years ago and you two knew each other then?"

Monica nodded. "We were inseparable in junior high, and kept in touch since by e-mail and phone calls. When she got the job at Highgrove, it seemed the perfect situation, and I found that really neat apartment for us."

"You must miss her a lot," Millie said softly.

"Every day." Monica wiped a tear.

"The police still . . . bothering you?" Kay asked, her expression compassionate but curious.

"I—wouldn't mind if questioning me could help them catch her killer. But I don't know of anyone who'd want to hurt Paige."

"So they think it was someone she knew, not just a thief who happened to pick your building?"

"I guess. I mean, Paige wasn't perfect. She might've had an enemy I didn't know about, but—"

"You've said she was a private person."

"Yeah. Close as we were, she didn't tell me everything." Monica drank more tea. "Much as I loved Paige . . . I probably shouldn't say this, but . . . Paige could sometimes be . . . a little vindictive."

"Vindictive. I don't think I've ever heard you say that about her."

"Yeah, well. Don't get me wrong, Paige was a good person. I don't mean she'd kill anyone, or seriously hurt them. But sometimes—if she felt someone had really wronged her—she could find some way to get even."

"Like how?"

Monica considered. "Well, there was this time in junior high when one of the girls in our class, Cindy, who was Paige's big rival in English class, spread it around that she'd helped Paige write one of her 'A' papers. She hadn't—Paige was a really good writer herself—but Cindy was trying to make herself look good at Paige's expense.

"The next time we had a theme due, Paige took Cindy's completed paper out of her backpack and hid it, so Cindy had no assignment to turn in. Paige later 'found' the paper on the floor in a hallway. But when Cindy turned it in late, the teacher figured she'd just claimed to have lost it in order to give herself extra time. She lowered Cindy's grade."

"I see what you mean by getting even, although the other girl kinda deserved what she got. You said you thought Paige was seeing someone. Were you able to give the police a name?"

"I—couldn't."

Couldn't? Or didn't? Millie wondered.

The portrait of Paige painted by Monica certainly differed from the impression the Highgrove crew had given of her. On the one hand, Monica might be carrying lingering resentment of her dead roommate. On the other, roommates probably knew each other in ways others wouldn't know either. Especially ones who'd known each other as long as those two had.

"How's Ashley's summer cold?" Monica asked, as if eager to

close the subject of Paige.

Millie could hardly blame her. Kay's questions had been pointed.

"Better. I'm glad she's sleeping a lot today."

The two chatted about the Reynolds children a few minutes. Kay freshened everyone's tea. The boys, apparently tired of playing on the swings, came in the kitchen for juice, then went to Kevin's room to play a video game.

"I'm so glad Kev's found a friend for the summer," Kay observed. "The boys get along really well."

Millie agreed. "I was afraid Danny might be lonely, being away so long from his Dallas friends. They e-mail each other often, but he seems satisfied here and Kevin's a big part of that."

"Guess I'd better get on home," Monica said, rising and placing her cup in the dishwasher.

"Got a hot date tonight?" Kay asked.

Monica smiled. "Hope it will be. I really like this guy."

"Do I know hm?"

"Probably not. We met at a party Paige and I threw a few weeks ago. He didn't seem especially interested in me that night, but he called later and we've been out a few times. I'll probably tell you all about him one of these days. Not ready right now."

Millie realized where she had seen Monica before: looking into a shop window downtown and holding hands with—

Whit Young.

"Sounds interesting—I expect a full report tomorrow," Kay teased.

"Don't expect it early. He's not a morning person," Monica said with a laugh.

Monica's guy couldn't be Whit, then, Millie thought. He'd said he *was* a morning person.

But maybe Whit had lied, either to her or to Monica.

Maybe Whit had only claimed to like mornings in order

to explain his early visits to Highgrove. If he really was seeking something specific on the grounds around the old dwelling, as Millie suspected, doing some of that searching in the wee hours before others arrived would make sense.

Kay frowned. "I hope this isn't another married guy, who'll break your heart like the last one did."

"I—don't think he is." Monica dropped her eyes as she spoke.

After she left, Kay went to check on her little girl and Millie continued looking out on the Reynolds backyard.

It was possible Monica's "hot date" wasn't Whit, of course. She might be seeing more than one man at the same time.

Maybe even another of the Highgrove crew. Nolan, perhaps? He wasn't attached, so far as Millie knew.

Or perhaps Luke? Jill had suspected him of involvement with Paige, but his excuses not to be with Jill, his resistance to becoming engaged, could as easily mean he was seeing someone else. Maybe even Paige's roommate?

No, it couldn't be Luke. He and Jill were going somewhere tonight.

What about Ron, then? He had a wife, but Monica had equivocated when asked whether her fellow was married.

Millie told herself not to rush ahead in her thinking. Monica's date could be someone unconnected to Highgrove. But if he was one of the crew, what if he'd been seeing Paige and her roomie at the same time? That could have given Monica Dusin a motive to harm her roommate. Paige might not have been the only spiteful one in that household.

Monica wouldn't have had to do the stabbing herself. But she might have helped plan it.

Millie scolded herself for thinking such things about the pleasant young woman who'd just left. Nor did Whit, or any of the Highgrove crew, seem the murderous type.

However, *someone* had killed Paige Oberlin. And from what Millie had heard of the Lynchburg Police's activities, it seemed they weren't buying the random-theft explanation.

# ✯ Chapter Seventeen

On Monday, Millie drove alone to the archaeology lab. Alice had had to see a dentist about a troublesome tooth and would come in later. Jill's door had been firmly closed this morning, the occupant apparently sleeping late after her date with Luke on Sunday night. Cynthia had said she'd lock all the doors and spend the day alone, cooking. Kay had picked up Danny and was taking the boys to visit Kevin's grandmother in a nearby town.

"Like to help me with screening again today, Millie?" Harold said when Millie entered the lab.

"Sure, if it's okay with Chas."

The lab supervisor, busy at his computer, waved permission, and Millie accompanied Harold to the dig. Together, they removed the sandbags weighting the heavy plastic that covered the excavation. All at once, Harold staggered back.

"My God!"

Lifting his corner of the plastic higher, Harold stared open-mouthed into the hole.

Millie gasped. Spread-eagled across the dig, twine grid markers ripped from their posts and tangled about her body, lay Jill Greene.

Her blonde hair was awry, her pink blouse disarranged,

and smears of dirt marred her tan shorts. Her eyes were closed, her usually rosy cheeks now pale, other-worldly. Both arms lay outstretched, palms up. One leg was bent at the knee, the other straight. She lay frighteningly still, making the dig appear to be an open grave.

Millie dropped her section of plastic and stepped into the hole, bending to touch Jill's wrist. Cool to the touch. No pulse.

Jill Greene's raucous laugh had been stilled forever.

The Bedford County Sheriff's Department arrived soon after Harold called. Their crime scene team cordoned off the dig, photographed Jill's body where it lay, and examined the scene for clues. Millie watched the activity a few moments, feeling numb. How could Jill, who'd been so full of life, of plans and ambitions, be gone? Millie felt she was in a bad dream from which she couldn't wake.

"Please be careful," Harold had urged the forensics people as they began their work. "This is an archaeological dig, and it's extremely important the site be disturbed as little as possible until we've finished excavating it. In collecting your evidence, you could inadvertently destroy centuries-old evidence."

The technicians assured him they'd be careful. An investigator asked Millie and Harold if they knew the victim. When Millie told him Jill's name and said they'd been housemates, he asked for more details. She explained the living situation and gave the names of the other occupants.

"Anyone home there now?" he said. "We'll need to take a look at the victim's room."

"Yes, Cynthia's there." Millie gave the address of the Victorian.

He spoke with two other investigators, who then left, and asked Millie and Harold to wait in the lab until needed for further questioning. They weren't to discuss the case in the meantime, he cautioned. They did as told, although Millie thought the warning futile in this case. Harold, Chas, and she had had opportunity to compare notes before law enforcement personnel arrived.

While Harold had phoned the police, Millie had told Chas of the macabre scene they'd found at the dig. Color had drained from the supervisor's face.

"No," he'd whispered, stunned into immobility. "No, not Jill."

Millie touched his arm in sympathy. "I'm sorry, Chas. It's an awful shock. While Harold's telephoning, why don't you and I sit down and have some coffee? Unless you'd prefer a soda or water?"

A solemn Harold, on completing his call, returned to the dig to await arrival of the authorities. Millie and Chas took cups of coffee to the small office at the back of the main room. He sat behind the desk, leaning onto it, she in front. Neither spoke for a few moments.

"I'm usually the first one in the main parking lot in the morning," Chas finally said, running a trembling hand through his red-blond curls. "But Jill's Cavalier was already there when I arrived today."

"Wonder how long it's been there?" Millie mused. "She and Luke were going to a movie marathon at a friend's house last night, and she'd said she'd be late getting home. I didn't hear her come in, and her bedroom door was closed this morning." She sipped thoughtfully. "Now I wonder if she ever came home at all."

An early-morning drive to Poplar Forest seemed an unlikely choice by Jill, much as she'd liked sleeping late. But her being at the dig at all was out of character.

Color returned to Chas's face, but the hand that held his cup wasn't quite steady.

"I never even got to give her the pendant I made," he murmured sorrowfully.

Millie searched for words of consolation. "Jill was excited about your making it for her, though. She told me you do lovely work."

"Really? She said that?" A half-smile touched his lips.

He looked like a vulnerable little boy, Millie thought, not a fortyish man with expertise in two specialized areas of knowledge.

"You shared Jill's passion for precious stones," she went on, hoping to soothe him further. "That was a huge interest of hers."

"Yeah. She even asked me to help her find someone to—" He broke off, set the cup down carefully, and stared at it.

"Someone to—?" She echoed his words, nudging him to go on.

"Nothing. She wouldn't want me mentioning that."

"Chas, it's fine if you don't tell me. But if it has any possible bearing on her death, you'll have to tell the sheriff's people."

He hadn't replied, eyes still on his cup. After a few minutes she'd decided he preferred to be alone in his grief and had gone out to keep Harold company.

On returning to the lab this time, Millie waved to Chas as he sat dejectedly in his office. She wanted to speak words of comfort to him but could think of nothing to say. Anyway, they weren't supposed to discuss Jill's death, so it might be better not to speak. She took a seat in the labeling room and began desultorily to mark artifacts. Soon, she heard a female investigator come in and ask Harold to accompany her to the main room for his interview.

Millie went on labeling, her mind struggling with the enormity of the grisly discovery. She wished she could call Alice, but would have to wait for the detective's permission. Who had murdered Jill? If the victim had been Cynthia, Millie would have immediately suspected Ted. But no such obvious suspect leapt to mind for Jill.

Cynthia and Jill had disagreed on occasion, but Millie couldn't believe that discord had led to murder. Jill had disliked Toby, but he'd shown no sign of returning the emotion. She had also seemed to resent the Highgrove crew, had been the one to quash Luke's proposal for regular meals. None of that seemed motive enough for murder.

But Jill had been afraid of something or someone. She'd claimed her room had been searched, had asked Millie to keep her valuable earrings.

And she'd asked that Millie make sure anything valuable of hers would go to her younger sister. "Just in case," Jill had kept saying, that day in the bookstore café.

In case of what? Her death? It seemed Jill had had a premonition that she'd be killed. And now she was dead.

Millie thought about her puzzling conversation with Chas. What secret had he and the victim shared? Why had she asked the lab supervisor's help in finding someone to—

To do what?

Whatever it was must have had to do with jewelry. As far as Millie knew, that had been their only common interest.

Chas came out of his office and plodded through the main room. Millie heard him climb the stairs to the library.

A crazy thought came to her. Could Jill's murder have been a case of mistaken identity, Ted thinking he was confronting Cynthia in the dark last night or early this morning?

No, that was a nutty idea. The women drove twin autos, but they themselves looked nothing alike, including size and build. Even in dim light, the differences should have been apparent.

And why had Jill been at the dig? Millie kept coming back to that. She must have been enticed there somehow. But how, and by whom?

Millie considered her own feelings towards the victim. She hadn't always been able to like Jill, who had had a selfish streak and been something of a know-it-all. But flashes of another Jill had appeared at times, hinting at a more caring, vulnerable woman than generally appeared.

And she had been a friend to Danny. Millie could forgive her much for that.

Anxiety for her son surfaced. This would be Danny's first real brush with death, the first demise of a human being to whom he'd been close. He was a strong kid, but Jill's death might hit him hard. At least he wasn't at home today, when sheriff's investigators would be searching Jill's room and presumably interviewing Cynthia.

Harold returned and told Millie she was wanted now. When she entered the small office where she and Chas had sat at coffee earlier, a tall, graying man introduced himself as Sheriff's Investigator Lou O'Steen and his colleague as Investigator Peg Vinson. He indicated a seat facing the desk, and Millie sat. He took the chair behind the desk, Vinson the one beside hers. Millie nervously cleared her throat. She had been interviewed by detectives before, after her mother's suicide and after murders of her fellow heirs in Philadelphia, but it never seemed to get easier.

O'Steen asked opening questions about Millie and her work at the archaeology lab, then had her tell about discovering the body. Vinson took notes as they talked.

"And you knew the victim, Mrs. Kirchner?" he asked when Millie finished her tale.

"I did." Millie again explained the living arrangements at the Victorian.

"So you four ladies share a house, and all of you volunteer at Poplar Forest?"

"Yes. Jill worked at the museum. Alice also works here in the lab but went to a dental appointment this morning—she should be here soon. Cynthia works on weekends in the Hands-On History Center. She's at home today, cooking."

"Have you any idea why the deceased would've been here at

Poplar Forest after hours, Mrs. Kirchner?"

"No, I've been wondering that, also why she'd have been at the dig at all. Jill wasn't much interested in archaeology. Far as I know, she never went out to the dig."

"What about this building? She ever come to the lab?"

"Only once that I know of, to bring sack lunches Alice and I had forgotten."

"So you and she just met this summer? You didn't know each other before?"

"No, we met when my son and I arrived here a few weeks ago."

Asked how Millie and Jill had gotten along, she replied that they'd been friends, occasionally had done things together, like going to Williamsburg last week.

"How did your other housemates get along with her?"

"Fine."

*Not exactly. Not all of you.*

"Except—" Millie began reluctantly. "Except there was friction between her and Cynthia."

"Over?"

Feeling disloyal to Cynthia, Millie mentioned the women's mutual interest in Luke.

"So it was a love triangle?" O'Steen nodded as at a familiar story.

"I wouldn't call it a triangle. Luke seems—seemed—committed to Jill. He and Cynthia flirted a little, but just that one evening." Millie hoped what she said was true, that Luke hadn't been leading Jill on.

Asked if she had any idea who might have killed the victim, Millie said she hadn't.

"When was the last time you saw Miss Greene alive?"

"Yesterday. She and Luke left to go to a friend's house around six. She said they'd be late getting home, since they'd be watching a movie marathon on TV."

"Do you know who that friend was?"

"No. Sorry."

"Where would we find Mr. Brooks today?"

"Probably at Highgrove." She explained about Luke's job and gave directions to the place.

Vinson jotted them down, tore that sheet from her notebook, and left. O'Steen asked Millie to remain where she was and excused himself to use the restroom. Soon both investigators returned and continued the interview.

"Mrs. Kirchner," O'Steen said, "do you know of anyone who had threatened Miss Greene, anyone she was afraid of?"

"No-o, no one who'd threatened her specifically. But we—all of us—were concerned about Ted Loftis." Millie went on to explain his pursuit of Cynthia.

"And you, Miss Cisneros, and Mrs. Ross all felt this Mr. Loftis was capable of violence?"

"Yes. He never made any outright threats, to my knowledge, but his hanging around, refusing to let go, is pretty scary. And after meeting Ted, Alice and I agreed he might be dangerous."

"What about Miss Greene? Was she worried about him?"

"She urged Cynthia to file a complaint against Ted, try to get him off the streets. But she never actually met him, far as I know." Millie took a deep breath. "Investigators, I need to tell you a few things. I don't know if they're relevant to Jill's death or not." She told about the intrusion into Jill's room and of the odd conversation she'd had with the victim at Williamsburg.

O'Steen frowned. "Would you say Miss Greene was frightened of one particular person? Or just generally afraid of losing her valuables?"

"I couldn't tell. But she did seem fearful of something or someone."

"So, you still have Miss Greene's earrings?"

"Yes."

"And she didn't tell you what this other valuable object she owns is? Or where it is?"

"No."

"From your knowledge of Miss Greene, have you any theories?"

"Only that it might be some kind of jewelry. Jill was crazy about precious stones, especially those with a colorful history. She read about gems in her free time, and she liked browsing in jewelry stores." Millie told about Jill's career plan.

The investigators asked a few more questions, and then O'Steen told Millie she could go for now. "Send in Mr. Locke, please. And when Mrs. Ross gets here, tell her we'll need to talk with her."

"Okay." Millie started to leave, then turned back. "Oh, will you be needing to question my nine-year-old?"

"Probably. But we'll talk to him at your house and will make it as non-threatening as possible."

"I appreciate that. Do you have any idea when you'll go over there? Danny's not home right now—he went somewhere with friends—but I want to be there when he learns about Jill's death. They were buddies, and he's already had lots to deal with this summer, so many new people and then the worry over Ted."

"Sure. It'll be later this afternoon."

"Thank you."

Millie climbed the stairs to the library and gave Chas the message. He was calmer than earlier but glum. They went downstairs, Millie to the labeling room, where she found Alice sitting at the table, eyes wide with unspoken questions.

"You've heard about Jill?" Millie asked in hushed tones.

"Yes, Harold told me you and he found her body. But he also said we aren't to talk about it until after I've been questioned." Her voice dropped. "Isn't it awful?"

"Ghastly. A nightmare." Shaking her head, Millie took a chair near Alice. "You get any help with your tooth?"

Alice smiled ruefully. "A filling's chipped. I go back to get it replaced in a couple of days."

"Can you stand the pain until then?"

"I guess. The dentist gave me a prescription in case it gets worse, though I told him I'd gotten by with aspirin so far. I don't like to take more medicine than necessary."

"Me either. But you shouldn't suffer unnecessarily."

Alice began labeling artifacts. Millie decided to work awhile before going home, since Kay and the boys weren't due back yet. She took an artifact bag to the kitchen and dumped its contents into a colander, glad of something to occupy her hands. But her mind continued to think about Jill.

Her body still wore the same clothes she'd left the house in yesterday evening, Millie realized. That suggested she'd been killed last night, since it would have been out of character for her to wear the same clothes two days in a row. If she hadn't come home at all last night, where and when had she and Luke parted company? And why?

Or had Luke murdered Jill?

Millie didn't want to think so. Although he'd behaved at times as if he felt less committed to the relationship than Jill, he'd seemed to genuinely care for her. Nor did he appear to be the violent type. He seemed too laid-back, too centered an individual. Furthermore, he was smart enough to know that, as perhaps the last person to see her alive, he'd be suspect number one.

As for a possible motive, Jill had been annoying at times, but people didn't usually get murdered for that.

Unless—

Unless Luke was truly smitten with Cynthia, and Jill's possessiveness had made him angry enough to strike her. Maybe he hadn't meant to kill her, had done so by accident.

But why had they even been at Poplar Forest? And why at the dig?

As for how she'd been killed, Millie didn't recall seeing a stab wound or a gunshot injury—no blood at all, in fact. Yet the soiled, unkempt appearance of her body suggested violence had been involved.

Another thought struck. The body had been found under the plastic that covered the dig. Had she been killed before the excavation had been blanketed for the night?

No, obviously not. It would have been covered Friday afternoon. This was Monday, and Millie had seen Jill alive on Sunday. So someone had removed the covering, placed Jill's body in its grave-like resting place, and replaced the plastic.

The killer must have coaxed Jill to the lonely spot and killed her, either last evening or early this morning. Or else she'd been slain elsewhere and her body moved to the dig. But why there at all?

# ★ Chapter Eighteen

Millie continued her washing chore for a couple of hours more, loath to leave in case she might miss hearing something relevant to Jill's death. But Harold professed not to have known the victim at all—although he had heard Whit mention her—or any reason anyone would be killed at the dig. Chas shut his office door right after his interview. When Alice finished hers, she could add nothing to what Millie already knew. Alice had taken a sleeping aid last night because of her bothersome tooth and hadn't heard Jill come in. Finally, when there seemed to be nothing else Millie could learn, she left.

Arriving home, she dropped her purse in the parlor and found Cynthia in the kitchen, stirring something on the stove. The tasty smell reminded Millie that, in the excitement, she hadn't eaten lunch. Cynthia looked up, her eyes red and wet. The women hugged each other, neither speaking at first, then took stools at the counter.

"Oh, Millie," Cynthia said, "this is so awful."

"I know. I still can't believe it. Danny hasn't gotten home, has he?"

Cynthia shook her head. "Not yet. Millie, those investigators seemed to think I might've had something to do with Jill's death."

"They have to interview people who knew her. Alice and I had our turns at Poplar Forest. Everyone who works at the lab was questioned."

"Yeah. Yeah, I guess. But you guys hadn't quarreled with her about Luke."

"The investigators have to consider every possibility. But they'll find out who really did it. For what it's worth, I don't believe you're guilty."

Cynthia smiled wryly. "Thanks for saying that."

"I mean it. Did you hear Jill come in last night?"

"I think so. I did hear someone in her room, late, but I was having a crying jag about Ted and didn't pay much attention. Him coming around here with that dog, trying to weasel his way in through Danny—that really worries me, Millie. And the worst of it is, there doesn't seem to be anything I can do about him."

"I know, Cynthia. At least we're all more alert now, and know how far he might go. You said it was late when you heard someone in her room. Any idea what time that was?"

"The investigators asked me that. I'd cried for a while before that, and kept on crying afterwards. One or two o'clock, maybe. Or it could've been later. Sorry, Millie, I was a real mess, crazy with worry, not thinking straight."

"Sorry you're having to go through that. Have you any idea who might've killed Jill, or why?"

"I don't. She and I had our problems, but I'm sorry she's dead. If I knew anything at all that would help solve her murder, I'd tell the investigators. Millie, if it's okay with you, I'd rather not talk about this anymore right now. I'll be on the terrace if anyone needs me." She went outside.

Millie remained at the counter, sitting dejectedly. Then she gave way to tears for the first time since finding the body. She cried partly for the victim and the waste of that young life, partly for Danny, partly for Luke, for Jill's family, and for others who'd cared for her, and partly for herself. Jill hadn't been a close pal, but Millie would miss her. She'd been a housemate and a person, who hadn't deserved to be murdered.

After a time, Millie roused and wiped her face. She was about to go upstairs when she heard a car stop in the driveway. She ran to the front door and peered out through a glass panel. Seeing Danny get out of the car, Millie went outside and waved to Kay and Kevin in the car. Danny came up the steps and submitted to being kissed and hugged. With another wave, Kay backed out and drove away.

"Hi, Mom. Whatcha doin' home early?"

"Tell you in a minute. Did you and Kev have a good time?" They went inside, into the kitchen.

"Yeah, it was fun. His grandma's pretty old and didn't say much to us, but Kev's mom got out some of her old games for us to play. I did pretty good at Chinese checkers."

"Glad to hear it. You hungry? Need something to drink?"

He had eaten but was thirsty. She poured milk for him, got herself an apple, and they sat at the counter. They had barely finished their snack when the front doorbell rang. He went with her to answer. Two men in suits stood there, badges in hand. The taller, older of the two, said he was Investigator Jim Zenith. He and his partner, Bob Loudon, were from the Lynchburg Police Department, part of a Bedford County/Lynchburg task force investigating the death of Jill Greene.

The change in her son's expression, from polite curiosity to a mixture of shock and fear, wrung Millie's heart. She should have prepared him for this moment, instead of acting as if everything was as usual, but she'd craved that last bit of normality for him and herself. Now, she let the investigators in and laid a gentle hand on her son's shoulder.

"Danny," she said, "the reason I'm home early is that our friend

Jill has been killed. The people investigating her death need to talk to anyone who knew her, so they can figure out who did it. I've already answered questions at the lab, and now these men need to ask you some. Try not to be frightened, Danno, just answer as best you can. I'll be with you the whole time."

He nodded somberly, eyes anxious.

Still gripping Danny's shoulder, Millie led the way to the library, saying it would be a quiet place to talk. The four of them sat at the rosewood table, she holding her son's hand for reassurance while Zenith asked him questions in a friendly, non-bullying tone. Millie appreciated his manner, although the interview produced no information beyond what she herself had told the other investigators. After they'd finished, Zenith asked if he and Loudon might remain in the library awhile, making phone calls and conferring. Hugging Danny to her, she agreed.

"I need to go upstairs and check my e-mail," she went on, "but can I get you anything first? Something to drink?"

They said no. She and Danny went up the spiral staircase to the second level and into her room.

"It wasn't so bad, was it, Danno?"

He shook his head, clearly struggling not to weep.

"It's okay if you need to cry, Danno. I'm really sad too."

While he started to snuffle, Millie sat in her desk chair and gathered him onto her lap. She hugged him and murmured reassurances into his hair.

When he was ready to sit up, she got him settled on her bed beside her with something to read, then booted her laptop and went into her e-mail program.

Several messages appeared to be SPAM, two were from friends in Dallas, one was from Scott, and one was from Jill.

Jill?

Sudden dread of what this message from her murdered housemate might say made Millie's heart pound. She took a deep breath and opened the message from Jill. It read, "Redrock, Viclib, blue ridge blossoms 4D, 12R."

Shoot, Millie thought, it made no sense. The e-mail must have gotten garbled somehow between Jill's laptop and her own. She checked the time the message had been sent. This morning, shortly after midnight.

This might be the last e-mail Jill had sent before her life ended. It should have been something important, Millie thought resentfully, something to help solve her murder, not a mess of meaningless letters and numbers.

Nonetheless, the investigators would need to see it.

Before going downstairs, she read the e-mail from Scott. Besides the usual sweet nothings, it voiced concern for Millie's safety—with Ted still on the loose—and eagerness for their coming weekend in Charlottesville.

Then he said he and Jolene were more and more worried about the company Larry was keeping.

*They* were worried.

Well, isn't that special, Millie thought snidely. She was dealing with the murder of someone she'd shared a house with, not to mention the possible traumatizing of her son, and Scott was speaking as if he and someone named Jolene were now a couple.

Millie immediately regretted the stab of jealousy. She should feel sympathy, kinship, for another single mother worried about her son's welfare. But she couldn't help resenting Scott's pairing himself with another woman, however innocent their relationship might be.

She saved Jill's e-mail to a flash drive, told Danny she needed to take care of something, and said, "I won't be gone long, sweetie. Want one of your action figures to curl up with?"

He shook his head. She hated leaving him, however briefly, but thought that would be better than dragging him behind her.

In the office, she printed out Jill's message. Then she went back downstairs, handed it to Investigator Zenith, and said she'd just found it on her computer.

"I've no idea what it means," she added with a regretful look.

Zenith scanned the e-mail, showed it to Loudon, and asked Millie when she had last checked her messages before finding this one.

"Probably around eleven last night, just before I went to bed."

He frowned at the paper. "Can you translate this for us?"

"I'm afraid I don't understand it myself."

"You sure? Think hard. Miss Greene evidently expected you would."

Millie spread her hands. "Then she gave me too much credit. I really don't."

He gave her a long sad look, apparently decided to let it go for now. "You will contact us if you figure out what it means?"

"Certainly." But she doubted she'd be making that call.

"We'll need to take your laptop, Mrs. Kirchner, as well as any other computers here, also all the cell phones."

"Really? But I have messages on my laptop I haven't even opened."

Zenith said she'd be allowed to read her new messages, with Loudon standing by. Millie and Loudon went to her room, where she opened and read her other e-mails—chatty notes from Dallas friends that didn't require answers. Then she packed up her laptop and gave it to Loudon.

Danny watched this all with curious eyes. She reassured him with a smile and promised she would return as soon as the investigators were finished with their questions.

She and Loudon went to the office, where she handed him the cell phone she'd carried in a pocket, since Ted's ploy with the dog, and packed the leased computer for him to take. He asked who had access to it.

"All of us, if we want," Millie said. "But Danny and I just use my laptop and, far as I know, Jill only used hers. Alice and Cynthia both use the office one."

The investigators who had been here earlier interviewing Cynthia had already taken Jill's laptop, Loudon said. He thanked her for her cooperation and said he and Zenith would be leaving the house now, but that she should call them if anything more occurred to her.

Millie went back to her room and cradled Danny in her arms. He looked at her with puzzled, scared eyes.

"You in trouble, Mom?"

"No, sweetie, there was an e-mail from Jill on my computer, maybe the last one she sent before she . . . died. The policemen took that and my computer, because those might help them figure out who killed Jill."

"You think that bad man did it? The one I'm not supposed to talk to?"

"Ted? I don't know why he'd want to harm Jill."

"Maybe because we wouldn't let him see Cynthia?"

She sighed. "Possible, I guess. We'll just have to be brave and hope the investigators catch whoever did it. And soon."

Dinner that evening was a somber affair. Alice and Millie struggled to make small talk unrelated to Jill but found it hard sledding. Cynthia said little, barely touching the excellent dinner she'd prepared. Danny, too, ate only a few bites. Millie wondered if the enchiladas were too spicy for him or if he was too upset to eat anything. When he asked to be excused, she decided some out-of-the-ordinary pampering was in order.

"Go ahead, Danno. And if you want to get some ice cream and take it with you, that'll be fine." She was violating her own rule of no dessert without eating a good meal first, but this was no ordinary day, for him, for anyone. "Just this once, okay? I'll be up in a little while."

His sad little smile touched her heart. When he had gotten ice cream and gone upstairs, the three women sat cheerlessly a few minutes over the remains of the meal.

Millie helped with dishes, then went upstairs. Hearing a sobbing sound coming from Danny's room, she went in and found him weeping into his pillow. She sat on his bed and held him close, and he transferred his sobs to her shoulder. They sat several minutes without speaking.

"Why'd Jill—hafta die, Mom?" he said at last, a catch in his throat. "She was fun."

"She was." Millie squeezed him tighter. "We're all going to miss her, and I'm very sorry you've lost her as a friend. I don't know why anyone would kill her, Danno. I hope the police find out soon who did it."

He hiccupped, a frequent accompaniment to his crying.

"Mom," he said plaintively. "Mom, you think somebody else'll get killed?"

"Somebody else? You mean me? Or Alice, or Cynthia?"

"You work out there too. All of you do. Where Jill got killed."

"Oh, Danno, sweetie, please don't worry. I know it's scary that somebody we know was murdered, especially not knowing who did it or why. But I really doubt I'm in danger, or Alice or Cynthia. It was probably somebody who was mad at Jill for some reason."

"Mom? Can we go back to Texas? I've finished my camp, and you don't hafta stay, do you?"

"You that scared, sweetie? Well, going home might be a good thing to do. But let's think about it some more and talk about it tomorrow. I'm not saying no, just that things may look differently then. For now, how about getting into your PJs, and I'll sing you to sleep, the way I used to?"

He did, and she sat on his bed, cuddling him and crooning soft lullabies. After a time, she heard the quiet, regular breathing of sleep. She waited a few minutes, making sure he was truly out, then eased her arm out from under him and drew up his covers. She slipped out of his room, shut the door, and stood in the hallway taking deep breaths.

And worrying. Danny had experienced the death of goldfish, also that of the woman who had taught him in kindergarten. He hadn't seen his former teacher, however, since her retirement a year before her death. Besides, she had been ill, and—to him—old.

Jill had been in the prime of youth, a friend, a housemate, a fellow baseball player, another connoisseur of knock-knock jokes.

Danny was a resilient kid, had so far taken new experiences and new people in stride. But she feared this might prove to be different.

The next morning, Danny told Millie he'd like to stay in Lynchburg.

"You sure, Danno? 'Cause I've been thinking about it too. I don't want you to have to stay if you'd be scared all the time. We could leave here and see other parts of Virginia, then drive on home."

"No, it's okay, Mom. Kev and I want to go back to Amazement Square. And I haven't shown you Hands-On History yet."

"Okay, then, if you're sure."

Relieved they wouldn't be leaving Lynchburg and Poplar Forest just yet, Millie called Kay Reynolds to ask if Danny could come to play with Kevin today. Jill's death had been covered prominently in the news, and Kay had heard Danny mention Jill, so she was full of questions. Millie answered, mostly with "I don't know." Kay readily agreed to Danny's coming over, so Millie and Alice dropped him by on their way to Poplar Forest.

The mood at the lab was somber. Harold worked the dig alone, while Chas holed up in his office and Millie and Alice washed and labeled.

That afternoon, Millie returned to Highgrove. She found the four men in the office, sitting around looking gloomy. Millie greeted them and crossed to a chair beside Luke's.

"I'm so sorry about Jill, Luke," Millie said. "It's hard to realize she's gone."

He nodded, his slender face drawn. The slump of his shoulders made him look lonely and vulnerable.

"Let's go, guys," Ron said, rising and waving to the other two.

Reluctantly, it seemed, the others followed.

Millie and Luke smiled sadly at each other.

"You don't have to console me, Millie," he said. "I know you miss Jill, too."

"Sure, but you'd known her longer and were closer to her. This must be agonizing for you."

"It's not fun," he acknowledged in a voice that quavered slightly.

"I don't want to increase your pain, Luke. But would it be okay if I asked you a few questions about Jill's death?"

He lifted one shoulder, then let it drop. "Why not? Everyone else has."

"Would you mind telling me what time you brought her home last night? I didn't hear her come in. I know you discussed all this with the investigators, but . . . "

He waited before replying, then heaved a shuddering sigh. "It doesn't put me in a good light. But you're curious, so let's get it over with. Jill and I had a fight. She'd been bugging me about getting engaged, and last night when she started in on wanting a ring, I kinda lost it. Jill's a neat girl—was a neat girl—" Luke broke off, swallowed hard. "But I thought her parents were right in saying she should finish college before we got married.

"Unfortunately, Jill has—had—two more years to go, and I didn't want to be engaged for two whole years. Plus, I couldn't afford to buy her a fancy ring, which she'd made clear was non-negotiable. I'd have to go way into hock to do it, and I couldn't see spending so much on a bauble just for show. Boy, did she get mad when I said that!"

If he'd used those words to Jill, Millie understood why her housemate had gotten angry. An expensive ring wasn't a priority for Millie, but it had been for Jill. She wouldn't have considered such a gift a mere bauble.

"Her folks are good people," Luke went on. "I called them after the investigators finished with me yesterday, and I learned Alice had already phoned her condolences. That was nice of her."

"Yes, it was. I've never met the Greenes, but Alice has mentioned talking to Jill's mother on the phone once and liking her."

"Yeah. Jill's death hit her folks hard, of course. Mrs. Greene was especially worried about the effect it would have on her younger daughter, Rachel."

"Jill mentioned a younger sister."

They sat in silence a moment.

"So, did you bring Jill home early last evening? She must've come home at some point and driven her car out to Poplar Forest, either last night or this morning. At least her Cavalier was found in the parking lot."

"I did bring her home, but not early. We were watching the movie marathon at Bruce and Yvonne's house, having a good time. Then during a break between movies, Jill started telling Yvonne about this fancy engagement ring she'd found online. Yvonne was egging her on like she always does, and Bruce kept stealing glances at me, waiting for me to respond. I tried ignoring the women, talking to Bruce about baseball, but they kept on and on even after the next movie started. I finally told Jill to shut up and let us all watch the show."

"Ouch," Millie said involuntarily.

He nodded ruefully. "Yeah. She didn't say anything for a long time, just looked daggers at me and tapped her foot against a table leg. I finally inquired, in a super-polite way, if she'd like me to take her home. She said, 'Yes, since your selfish attitude has ruined the fun for the rest of us.'

"On the drive home, she asked—ever so formally—if I had ever loved her at all. If I had, she said, I should've been glad to shower her with whatever would make her happy."

He sat back, limp against his chair. "Obviously, I should not have said a word at that point. But all the good sense I've ever had must've left. I told her honestly how I felt about expensive rings and long engagements. I had hinted at my feelings before, but last night I laid it all out, plain. And then—then I said if she wanted to go on seeing me she'd have to drop all references to rings and engagements." He winced. "That did not go over well."

"And that surprised you?" Millie stifled a chuckle.

"Not really. I was just so mad—" He wiped a hand over his face.

"But if we hadn't—hadn't had that fight, Jill might still be alive. She might not've gone to Poplar Forest, might not've been—" He raised his hands to his eyes and rubbed them hard. "God, what a fool I am."

Millie laid a hand on his arm, finding no words to comfort him.

"The rest of the drive home," he went on miserably, "neither of us spoke. And as soon as she got out, I drove off. I know, I know, you can't be any more critical of me than I am."

This was something she could, and should, respond to. "Luke, please don't beat yourself up over this. Jill was obsessed with real gems—unreasonably so, in my opinion—and that argument was bound to happen eventually. I'm sure you did the right thing to tell her honestly how you felt."

"You think so? Thanks, Millie."

After a minute, she asked if he had any idea why Jill would have gone back out by herself, late at night. "And why Poplar Forest?"

He shook his head, clearly at a loss. "As for going out, when we used to fight back in Maryland, she'd drive around for hours, trying to clear her head. I figure that's what she did last night. But Poplar Forest? Beats me.

"Especially her being at the dig. Jill disliked my chosen profession and hated getting dirty, except for sports."

"What time did you get to the Victorian?"

"Little before midnight, maybe 11:30, 11:45. I got home a little after twelve. Ron wasn't back from wherever he'd gone."

"Is it unusual for him to stay out late?" Millie hadn't figured Ron for a night owl.

The ring of the telephone prevented Luke's response. He answered, gave a curt reply, and hung up.

"Reporters! They've been calling since the news of Jill's death broke yesterday. I say 'no comment,' but some are persistent. What was I—? Oh, yeah. It is unusual for Ron to be out late, but we don't ride herd on each other. I wouldn't want to have to account to him for every move I make."

"Well, guess I better get to work. Let me know if I can help somehow."

Millie donned her hat and a pair of gloves and went to the dig. Whit stood alone at the shaker screen. She assumed Ron was now working inside the house. And Nolan? Glancing around, she saw him sitting with two policemen in the lawn chairs, conversing in low tones. She looked back at Whit, who raised his eyebrows expressively.

"Are they interviewing Nolan about Jill's death?" Millie said.

"Those two didn't seem to have much to do with each other."

Whit shook his head. "I don't think so. These particular investigators have been working on Paige's murder. I suppose they could be on both cases, though."

"Is Nolan the only one they've talked to today?"

"So far. But I may be next."

After a time, Nolan rose, came to the dig, and motioned for Whit to take his place in the lawn chair.

"Hey, Millie," Nolan said as he joined her at the sifting task. "How you doing?"

"Okay, I guess. Still stunned over Jill's death."

"Yeah, that was a shock. Any idea what happened? Why she'd have been out there?"

"No, it's all a mystery. No scenario I come up with makes sense. You think the police are getting anywhere on Paige's death?"

He shrugged. "Who can tell? It's a huge waste, isn't it? Two beautiful young women murdered, and we don't know why. Maybe Paige really was killed by a thief, since her purse was taken."

"But Jill's death can't be explained that way, and I'll bet there's some connection between the two. It would be super-coincidental otherwise."

"Yeah. Though coincidences do happen in real life."

Presently, Whit came back to the dig and, without a word to Millie or Nolan, began screening. The investigators rose from their seats and strolled to the house. Nolan took a cigarette lighter from his jeans pocket, got cigarettes and his lidded ashtray from his car, then walked some distance behind the vehicles to light up. After a time, Millie went to the kitchen for a drink and noticed the office door was shut. A murmur of voices came from behind it, but she couldn't distinguish words.

Millie screened a while longer, had about decided to call it a day, when the investigators left the house by the front door. Ron was walking in front of them. They reached the police car parked beside her Prius, and one investigator motioned for Ron to get into the back seat. He did, and the other men climbed into the front. Millie watched them drive away, wondering what was going on.

Then it hit her: Ron had been wearing handcuffs.

# Chapter Nineteen

"They've arrested Ron," she said to Whit and Nolan, not believing her own words. "Why?'

The men looked at each other, then sheepishly at her. Neither spoke. Millie whirled and stalked off. She found Luke still in the office.

"They've arrested Ron," she repeated. "Do you know why?"

Luke squirmed in his chair. "I'm not sure I should say. I'm hoping they'll realize they've made a mistake and release him."

"But why, Luke? Do they think he killed Jill? Or Paige?"

He stared at his hands, then raised his eyes to hers. "I suppose it'll get out anyway. Ron and Paige were lovers. The police evidently think he killed her because she was going to tell his wife."

"Is that true? Were they having an affair?"

He nodded. "Yeah. But I can't believe Ron killed her."

"You withheld information from the police? Until today?"

"It sounds bad when you say it like that."

Millie gritted her teeth. "It would sound bad however I said it. How could you do that, Luke? This is a murder investigation."

"But Ron's not guilty. So I didn't want the police to waste time following that trail."

"How do you know he didn't do it? Were you there?"

A muscle worked in his jaw. "No, I was not there." He emphasized each word. "But Ron and I have worked together before, and you get to know a guy working side by side with him."

The concern in his voice touched Millie. "Still—"

"I know you're right. I shouldn't have lied to the investigators. But I wasn't the only one. Whit and Nolan knew, too, and didn't tell. When the police came back today, already knowing about the affair—they evidently got an anonymous tip or something—we had to 'fess up."

"Maybe Ron has an alibi for the time of Paige's death. Were you and he still here at the time?"

"Unfortunately, no. He'd left work early that day to take care of some errands, and he said he didn't run into anybody who knew him."

"What kind of errands? Would a security camera somewhere have caught him?"

"I'm sure the police'll check all that. I don't know."

Millie thought all the way back home about Ron's plight. Ron and Paige. Maybe he did kill her, she thought. He didn't seem the type, but probably few murderers could be picked out of a crowd as being "the type."

She thought about the times she'd talked with Ron, his interaction with others. He was affable, serious about his job, apparently committed to his wife—

Apparently. Were Ron's fond mentions of his wife too good to be true? Was Ron the one Monica had been with Sunday night, the reason he wasn't home when Luke arrived?

She tried to recall if Ron had ever said anything, pro or con, about early mornings, since Monica had said her guy wasn't a morning person. She couldn't remember his ever saying.

Millie thought back to the evening the Highgrove crew had come to dinner at the Victorian. Ron had been pleasant to Danny but hadn't gone out of his way to make a friend of him the way Whit had. Ron had been especially taken with the mansion library, had returned to look at it after Alice's "tour" finished. In fact, he had spent considerable time in there alone while others were preparing for the ball game.

Had he been in the library that whole time, or had he gone up to Jill's room to look for something in her chest of drawers? That had been a Wednesday, and Jill had noticed the intrusion in her room on Thursday but hadn't been certain whether it had happened the day before or on Tuesday, when Toby had been there.

How would Ron, or Toby for that matter, have known which room was Jill's? Oh, yes, all the men had been given tours of the impressive old house.

Stop it, Millie, she told herself. Ron gets arrested—probably unfairly—for one crime and you immediately have him guilty of another. If any of the Highgrove crew had been Jill's intruder, it could as easily have been Nolan or Whit.

Or even Luke. All the men had excused themselves at various times to use the restroom.

Millie's mind continued replaying that Tuesday evening, including the scene at the dinner table: the banter, Luke and Cynthia flirting, Jill's annoyance—

And her long, long look at the tablecloth beside Ron's plate. Staring at his left hand, perhaps?

His ringless left hand?

Millie recalled the photo of Ron and Paige on the wall in the project office. He had worn a wedding band in that picture—she remembered how the sun had glinted on it. She didn't think he'd been wearing one that night at the mansion.

Trust Jill to notice jewelry on people's hands. Or the lack of it.

Had that jewelry fixation led to Jill's death, Ron fearing she'd guess he had removed his ring to cheat on his wife more easily while away from home? Had he worried that Jill would, out of pique perhaps, tell his wife he hadn't been wearing his ring?

If Ron had killed Paige, whom he presumably had cared about, to prevent his wife's learning he had strayed, would he have hesitated to murder Jill, whom he hadn't loved?

That evening after dinner, for a change of subject, Alice called Millie to her room and showed her several pages in one of the red-backed journals. In the first entry, Prissy had hardly been able to contain her excitement that Effy was coming to Lynchburg, much sooner than expected. And he was bringing her a present, something she'd love, something in her favorite color.

"Red," Millie guessed, on reading the passage. "At least if those clothes that were with these diaries belonged to Prissy."

"Exactly. But that was apparently the only clue he gave her about the gift."

Millie went on reading. "Hmm, interesting. In the same letter in which Effy told her he was coming and bringing a gift, he enclosed a newspaper clipping about a stagecoach accident."

She looked at Alice, who shrugged.

"The incident happened near St. Louis, where her beloved was living, so it seems natural he'd find it interesting." Millie laughed. "Could it be that Miss Prissy was the teensiest bit self-centered, uninterested in anything that didn't concern her directly?"

"You think? But she does figure out a reason for his sending the article. See here?"

Millie read the part indicated. "Ah. Two women were thrown free of the coach and one of them, lady's maid to the other, lost something valuable belonging to her mistress, which she'd been carrying to try to fool would-be thieves.

"And Prissy figured the present he was bringing must be something valuable, so he sent the clipping as a warning to her not to travel with whatever it was. Or at least not to entrust it to her maid. I suppose that could be the explanation."

"Maybe. But from reading Prissy's journal so far, I don't have the impression she was overly bright—or maybe she was just self-involved, as you said—so he could have meant something else entirely."

"Keep reading, Alice. Now I really want to know what he brought her, and whether she was right about why he included the cutting."

"I will. I'm dying to know, myself."

The next day, Millie was well into her washing task at Poplar Forest when Alice came in and said her tooth was bothering her more today and she was going to fill her prescription for pain pills, then go home and rest, to give the medicine a chance to work. She'd ask Cynthia to drive her back over later, and they'd pick up Millie.

"Don't worry about coming back for me," Millie said. "I'll get Chas to bring me home. You need to rest, and we don't want Cynthia driving alone, in case Ted's around."

"Well, we'll see. I'll call you later."

"Take care of yourself."

After Alice left, Millie continued cleaning artifacts until mid-morning, then went to check on Chas. All day yesterday and earlier today he'd been in his office with the door closed. Now, however, his door was open, suggesting he was at least open to conversation. Millie tapped at his door and invited him to join her for coffee. He looked up with a woebegone expression, shook his head, then sighed and put down his pen.

"Yeah, okay. Sounds good, now you mention it."

They carried cups of coffee to the main workroom and sat at the big table.

"How are you doing, Chas? Really." Millie said. "I know Jill's death was an awful shock."

He ran a hand through his reddish curls. "They say time helps—though I can't imagine right now that anything could."

"You didn't have to come to work today, you know. I'm sure Harold would've understood."

"Trying to focus on work distracts me a little. It's better than sitting home staring at the walls." He sipped coffee, set the cup down, picked it up again. "Millie, I'm guessing you think Jill was just stringing me along, pretending to like me when she really didn't."

Millie said nothing. She did think that. In fact, Jill had admitted as much.

"She was interested in my jewelry, not in me. I knew that."

"You did?"

"Sure. Why should a pretty young woman like her be attracted to an old bachelor like me—a guy with two part-time jobs and no money, awkward and unsure around women? But I am a darned good lapidary. That was my ace in the hole."

"Jill said you're really talented."

"At making jewelry, yeah. My mistake was letting myself think our spending time together, sharing a mutual love of gems, could lead to something more. But whether or not anything ever developed between us, I'd've been happy to see her wearing jewelry I'd made."

Millie cleared her throat. "Chas, you started to tell me before about helping Jill find something or someone. Do you think whatever it was you were searching for could've led to her death?"

"Jeez, I hope not."

"Did—did you find whatever it was?"

"I did." He grinned wryly. "You're trying to ask, every way except straight out, what that something was. Okay, Millie, I've already told the investigators. I guess it doesn't matter anyway, now Jill's gone. She told me she had acquired a very fine piece of jewelry, but for personal reasons she didn't want it to be recognized by anyone when she wore it. She asked me if I'd re-cut it for her.

"I said I was flattered, but if it was a really special piece I'd be reluctant to try it. I'm good, Millie, darn good, but she seemed to need an exceptionally fine cutter, a real expert, with way more experience than I have."

Millie held her breath, hoping he'd continue.

"So she asked if I could find someone for her, someone who wasn't too inquisitive about where a stone came from. Obviously she had gotten it by less-than-honest means, and she was asking me to break the law by helping her get the stone re-shaped to hide her crime. I knew all that, and I'm basically an honest guy. So why didn't I tell her no, maybe even turn her in to the authorities?"

"You're not the first to let love, or attraction, determine his actions," Millie said gently.

He cradled his cup in both hands, taking small sips from it.

"So," she finally asked, "did you find a lapidary for Jill?"

He nodded. "Yeah. I've got contacts with other cutters, and word gets around about who isn't picky regarding the niceties of the law. A guy named Art Corcoran—A. C., as he likes to be called—was mentioned to me more than once. I got in touch, gave him Jill's cell-phone number and his to her, and said they could work things out between them. I wanted no part of making the actual deal."

"Do you know if they ever made contact, arranged for him to re-shape the stone?"

He shook his head.

"Did you ever see this special gem?"

"Nope. Jill trusted me only so far."

"Do you know anything about how it was set? As a pendant, a ring, or what?

"I really don't know, Millie. And shady as the whole thing

sounded, I didn't want to know a lot."

After Millie returned to work, she thought of little except the information Chas had confided. So Jill had had a special jewel. Millie didn't doubt Chas was right, that she'd acquired the gem in a way not strictly legal.

That must have been what the intruder had been searching for in her room. But who? And how had he, or she, known what Jill had?

Millie recalled her joking question when her housemate had mentioned someone's being in her room: "You don't have the British crown jewels stuffed into an old boot, do you?"

Hearing that, Jill had choked on the soda she was drinking. So that reference to crown jewels must have been too close to actuality for comfort. Not crown jewels, of course, but jewels. Or a jewel.

Millie's thoughts returned to that day at Williamsburg, when Jill had given her the diamond earrings to keep. She'd added that she also had something else of value, and Millie must see that her younger sister received *anything* valuable she owned. Just in case.

Jill had feared for her life, because of a jewel she had obtained illegally.

What? And from where? She must have stolen something from a jewelry store, one day while browsing. But how? Shops had safeguards against theft. Their staffs undoubtedly were taught not to leave a customer alone with expensive jewelry. Not stolen from a store, then.

Millie continued to worry about Jill's mysterious gem but could get no further on the puzzle.

Ron was released after a security tape turned up, showing him buying gas at a convenience store about the time of Paige's attack. He returned to work at Highgrove, much chastened by his experience but refusing to talk about it.

A television reporter broke the story that Jill had died from sudden cardiac arrest, caused by an "incredibly timely" blow to the chest "at just the wrong moment, the precise millisecond between heart contractions." From such a timely blow, the report said, an abnormal heart rhythm called ventricular fibrillation, or VF, could result, stopping all circulation and "instantly depriving the brain and other vital organs of oxygen."

Such a rare event could happen even in an apparently healthy individual such as Jill Greene had been, the newsman added.

Wow, Millie thought. Jill's murderer couldn't possibly have timed that blow with such precision on purpose. He, or she, might not have intended to kill her. But Jill was just as dead as if it had been meant.

The reporter also said Jill's body showed signs of having been moved from somewhere else after death occurred. He theorized that the murderer had used one of the archaeologists' wheelbarrows, kept when not in use in open-air storage on the Poplar Forest grounds, to move her lifeless body to the dig.

Uncomfortably, Millie remembered Luke's telling about their fight that Sunday night. Perhaps he'd struck Jill in anger, not meaning to kill her, then had panicked on seeing what he'd inadvertently caused.

She still didn't see why he'd have taken her body to Poplar Forest, though, or to the dig.

Wait. Maybe that had been an ironic commentary on her dislike of his occupation, her being discovered in an archaeological dig herself at the end. He wouldn't have used his own excavation, of course. But the one at Poplar Forest had been handy, and he'd know the terrain from his visits there.

She had only speculation, however, nothing to take to the police. Anyway, they undoubtedly were way ahead of her in considering Luke Brooks as a suspect.

Jill's mother and sister Rachel came by the Victorian to pick up her clothing and other belongings not taken by the police. Alice showed the two women to Jill's room, Millie trailing behind, hoping to be of use. And curious.

Mrs. Greene was a big woman with a no-nonsense exterior, but as she folded a blouse of Jill's and tenderly laid it in a suitcase, her bottom lip began to quiver.

"You don't have to do this, Mrs. Greene," Alice said from the doorway. "Millie and I would be glad to pack up your daughter's things for you."

"Sure," Millie seconded. "The two of you can wait downstairs, and we'll bring the filled suitcases and boxes down and put them in your car."

Mrs. Greene straightened and said with dignity, "I appreciate the offer, both of you. It was nice of you to suggest it when you called me about Jill, Mrs. Ross. You've been a wonderful mother figure to all these young women. But let me do this one last thing for my girl." She went back to work, clearly determined to get through the unpleasant chore with no pause that might make her unable to continue.

Jill's sister hovered near her mother, seemingly unaware of the tears coursing down her thin cheeks. She pulled a sweater from the closet and held it to her face, drinking in Jill's scent, and sobbed aloud. Mrs. Greene gently took the sweater from her and told her to wait for her downstairs. Millie moved from behind Alice and put out a hand to Rachel.

"How about joining me in a soda or cup of tea? Whichever you prefer."

Eyes averted, slight body shaking with emotion, Rachel followed. When they reached the kitchen, Millie offered several choices and Rachel selected an herbal tea. Millie carried both full cups to the terrace, where the women sat facing the house next door. Also Victorian in style, it was painted lavender with mauve and navy trim. Its owners, obviously avid gardeners, had carried out the blue/purple theme in their yard with larkspur, impatiens, salvia, hydrangea, lobelia, periwinkles, wisteria, and grape hyacinth. Millie found the riot of color oddly restful.

"I'm so sorry about your sister," she said, laying a gentle hand on Rachel's knee. "Jill spoke of you sometimes, and I know she loved you a lot."

Rachel nodded without making eye contact, her shoulders jerking with sobs. Millie reached into a pocket and brought out Jill's diamond earrings.

"Jill wanted you to have these," Millie said. "They were her favorite earrings, but she hadn't been able to wear them lately because of a rash on her ears. She asked me to hold onto them for her and see that you got them, if—if anything happened to her."

Rachel's eyes widened, and her weeping stopped. She took the gleaming baubles and turned them about in her hands, then looked at Millie.

"She loved these, and she'd told me she'd leave them to me in her will. But . . . I don't understand . . . why . . . did she expect something to happen to her?"

Millie had dreaded this part. "I believe she did, though she wouldn't tell me much. She did say she had something else, something even more valuable than these earrings, that she also wanted you to have. Did she ever tell you about that?"

Rachel opened and closed the hand that held the ear bobs. "Maybe. She sent me an e-mail a couple of weeks ago, saying she'd found something really nice, really pretty, that she wanted to show me the next time we saw each other."

"Found something. That was the word she used, 'found'?"

"Yeah."

"Hmm. I think the special item may have been a jewel of some kind. Did her message suggest that?"

"No. But it didn't say it wasn't jewelry, either."

"Did she indicate where this special piece was?"

"No." Rachel chewed her lip. "No."

Millie told her what Jill had said about the valuable item's being in a safe place but one she couldn't readily get to, at least not all the time. "Does that suggest any place to you? Maybe a spot at your house where she used to hide things she loved?"

Rachel shook her head, her long hair swinging. "No. She just said she was keeping it safe, somewhere that nobody could find without her telling them."

Tears gathered in her eyes again. "It's not fair," she murmured. "Jill was getting her life together after—"

"After?"

Rachel looked at Millie a long moment, as if wondering whether to say more. She evidently decided she could trust Millie, given their exchange of Jill's confidences.

"An uncle of ours did . . . things to Jill when she was a young girl. Told her not to tell or he'd hurt me. And she didn't—not for a long time. She finally did tell our mother, and Mom had that uncle arrested and prosecuted. Jill got counseling, but she's had a hard time trusting people, especially men. Her life seemed to be getting better, though, and now—"

Rachel wept quietly, as if joining her stillness to that painful silence Jill had endured as an abused child.

# ✯ Chapter Twenty

The rest of Millie's week was a blur of work. She spent more time with Danny, who clung closer to his mother than before, and worried about the many unanswered questions regarding the two murders. But her Charlottesville weekend with Scott loomed, and her excitement about it grew. Thursday evening, he phoned.

"Everything still on track for this weekend?" his dear voice asked. "You haven't decided to cancel on account of Jill's murder?"

"If my staying here would help catch her killer, of course I'd stay. But I've been interviewed a couple of times and told the police all I know. Wish I could figure out that strange e-mail from Jill, but so far I haven't."

"The whole thing seems odd. But I'm glad you can meet me in Charlottesville." Scott said he would fly there Friday evening and see her and Danny Saturday morning.

"Great! We'll pick you up around eleven. I have the MapQuest directions to Brian's house."

"Can't wait. Love you, sweetheart."

After the call, she decided to do online research about the University of Virginia. She felt well prepared to see Monticello, having gone to its Web site several times, but felt the need to know more about UVA. On its Web site, she took a virtual tour of the campus and read information about its classes, buildings, and famous founder. She learned it had a number of libraries, some devoted to specialized materials. Among the exhibits currently in a Special Collections Library named for Albert and Shirley Small, she noted, was a recently donated collection of early newspapers published in the West.

Hmm, Millie thought, wondering if it would have anything published in the territory that became Missouri.

Unlikely though the possibility of learning something related to Ephraim Hayes was, Millie was elated. She looked forward to her time in Charlottesville with even greater eagerness.

Late-afternoon sun lit Scott's rugged features as he smiled at Millie from the passenger side of her car.

"Sorry Danny caught a summer cold," he said, "but I'm awfully glad to have this time alone with you."

"Me, too," she said, laying her hand on Scott's.

She had driven from Lynchburg that morning and picked up Scott. They had looked around Charlottesville, had a leisurely lunch in a quiet soup-and-salad place, and taken a guided tour up Montalto, the mountain that neighbored Monticello and towered majestically above it, and which Jefferson had once owned. He had harvested timber from his "high mountain," had watched progress on construction and remodeling of his beloved home from this peak, and had planned an extensive park here, connected to Monticello by a bridge and a road. The latter plan had never come to fruition.

Along with the tour, Millie and Scott had strolled around the mountaintop and sat on a grassy verge at one side of it, enjoying clear air, the absence of traffic noise, and the sight of birds gliding and swooping around the mountain face. From high above modern Charlottesville, they looked down on the Jefferson Library, a small brick building at the base of Montalto that housed sources used by serious Jefferson scholars. She daydreamed about one day doing research there.

After dropping Scott at Brian's to change for the evening and checking into her motel, Millie had phoned to check on Danny.

"He's doing okay," Alice said. "Coughing, sneezing, irritable. Who isn't with a yucky cold? You and Scott having a good time in Charlottesville?"

"We are. I think Scott's glad he took a break from studying."

"Good. Want to speak to Danny? He's asleep, but I could wake him."

"No, let him sleep. I'll call back later."

Millie had picked Scott up again for the drive out to Monticello, her anticipation growing as they approached the turnoff to it. She drove through a gate, stopped to let a uniformed guard check their names off his list and be waved on, then proceeded slowly along the winding, woodsy lane. The Signature Tour, available only on Wednesday and Saturday evenings in summer, was a guilty pleasure she was allowing herself. Its "perks" included driving all the way up to the historic house, rather than parking below and riding a bus up, as on a regular tour.

When she had initially researched Monticello tours at its Web site, Millie had been tempted by this tour, which promised a fuller, more leisurely look at the house, an hour or more in a group of twenty, instead of a half-hour with forty-five on the daytime tour. But she'd regretfully decided Danny would be bored. A shorter Tour for Children and Their Families, offering a hands-on look at Monticello from a child's point of view, seemed more appropriate.

But Friday morning Danny had waked up with a sore throat and sniffles. Millie had felt sure it was only a cold, but he wouldn't be up to a weekend excursion. Reluctantly, she'd started to call Scott to cancel, but Alice had offered to do nurse duty and insisted Millie go. After some hesitation, she had let herself be persuaded. With her promise to bring gifts and take him to Monticello later, Danny had agreed. She had phoned Scott, explained the change, and suggested they take the Signature Tour. He'd thought the additional cost—forty-five dollars as opposed to fifteen—well worth it.

"Of course, I wouldn't have had even the fifteen dollars before Nathan Henry's legacy changed my life," he'd said with a laugh.

"I know. I feel guilty splurging, since some people can't even afford the basic tour, but I do think old Nathan would approve of our spending part of his wealth this way. Besides, I want to do it."

"Me, too. And if he wouldn't approve, who cares? He's not coming back to reclaim his money. Don't feel guilty, sweets. Let's just enjoy it."

She had booked their tickets online but had nearly backed out when Danny waked up Saturday morning feeling awful and out of sorts. Alice had gentled him into a better mood, however, and sent Millie out the door.

Now, steering around a curve in the quiet, stately woods, Millie indulged her favorite fantasy when visiting any historic location—imagining she had lived at the place in its heyday. Today, she saw herself as one of the enslaved people at Monticello, trudging through the forest looking for mushrooms for Jefferson's table. Fortunately, Scott understood her need to "re-live" the past and allowed her quiet time to wool-gather.

Soon, she began talking again, signaling her return to the present. "I owe Alice Ross big time. She does lots of nice things for Danny and me. Hamilton's murder was an awful blow, but she and I got to know each other because of it."

"Hope I'll meet her some day."

"You could change your plans and drive back to Lynchburg with me."

"Boy, is that tempting, but . . . I'd better not."

"How's the studying going?"

"Okay, I guess. There's just so much to cover, so many things my committee could ask. But I'll get through it. Other people do."

"Many who aren't as bright as you, I'm sure."

"Thanks. But I'm afraid my less-sharp peers have mostly found other lines of work, or have settled for a master's as their terminal degree. People who take doctoral comps tend to be both smart and determined. Even so, some get weeded out. After studying like fiends, maybe taking comps more than once, they finally give up."

"Are you preparing an 'out' for yourself, in case you flunk?"

He grinned. "Never hurts to have an excuse ready. But I'd hate myself if I just barely failed because I'd spent a few too many days playing."

"You really think you're cutting things that fine? That a day or two more of studying could mean the difference between passing and failing?"

"Probably not, but I need to give this my best shot. I want to pass the first time and get this hurdle behind me."

"Okay, I'll quit tempting you to loaf."

They parked, walked up a path beside a truck garden, climbed steps, and arrived in front of the Museum Shop at 6:05. They had been told to arrive no later than 6:15 for the 6:30 P.M. tour.

Other tourists occupied two park benches or perched on a nearby rock wall surrounding the famous residence. Millie had seen pictures of Monticello from many angles, had caught glimpses of it while driving up the mountain, and had seen it from above at Montalto. But now, finding herself so near the graceful columned dwelling almost took her breath away. Monticello was bigger and grander than Poplar Forest, but the two had clearly been fashioned with the same love of beauty, eye for detail, and striving for perfection.

She took advantage of the wait to nip into the Museum Shop, buy a game for Danny, and stow it in her car.

"Glad we chose this evening tour," Scott observed when she returned. "Brian says hordes of people take the daytime tours in summer. Sometimes one group comes into a room just as another's leaving."

"So Monticello's overrun with visitors," Millie said, "and most people aren't aware Poplar Forest exists—much like when Jefferson was alive."

"Yeah. I'd never heard about his second house until you said you were going there, and I'm reasonably well informed. Wish I had time to see Poplar Forest this trip, but I better wait on that until comps are over. If they ever are. Right now it's hard to envision my life beyond them."

Two people, a woman carrying a clipboard and a man wearing an official-looking smile, came down the gravel path towards the group. The sixtyish woman, short and round-shouldered, welcomed the group and introduced herself as Susan, and her taller, older colleague as Henry. Susan said they'd see parts of the house not on the standard tour, including the famous dome room, and participants should feel free to ask questions of either her or Henry.

She led them along a path between the rock wall and the museum shop, the same route guests would have taken when Jefferson lived here. In those days, she said, visitors had traveled concentric circles called roundabouts coming up the mountain, a difficult journey then. She paused near a corner of the yard, at a vista that had been a favorite of Jefferson's. This was where a white sheet had been hung on July 4, 1826, she said, to notify family members staying at nearby Tufton Farm that Thomas Jefferson, gravely ill for several days, had died.

She briefly summarized the history of the house. Then they circled it and climbed the front steps, Henry taking over to tell about the two Monticellos. The first had been planned when Jefferson was a young man and remained unfinished when his beloved Martha died eleven years into their marriage. The second, more sophisticated version he'd designed years later, after traveling to cosmopolitan places such as Philadelphia, Annapolis, Paris, and Italy. He hadn't been a great innovator in architecture, according to Henry, but had copied and re-interpreted elements he liked in buildings he visited.

"He worked on Monticello off and on for about forty years and considered it his 'essay in architecture.' Of course, a good essay must be revised."

Inside, they saw an impressive two-story entry hall, with Jefferson's calendar clock, its day-of-the-week wall markings descending to the floor below.

"Seems like it would've been easier to change his design than to cut a hole in the floor," a visitor remarked.

Henry smiled. "It's true he could have re-calibrated the weights and days, but he wasn't here when the clock was being installed. So he wrote the installer to let the weights descend into the basement."

Millie knew Danny would be interested in the buffalo robe draped over the balcony rail, as well as the elk antlers and Indian beadwork displayed, all reminders of Lewis's and Clark's encounters with Indian tribes. The entry hall had been used by Jefferson as a museum for edification of his visitors, the guide said.

"The concept of extinction of animal species had been proposed by that time, but Jefferson didn't want to believe it. Among the things he asked Lewis and Clark to look for in their travels was evidence of extinct species, including the unicorn."

*Unicorns? Please!* Sylva's voice said.

They saw the South Square Room, used by Martha Jefferson Randolph as a sitting room and classroom for her eleven children. A stand displayed an elaborate copy of the Declaration of Independence, one of three at Monticello.

Then came the library, which had housed many of the nine-thousand-plus books Jefferson had owned in his lifetime. His books, along with most of his other belongings, had been sold at his death, but some had been bought back and were now behind glass doors in what he'd called his book room.

"Some volumes still have Thomas Jefferson's fingerprints in them," Susan observed.

The third president had read seven languages, she added, including ancient Anglo-Saxon, which he had learned from George Wythe, his mentor and sometime law partner.

"It's been said," Susan noted, "that Wythe, along with two other influential men Jefferson used to dine with when a student in Williamsburg—Dr. William Small, math professor at the College of William and Mary and Jefferson's surrogate father, and Francis Fauquier, the worldly royal governor—'created' Thomas Jefferson. Certainly all were learned men who encouraged and enlightened young Tom through witty, literate dinner conversations."

From the book room, they could see into the light-filled greenhouse, where Jefferson had grown plants and made locks and chains at his workbench, and where his pet mockingbird had probably lived.

As fellow tour members looked over the greenhouse and book room, Scott murmured to Millie, "How's everything at your house? Had anymore late-night skulkers?"

"Fortunately, no," she replied, low-voiced as he. "We're all nervous, of course, especially after Jill's murder. She had finally told Alice and Cynthia about the intrusion in her room, but none of us can figure out who it was. Of course we hope Ted's left town but can't be sure. We're persevering, though."

"I'm worried about you, you know. Any chance you'd cut short your stay in Lynchburg?"

"That's always an option. I've talked about it with Danny, and with Alice, and we've agreed we probably aren't in real danger. We'd be off like a shot if I thought we were."

"If you say so. Just be careful, really careful."

They saw Jefferson's private suite, his bedroom and office—or "cabinet," as he'd called the latter—the two separated by an alcove-bed wall. The cabinet contained his collection of early-nineteenth-century scientific instruments and, like the library and a few other rooms, was shaped like the end of an elongated octagon. In the bedroom, they saw an over-the-bed closet, reached by stepladder and ventilated by oval holes near the ceiling. Mirrors on one wall reflected natural light that entered, somewhat dusky now, from a skylight and triple-sash windows.

Monticello contained thirteen skylights, Henry said, "some of the first in the country." He confided with a smile, "They leak just a little."

He told about Jefferson's daily routine, rising with the sun, checking and recording the temperature on a thermometer by his bed, and then, no matter how freezing the weather, plunging his feet into cold water.

"Perhaps he was onto something," the guide added. "He had very few colds."

Susan showed them the parlor, an airy, spacious room shaped like the end of an octagon. It featured a Jefferson-designed parquet floor, a harpsichord Patsy Jefferson had often played for guests, the siesta or "Campeachy" chair its owner had used during troublesome bouts of rheumatism, and busts and portraits of famous men. Two of the busts, on pedestals flanking doors to the west portico, were of Tsar Alexander I of Russia, whom Jefferson had admired, and Napoleon Bonaparte, whom he had not. Their owner had placed the two busts in opposition to each other, the guide said, as a contrast between good and evil.

Napoleon, Millie thought, the ruler who had sold Jefferson the vast lands of the Louisiana Purchase. Happy though the third president had been at the acquisition of those Western lands, he'd considered Bonaparte cold-blooded and unprincipled.

As Millie gazed at Napoleon's likeness, she thought about Jefferson's relations with France over the years. An unabashed Francophile, he had lived with his young daughters in France for years, returning home on the eve of that country's revolution. Though he had initially applauded its echo of America's own quest for liberty, he'd been horrified by the loss of lives and property during the Reign of Terror.

Lives and property, Millie thought. Property—

The glimmer of a memory came to her, something that had been lost during the French Revolution. What was it?

Probably unimportant, Millie thought. But she couldn't shake the feeling it was something she needed to remember.

"Think you could stand to live here?" Scott asked as they strolled through the elegant room.

"Hmm," Millie said, finger to cheek as if considering. "A stately, one-of-a-kind house, great views from every window, books everywhere. I could force myself."

"You wouldn't have liked the place in its original state, *sans* central heat and air-conditioning."

"I wouldn't have enjoyed walking around piles of lumber in an unfinished house either, which Martha Jefferson had to do much of her married life."

"Must not've bugged her too much. Apparently it was a happy marriage."

They saw the dining room, a light-infused space with a lazy-Susan door that had allowed food to go from kitchen to dining room without intrusion by servants on mealtime conversation, also dumbwaiters in the fireplace mantel that had brought wine from the cellar. Millie escaped for a moment to her fantasy world, imagining she was Jefferson himself, proudly serving an elegant French dish prepared by his chef, Sally Hemings's brother James.

Susan told them about the many new foods Jefferson had introduced to the American table, including ice cream, macaroni, and olives. As many as twenty-five family members had sometimes lived and dined together here, the guide said.

"And with the many, many visitors Jefferson entertained, his daughter Martha might serve up to fifty people at a meal."

Wow, Millie thought. Even with servants, Martha must have kept busy morning to night ensuring that the household ran smoothly. Maybe Jefferson's three brilliant male dinner companions in Williamsburg had created the nation's third President, but women and slaves had also helped him be the Thomas Jefferson of history.

They saw the light-filled tea room; the north octagonal bedroom, called "Mr. Madison's room" because Jefferson's good friend James Madison and his wife Dolly had often stayed there; and the North Square Room, another alcove-bedded space. Then they climbed two flights of narrow, twisting steps to the third floor.

Millie remembered what Luke had told her, that Jefferson didn't like stairs because they occupied too much space.

In response to a question about their narrowness, Henry confirmed this, adding, "We can't include the dome room on regular tours now because many people can't negotiate the steps."

Eventually, they emerged on the third level. As Millie and Scott waited for others to finish the climb, he asked if anything more had come to light about whether Highgrove was a Jefferson design.

"Luke seems inclined to think it is, but he's a cautious professional. I hope it is, of course."

"I know you're interested in the puzzle, sweets, but I can't say I'm keen on your continuing to work at Highgrove. The two murdered women were both involved with guys who're on that crew."

"I know. And I do think about both Paige and Jill when I'm there. But I really don't think I'm in danger, Scott. If I did, rest assured I wouldn't go there anymore, Jefferson house or no."

"But you could be wrong. If you don't want to tell Luke you're afraid to work there, I'll happily be your excuse. Just say your boyfriend's jealous and doesn't like you working around four guys. Which is kinda true."

"It's sweet that you're jealous, Scott. So long as you don't start obsessing. Like Ted."

# ★ Chapter Twenty-One

On the third floor, they saw a weathervane that connected to a dial in the porch ceiling downstairs, used by Jefferson to record wind direction each day. Millie commented on how many aspects of science, politics, the arts, and learning in general had interested Jefferson.

"He was a true Renaissance man," Susan agreed with a smile.

In the dome room, even at twilight, enough illumination poured from the big porthole windows to give the space a soaring, airy quality. A high ribbed ceiling curved to an oculus window at the top. Thomas Jefferson's spirits must have lifted on entering his "sky room," Millie thought. But spectacular as the chamber was, the inadequate stairs up to it had meant it was mainly used for storage and as a playroom for the Jefferson grandchildren.

They descended the other set of steps to the basement, and Susan invited them to see the exhibits there, the adjoining "dependency wings," and the stables and grounds on their own. Henry and most of the tourists left, but Millie stopped Susan with a question.

"I'll be bringing my son, Danny, later. Can you tell me what we'll see on the children's tour?"

Susan's face lit with interest. "It happens I'm also a guide on that tour. The families walk through the house as we've done but don't go to the dome. Kids' tours are thirty minutes, usually eighteen in a group. It's especially neat when grandparents come—they love to see their grandchildren engaged and learning.

"Most museums are difficult for children, because they can't touch things. But here, we emphasize touching." She gave examples. In the dining room, children held a pewter sippy cup to see how heavy it felt and smelled a vanilla bean while Susan told about a recipe for vanilla ice cream Jefferson brought home from his travels abroad.

"Neat," Millie said. "A guide who references ice cream will be talking Danny's language."

"I also use stuffed animals, like letting the kids feel the shape of a bison's hump while I tell about the buffalo-hump shield in the entry hall, which is like the one Lewis and Clark brought back."

In the book room, she said, children drew straws as Jefferson's grandchildren did to see who would get to read the book first.

"Jefferson must've been a neat grandfather to have," Scott said.

"He doted on his grandkids and led them in playing games. Some of the male guides demonstrate his technique for foot races. He'd line the grandchildren up by height, give the smallest a little advantage, and award each a prize."

"I can't wait to bring Danny. Thanks."

Millie and Scott walked through the basement, seeing a display about Shadwell, where Jefferson had grown up. His ancestral home had been destroyed by fire when he was a young man, taking with it the records of his early life. They also looked at wine and beer cellars, the ice house and stables, and Mulberry Row, where slave quarters had once stood.

As they rode back down the mountain, Millie sighed with

contentment. "That was lovely. I almost feel I've had a visit with Jefferson."

"Yeah. But all that talk about ice cream and French food made me hungry. Don't spare the horses getting to the restaurant."

He had researched Charlottesville eateries online and made a reservation at a Continental restaurant. Millie realized she was ravenous, too.

Glancing at Scott, she thought how much richer her life was for knowing him. He loved good food and the ambiance of fine dining just as she did, but he always considered Danny's tastes when the three of them ate out together. They couldn't force Danny to accept him, but she appreciated Scott's efforts to get to know her son.

At her insistence, however, he didn't ply Danny with gifts. Since receiving the Henry legacy, she'd resisted giving her son lots of "things," wanting him to grow up with no sense of entitlement, able to empathize with those less fortunate. Scott respected her struggle with the question of how much was too much and gave Danny only the occasional token gift.

Tonight, however, she was looking forward to a "grown-up" evening.

Before going into the restaurant, Millie again called Lynchburg. This time Danny was awake. He grumbled that he felt awful, and she heard congestion in his voice. But she trusted Alice's assurance that he was doing okay.

"You bringin' me somethin', Mom?"

She said she'd be bringing him a game of skittles, which was popular with Colonial children and which she thought he and Kevin would enjoy playing. That satisfied him, and they said goodnight.

The restaurant was attractive and quiet, and Millie enjoyed her meal of grilled salmon, asparagus, Caesar salad prepared tableside, and chocolate soufflé.

"I'm glad Danny gets along with your housemates," Scott said.

"Yes, he's gotten something good from each of them. Alice is the grandmother he's never had, although my friend Sylva's a kind of *great*-grandmother to him. He and Cynthia have bonded over plants and the kids' camp. Jill likes—liked—the same jokes and sports he does."

"How's Danny dealing with her death?"

"Not too badly. He gets sad sometimes, misses the way they used to joke, and clings to me more now. But he's a strong little kid. My own view of Jill has changed since I learned she was abused as a child. I see now why she didn't always give people the benefit of the doubt. Anyway, she was a friend, and you can't expect friends to be perfect."

"Except for me."

"Except for you."

Millie gazed around appreciatively at the restaurant. Soft lamplight brought out the richness of dark woods, glinted off the gold fleur-de-lis pattern on the ivory wallpaper. She felt herself growing drowsy . . .

Her eyes flew open. Fleur-de-lis. That explained the partial memory that had nagged her since seeing Napoleon's bust at Monticello. Jill had told Millie, just after her arrival in Lynchburg, about a famous jewel carried in a pouch with a fleur-de-lis pattern. It had once belonged to crowned heads in both France and England, had been lost during the French Revolution, then had turned up in the possession of an English lady traveling in Europe. Later, it had been seen in this country but had disappeared again.

What was it Jill had called the stone? The Scarlet something. Oh, yes, the Scarlet Star. It had been a star ruby.

Poor Jill, Millie thought. How she would have liked to own the Scarlet Star, even to see it, touch it.

The next day, Millie picked up Scott and they ate a leisurely breakfast, then drove through bustling Charlottesville to the campus of the University of Virginia. It was a mixture of modern and classical buildings until they reached the original part of the school, recognizable by its cluster of Greco-Roman structures and the dome of the Rotunda, which towered above nearby rooftops. Fortunately, they found a parking spot within easy walking distance of Jefferson's "Academical Village."

Millie felt excited, not only about seeing Jefferson's college but because of her plan to check out the Small Library. She hadn't mentioned this to Scott, superstitious about jinxing her chances of finding useful information there.

As they walked beside one of the college's distinctive serpentine walls, she peered over its undulating top at an attractive yard with flowers, trees, and a bench that invited contemplation.

"This curvy wall's pretty," Scott observed, "but how practical is it?"

"Very, apparently. Since it's one brick thick instead of two, it saves on materials, yet the curves make it stable and sturdy. Jefferson copied the idea from walls in Europe. These gardens and walls separate the Pavilions—faculty housing—from the Ranges, where student dorms and dining facilities are."

"Neat. I wouldn't mind studying here myself."

"Me neither. But given our ties elsewhere . . ."

They passed through an archway and entered what seemed a separate town from another age. Buildings in various versions of the Jeffersonian Classicism style ranged around a long central rectangle of clipped, tree-dotted grass. Two young men in jeans and T-shirts tossed a Frisbee in a corner of the lawn, the only reminder that this was a functioning twenty-first-century university.

Gazing at the graceful buildings, Millie felt her heart lift. This was Thomas Jefferson's dream, the college he had founded and overseen in his old age. At the north end stood the impressive Rotunda. On the east and west sides, facing each other at intervals, stood ten Pavilions featuring columns, second-story terraces, and covered brick sidewalks, no two buildings exactly alike. At the south end, which Millie knew Jefferson had intended to leave open to symbolize the limitless freedom of the human mind, three newer buildings stood.

"With modern Charlottesville all around, who'd expect this here?" Scott said reverently.

Millie smiled, seeing in her mind's eye an aged Thomas Jefferson striding about the collegiate town he'd created, nodding in satisfaction.

They entered the lower level of the Rotunda building, where Scott's friend had said campus tours began, and waited with a few others.

"You still tutoring Larry?' Millie deliberately kept her tone unemotional.

Scott's face darkened. "Yeah, but he's a big worry to his mom and me. He's been hanging with a couple of kids who are known trouble-makers."

Millie squelched the twinge of jealousy she felt on hearing him say, "his mom and me." As if they were a couple, worried about their son. She forced a sympathetic smile.

"You said his mother's working two jobs?"

"Yeah. After Jolene's shift at the nursing home ends, she clerks at a convenience store. Gets home late, dog-tired. I've taken Larry to the movies and to a ball game, but with teaching and studying myself I can't give him much time either."

"He making any progress in his reading?"

"A little. We found a book at the public library that he seemed to actually enjoy reading. He needed help with lots of words, but I think he's begun to get a glimmering that reading can be fun."

"That's wonderful." Millie considered. "Larry's a couple of

years older than Danny, but Danny reads well above grade level. They might enjoy some of the same books." She gave him a few titles Danny'd liked and said she'd give the question more thought. "I can e-mail you other possibilities."

"Thanks. I doubt that reading better could solve all Larry's problems, but I bet it'd help."

"What about kids' activities at the parks or YMCA? There must be things he could participate in that would help him make different friends."

"Yeah, I guess. Problem is, Jolene has no time or energy to investigate what's available. Maybe I'll try to do some of that for her."

"Jolene's lucky to have your help." Despite her brave words, Millie felt a sinking feeling at the thought of his spending more time with Jolene.

On their tour they learned that the campus design resulted from Jefferson's dislike of the system of distancing college professors from students. Hoping to promote one-on-one exchanges between the two, he had placed faculty and student housing, classrooms, library, and dining halls all in close proximity around a shared lawn. He had intended UVA to be a private university, but the expense involved made him turn his college over to the state of Virginia.

Jefferson hadn't been a fan of corners because they trapped light, so he'd emphasized circular and oval shapes in his Rotunda, both outside and inside. The building had originally been classrooms, except that the dome had housed the university library.

The Rotunda contained two small ovens that had produced gunpowder during the Civil War, and a large bronze bell that, in the early years of the university, had rung each morning to summon students to class. The bell bore a crack, from water's collecting in it and freezing, and a bullet hole from when boisterous students had fired at the nearby university clock and missed.

A life-size statue of Thomas Jefferson reigned from a pedestal in the hallway. The Rotunda had been largely destroyed by fire in 1895, but UVA students had managed with heroic effort to save the statue. They'd first lowered it onto a library table, which had collapsed under its weight, then lined one side of the staircase with mattresses and wrestled the heavy marble object downward, breaking stairs as they went. Unfortunately, the head had lodged in a fireplace niche in a curved upper wall. Meantime, a professor had tried to dynamite a bridge between the Rotunda and an annex, hoping to slow the flames' progress. The considerable explosion he produced failed to keep the fire from spreading but did blast Mr. Jefferson loose. The students escaped to the lawn with him just in time.

*Quite a story for those students to tell their grandchildren,* Sylva commented: *"The time I helped rescue President Jefferson."*

Climbing a dramatic curved staircase, they saw the dome room, a huge circular space lined with columns and a railed balcony, all lit from above by rays from an oculus skylight. Rows of folding chairs, placed as for a lecture, covered a portion of the shiny hardwood floor. Millie and Scott fell silent, awed by the Rotunda's majesty and vastness. She turned slowly around, trying to take it all in.

"This dome room is considered one of the seven historical wonders of the United States," their guide said.

Scott and Millie strolled about, peering into study alcoves. "I would love to study here," Scott said wistfully. "I almost feel Jefferson could show up at any minute. But I need to be with Aunt Charla as much as possible. She doesn't know me part of the time—thinks I'm Orvis, one of the many students she taught. At least Orvis was one of her favorites. And now and then, she calls me by my right name."

"She raised you, and, Alzheimer's or not, she's still your aunt."

"She and your Sylva would've liked each other if they'd met a few years ago. After meeting Sylva that one time I visited, I see why you're devoted to her."

*Yeah, I'm a sweetheart, all right.*

The tour moved down the stairs and out of the Rotunda building, onto the colonnaded walkway, where they stopped in front of a Pavilion and looked through a picture window at the resident's comfortable living room. The Pavilions were now assigned to distinguished faculty members. As for students, "living on the Lawn" was now a privilege granted to a few, based partly on the student's grade-point average, partly on his or her service to the university and the larger community.

When the tour was over, Scott and Millie walked with their guide back to the Rotunda. She asked where the Small Special Collections Library was.

"I read about it online," she explained, on seeing Scott's quizzical glance.

The guide gave directions and mentioned the collection of rare early periodicals published in the American West that was now on display.

Understanding dawned on Scott's face. As soon as their guide left, he said, "Interested in the library, eh? Not in old St. Louis newspapers?"

"Can't put anything past you."

"And don't you forget it. Let's go check out the exhibit."

As they neared the library, they passed four rectangular wooden boxes spaced across the lawn, each holding a panel of heavy glass. Scott looked a question at Millie.

"Skylights," she said. "The Small Library is under ground." Peering through one of the panes, she thought she saw movement below.

They entered the building, passed a big gallery on the right holding a collection of maps, and descended a dramatic spiral staircase. At the bottom, they found themselves in a barrel-vaulted gallery. An exhibit on their left, according to a sign, displayed materials related to the Declaration of Independence, including a copy of the rare Dunlap broadside of the famous document, Jefferson letters relating to it, and pages of newspapers from 1776 that mentioned it. Millie was intrigued but decided she hadn't time to browse today, maybe when she came back later.

In the gallery proper, they found the Wade Heaton Collection, which an explanatory sign said was a recent acquisition, willed to the library by Mr. Heaton, who had recently died. Heaton had been a devotee of the Old West and a student of influences that shaped it. His focus had been periodicals published in various locales that would become the Western states, and he'd collected mainly front pages. These early papers had been published at differing intervals and in varying sizes, the sign said, depending at least partly on the size of paper available to their printers.

Millie and Scott walked from one display case to another. Several small-sized sheets in one caught her eye, and she stopped for a better look. The three front pages were from the *Missouri Dispatch*. Published in St. Louis, they were printed on pages about eight by twelve inches in size, with three columns to a page.

Hardly daring to hope, Millie looked for the dates of publication. Two were from late 1808, the third from April, 1807. She quickly ran her eye over the 1807 front page, which contained several brief items, one about the trial of a horse thief in the area, another about prices trappers were receiving for animal pelts, compared to the previous year's prices.

A third told of the mysterious disappearance of a bricklayer who worked for a prominent local builder. Mrs. Edith Blevins, the bricklayer's landlady, had reported her lodger's disappearance, saying he was a steady young man, despite being behind on his rent, and she feared foul play.

But what had made the item newsworthy in the editor's eyes,

apparently, was the notoriety of Mrs. Blevins, known throughout the area as an agitator for abolition. For that same reason, evidently, the police had discounted her story.

The name of the missing man was Ephraim Hayes.

Millie's heart skipped. She poked her palm with a fingernail, to make sure she was awake. Wordlessly, she pointed at the item. Scott read it, grinned, and gave her a hug.

"How about that!" he said, trying to whisper, but the intensity in his voice drew the attention of a woman at a nearby display case. She frowned at him.

Millie hugged Scott back, then drew away and read the item again to make sure she had really read what she'd thought. Sure enough, one Ephraim Hayes had disappeared from St. Louis in April of 1807. Had he come on to Lynchburg then?

Partly out of curiosity, partly to calm herself, Millie skimmed the other articles on the page. One concerned a stagecoach accident that had happened in the vicinity. The coach had been traveling over rough ground when an axle broke and the stage turned over, throwing two female passengers clear. One was a Lady Jane Peale, lately arrived in the country from Bavaria, the other her maid, Samantha Goodhue.

Stagecoach accidents must have been fairly common then, Millie thought. But a sense of familiarity with the situation made her read on. She learned that both women had been hurt, the lady with a concussion, her maid with multiple cuts and bruises. The maid had been frantic, the article said, because in the accident a valuable item that belonged to her mistress had dropped from Samantha's bustle, where it had been hidden to foil thieves.

Lady Jane had been unconscious for a time, but on awaking and learning of the loss had demanded that St. Louis authorities find her property, as discreetly as possible. A thorough search of the area where the stage mishap had occurred had proved futile. One searcher wasn't as close-mouthed as the lady could have wished, and a *Dispatch* reporter soon had the story.

The owner of the missing item had described it as a small pouch, brown with a fleur-de-lis pattern in gold, holding a ring—an inexpensive bauble, Lady Jane said, but one with great sentimental value. The enterprising reporter, however, had bribed the maid and learned that the piece was in fact a very valuable gold ring set with a large star ruby called the Scarlet Star.

All at once, Millie felt faint. She reached for Scott's arm and took deep breaths, trying to regain her equilibrium. Presently, she felt better, enough to stand on her own. Scott held onto her, his eyes full of concern and curiosity.

"Scott, I can't believe this!" she said in low tones. "The Scarlet Star is a stone Jill told me about, right after I arrived in Lynchburg. Let's sit down. I need to absorb this."

They found chairs in a nearby reading room, and Millie sat with face in hands, trembling, until the shock of the discovery began to dissipate. The Scarlet Star.

And it had disappeared about the same time Ephraim Hayes had. Could there possibly be some connection?

Millie looked up at the ceiling, at one of the skylights she and Scott had seen above ground.

Maybe Ephraim had found the Star before the all-out search began, she thought. If he'd guessed its worth—the elegant carrying pouch would have been a strong clue, in addition to the stone's size and brilliance—he might have made off with it, perhaps intending to ransom it to its owner. But then, something might have happened to prevent his doing so, perhaps the fear he'd be arrested for theft.

Or—?

Prissy.

She felt sure she was right. Prissy's Effy was Ephraim Hayes. And the gift he'd promised to bring her had indeed been something in her favorite color. Red.

Scarlet.

The article in the *Dispatch* must be the same one Effy had sent Prissy, a clue to the gift he was bringing. Poor, dense, self-absorbed Prissy hadn't made that connection.

But why be critical of her, Millie thought more charitably. Millie hadn't seen it herself. Nor had Alice.

Millie managed to pull herself together enough to tell Scott of her discovery. His amazement and glee matched hers, and they silently squeezed each other's hands.

Then they spoke with a librarian and filled out a request for a photocopy of the front page in question, giving both Millie's e-mail and snail-mail addresses. The librarian explained it would take a few days to complete the request, but then Printing Services would e-mail Millie an invoice. On receipt of payment, the copy would be mailed to her.

Scott and Millie left the building, holding hands and talking about her discovery.

"You'll definitely get an academic paper out of this," Scott said. "It'd be even better if you could account for Hayes's time between April of 1807, when he disappeared from St. Louis, and July of 1807, when he died in Lynchburg. But you can't have everything, I guess."

They had talked earlier about going to see the Edgar Allan Poe room, where the famous novelist was thought to have resided during his short tenure as a UVA student, but both felt too flustered for more sightseeing.

They had lunch, nearly too keyed-up to eat, and strolled around the shops adjoining UVA, then returned to Millie's car, planning to rest and change for dinner at a different "grown-up" restaurant. They intended to see the ruins of a Jefferson-designed building at nearby Barboursville on Monday before returning to their respective homes. But as they neared the car, Scott's cell phone rang. From his end of the conversation, Millie gathered it was Jolene, upset about something. Annoyance tightened Millie's lips.

When Scott ended the call, he looked gloomy.

"Afraid I'll have to cut this weekend short, sweetheart. Larry's been picked up for shoplifting, and Jolene's nearly hysterical. She says he's trying to act 'cool,' but she's sure he's terrified as well."

Millie didn't say anything. It was all she could do not to lash out in anger. She tried to tell herself that, if it were Danny who was in trouble with the police, she'd be frantic too.

They got into the auto, Millie feeling she'd swallowed a stone that had lodged in her throat.

"Sweetheart?" Scott said. "You okay with this?"

Millie decided she couldn't pretend that ending their time together early because of Jolene didn't matter to her. She swallowed hard, then said in a steady, though chilly, tone, "Actually, I'm not. I understand Jolene's worried about her son, but it seems to me she's becoming too dependent on you."

He didn't speak at first. Sneaking a glance at him, Millie saw his jaw was set.

"As a single mother yourself," he finally said coolly, "I'd have expected you to be more sympathetic."

"I do sympathize with Jolene. But I've had to learn to depend on myself. Being a single mom doesn't mean you can cling like a leech to the first sympathetic man you meet."

"Leech? That's pretty harsh."

"Maybe. But I think calling you home early from the first fun weekend you've allowed yourself in months is a lot for her to ask."

"I see. Then I guess we'll just have to disagree about that."

Neither spoke for a time. They reached Brian's house, and Scott climbed out.

"You planning to fly back today, then?" Millie asked without expression.

"If I can get a flight."

"Then I'll drop you at the airport and head on back to Lynchburg."

"Okay."

Scott secured a reservation on an early evening flight and phoned Millie at the motel to give her particulars. She packed her bag, checked out, and collected Scott. They drove to the airport mostly in silence. At the terminal, Scott lifted his bag out, set it near a check-in point, and came around to the driver's side of the car. Spreading both hands on the door frame, he looked at her, his expression a mixture of sadness and frustration.

"I am sorry about this, Millie. But I couldn't enjoy sightseeing here if I knew I was needed in Boulder."

Millie gazed at him a long moment, her heart in turmoil. She wanted to kiss him goodbye but couldn't bring herself to, with this unresolved problem between them.

"I hope things work out okay for Larry," she said. "Maybe this'll be a wake-up call for him."

"Let's hope." Scott turned away, then came back. Lifting a strand of Millie's hair, he touched it to his lips. "Be careful driving back to Lynchburg," he said. "And don't take any chances there, till that killer's caught."

"Sure. You have a good flight."

He watched her a moment longer, then slapped a hand on the door frame and walked away.

# ✭ Chapter Twenty-Two

Millie had an easy drive back to Lynchburg, except for tears and self-scolding. Maybe she should have pretended Scott's decision to return early hadn't bothered her.

No, if they couldn't be honest with each other, they didn't belong together.

She pulled off the highway and got a soft drink in a convenience store. Before starting off again, she called Sylva on her cell phone. They'd had several conversations since Millie's arrival in Virginia, and Millie felt particularly in need of the elderly woman's counsel.

After their greetings, Sylva asked how the weekend in Charlottesville was going.

"It was going great. Until Jolene called." Millie summarized the situation and what she and Scott had said.

"Ah."

"Sylva, I came across as a harpy who cares only for herself and what she wants."

Sylva chuckled. "I very much doubt that."

"Well, I could have been more understanding. I didn't much like myself."

"So you are human, after all."

"Please don't make light of this, Sylva. Why couldn't I at least have kissed Scott goodbye? And why'd I have to run my mouth calling Jolene a leech?"

"Millie, dear, I agree it wasn't your finest hour. But in the end, we have to forgive each other and ourselves for being human. I'm sure once Scott has time to think things over, he'll see that what you said was valid. Sure, you could've phrased it better, but you did have a point."

"So you don't think I was totally unreasonable? Jealousy's such an ugly emotion."

"Can be. But it's also flattering to Scott. Besides, the shoe's on the other foot sometimes. He's not crazy about your working so closely with several young men."

"I know. But I've assured him we're just friends."

"Are you certain he fully believes that?"

"You're saying we need to cut each other some slack."

"I am. A long-distance relationship is tough to maintain. On the one hand, the times you're together are especially sweet, because they're rare. On the other, no matter how often you call and e-mail, you miss big chunks of each other's lives. You let your imagination fill in the blanks, and that makes it harder to trust."

"Sylva, I do love Scott. And one of the things I love about him is that he cares about other people."

"Then you may want to let him know that, when you've both had time to cool off."

"I will. Thanks, Sylva."

When Millie reached home, she found Danny lying on a couch in the parlor, drinking orange juice and watching a DVD Alice had rented. They hugged, and Millie gave him the game she'd bought for him at Monticello..

"This looks fun. Thanks, Mom."

"So you're feeling better, huh?"

"Yeah, some."

"Much more to go on the movie?"

"It's nearly over."

"Good. Then it'll be bedtime."

Millie went to the kitchen, where Alice was mixing cake batter. At Millie's entrance, she shut off the mixer and came to hug her.

"He seems better," Millie said. "Thanks so much for looking after him, Alice."

"Happy to." She gave Millie a long look. "Did you leave your smile in Charlottesville?"

Millie smiled half-heartedly, then told about the shortened weekend. "I didn't handle it well. So I'll call Scott when he's had time to get home."

"Probably a good idea."

Millie told her of the exciting discovery she'd made at UVA.

"Get out!" her friend said. "That is truly amazing. That ruby really could have been the gift he promised her."

"I know. I can hardly believe it myself, but I really do think I'm right. Have you found anymore in Prissy's journal about Ephraim?"

"Impatience for him to arrive, anger that her dad refuses to let them see each other when he does. She can usually get 'round Papa, she says, with a mixture of little-girl pleading and grown-up sighing, but so far not this time. Ephraim was probably hoping to overcome her father's objections by producing the Scarlet Star."

"Could be. But he'd have had to come up with a good explanation of how he happened to have it. 'I found it' hardly seems enough to explain such a spectacular stone."

"Yes. Prissy's father sounds like a suspicious fellow who wouldn't simply take Ephraim's word. He'd check with the authorities to see if a one-of-a-kind ring had gone missing, and Lady Jane Peale's loss could surface. Then Effy would have been in trouble, for sure."

"But I suppose that was his problem. Taking the ring might have seemed like a good idea when he found it, but once he got here, he must have realized the difficulty of producing it. Keep me posted, Alice, the second you find out anything more from the journals."

"I will."

Millie saw Danny to bed, making him as comfortable as possible with a still-stuffy nose and the occasional coughing spell, then went to her room. She checked her watch. Scott should be home by now. Taking a deep breath, she dialed his land line. He answered on the third ring.

"Hi, Scott, it's me. Glad you made it home safely."

"I did, thanks. And you did, too?"

Formal. Not a good sign.

"Yes, and Danny's somewhat better."

"Good to hear."

"Scott, I'm sorry my jealousy ruined our parting. You were right to go home and try to help Jolene and Larry."

"I appreciate your saying that, Millie."

"How're they doing?"

"Not too bad, I guess. I talked to Jolene soon as I got back, and she's calmed down some. Larry's home, released into her custody, but they both have to appear in juvenile court tomorrow. Apparently he's one scared kid. I recommended Jolene talk to an attorney, see what options Larry may have." Scott hesitated. "I know you probably won't think I should've done this, but I offered to pay the lawyer's fee."

"Okay."

"Is it really, or are you still pissed?"

Millie took a moment to answer. "I'm not 'still pissed,' as you put it. I guess I do still think there's a danger of Jolene relying too much on you. But that's not for me to decide. So I just hope things work out happily for Larry. And for Jolene."

"Thanks, Millie."

"And I hope you'll soon be able to get back to studying."

"Me, too. Thanks for calling." He paused. "I really enjoyed being with you in Charlottesville, seeing Monticello and UVA together. And I'm thrilled for you, learning what you did about Ephraim Hayes."

"Thanks. I loved all that, too. Have a good evening."

"Good night."

So, she thought as she hung up. No sweet nothings, no pet names.

But at least you're still speaking.

Monday, Millie took off work and stayed home with Danny, so Alice could go to work and Cynthia with her to study in the Poplar Forest library. Danny seemed better, yet he wasn't fully well. He was tired of staying in the house, and Millie kept busy trying to keep him occupied but quiet.

When Alice and Cynthia came home in the early afternoon, Cynthia went to her room, saying she'd be going to Toby's parents' house for dinner, so Millie shouldn't cook enough for her. Alice, too, had plans, helping Belinda host a dinner for her Sunday-school class. Until time to leave, however, Alice said she'd take over nurse duty and let Millie get out for a while. Noticing Danny needed more cough medicine anyway, Millie took her up on the offer. She bought the medicine, then drove around in one of the old sections of Lynchburg.

She found herself passing the brick Methodist Meeting House she'd noticed before. On a whim, she got out and looked it over more closely. It might go back to the earliest days of the city, she thought. Then an idea came to her. Crazy, probably, a real long shot, but it seemed worth checking.

She went inside and found the church office. A slim, white-haired lady with a gentle smile greeted her and asked if she could help. A sign on the desk said she was the church secretary.

"I'm . . . not sure. Can you tell me how old this church is?"

"Certainly. It was established in 1806."

Millie cleared her throat, trying to calm her fluttering pulse. "The same year Old City Cemetery was founded," she observed.

"Exactly," the church secretary replied. "The same religious fervor and focus on the spiritual that prevailed at the time brought about both. Are you a researcher?"

That term applied to herself startled Millie. But yes, she was a researcher. She was doing research.

"I am. Can you tell me if the church has records that go back to the founding? I'm trying to trace someone who died in 1807. Would you have a list of people who attended the church back then?"

The woman frowned. "Not of attendees. We do have membership rolls, as well as records of baptisms, weddings, and funerals. Could your research subject have been involved in one of those?"

"His funeral, perhaps. And he might have been a member."

"I'll need to get the old records out of storage. Have you a little time, or shall I call you with the information?"

Millie said she had some time now. "That is, if I'm not taking you away from something else you need to be doing."

The secretary smiled. "Nothing pressing. Whom are you researching?"

"Ephraim Hayes." Millie gave the date of death from the tombstone in Old City Cemetery.

"Ephraim Hayes . . . Ephraim . . . hmmm, I think I've seen that name somewhere recently. Oh, yes, one of our church members was gathering information for a history of the church, and I helped him go through the old books. I'll just go check. Please make yourself comfortable."

Millie sat, thumbing through a magazine and fidgeting. Finally, the secretary returned with an old ledger.

"I found him," she said, a note of animation in her voice. "He wasn't a member, but his funeral was held in this church. The pastor at that time officiated."

"Really. Can you tell me anything more? How many attended, who arranged for the funeral?"

She opened the book, read a passage, then showed it to Millie. "Nothing about the number attending. But a Mr. Patrick Kavanagh made arrangements. He was one of the first deacons of the church and very faithful in attendance and tithing."

"Patrick Kavanagh. Hmmm, I wonder what the connection was between Hayes and Kavanagh."

The secretary smiled. "I can tell you that. After reading this entry about Mr. Hayes's funeral, I remembered where I'd seen the name Ephraim Hayes before. When the church was being built, the contractor made a mess of one of the brick walls, and Mr. Hayes repaired it. He was working for a Mr. Hiram Wixon at the time, building Mr. Wixon's own house. Because a good bricklayer was needed for this job, Mr. Wixon was kind enough to lend Mr. Hayes's services to the church. The member who's writing our church history was quite taken with the incident and plans to use it in his book."

Wixon, Hiram Wixon. Millie knew that name.

Yes, he was Nolan Unruh's ancestor, the one who had built Highgrove.

"Can you tell me anything about the house Mr. Wixon was building for himself?" Millie's voice shook so that she wasn't sure her words were intelligible.

"Only its name. It was called Highgrove."

Somehow, Millie managed to ask the church secretary for copies of the pages that mentioned Ephraim. The church's copier was out of order, she said regretfully, but took Millie's contact information and said she'd send them when it got repaired. Millie gave her much more money than would be needed to cover the cost of copying and mailing. When the secretary protested it was too much, Millie asked her to contribute the rest to the church, as her grateful donation.

Highgrove, Millie thought as she walked to the car. Ephraim Hayes, a temporary member of the Lewis and Clark Expedition, had helped build Highgrove. Her mind reeled with implications. Not only had she found the link between St. Louis and Lynchburg, not only had she proof of how one expedition member had ended his days, but—

She knew for sure Highgrove had been under construction in 1807.

When Millie reached home, Cynthia had already gone and Alice was clearly eager to get away, to help Belinda before the dinner, so Millie decided to wait until later to tell her the newest revelation about Ephraim.

Danny and Millie played a game and watched a little TV; then he went upstairs. He seemed to be feeling much better, but she didn't want him to do too much too soon. While he got ready for bed, she changed her running shoes for house slippers and emptied her slacks pockets for greater comfort. Going back to check on Danny, she found him sitting up in bed, reading a book Alice had gotten him at the public library.

"I'll be downstairs in the library if you need me. Don't read too late. Half an hour, then sleep."

"Aw-w, Mom, this is really good. Can't I finish it?"

Millie smiled, recalling times she'd said those same words to her mother. Seeing that he didn't lack a lot more, she tousled his hair and gave him a reprieve.

"Okay, but lights out as soon as you're through. Okay?"

He nodded, eyes already on his book again.

Millie walked to the second-floor entry to the tower and entered the upper level of the library. She sauntered along the catwalk to the stairs at the opposite end of the room from the door and stood for a moment looking down on tiers of book-filled shelves, comfy chairs, and elegant paneling. A library, the most peaceful of rooms, a sanctuary from the world, she thought. All it needed to complete the picture was a roaring fire in the fireplace.

But it was hardly skiing weather, even though temperatures in Lynchburg weren't what they'd be in Texas at this time. Regretfully, she nixed a fire.

Millie descended the stairs and, curling up in a deep chair in one corner, opened a book from the Poplar Forest library called *Lewis and Clark Through Indian Eyes,* edited by Alvin M. Josephy, Jr. Flipping through it, she found several mentions of Sacajawea, the Indian woman who had guided Lewis and Clark, including two versions of her life told by her own descendants. Her name was spelled differently, however, sometimes as Sacagawea, sometimes as Sakakawea.

One version said Sakakawea was stolen from her Hidatsa village by Shoshone Indians when she was small but escaped while still a young girl and made it back home with help from a wolf. Another didn't mention a capture but said Sakakawea was given by her father to a white man named Sharbonish when she was eighteen. Both versions agreed she was Hidatsa, not Shoshone, and neither version called her a slave.

Interesting, Millie thought. And oral history had sometimes been found to be more reliable than documentary evidence. Reading on, she soon nodded over the book.

Sudden sounds woke her. She heard light footfalls, someone moving stealthily through the library.

Millie looked about the room, confused as to the source of

the steps. Outside the circle of lamplight surrounding her chair, the room was dim. Her eyes paused at each dark recess or corner, straining to see into the gloom. Apprehension raised chill bumps on her arms. She thought of calling out "Who's there?" but realized that would be pointless. If this was an intruder, trying to stay hidden, he'd hardly respond.

Ted. It must be Ted. Had to be.

# ★ Chapter Twenty-Three

But Cynthia had gone out. If Ted were monitoring her movements, he'd know that. Unless he hadn't been around at the precise moment she'd left with Toby. Or unless his goal was to take revenge on the two housemates he blamed for keeping Cynthia from him.

If he'd been watching the house, he'd know Alice was out, too, that Millie and Danny were here alone. So if the two women were his targets, he must plan to pick one off now, the other later.

A jolt of fear went through Millie. Her new cell phone was upstairs, where she'd left it on emptying her pockets. With the doors all locked, she'd assumed she and Danny were safe. How had Ted gotten in?

And if he wasn't Ted? That seemed scarier yet, adding more uncertainty about his intentions and capabilities.

She had to get to a phone and call the police. A desk-style telephone sat on one corner of the rosewood table, but Millie didn't dare try to call from this room. Laying down her book, she forced herself to stand and walk calmly towards the stairs.

As she neared them, a man stepped from the shadows. Millie froze.

He was sturdily built and wore a raggedy long-sleeved shirt

and jeans. He had graying hair, a droopy moustache, and cauliflower ears. His posture was ramrod-straight, with shoulders back and chest thrust out. She didn't recognize him, though something about the way he held his head seemed familiar. And there was something else about him, something she couldn't pinpoint.

His right hand clutched a knife, sharp-pointed and ugly. He tapped the blade casually against the open palm of his left.

"Who are you?" she managed to croak.

He shrugged. "Well, milady, so you thought you'd outfoxed me."

His bad version of a British Cockney accent was a poor attempt to conceal his own speech pattern. So he had to be someone she knew. Not Luke or Toby—both were too slender. She thought of all the stocky men she knew besides Ted and came up with four: Chas, Whit, Nolan, Ron.

This man exuded a self-confidence she didn't associate with Chas. Neither did he move with the swagger Whit affected. Nor did he slouch like Nolan. As for Ron, this fellow's attitude was anything but lackadaisical.

*All those behaviors can be faked.*

True. Probably even Ron would be animated with a knife in his hand and adrenaline coursing through his body.

"Where is it?" he demanded.

"Where is what?"

"Don't play innocent with me. It wasn't in her car, so she had to be keeping it with her."

She, who? Cynthia? Someone had rummaged in her glove compartment. This was Ted, then. But what had he been looking for in her car?

"Come on, give me the ring, and I won't hurt you."

A ring? Had he lost the engagement ring he'd shown her and Alice, the one he'd thought would win Cynthia back?

"What ring? I don't know what you mean." If he meant

Cynthia's engagement ring, why in the world would he think Millie had it?

He grinned. "Yeah, right. Give it to me. Now."

She racked her brain trying to think what he might mean. A memory flashed into her mind: Ron talking on his cell phone about a ring he couldn't find, a very special one. He hadn't worn his wedding band lately. Had it disappeared and he thought Millie had taken it? Ron, then, not Ted? Granted, losing a wedding ring would be unfortunate, but hardly worth threatening someone with a knife.

"The ring Jill had. Get it for me."

*Jill's murderer.*

Millie's knees began to shake. "I still don't know what you're talking about."

"Cut the stupidity act. I want the ring Jill gave you in the bookstore café."

"Bookstore—?" Millie's mind raced back to that puzzling conversation, Jill's mysterious confidence. This man must have seen the women together, seen Jill hand her something.

That fellow she'd noticed repeatedly in Williamsburg. Could this be the same one?

He didn't look at all the same. The features of this man were of normal size, unremarkable save for the deformed, "cauliflower," look of the ears.

A disguise. Of course. And his current scruffy appearance was another.

"You—you were at Williamsburg, going to all the same places Jill and I did."

He laughed unpleasantly. "Of course. Women lose purses all the time, don't they, especially sightseeing. So that seemed a good place to steal Jill's. But when I got her bag, the ring wasn't in it. Then I saw her take it from her bottle caddy and pass it to you."

Jill's earrings. For some reason, he thought Jill had given her a ring instead. This could not be Ted. He wouldn't even have known the women were going to Williamsburg. And he'd never met Jill.

The other four men had known Jill, and they'd known about the Williamsburg trip. The women had made no secret of their plan.

"I don't know about any ring. All Jill gave me was some earrings. And I don't even have those anymore."

"I'm not here for any damned earrings." He lowered his voice, spoke so softly she barely heard him. "Now, give me the ring and no one gets hurt."

She stared at him, trying to process the shift in his behavior. From acting threatening and angry, he was now almost pleading.

Then his demeanor altered again. Baring his teeth, he brandished the knife. At Millie's involuntary step backwards, he grinned.

Was he quite sane? But maybe the swift changes were his way of keeping her off balance? Who could it be?

Question, ask him a question, Millie thought.

"Why such a memorable disguise at Williamsburg? Seems like you'd have wanted to be as nondescript as possible, blend in with the crowd."

He seemed flattered by her query. "That's one way to go. Another is to confuse any witnesses by giving yourself distinctive but false characteristics, like big ears and nose. Add a green cap, and those are the details you remembered. Right?"

She slowly nodded, ashamed to have been so easily misled.

"How'd you get in?" As she spoke, Millie saw the answer. He had jimmied the lock on the French doors. They hadn't quite closed after him. A shaft of darkness separated the edges.

"I'll ask the questions. What'd you do with that ring Jill gave you? It's not in your Prius. I checked just now."

"You got into my car? But I locked it, I'm sure."

"Car alarms can be disabled, and locks opened. Now, where is it?"

"I tell you, I don't know. Jill didn't give me any ring. I've no idea where she'd have hidden one."

"Bullshit! She sent you an e-mail telling you where it is. You know the code, so what'd her message mean?"

He knew about the mysterious e-mail, then. Jill must have told him, having been tricked or intimidated into doing so.

"You didn't have to murder Jill. She didn't deserve that."

He snickered. "You think I meant to kill her? Well, here's a flash that'll make you feel better. I hit her, all right, trying to make her tell me where the ring was, but not hard enough to kill her. She just suddenly collapsed."

So he hadn't intended murder, Millie thought. Much good that would do Jill now.

"I'm warning you." He waved the knife. "You don't want me taking out my frustration on you. Or your kid." He glanced up at the second level of the library.

Danny! He was the only other person in the house. She had to protect him, even at risk of her own life. Her head whirled with questions, but that one thing she knew for sure.

Then she realized what her subconscious had been nagging her about ever since the man had stepped into her path, a detail that gave away his identity. A faint odor of tobacco smoke clung to him. And only one of the stocky men she knew was a smoker.

Nolan Unruh.

Not Ted. Not Chas. Not Whit. Not Ron. Nolan.

It made sense, now. Nolan, who knew makeup, wigs, and other pieces of disguise from playing Jefferson.

She tried to pretend she hadn't guessed. But her eyes had involuntarily widened at the sudden knowledge. Watching her keenly, Nolan apparently read something in her face.

"You know, don't you? You know who I am."

But he'd resumed the false accent, so he must not be sure. She shook her head, tried to sound genuinely puzzled. "No. Who are you?"

His scornful half-grin told her he didn't buy the lie. Pushing up his left shirt-sleeve, he sheared a few hairs off his forearm with the knife.

"See how sharp it is? Keen enough to slit a kid's throat." He glanced up at the catwalk again.

Just when she needed most to think clearly, her mind seemed a tangle of non-functioning circuits. She could focus on only two things: that knife and the threat to her child. She fell back on the one idea that came to her: stall, buy time, hope her brain would begin to work again.

"Why'd you kill Paige?"

A flicker of regret crossed his face. "She saw me scraping bits of plaster off a wall and realized I had a hidden agenda at Highgrove. She was going to tell Luke and my aunt, get me thrown off the crew. Fortunately, Luke wasn't there that afternoon; he'd gone to Richmond. But I couldn't risk her telling. I had to keep my volunteer gig.

"Maybe I should've found a way to discredit her, instead. She was a good kid. But she also had this thing about poking around old buildings, especially churches. If she'd found the link between the old Methodist church and Highgrove—that doesn't prove whether Jefferson designed the house or not, but I didn't want Luke and Ron to get that far—the longer it took them to figure out Highgrove's history, the more time I'd have to find it."

"Find what? What were you looking for?"

All at once, Millie's brain unlocked. Bits of information that had seemed pieces of separate jigsaws now joined together.

Ephraim Hayes had helped build Highgrove, after bringing the Scarlet Star here for his lady love. But Prissy's father had forbidden the lovers to meet. Maybe Ephraim hadn't been able to present his fabulous gift, had hidden it temporarily—for safekeeping?—inside a wall he was building.

And Jill Greene had found it two centuries later. Jill, one of the few people in the world who'd recognize that stone and the pouch that held it. That's what she had surreptitiously carried to her car that day, had hidden in her glove compartment.

That was the valuable item she'd told Millie was in a safe place, but one she couldn't get to readily, not whenever she wanted.

"You were hunting the Scarlet Star, weren't you? In the—the fireplace wall."

His silence gave assent.

"How'd you know Jill found it? Did you see her?"

"Yeah. She sensed someone was watching—kept glancing around—but never saw me. I can't believe you knew the ring Jill had was the Star, though. She must've let it slip somehow."

No wonder Jill hadn't wanted to be around the three crewmen after that, since she must have suspected each of having seen her make off with the ruby. Except for Luke, who she'd have known was still showing Millie around.

"If you gals had come out just a little later that day—the break in that fireplace exposed a corner of the brown pouch and its gold pattern, but I only noticed it because I knew what I was looking for. When I spotted it that morning, Ron was about to start work there, but I asked him a question he'd have to go to the office to look up. While he was gone, I tried to get the pouch out. It didn't have much mortar holding it, and I almost had it loose. But then you two showed up, and I knew Luke'd be bringing you right in to show the place off."

"So you tried to get everyone out to the dig, hoping we'd stay long enough so you could finish getting out the pouch."

"Yeah, when Luke starts lecturing, he can go on and on. But he didn't take my suggestion that day, had his own plan for showing Highgrove."

"When Ron did examine that cavity later, he must've wondered about that depression in the mortar where the pouch had been."

Nolan nodded. His eyes strayed upwards to the catwalk again. Worry for Danny made Millie faintly sick, but she had to keep Nolan talking.

"But how'd you know to look for the Star at Highgrove?"

He snickered, enjoying his control over her. "My ancestors weren't as bad about throwing things out as I claimed. In fact, I have a book of family memories Granddad gave me. Most of our family couldn't care less about old stuff—that part's right—but one in each generation cared enough to keep that book. I'm the one in mine.

"Granddad meant me to have Highgrove, too—told me so. But he didn't trust lawyers, so he left a handwritten will. Big mistake. He was clear enough in dividing other property among his kids, but his wording about Highgrove was ambiguous. He never put Grandma's name on the deed, but she always favored Aunt Julia and swore he'd meant the place for her. She couldn't produce anything in writing, of course, so the courts got the case. Grandma's the one who gave my aunt the house plan for Highgrove."

Millie listened with one ear, her mind considering and rejecting escape routes. But Nolan was into his story and didn't seem to notice her attention drifting.

He told how his ancestor, Hiram Wixon, had told his grandson Andrew, when Hiram was on his death bed, that valuables were hidden in a fireplace at Highgrove. He said his little son, Andrew's father, had claimed to have seen "the brick man" put a ring and a paper in a sack and hide it in a wall. Discounting the lad's story at the time, since he often made up stories, Hiram had later questioned his boy, who couldn't recall then what he'd seen. So Hiram had gone to his grave thinking it might be true. He couldn't ask the bricklayer, because the man had been killed on his way home from work one day.

Ephraim killed? For a moment, Millie almost forgot her own peril in imagining Prissy's grief.

"It's not clear whether Andrew believed all Hiram told him, a sick old man rambling about something long past, but he found the story interesting enough to include it in a family-memories book he was compiling for his kids and grandkids."

"The same book your Granddad left you?"

"Yep."

"And it told you the Scarlet Star was at Highgrove."

Nolan snorted. "I wish. It didn't even give the bricklayer's name. But the memories book also said Hiram had lent the man's services to repair a wall at the Methodist Meeting House, which was new then. I checked with the church, and they told me the fellow was Ephraim Hayes. I recognized the name from my Lewis and Clark reading, also knew Hayes had been a bricklayer in Kentucky."

"I found that church record, too," Millie said, hoping to reach her captor through his vanity as a researcher. "You must've been thrilled, finding a connection between the expedition and your own family.".

He grinned. "Yeah, also finding his grave in Old City Cemetery, plus an old newspaper in a museum in St. Louis that mentioned him."

"The *Missouri Dispatch,* April, 1807."

His eyes widened, then narrowed. "Yeah. How'd you know that?"

She told about seeing the same paper at UVA and making the same connection he had between Ephraim's disappearance and the Star's. She thought she saw respect in his eyes.

"If you'd won the court case," she said, "you wouldn't have

started tearing down the place, would you, to find the Star?"

His face softened for an instant. "Not Highgrove. I do love it, you know. But there's X-ray technology that can find things buried underground or in concrete. Why not in a brick wall? If that wouldn't work, I guess I'd have started examining each fireplace, brick by brick. I'd have found a way."

He resumed slapping the knife blade on his open palm. Millie realized he was growing agitated again. She didn't doubt Nolan would harm her son if he thought that would help him get the ruby. The tension was almost unbearable. Her spine and stomach were in knots, her mouth desert-dry.

Stalling was still the only plan that occurred to her.

"Why'd you kill Jill at the dig? And how'd you get her out there?"

He frowned. "I called her cell that night after Luke brought her home. I'd followed them to their friends' house, because I knew there was a good chance they'd fight—Luke had told me Jill was worse about engagement talk when they were with these people—and that could work to my advantage. Sure enough, they came out practically spitting at each other. I'd heard enough about Jill from Luke to know she's reckless when pissed.

"So I phoned her, pretending to be the crooked lapidary and telling her to meet me outside the Poplar Forest museum to give me the ring and instructions for re-shaping it. She was reluctant, said that would be too isolated late at night. But I insisted, and she finally agreed."

"So what happened? You didn't get the ring from her then?"

"She didn't bring it. Said she wanted to size me up before turning over something so valuable."

"Must've been frustrating, after everything you'd been through."

"Damned straight. But I was cool, told her I had plenty of other work, figured she'd think if I wasn't pushing her I must be okay. But she said she'd decided to wait, told me I should go ahead with other jobs while she thought it over. That's when I lost it, seeing all my careful planning evaporate."

"But this was outside the museum shop, right? How come her body was at the dig?"

"That was my little gift to Chas, making him suspect number one in her death."

Nolan was moving restlessly now, his tennis-shoe-shod feet shuffling, the knife blade slapping his palm. Millie realized he probably wouldn't stand for anymore attempts to distract him.

His head jerked upwards, as low sounds came from the catwalk overhead. Someone had entered the tower on the second floor and was moving around the room towards the stairway.

Danny. Millie's heart plummeted.

"Danny, go back!" she yelled. "Run to my room—dial 911—"

Nolan grabbed Millie and clapped a hand over her mouth. She struggled to free herself, but he was too strong. She felt the knife point prick her shoulder blade, felt the intensity in the taut body so near hers.

The movements above paused. Millie guessed Danny was wondering if her shouted command had been serious. Terror for him surged through her like electrical current.

"Now," her captor muttered in her ear, "you're going to take that back. Tell your boy you were kidding. Tell him to come down here, you want to show him something." Nolan moved the knife around Millie's body until the point grazed her throat. "Make him believe it. Or Danny loses his mom in a painful, horrible death. You got that?"

She hesitated, then nodded vigorously. He eased his hand off her lips.

"Run, Danny!" she screamed. "Call the police! Quick!"

Snarling, Nolan flung her aside and dashed up the stairs. Millie heard Danny run along the catwalk, back the way he had come. In the moment she struggled for balance, she considered racing to the phone on the rosewood table and dialing 911 herself.

But Nolan might catch and harm Danny while she was doing that. She had to help her son get away. She sprang up the steps.

Nearing the top, she saw a small pajama-clad body disappear through the door into the second-floor hallway. But Nolan was streaking around the catwalk. She'd never reach him in time.

"Wait!" she called. "Wait, Nolan! I know where Jill put the jewel. It's here, in this room!"

As she said the desperate words, she realized they were true. That mysterious e-mail had contained clues directing her to the jewel's hiding place. But until this moment—until fear for her son heightened all her faculties—she'd been too dense to understand.

Nolan halted. He wavered, glancing from her to the still-open door into the main house, torn between two options. Then, with a last look at the doorway, he turned and ran back to the stairway. Grabbing Millie's arm, he brandished the knife in her face.

"If this is a trick, you'll regret every one of the few seconds you live. But get me that jewel before the police get here, I'll let you go."

Trembling all over, Millie preceded him down the stairs.

"Okay, where is it?" he demanded as they reached the bottom.

"I—let me think a second. Jill put the clues in an e-mail—"

"I know all that already, from hacking into your e-mail. What'd it mean?"

He'd hacked into her e-mail?

"I think—think it told where in the library she'd—hidden the jewel. I think the numbers referred to—-the number of rows down and the number of books along a row." Millie felt her quavering slow, then cease, as her brain worked out the details of

Jill's message.

"You think? Great. Counting from where?'

"The message mentioned 'blue ridge blossoms.' I think that refers to a gardening book I saw Jill with, right after she would've brought the ring from Highgrove. Jill wasn't a gardener, you see."

"Who cares about her hobbies? Hurry up, we're wasting time. Locate that jewel."

Millie hastened to the area where Jill had been standing as she'd leafed through the book on plants. She'd stood about here, Millie thought. She fumbled along a shelf or two, trying to recall details about the book. A blue cover, maybe. The words "Blue Ridge" in the title, she felt sure.

*Horticulture in the Shadow of the Blue Ridge.* That was it. Millie drew the tall blue-backed tome from its shelf and felt behind it. But her groping fingers found nothing. No piece of jewelry, no small bag that might contain one.

God, no, she thought with renewed panic. Nolan would think she'd been feeding him a line. Glancing at his dark eyes, she saw suspicion and anger.

Wait. She'd forgotten the rest of the e-mail, the numbers. "Three down, ten right."

She counted down four rows below the slot where the horticulture book had been, then counted off twelve books to the right. Taking a deep breath, she removed the book her finger rested on.

*Northanger Abbey,* by Jane Austen.

Millie almost laughed aloud. In that book, Austen satirized gothic novels popular in her day, portraying a naïve young heroine who unfairly suspected dire doings in a grand old mansion she visited, all because she was too caught up in reading sensational novels.

Nolan impatiently shoved Millie aside and pitched books

from that shelf to the floor. He scrabbled around on the empty shelf, then turned furiously on her.

"You connin' me? There's nothing behind any of these books."

Millie's heart dropped. She must've misinterpreted Jill's message. She'd felt sure this was right, but if the shelf was empty—

Frantically, she passed her own hand along the shelf. He was right—nothing there.

But she couldn't give up. She ran her shaking fingers over the wall behind the shelf. One fingertip touched a button a few inches up from the shelf. A button? What—?

She pressed it. A line of books a foot from her right hand broke from the surrounding shelves and began to inch outward.

Actually, a whole column of books was gradually pushing away from that side of the room. Millie felt briefly disoriented, as if the earth had shifted beneath her. What in the—

In her befuddlement, she heard a vehicle stop outside. Please let that be help arriving, she prayed.

Then she realized it might be Alice, or Cynthia returning. Would either be able to help, or would Nolan kill them too?

Hearing nothing more, she decided she had imagined the car's stopping, from wanting a rescuer so much.

Nolan didn't seem to have heard anything. His whole attention was riveted to the section of bookshelves about four feet wide that slowly, steadily, left the rest of the wall behind.

Peering into the widening aperture, Millie saw that a cubicle of some kind lay behind the moving shelves.

A secret compartment, maybe a secret room. Of all things.

It turned out to be a mere closet of a room, its interior unlit. But rays of light from the library let Millie make out a few furnishings: a small marble-topped table, supported by an intricately carved center spindle; an armchair with a carved backrest and pink-and-gray floral upholstery, the mate to one in the parlor that

Alice called a “gentleman’s chair”; and, on the table, an amber-globed hurricane lamp, a metal ashtray, a couple of old books, a cigar box, and lots of dust. A crocheted blue afghan lay folded on the chair seat. A musty odor, combined with traces of stale cigar smoke and something oily-smelling, assailed her nostrils.

A hideaway, Millie thought. Someone—perhaps the original owner of the house—must have used this chamber as a private retreat from life’s hustle and bustle. In any other circumstances, the possibilities would have intrigued her.

Gripping her shoulder, Nolan pushed her into the tiny room. She realized she should have attempted to flee while he was focused on the astonishing apparition. Now it was too late.

They reached the table, and he thrust her aside. Opening the box, he drew forth a small brown pouch patterned with gold fleurs-de-lis.

Wearing a triumphant smile, he laid the knife on the table, opened the pouch, dropped it and a paper from inside it on the table, to clutch a tiny drawstring sack he had found inside. Yanking the little bag open, he took out a gold ring, centered with a large red stone.

Millie edged backwards, as quietly and unobtrusively as she could.

“Yeah,” Nolan breathed, cradling his prize in one palm. He bent to switch on the lamp, groped all around its lower globe, then the upper one.

“Damn, it’s an oil lamp!”

With slow, careful progress, Millie had almost made it out of his reach. But he noticed her movements, grasped her arm, and pulled her back into the secret room. Releasing her, he took his cigarette lighter from a shirt pocket and flicked it on. Crimson sparkles flashed from myriad facets as he turned the gem first one way, then the other.

“Yeah,” he said again and grinned. “Yeah.”

So this was the Scarlet Star, the cause of so much sorrow. Millie saw why such mystique surrounded the stone. It was indeed spectacular.

While Nolan gloated over his trophy, she began inching away again, but, pocketing the ring, he grabbed for her wrist. This time she resisted. They struggled, his iron grip crushing her tender flesh. Summoning all her strength, she landed her other fist hard on his jaw. In that moment of shocked surprise, he dropped the lighter. It fell onto the tinder-dry paper, sending flames shooting upwards.

"The manumission!" With a strangled cry, Nolan grabbed the afghan and smote the paper one-handedly, maintaining his grip on Millie with the other. The fire wavered but still burned.

She dug her fingernails into the fist that held her tight, at the same time pulling with all her might on her captured wrist. He yelped, dropped the afghan, and grabbed the knife off the table. She tried her best to wrench her hand free but couldn't break his hold. He waved the weapon near her face, his expression full of rage. She stopped struggling.

"Okay, Millie, now you're going to smarten up and help me get out of here. You'll be my shield. If we get completely away, I may let you go."

"No, please—let me stay here. I won't tell the police who you are. I'll send them on a wild goose chase. I promise."

"Yeah, like I can believe what you say. You were gonna call Danny downstairs a while ago, too, weren't you?"

"You're not a mother. If you were, you wouldn't expect me to choose my safety over Danny's. But I'm telling you the truth now—I won't give you away."

"Yeah, sure. Let's go." He pushed her across the room ahead of him, the knife point digging into her shoulder.

She mustn't go with him. Whether Danny had understood her shouted order and called the police or not, she'd stand a better chance here, in this house, than on some lonely back road with Nolan.

Delay. She'd try that once again. She paused, turned towards him.

"Please tell me who designed Highgrove, Nolan. Was it Jefferson?"

"Shut up." Nolan nudged her forward, and they neared the French doors. He reached a hand towards the handle, but she blocked him with her body. He forced her aside and twisted the knob.

As he flung the door open, she tried to retreat. But he stuck the knife hard against her spine. Millie felt it pierce her flesh. Renewed fear paralyzed her legs, left them weak, insubstantial.

"I said move it!" he said. "Or you die right now."

Somehow Millie managed to make her legs work. She stumbled through the door, head down, trying to think of another plan. But the fright that had immobilized her legs now numbed her brain. Robot-like, she staggered forward.

"Hold it there!" a stern voice said. "Police!"

Nolan hurled Millie to one side and started to run. A uniformed cop stepped from the shadows into his path, gun drawn. Nolan's shoulders sagged. His knife hand dropped to his side.

Millie sank to the terrace, all strength and adrenaline gone.

# ★ Chapter Twenty-Four

Millie spent much of the rest of that evening answering questions from the police and comforting Danny, whom she'd found cowering in her closet. When he was finally asleep, she phoned Sylva, told her about the resolution of the murders, and reassured her she and Danny were both okay. Millie considered phoning Scott, too. But given the way things stood between them, she decided to wait. Alice and Cynthia came home late and had to hear all about the evening's events.

"You were amazingly coolheaded," Alice said, hugging Millie. "Hamilton would have been proud."

"Thanks. That means a lot. But I was anything but cool. If I hadn't had Danny to think of, I'd probably have curled up in a whimpering ball, or melted into a pool of my own sweat. Or maybe I'd have upchucked all over Nolan's tennis shoes."

"Maybe you should've tried throwing up on his tennies," Alice said. "He wouldn't have been expecting that."

They talked a long while about Millie's close call, sitting over cups of herbal tea in the kitchen. Then, from a sack she'd brought in with her, Cynthia produced two hand-painted ceramic beer steins, which Millie thought looked familiar.

"Toby gave these back to me," Cynthia said. "He admitted

stealing them the night he brought over his mom's cake."

"So that's where he was that night," Millie replied. "Danny said Toby wasn't in the kitchen when he went to the bathroom. Toby was busy, all right, but not doing dishes."

"Yeah. He moved the other steins around in the cabinet to cover his theft. I suppose none of us was interested enough in that collection to notice. He wrapped the foil from his cake around these, set them on our porch, and picked them up after saying his goodbyes on the terrace."

"At least he finally owned up," Alice observed.

"We can credit his mom for that," Cynthia said scornfully. "She found out and insisted he bring them back." She sighed. "I can't stand that kind of sneakiness. Toby and I are history."

The next morning, Millie and Chas sat in the main room at the lab, drinking coffee and discussing the events that had been reported in all the media. Alice had taken the day off and gone shopping in Richmond with Belinda. Danny, much better from his cold in spite of his evening adventure, was with Cynthia at home, surfing plant and animal Web sites.

Chas smiled more than he had since before Jill's death. He'd wisely been honest with the investigators from the first, about his relationship with Jill and helping her find a lapidary, but his inability to tell more about the stone she'd wanted re-cut or why her body had been in the Poplar Forest dig had insured he remained a "person of interest." Now, with Nolan's arrest and Millie's incriminating information, Chas had high hopes he'd soon have his old life back.

"Stupidity over a woman is a good defense, isn't it?" he joked to Millie.

"If it were, prisons would probably be much less crowded. But the e-mails on your computers will surely prove what you did for Jill, and didn't do."

"Yeah, it's all there. As Nolan found when he hacked into my e-mail."

"Yours too? But why yours?"

Chas sighed, ran a hand through his curls. "He was at the sandwich shop that Friday Jill and I went there after work, probably overheard some of our conversation. Nolan and I go way back. We both grew up here—not in the same class; I'm several years older—and we were both always interested in Jefferson, so our paths crossed often. We've always rubbed each other the wrong way. That all came to a head in the Jefferson Geniuses competition; he hated the fact I won the last contest."

"I suppose he knew you were training as a lapidary?"

Chas nodded. "And since he knew Jill had the ruby, what he overheard that evening probably told him all he needed to know. Then he'd have hacked into my e-mail program and probably Jill's, too. He's been a whiz with computers ever since I've known him, used to brag about going into teachers' computers to get their tests early.

"I'm guessing he called A.C., the lapidary I found, pretended to be me, and told him Jill wouldn't be needing his services after all.

"I'd told Jill A.C. was unpredictable, but said he was so good it would be worth putting up with his crap. So she wouldn't have been surprised when he suggested an odd meeting place."

Millie sipped her coffee. "All Nolan had to do was wait for a good time to get her alone, without Luke or anyone else around. Even if Jill got suspicious, she couldn't report him to the police."

Millie went by the police station to file a formal report, then drove out to Highgrove. She found Luke, Ron, and Whit sitting in the lawn chairs with Miss Julia. Whit brought another chair from the shed, and Millie joined them.

"So you're the one responsible for my nephew's arrest." Miss Julia fixed Millie with a stern eye, her severe tone suggesting displeasure.

"I suppose."

"Good for you." Highgrove's owner broke into a tiny smile. "I've never trusted him, you know. He was a sneaky child and became a deceitful adult."

Millie cleared her throat. "If you felt that way, may I ask why you allowed him to work at Highgrove?"

"From what Luke told me, he was an excellent worker, and free labor's not to be sneezed at. But I insisted Luke watch Nolan closely at first, and I didn't allow him to have a key. I wanted to be sure someone else would be around when he was here."

"But didn't you also refuse Whit a key?"

Millie had thought the elderly woman might find her questions impertinent, but the liveliness of Miss Julia's expression suggested she appreciated others being as direct as she.

"I did. And Paige. And you, if you'd ever asked for one." Miss Julia smiled again. "Oh, it's not that I didn't trust you, Whit, or Paige, but I didn't want to be too obvious about excluding my own nephew. I loved his mother, and for her sake I've tried to tolerate him."

"So why'd you think he wanted to help at Highgrove?

"Not from the goodness of his heart, certainly. But I didn't suspect he was looking for something here. I thought he might try to vandalize the inside, to spite me."

Millie glanced around at the three men. "Nolan wasn't the only one searching for something at Highgrove. Whatever gave you the idea to look for York's manumission here, Whit?"

Whit looked sheepish. "One of the letters in my dad's L&C collection said William Clark gave Ephraim Hayes a paper to carry back to St. Louis for him, right before the return party left."

So Harold had lied about what was in those letters, Millie

thought. York's manumission and Clark's commission to Hayes would certainly qualify as new information about the expedition. She remembered Harold behaving oddly that day, mentioning the letters, then backing away from the subject, as if he'd begun a conversation he didn't want to finish.

"The letter writer didn't know what that document was," Whit went on. "But he guessed it might be York's manumission, given to Hayes to hold in case York returned safely from the mission but Clark didn't. Why the writer thought that, whether Clark had idly commented he might free York one day, or what, the letter didn't say."

"But why at Highgrove?" Miss Julia asked.

Whit explained that he and Harold had seen Ephraim's grave and, knowing Hayes was a bricklayer, had researched all buildings in the area that had been under construction from 1805 through 1807. That had led them to the old Methodist Meeting House. The current secretary there had been on vacation when Harold had phoned, but her substitute happened to be the woman who'd retired from the job, come back to fill in. She was familiar with the oldest records and recognized Ephraim's name.

"So you and Harold, Nolan, and I all used the same sources, but came at them differently," Millie said. The two male researchers the cemetery curator had mentioned must have been either Nolan and Whit or Nolan and Harold, she realized.

Ron commented on the irony of his having been the only person Nolan had tried to hurt with his ladder ploy, since Whit and Harold were conducting a secret search, too. "Nolan must've heard me talking about looking for my wedding ring and thought I meant the Star. He knew Jill already had it but must've figured I knew about the ruby and might let out his secret. Wonder who he thought I was talking to about it, though? Michelle or some other confederate? Anyway, he tried to take me out of commission for a while."

Millie nodded. "Nolan was desperately afraid of any publicity about the house, at least until he got the Star safely out and hidden again."

"Amazing, isn't it?" Miss Julia said dryly. "That with all those searches going on, any work got done on my house at all."

"Why were you hunting outside for the manumission?" Ron asked Whit.

"I'd looked around inside quite a bit when we first began work here, as I had opportunity. You and Paige helped me there, since you were so focused on each other."

Ron glared at him a moment, then shrugged. "I guess everyone knows about that. We must not've been as discreet as we thought."

"Nolan evidently overheard Harold and me talking about the manumission," Whit said, "and knew I was looking for it. Looking outside was Harold's idea. He'd worked in construction and guessed Ephraim might not have found privacy enough to hide anything inside. So Harold figured he'd wrapped it in oilskin for protection and hidden it outside."

"If Clark did sign and send back York's manumission," Millie said, "that would speak well of him, providing for York in case he himself didn't make it."

"Yes," Luke conceded. "But I'm guessing he wouldn't have told York he'd signed his manumission."

"Maybe he did," Whit said, "and that would help explain why the two of them fell out after returning from the mission. If Clark reneged on a promise that important, York couldn't just let it go."

Ron shook his head. "You're all making this huge assumption, because you want Clark to have planned to free York. But that document could've been lots of other things, a handwritten will, maybe a deed to property back home. Wouldn't have been many notaries in the wilderness, but in those days a couple of witnesses' signatures would have sufficed."

"So what's the story on your ring, Ron?" Luke asked. "You ever find it?"

Ron looked at the dig, then at the house. "No. Paige hid it so well I may never find it. She took it one day after I removed it during our—interlude. It bothered me to wear it when she and I—"

He sighed. "Paige was demanding I get a divorce and marry her. Threatened to tell my wife about our affair if I didn't. My ring was going to be her proof I was cheating. But now I've told Michelle the truth and explained why I don't have my wedding band. She'd suspected, anyway, and that's why she gave me such a hard time about losing the ring."

"So did your wife forgive you?" Miss Julia asked bluntly.

"We—we're talking about that."

"What happened to Hiram Wixon's memory book?" Millie asked Miss Julia. "Do you have it now?"

"The police took the actual book as evidence, but did let me get copies of some parts. I've never been much on family history—what's done is done, and much of it's better forgotten—but I do find Hiram's recollections interesting." She summarized for the men what Nolan had already told Millie about the "brick man."

"Nolan's been a Lewis and Clark fanatic ever since high school and loves researching on the internet. He must've worried at that family story every which way, till he finally came up with information and a theory that made sense."

She glanced at Luke. "And you weren't aware of any of this going on under your nose?"

He grinned. "I'm lots better at detecting past secrets than present-day ones."

Millie decided the time was right for the big question. "Nolan said he learned from the memories book who designed Highgrove. Would you please tell us who that was?"

Miss Julia smiled. "I may just tell Luke. He's the one who's had to put up with my carping about wanting quicker results. If he chooses to tell others later, he may. But I feel he deserves to know first. I'll bring you my copy of that part of the book tomorrow, Luke."

"Not even a little hint?" Millie pleaded.

"Sorry, no."

That evening after dinner, Alice asked Millie to come to her room to see more of Prissy's diary.

"Since you told me Ephraim was killed coming home from work," she said, "I've skimmed the journals as fast as I could, looking for mentions of Ephraim, and found several."

The first she showed Millie said Ephraim had been gravely injured, set upon by two men as he walked home from work, and was in the hospital. His friend and co-worker, Lew, had brought the news to Prissy at home.

"Finally," Alice said, "I learned our diarist's full name. See, she says when she heard a man had asked to speak to a Miss Priscilla Kavanagh, she knew it was serious, since everyone she knew called her Prissy."

"Kavanagh," Millie said. "That's the name of the man who arranged for Ephraim's funeral."

"Decent of him," Alice observed wryly, "considering he'd kept Ephraim and Prissy apart so long."

Lew had been walking home by the same path Ephraim had taken and surprised two men in the act of turning out his friend's pockets. From the few words he caught before they ran away, he gathered they were looking for something specific.

"The Scarlet Star," Millie said. "Those men may have followed Ephraim all the way from St. Louis."

Alice nodded. Reading on, Millie saw that Lew had gotten Ephraim to a doctor's house, where he was treated for multiple serious injuries. One of these, a knife wound to his throat, made talking difficult. He communicated through sign language and written notes, Lew told the Kavanaghs.

In view of the extreme circumstances, Papa Kavanagh relented and let his daughter visit her beloved, accompanied by her brother for propriety's sake. On seeing how badly hurt Ephraim was, Prissy grew distraught, could hardly attend to his desperate efforts to tell her something. He was weak from loss of blood, slipping in and out of consciousness, and his pitiful efforts at sign language conveyed no clear message.

Soon, a nurse told Prissy she'd have to leave, that the patient needed rest and her presence was over-exciting him. Wild-eyed, Ephraim grabbed at Prissy. She kissed him, trying to quiet the frantic movements of his right hand on the sheet. His trembling fingers found paper and pen where they'd fallen on the bed after an earlier attempt to converse with a nurse. Feebly, he made a few scrawls on a scrap of paper, but then his strength failed. The pencil slipped from his grasp.

Prissy thought he had lost consciousness again. But then his eyes opened, and he motioned her to pick up the paper. She started to read it, but he shook his head. She asked if she was meant to take it with her, and he nodded yes. She put it in her pocket, kissed him all over his face, and tearfully let her brother lead her from the room and the doctor's house.

Nearly hysterical, she sobbed all the way home in the carriage. Later that evening, her maid found Ephraim's note in the pocket of her mistress's dress as she was hanging it up and placed the paper in a drawer of Prissy's dressing table. An exhausted Prissy took a sleeping draught and slept through the night.

On waking the next morning, Prissy poured her anguish out in her diary while taking breakfast in her room. Would her beloved recover? Would he be able to work again, become the success Papa Kavanagh demanded? Even if Papa relented and agreed the lovers could wed without Ephraim's passing the test, would Prissy still want to marry, knowing she might end up caring for an invalid for years? The young woman who had mainly thought of new dresses and bonnets before, now found herself dealing with disaster in her life.

Prissy's account ended abruptly, seemingly in mid-thought. Then came a gap of some weeks in dates on journal entries. When she again took up her pen, it was to write of her devastating sorrow. The reason she had suddenly stopped writing before was that Lew had brought her awful news: Ephraim had died during the night.

At first, the diarist wrote, she had hardly been able to function, sometimes feeling numb, sometimes dissolving into tears with no apparent provocation, always burdened by the knowledge that her true love was no more. Anxious as she'd been about whether he'd be the same man if he'd lived, the finality of his death crushed her spirit.

Then one day, feeling a little better, she searched for a favorite hair ribbon in her dressing table and found Ephraim's note. When she read her dead lover's handwriting—shaky though it was—she trembled all over with renewed emotion.

The note made no sense to her: "Fire—" Something illegible after that word, or portion of a word, then, "Look. High—" That was it.

Puzzled, Millie considered the cryptic message. "Fire" what? Look for what, and where? "High" could be the start of a phrase, such as "high up," "high mountain," or "high plains." Had Ephraim meant Prissy to look for something high up?

No. He had tried to tell his beloved where to find the wonderful gift he'd carried from St. Louis to Lynchburg for her, the precious stone in her favorite color, the blood-red ruby known as the Scarlet Star. "High—" was the beginning of "Highgrove," "Fire—" the start of "Fireplace."

Millie saw why Prissy hadn't grasped what Ephraim had tried

with almost his last breath to tell her. But how much better, she thought, if Prissy had only understood.

The next morning Millie went out the front door of the Victorian to get the morning mail and nearly fell over a large dog tied to the door handle. His tail waved in a friendly manner, and his liquid brown eyes looked up imploringly. Killer.

She bent to give him a pat and saw a note affixed to his collar. It read, "For Danny."

Another of Ted's tricks, undoubtedly. But how cruel to use her son and this appealing animal as his pawns.

The golden retriever-collie mix gazed expectantly at Millie, still wagging his tail. She stood up and peered around at the street and the neighboring houses, expecting to see Ted somewhere. But if he was out there, he was well hidden.

Danny wasn't up yet, fortunately. He mustn't see the dog until she'd had a chance to figure out what was going on. She went inside, filled a bowl with water, and set it in front of Killer. He lapped thirstily. She went back inside and told Alice and Cynthia what she'd found on the porch.

Then Millie noticed a transformation in Cynthia. Her petite body seemed to float rather than walk between refrigerator and counter. Her grin suggested she'd just won a sweepstakes prize.

"Oh, I know about that!" she said with shining eyes. "I got an e-mail this morning from Ted. He says he's gone back to New Mexico. His dad died suddenly, and he went home, expecting a court battle with his siblings over property. That last part definitely sounds like Ted, demanding every last penny he thinks he's entitled to.

"I hesitated to even read the e-mail, but at least it came openly from him, not from this TOAF character he'd adopted. When I did read it, of course, I thought it was a scheme to throw me off my guard."

"Logical, given Ted's behavior so far," Alice muttered.

"I called a friend in New Mexico who also knows Ted. She says it's true about his dad dying, and a likely court fight. She and Ted actually ran into each other at the Santa Fe airport last evening, when she'd just flown in from L. A. They had drinks together.

"I know this news doesn't prove Ted's out of my hair forever, but at least it's a reprieve."

Millie hugged her. "Cynthia, that's wonderful! I'm glad for you."

"And Ted said he left Killer for Danny. He'll have his dad's hunting dogs to look after now, anyway. I think Ted actually has a soft side, at least when it comes to animals."

It seemed too good to be true, as far as Millie was concerned. Ted was too much like Jack for her ever to fully trust him. But that darling animal needed someone, and her son desperately wanted a dog. The only alternative seemed to be to take Killer to a shelter, where he'd been before Ted had come along. And she'd promised Danny a shelter dog as soon as they arrived home. Much as she dreaded trying to get that large animal all the way to Dallas in her small car, she decided she'd find a way.

Danny could have his dog.

Millie had planned to work at Poplar Forest today, but in view of this development told Alice she'd go in tomorrow instead. Alice and Cynthia drove to Poplar Forest together, and Millie put the well-mannered animal and his refilled bowl of water into the fenced backyard.

When Danny awoke and Millie told him the news, he ran to the backyard and fell on Killer's neck, hugging him and grinning ecstatically. The dog's tail thrashed wildly, and he licked Danny's face and arms until they gleamed. Danny renamed him "Harris" on the spot, after his favorite fictional boy, the title character in Gary Paulsen's laugh-out-loud novel *Harris and Me.*

Millie and Danny went to buy dog food and fed the hungry

canine. Then Millie called the animal shelter where Ted had said he'd gotten Killer. The kindly woman she spoke with remembered the dog. She said that before Ted adopted him he'd belonged to an elderly man who'd trained him well but could no longer care for him, and that the animal had had his shots. She gave instructions for caring for Harris, since Millie explained she and her son hadn't had a pet before.

So far, so good, Millie thought; now if Ted doesn't show up one day, demanding "Killer" back.

That evening, she decided to call Scott. They hadn't talked since she'd called him Sunday evening to apologize for getting so upset about Jolene, and she had expected he'd call her yesterday.

He hadn't. If he responded now with gruffness over his interrupted studies when she told him about nearly losing her life last night, that would tell her all she needed to know about any potential future with him. She dialed his number, and it rang a few times. She was about to disconnect, leaving no message, when he came on the line.

"Millie," Scott's deep voice said. "Sorry I haven't called you. I've been spending a lot of time at Jolene's house."

Hearing those words, she almost hung up. But she decided that would be childish. "I thought you might be interested in what happened here Monday night," she said in a carefully neutral voice. She told the story matter-of-factly, starting with the fact of Nolan's guilt in the two murders and his motive, ending with his breaking into the house and threatening her with a knife.

She heard a quick intake of breath. "Wow!" Scott said. "Wow! Are you okay? Is Danny all right?"

"I'm fine. Danny's fine. Everyone's fine, I suppose, but Nolan."

"I'm so glad you're safe, sweetheart, so glad. Danny too. This Nolan character must be a really evil guy."

Sweetheart. Scott had called her sweetheart.

"Evil, maybe," she said. "Greedy, definitely. Probably if he'd known exactly where at Highgrove the jewel was, he'd've broken in and taken it, court order or no. But he didn't know exactly, and for so long he hoped he'd be getting legal title to the place."

"It must've eaten away at him all that time the court case was pending. But so be it. At least he's caught and you don't have to worry about him anymore. What about Ted? Is he still sniffing around?"

"No, that's another good development." She told about Cynthia's news and about Harris.

"That's great. I know Danny's excited."

"He'd probably spend his nights sleeping outside with Harris if I'd let him." Millie took a deep breath and plunged. "How're things in Boulder?"

"Much better. Jolene and I talked to an attorney, and he helped get Larry enrolled in a program that's part community service, part restitution. He'll spend a few hours a week cleaning up one of the parks, and will even earn a small wage, enough to pay back the shop for the items he stole. Little by little."

"And this is okay with Larry?"

"Oh, yeah. His brush with the law scared him straight—at least for now. Also, Jolene came up with an idea to help not only herself but also several other mothers in her neighborhood. All these women have to work, but they're worried about their preteen boys being unsupervised for long periods. They've found an older man in the neighborhood, a retiree, who's willing to take the boys after school and show them how to repair a classic car he's been restoring."

"That sounds wonderful, Scott. Jolene must be pleased to have worked out such a sensible plan." Millie hesitated. "Or was that your suggestion?"

"All her idea. I only said it seemed to me Larry needed somewhere to go when she was working, some place where he'd have wholesome, supervised fun. Jolene came up with the actual plan." She heard him take a deep breath.

"Millie, I decided you had a valid point about Jolene's depending on me too much. I told her I'm getting behind in my studying and have to really buckle down. I said I'll still tutor Larry, but that might be all I can do with him for quite a while."

"How'd she take that?"

"Better than I expected. She said she appreciated the time I've already given Larry, and insists on paying me back every penny of the lawyer's fee. I told her not to worry about that now, not until after the shop's paid back, but then maybe she and Larry can split the cost of repaying me. She liked that idea, and Larry's even okay with it. I think it makes him feel grown up to know he'll be helping his mom pay bills."

"So all's well that ends well?"

"Not quite." His voice grew husky. "I need to know you and I are okay, Millie. Sorry I acted like a jerk. I get jealous when other guys get to spend time with you and I don't, so I should've understood your feelings about Jolene. Forgive me?"

"Only if you'll forgive me. Whatever the feminine of 'jerk' is, that applied to me."

"Thanks, sweetheart, for being so terrific about this. I love you, you know."

"And I love you."

They chatted a few minutes more. Then with words that would have made Danny roll his eyes in embarrassment, Scott rang off.

*The first lovers' tiff, dealt with and survived. A milestone.*

That evening after Danny had gone to bed, Millie sat with Alice on the side terrace, drinking decaf coffee and talking over recent events. Cynthia had gone with Luke to a ball game.

"This isn't a date," she'd said firmly as he had come up the walk to get her. "We're just going as friends. Jill's death is much too fresh for anything else. Anyway, we may decide we can't stand each other on closer acquaintance."

But Millie had noticed her working especially hard to get her hair just right.

"Had you any idea that secret room was here?" Millie asked Alice now. "I wonder when Jill found it."

"Some time before you and Danny arrived, evidently. And, no, it was a complete surprise to me. I'm not sure why Jill didn't tell me or Cynthia about it. We were all just getting to know each other then, though, so perhaps she didn't fully trust us yet. And her history with that uncle may have gotten her into a habit of keeping secrets."

"Could be."

"So are you going to write up what you've learned about Ephraim Hayes, submit it to a professional journal or deliver a paper at a history conference?"

"I hope to. Maybe Whit and Harold would be interested in publishing something with me; they did a lot of research on Ephraim. Whit's granddad would love to have his letters collection footnoted. And you and Prissy's journal should get credit, too. I guess Nolan should, for that matter. But somehow, I'm not disposed to include him in the laurels."

*So you're letting a little thing like two murders and two more attempted murders sway your thinking? How petty, Kirchner.*

Yeah, Millie thought. So sue me.

She and Alice sat in companionable silence a while. Then Millie summoned the courage to raise a subject that had been on her mind for weeks.

"Alice, what do you really think about Thomas Jefferson? Him and slavery, I mean. I know the arguments in his favor, that he condemned the institution many times, that he inherited slaves along with staggering debts, that one big landowner in the South couldn't buck a whole system, and so on. Maybe I keep wanting him to've been better than he could've been, given his situation and the century he lived in.

"But somehow it seems too easy to say he was a man of his time. Some people have managed to rise above time and place. Do you . . . think much about that side of him when you're working at Poplar Forest? At a place where members of your race were enslaved?"

Alice gave a long sigh. "The first time I visited there, took the tour, I left with a mess of conflicting emotions. Yes, he did treat people of my race as his inferiors, his property. No one has the right to own another human being.

"But he did allow his slaves opportunities that most masters didn't. He saw that some learned to read, he sent James Hemings to culinary school in Paris, and John Hemings developed into a master craftsman by working on Jefferson's building projects. It's true that those skills benefited the master as well as his slaves, but at least he saw them as individuals, with differing abilities.

"In many ways, Jefferson was a great, great man.

"I abhor some of what I know about him. But other aspects delight me: his lofty thoughts, his inquisitive mind, his love of beauty, his devotion to family. And he was probably the president this country needed at the time.

"I also try to remember I don't always live up to my own highest ideals. I think if we refuse to acknowledge the great good any human does because he also makes great mistakes, that's a judgment we don't have a right to make. Who made me, or you, the all-high judge of any of our fellow beings?"

*I knew I liked this woman.*

Cynthia and Luke came in for coffee after their non-date, sitting at the kitchen counter with Millie and Alice. Luke seemed happier than could be explained by the fact his team had won. Cynthia, too, smiled a lot, as if she shared some hidden knowledge with him. Their behavior towards each other was that of mere buddies, not lovers, so Millie wondered what was going on. After a few minutes, Luke could apparently keep the secret no longer.

"Highgrove was designed by Thomas Jefferson. Miss Julia told me just before I came to pick up Cynthia."

Millie and Alice jumped up, waved their hands in the air, and cheered. Luke and Cynthia joined in, and Millie wondered if the shouts would wake Danny. But he didn't come stumbling into the kitchen, and finally they all sat again.

As Luke told the story, Jefferson had designed a house for his friend Josiah Bradshaw. But that worthy had kept the plan a while, then returned it with thanks, saying his new wife wanted a house of a different design. However, Josiah, justly proud of having a house plan designed by a President of the United States, had shown it liberally to friends and neighbors. One of those had been Hiram Wixon, who borrowed the drawing to show his wife. Wixon had taken that opportunity to make a copy for himself. A poorer draftsman than Jefferson, he had produced a sketch that, though poorer in execution, retained much of the quality of the original.

Highgrove, Millie thought, a Jefferson design after all. She imagined Thomas Jefferson striding around the dwelling, nodding at a graceful column, tsk-tsking at the added-on attic that spoiled the roofline.

What would he say about the United States of America now, two centuries after he'd helped bring it into existence? Would he be surprised it had become so powerful among nations, proud of its finest hours, chagrined at its worst? He certainly would be proud of the fact that it had elected a black man as president, or more precisely a man who was only half-white. As Barack Obama himself said, a mutt.

The country wasn't unlike Jefferson himself, Millie thought, with huge aspirations, marvelous energy and ideas, for the most part good-hearted, but ultimately imperfect, as all countries and individuals are.

THE END

# ★ Author's Notes

In portraying both historical and modern events, places, and persons, I've adhered to known facts, except in a few instances for the sake of the story. For example, the *Missouri Dispatch* was St. Louis's first newspaper, but it didn't begin publication until 1808. Stagecoaches served St. Louis, but the first didn't arrive there until 1820. The Rivermont section of Lynchburg, Virginia, contains many impressive Victorian houses, but both the dwelling where Millie and her housemates live and the one next door are imaginary.

The Lewis and Clark Expedition, or Corps of Discovery, numbered as few as thirty-three persons and perhaps as many as fifty-nine (including Sacagawea's infant son, Jean-Baptiste Charbonneau) at various times, with some members leaving or joining during the long journey. A "temporary party" led by Corporal Richard Warfington did make part of the trek to the Pacific Ocean and returned to St. Louis in 1805 from what is now North Dakota. William Clark was from Kentucky and did recruit some expedition members there, but no one named Ephraim Hayes was ever a part of the Corps. He is fictitious, as are several other characters in his plotline.

I consulted many references regarding the Expedition, but

much of what Millie learns comes from one book, *The Fate of the Corps: What Became of the Lewis and Clark Explorers After the Expedition,* by Larry E. Morris. Occasionally, I portrayed material from this source as coming from another, unnamed source, when the plot demanded that Millie discover portions of the information at different times. The phrase "masterful planning," to describe Jefferson's preparations before the Expedition, is Mr. Morris's. The other book specifically cited as one read by Millie, *Lewis and Clark Through Indian Eyes,* edited by Alvin M. Josephy, Jr., is real and was a useful source;, however, the book Jill holds in the library, *Horticulture in the Shadow of the Blue Ridge,* is imaginary.

Highgrove is fictitious, and no such house is known to exist in Bedford County, Virginia, or elsewhere. Poplar Forest, however, is real. Thomas Jefferson's retreat near Lynchburg, Virginia, has been carefully restored and is open for public viewing (see www.poplarforest.org). Jefferson did design many buildings other than his own two residences, including several houses for relatives and friends.

Old City Cemetery at Lynchburg was really established in 1806 and does contain a few graves of Revolutionary War veterans. The Methodist Meeting House in Lynchburg was built in 1806, and a brick wall there actually did require repairs because of inferior work by its first contractor, but these would likely have been done in 1806, not 1807.

The Wade Heaton collection of early Western newspapers is fictitious, but the Albert and Shirley Small Special Collections Library at the University of Virginia does contain among its holdings a permanent exhibit of materials related to the Declaration of Independence.

The Scarlet Star is from my imagination, although events surrounding it were suggested by histories of actual gems such as the Florentine and Hope Diamonds. I chose the fleur-de-lis pattern for its pouch because I was connecting the gem to St. Louis; that three-petalled symbol is used in the city's flag to represent the convergence of three rivers there (the Mississippi, the Missouri, and the Illinois).

I'm indebted to many people for generous sharing of their knowledge and expertise, including the staff of Poplar Forest, especially Jack Gary, Director of Archaeology and Landscapes; Gail Pond, Collections Manager; Travis McDonald, Director of Architectural Restoration; Octavia N. Starbuck, Director of Interpretation and Education; Dianne Kinney, Manager of Visitor Services and Volunteers; Dr. Barbara Heath, former Director of Archaeology and Landscapes; Keith W. Adams, former Senior Staff Archaeologist; Liz Paull, former Staff Archaeologist; and Rachel Deddens, former Education Assistant.

Major Ricky Gardner of the Bedford Sheriff's office in Bedford County, Virginia, gave invaluable advice about investigative procedures and personnel.

Many people in Lynchburg also contributed, especially Ted Delaney, Archivist and Curator; Jane White, Director Emerita; and Dawn Fields, Visitor Services Manager, all at Old City Cemetery; Lewis Hobgood Averett, Coordinator of Public Services at Jones Memorial Library; and Cathy Beeson of the Lynchburg Chamber of Commerce.

At the University of Virginia, these individuals helped: Karin Wittenborg, University Librarian; Holly Robertson, former Director of Preservation, UVA Library; and Heather Moore Riser, Director of Public Services for the Albert and Shirley Small Special Collections Library. Other assistance in Charlottesville came from Malika Bouhdili, former student guide at UVA; and the staff of The Jefferson Library, especially Anna Berkes, Research Librarian.

Many docents and guides at historic sites contributed, especially Liz Marshall and Catherine Neelley at Monticello, Irene

V. Soderquist at Montalto, and Shirley Raynes and Tom Shultz at Williamsburg, as well as Susan Marcinkus, former Events Coordinator at The College of William and Mary Bookstore, Williamsburg.

I also appreciate the help of personal friends Carolyn and Bruce Cameron of Chalice Art (www.chaliceart.com), for information on gems and lapidaries; Dr. Dan Althoff of Southeastern Oklahoma State University, for help with Spanish phrases; Lisette Rice, Tulsa librarian and Jefferson aficionado, for suggesting source materials; and Dr. Patrick Fontane and Dr. Marilyn Fontane of St. Louis College of Pharmacy, for showing me St. Charles, Missouri, and starting me thinking about Lewis and Clark as a plot element.

—Marion Moore Hill